CRY WOLF
NATHALIE GRAY

ELLORA'S CAVE
ROMANTICA PUBLISHING

What the critics are saying...

ɛͻ

WOLFSBANE

Winner, 2006 Reviewers Choice Award

5 Stars "Like a stroll through the garden at midnight on a moonlit night; full of surprising beauty" ~ *Ecataromance Reviews*

Winner, 2006 Gold Star Award

"I strongly recommend this highly exciting, enchanting book. Its sexual fury, gripping plot, and attention-grabbing characters are both memorable and satisfying" ~ *Just Erotic Romance Reviews*

Winner, 2006 Recommended Read Award

5 Angels "Exceptionally well-written […] one of the best paranormal, gothic type stories I have read in a long time" ~ *Fallen Angel Reviews*

5 Euros "Fascinating" ~ *Euroreviews*

"magical […] Wolfsbane will enchant you" ~ *Joyfully Reviewed*

4 Roses "A dark tale of courage and love in the face of adversity" ~ *A Romance Review*

BAIN'S WOLF

Nominated, 2006 Reviewers Choice Award

5 Stars "Delicious [...] a rich tapestry" ~ *Ecataromance Reviews*

4 Kisses "The plot twists worth of a Hollywood blockbuster kept me reading well into the night" ~ *TwoLips Reviews*

4.5 Blue Ribbons "The twists and turns are never ending in a plot that will hook you from the first page" ~ *Romance Junkies*

"Gray's excellent writing will pull you in and carry you along a fantastic tale. If you've read Wolfsbane, you really shouldn't miss Bain's Wolf" ~ *Joyfully Reviewed*

5 Angels "Although werewolf tales are quite common lately, Bain's Wolf most certainly is not!" ~ *Fallen Angel Reviews*

4 Stars "A wonderful grasp on her craft [...] This is this first Nathalie Gray that I have read, but it won't be the last" ~ *Just Erotic Romance Reviews*

An Ellora's Cave Romantica Publication

www.ellorascave.com

Cry Wolf

ISBN 9781419956362
ALL RIGHTS RESERVED.
Wolfsbane Copyright © 2006 Nathalie Gray
Bain's Wolf Copyright © 2006 Nathalie Gray
Edited by Mary Moran
Cover art by Syneca

Trade paperback Publication June 2007

This book is printed in the U.S.A. by Jasmine-Jade Enterprises, LLC.

Content Advisory:

S – ENSUOUS
E – ROTIC
X – TREME

Ellora's Cave Publishing offers three levels of Romantica™ reading entertainment: S (S-ensuous), E (E-rotic), and X (X-treme).

The following material contains graphic sexual content meant for mature readers. This story has been rated E–rotic.

S-*ensuous* love scenes are explicit and leave nothing to the imagination.

E-*rotic* love scenes are explicit, leave nothing to the imagination, and are high in volume per the overall word count. E-rated titles might contain material that some readers find objectionable — in other words, almost anything goes, sexually. E-rated titles are the most graphic titles we carry in terms of both sexual language and descriptiveness in these works of literature.

X-*treme* titles differ from E-rated titles only in plot premise and storyline execution. Stories designated with the letter X tend to contain difficult or controversial subject matter not for the faint of heart.

Also by Nathalie Gray

ഇ

About the Author

I am a mother, spouse, older sister, writer, ex-soldier, high school drop-out, dog owner (or dog owned), half couch potato/half intermittent jogger, wannabe renovator and avid reader who watches too much television, sinks too much money in clothes, likes animals more than humans, recycles, wore braces, never downloads copyrighted stuff, was a nerd without the grades, has a belly laugh that turns heads in theaters, can't stand bullying, is mother hawk more than mother hen, votes even if candidates aren't that great and thinks formal education is highly overrated (probably because she has none).

Nathalie welcomes comments from readers. You can find her website and email address on her author bio page at www.ellorascave.com.

Tell Us What You Think

We appreciate hearing reader opinions about our books. You can email us at Comments@EllorasCave.com.

CRY WOLF

 හ

WOLFSBANE

BAIN'S WOLF

WOLFSBANE

Chapter One

ℬ

Hot tea splashed on his hand. Fredrick stifled a curse. No use giving the nasty little swine satisfaction.

"Oh please do receive my apologies, Master Fredrick," the servant sneered. He tossed on the tray the serviette wrapped over his forearm. The resulting whip of air caused the tiny flame of the candle to sputter and fret. Hurriedly, the man took it away from the table and shielded its flame with his cupped hand.

Fredrick took pleasure in this small triumph. Light was precious to everyone in the darkened tower. Except to him.

Fredrick dabbed his burning hand where already the pale skin was turning a sunburn shade of red. "If you're going to torment a chained man, at least don't pretend to be sorry." He slid the tray, which the servant had placed within his reach, to his end of the table. The length of chain digging in his ankle clinked dully on the expensive rug.

A malicious grin tugged the servant's mouth. He mock-bowed. "As you command."

If Fredrick could only reach out and close a hand over the man's throat. That's all he'd need, one hand. Fredrick couldn't remember the man's name nor did he want to. The face looking at him now was familiar, of course, he'd been coming there twice a day, bringing in food and taking out the refuse. But no name. No use learning them.

How many servants would his cousin send in, hoping to force him into her schemes? The first one she'd sent had been his real manservant, an honest man with thirty years' honorable service. The old man's death—his *murder*—still haunted Fredrick's dreams. Then there'd been two maids and a young servant. When trying to win his consent by using friendly faces had failed, his cousin's tactics had turned even more vicious. No more loyal servants from his own house had been allowed in the tower. Only her own handpicked sort. Thugs and ruffians from the city streets mostly.

Disposables.

Rage seeped into Fredrick's heart. He forced it down. Rage meant he'd lose control, would allow his darker side to rule him. It was what his cousin wanted most—to break him. And this he could *not* let happen.

"Thinking of revenge again?" the servant asked, too close to the truth. His dark eyes gleamed with malice above the tiny flame.

"Cousin quickly tires of the likes of you," Fredrick replied, enjoying the hatred tightening the servant's mouth. It was one of his few pleasures left—taunting his tormentors.

A small step brought the careless servant dangerously close to Fredrick's reach. *A mere foot away—yes, that's it, come closer. It wouldn't take long.*

The man must have sensed the imminent danger for he hurriedly backed away several paces. "Maybe I should pour the entire pot on your ungrateful head."

"Come here and do it." Fredrick turned the teapot so the handle faced the other man.

Alarm crept in his expression. Fredrick could smell it from where he sat. The stench of fear. "That's what I thought."

This one had been in his cousin's service for almost three months. He'd begun his duties as a genuine servant would, then had become bolder by the day. The sneaky type, it'd started slowly, like using icy-cold water for his bath, or bringing only small amounts of food. The servant kept blaming the kitchen staff, of course. Because Cousin never tried to discourage the behavior, the verbal abuse had begun then the whole thing had spiraled downward. Cold meals, wine that smelled of urine, burning tea "accidentally" spilled on his hands. Fredrick could only guess the things that ended up in his food. But he had to eat. If only to remain strong in case…

"You're going to die here, you know that, don't you?" the servant said after a while. His slicked-back hair looked greasier today. "She'll grow sick of playing nice."

"I have already grown sick of 'playing nice', as you so ineptly put it," a woman's voice said from beyond the darkened doorway.

Fredrick leaned back in his chair and crossed his legs. "Good day, Cousin. How's life in *my* castle?"

His emphasis on the pronoun didn't escape her for she scowled, which accentuated the hard lines of her beautiful face. "*Our* house, if you were not so stubborn."

Fredrick could have laughed. So predictable. "My house it shall remain then."

"Unfortunate," she replied, seemingly gliding into the room, robes which hid her feet rustled on the imported carpet. "Leave us," she said without looking at the servant. "The candle stays here," she added when the man seemed to hover uncertainly near the door, still cupping the flame with his hand. He came back to the nearest end of the table and set the precious candle down.

"Too bad she'll kill you quickly. I would've made it last," Fredrick called over his cousin's shoulder.

By the look on the man's face, Fredrick knew his meal would be particularly disgusting tonight. He sighed.

Using her silver cane like a pivot, she circled it twice before settling down at the other end of the table, well out of his reach, and toyed with the candleholder. A bead of hot wax glided down the length of the candle. Fredrick followed with his eyes until it hardened on her lacquered fingernail. He could remember what those had felt like on his back. A shiver prickled the fine hair along his forearms.

"What will it take for you to see the light?" she asked, scoring a tiny notch in the wax with her glistening nail. "I have gone to great lengths and am prepared to go even farther."

"You'll never go far enough to break me, Cousin. Even with the poison your charlatan gives me. But you already know that." He knew exactly what they were giving him. Wolfsbane. How ironically appropriate.

"My physician only puts a tonic in your food. It is your illness that makes you—"

He threw her a menacing glare. "Don't insult my intelligence. You're poisoning me so I'm just lucid enough to be entertaining but not enough to be dangerous." Fredrick knew his food contained a small amount of poison—tonic, indeed—but he couldn't stop eating, even if it meant being in a constant state of stupor. Starving would achieve nothing.

She shrugged, which dislodged a strand of raven-colored hair from behind her ear. Bringing the silver pommel of the cane to her lips, she let it glide over her chin, down the length of her graceful neck then farther between her breasts, which swelled out of a tight, midnight blue corset. Straightening her long legs, she angled one outward, toward him, and ran the silver butt along the inside of her thigh, which poked out through a slit in the dress.

His cousin may have been a greedy demon, but a beautiful, alluring woman she was also. And she knew it too, often using it on men. On him, much to his shame. By the time he'd realized she was seducing him, her trap had already been sprung and he'd woken up prisoner to his own tower, with Cousin bent on getting her claws into the family fortune. His family fortune. That was almost two years ago.

"You may stop at your convenience, Cousin," he said with pretend levity. He wouldn't even call her by name. The mere taste of it revolted him. She despised him for it, had often tortured him to make him say her name. She hadn't succeeded so far. And she wasn't even his real cousin, only shared the family name. Strictly speaking, she was his cousin's descendant. But flaunting about that bit of genealogy could mean people would figure out his real age. Something he couldn't afford to do. Only four people knew who he was—two of them were in this very room. So she'd begun calling Fredrick "cousin" to taunt him, with him returning the favor.

"What makes you think I do this for *your* pleasure?" The silver butt snaked through the velvet slit of her dress, which parted wider and allowed him a view of her long, pale thigh.

Fredrick took his glass, brought it to his lips. Thankfully, the wine tonight smelled like nothing else but wine. And a good year it was, as well. From his own personal cellar, no doubt. Maybe that charlatan hadn't poisoned his meal tonight. Maybe he'd get a chance. Fredrick tried not to get excited at the prospect of having a clear mind for the first time in a long while. He tried not to *hope*.

Fire accompanied the liquid down his throat. Peculiar. Licking his numbing lips, he brought the glass down and noticed his hand shook slightly. The witch.

"Someday..." Fredrick snarled. Already, his vision clouded.

His cousin smiled as she ran the length of the cane back and forth between her thighs. "It is just something to make you docile as a kitten—or should I say as a puppy?"

Fredrick's tongue felt heavy, his throat tight. He cleared the tabletop with a swipe of his arm, stood on shaky legs and stumbled at the end of his chain, straining to reach her, squeeze her detestable throat until she turned blue. The old, familiar burn at his ankle didn't bother him much. Not with the drug this demon had put in his wine. He knew what was coming and hated her for it.

She'd steal his seed again, futilely trying to get a proper heir, and violate him while the drug kept him the obedient dog. But she'd never succeeded in getting with child. Did she think he had lived all these years willingly alone, wifeless, childless, barren as a field in winter? He couldn't *have* children.

And even if he could, he'd never curse someone to a life such as his. But if Cousin came to learn she couldn't get a proper heir to inherit the von Innsbruck name and fortune, he'd be dead within the hour. So he kept the knowledge to himself, hoping Cousin would merely torture him so he'd sign the deed. Torture was better than the thought of her raising his child. Any child.

"How I love watching you like this," she said. A maniacal glint made her pale eyes striking.

The poison's effect began subtly — as with the last times — then grew in intensity. His belly constricted around the base of his member, tightened into a searing ring, and burned what little resolve still clung to his fogged mind. He had to fight it. At least try. But his instincts were taking over. Lust flared inside him.

Never love, though. He'd never love this woman or any other. Treacherous creatures, all of them!

"Come here," he heard his raspy voice say, though he would've preferred killing her with his bare hands.

His fingers reached out of their own volition and clutched at the air while thoughts of her filled his head, flailed his heart, swelled his member. "Come...*here*."

The silver butt of her cane — *his* cane, damn her — emerged glistening from her dress. With a feral lift of her ruby lips, she brought it up to her face and flicked a forked tongue at it.

Logically, Fredrick knew the woman's tongue couldn't have been forked. But try as he might, he couldn't clear his mind. He was slowly losing his grip on reality. He didn't even know what he'd been given, only that it reduced him to a throbbing, lusting beast. That charlatan of a physician she kept around! It was his doing. If there ever were a day Fredrick broke free of his prison, there'd be no hole deep enough for the snake to crawl into.

A groan escaped him when he collapsed onto one knee, the chain still taut behind him, tearing his ankle, reminding him who was in control. Sounds came to him muffled and distorted. Light from the lone candle atop the table intensified, turned crimson, chased shadows to the ends of the circular room. Everything began to spin. Fredrick felt as though his member would explode from the strain. Demonic spawn. How he hated her.

She stood, but left the cane on the table. Coming closer but just out of his reach, she knelt facing him and parted her dress so he could watch her introduce a finger into her orchid-pink flesh.

"Sign the deed and make me your wife, and you can have it anytime you wish, Fredrick." Lacquered nails pulled at her lips, circled the engorged bud. "I would let you do all the things you have ever wanted to do to a woman but were afraid to. You would wake up in the middle of the night with your flesh sunk deep in mine." She moaned deep in her throat. "Husband and wife, Fredrick, would that not be thrilling? And after your untimely passing, it would all be mine," she murmured while giving herself pleasure.

His name and lands. Castle Innsbruck. His beloved people.

His mind was fogging up. Fredrick clutched at his forehead, fisted his hair. "No."

"No?" she replied with a short laugh. "You want me more now than you can bear. I know the effect of what flows in your veins for I use it too."

"Go to Hell," Fredrick snarled.

She laughed again. The sound of a cracked bell. "All in good time. First, you will take me to Heaven."

The door opened and in came a man. His features were chiseled and hard, his eyes gleaming. "Just in time, I see," he said with a rich voice.

Fredrick's rage reached the boiling point. He pointed an accusing finger at the man. "Lothar…demon. I'll get you…"

Lothar smiled widely. "And I *am* looking forward to that day."

His cousin bent far back when Lothar came up behind her and let his hands caress her breasts through the bodice. His ponytail spilled over his shoulder. Then his fingers snaked lower, to the place where Fredrick wanted to sink his flesh so much it hurt. Breathing hard now, Cousin let the man slip his fingers into her while her eyes never left Fredrick's face.

Gathering her gown in one hand, she pulled it up, giving Fredrick an explicit view. Her knees spread wide when she arched back. Lothar also kept his gaze on Fredrick while he stabbed his fingers into the panting woman. She yanked her bodice down under her breasts and squeezed her nipples hard. Fredrick saw the bruised flesh turn red.

Fredrick squeezed his eyes shut, gritted his teeth. If he could only control his response the way he did when...

"Watch me." His cousin's command made him flinch.

A drug-induced snarl of excitement rumbled in Fredrick's chest when Lothar wrapped a thick fist around her long hair and pushed her down on her elbows. While he kept her down, with his other hand he undid the buttons on his trousers. His thick member sprung out of its confines and glistened threateningly over the woman's denuded backside. But instead of sinking it into her—something Fredrick was ashamed to realize he wanted more than anything—the man raised his large hand high. The clack of skin against skin resounded in the circular room.

"Harder," she snarled, her gaze riveted to Fredrick's.

The man slapped her cheek again, hard. Roughly pulling her around so Fredrick could get a full view of her glistening sex and spread-wide behind, the man slapped her again, this time so hard she cried out. Again and again his hand came down. Again and again, the woman snarled for him to hit harder, even taunting him with unspeakable words.

The poison in Fredrick's veins melted away the last of his resolve, of his pain and rage and frustration. With a snarl, he tore open his long black tunic. Buttons landed everywhere with small clicks. Smells of her reached him, tiny sounds from her throat made him claw at himself. He was already kneeling but he collapsed on his hands as well, a monstrous erection hanging heavy between his thighs. Yet Fredrick couldn't keep his gaze away, even if at the same time, a small, faint part of his brain told him to fight the poison, to clear his thoughts.

His cousin reached behind her and grabbed the man's shirt, pulling him down on top of her. In a golden brown cascade his ponytail grazed her back. "Savage me."

He did.

Fredrick gasped at the sight of the man clutching two handfuls of her gown and using these as anchors to violently thrust himself into the writhing woman. Her knees left the floor.

Visions exploded in Fredrick's brain.

His cousin was on her knees, bucking back against him. Pleasure ripples clutched at his shaft. He was digging his fingers into her flesh. She arched back. Screamed. Then a searing rod impaled him from behind, breached the sensitive skin of his anus. Fredrick growled in pain yet continued thrusting himself into his cousin, hoping to quench the poisoned yearning. Behind, Lothar hurt him with his too-hard thrusts. Fredrick felt his hair being pulled back. Lothar bit him on the shoulder, triggering monstrous arousal that scared Fredrick. He, in turn, imagined he bit his cousin on the shoulder. Blood flowed from the hideous wound.

Fredrick gasped in pleasure and shock. Licking his lips, he continued pounding himself into her welcoming flesh while he mentally rendered it with claws and fangs.

A cry tore up his throat. Feral. Inhuman. It curdled his blood, made his seed explode from him. Another cry soon followed his — Lothar pulled out of Fredrick, leaving behind only hurt and shame.

Then like a blanket of ash falling over the world, the light went out. And Fredrick was falling into Hell.

Chapter Two

ର

Scarlet wouldn't scream. Knowing it infuriated her "master", she relished in this one small victory. They could have her body but they sure wouldn't get her soul. Nor the coins safely tucked away in the hollow heels of her wooden shoes. When he pulled out of her, she had to stifle a small snort of triumph. It wouldn't do to anger him further.

With a stinging slap on the backside, Werner pushed her hard against the brick wall. His breath smelled of onions and ale when he tugged on her hair, leaned his chin over her shoulder. "I'll go get somethin' to drink. Then you and me'll meet with the patron I talked to you about. Meanwhile, poppet, you stay right here."

She didn't watch him leave, but heard the jiggle of belt buckle and scabbard as he pulled himself back in. She didn't even know what the new work entailed, but would've preferred keeping her old one. Stealing may be a sin, but one she knew and had learned to accept. And one she was good at.

"Don't try to escape, Scarlet, I'd only find you again—and this time, I might not be so nice," he called over his broad shoulder.

She cursed him under her breath, hating every single hair on him. If he hadn't been one of the bailiff's men—therefore powerful and well-connected—she would've made him pay. Somehow, he always managed to find her, no matter what good hiding spot she thought she'd found. Probably, he had moles working for him who gave her away in a second, her being a mere thief. She *had* to steal just to survive. Couldn't he understand that! And now she would have to…Heaven knew what.

Scarlet shivered at the horrid visions. A wealthy patron coming to take her away. She could well imagine why. Be a slave in some dungeon, at the mercy of every base thing they'd want her to do, to *be*.

Well, she wouldn't take it idly. After a short moment, Scarlet rearranged her dress the best she could and snuck out of the alley behind the guardhouse. If she were quick about it, she'd be across town before he realized she'd gone. She may be a thief, but she would be no one's whore.

Vulgar male laughter wafted in through the maladjusted door and chased her down the slimy cobbled lane flanked on either side by decrepit half-timbered houses. What she wouldn't do to see the countryside. Taste the sweet air of grass and sea. Scarlet looked up at the moon and sighed. Enough dreaming. She was here and now and getting away from Werner was the only thing she should have in mind.

As she rounded the corner of the narrow alley, Amsterdam's urban canal greeted her with its offensive smells and glittering reflections. She hadn't gone ten steps when a male voice she knew too well stopped her. Fighting against cold fear clamming her palms, Scarlet half turned, half crouched.

Werner was charging down the alley, slopping ale and cursing. Without thinking, Scarlet ran.

She could outrun the thickly muscled man easily enough, but his hollering would soon bring attention. She'd be caught again. Horrible images danced in her mind's eye. Maybe being taken away by this rich patron wouldn't be so bad after all. Compared to what Werner would surely do to her.

Sweet Mary, help me!

Lungs burning, she dashed down the mud-slippery alley and was about to cross the wider street to the safety of the canal when a loud sound thundered around her. A team of black horses exploded to her left, gleaming and frothing at the mouth, and reeled to a jittery, chaotic stop. The carriage's driver yelled something at her, but Scarlet couldn't hear anything over Werner's voice as he closed a ham-sized hand over her neck. This time she yelped.

"You little viper!" he hollered, giving her a rough shake. "I'll teach you."

With hot breath from the restless horses blowing across her face, Scarlet fought against the much larger man as he dragged her back by the scruff of the neck toward the side of the road. Scratching and biting and kicking as much as she could, Scarlet only managed to make Werner laugh.

"You've some spirit about you, girl," he panted, gathering both her hands in one of his and pulling her to him. "But you can't always get away. Sometimes, you lose. I warned you, Scarlet, I did. Now look what you're making me do." He unbuckled his belt.

"No," she snarled, kicking him in the shin.

"What is going on?" a rich female voice demanded loudly.

Behind Werner, Scarlet spotted a woman coming out of the black carriage. The air about her as she stepped down and put gloved fists on narrow hips! Scarlet would have stared in awe had she not been fighting for her life.

"My lady," Werner said, dragging Scarlet with him as he whirled around and bowed. "I thought you were at the—"

"Silence," snarled the woman, stepping down. She was as tall as Werner, slender, with long black hair loose about her athletic shoulders. A cane with a silver pommel glistened in her gloved hand. Scarlet couldn't take her gaze off her.

"My pardon…I didn't mean to offend." Werner stopped, stared daggers at Scarlet then loosened his grip on her hands.

She snapped them out and took a step away from him.

The tall woman advanced, her midnight blue cape fretting around her ankles. "Is this the girl you told me about?"

So this was the wealthy patron come to take her away? Scarlet had expected a fat, bald man dressed in gaudy clothes.

"She is, mistress," Werner replied, pawing behind him for Scarlet.

Turning, the tall woman set her icy blue gaze on Scarlet. "I need someone who has stamina and is not afraid of darkness. Can you handle that, young woman?"

"I'll be no one's whore," Scarlet snapped back, not caring about her tone.

Werner meant to backhand her but she snuck under his swipe.

"That will be enough," the woman said. A grin tugged at the corner of her mouth. "Then you shall be no one's whore. What is your name?"

"Scarlet."

"Scarlet," the woman repeated, eyeing her from head to toe then back up again. "A fitting name. As I said, you shall not be asked to bed anyone — unless you wish to, which is none of my concerns. Your duties will involve cleaning and taking care of a very ill man."

Scarlet didn't even need to look at Werner to see her death in his eyes. There'd be neither safety nor future in Amsterdam for her. Might as well take a chance and follow this strange and magnificent woman.

"Well?" the woman asked, patience clearly not one of her virtues.

Without a look at Werner, Scarlet nodded. Before she could follow the woman back to the coach, Werner grabbed her wrist and squeezed so hard Scarlet moaned. "I'll find you again when they're done with you."

A terrifying glare from the woman had Werner retreating by a step.

Scarlet rubbed at her bruised wrist as she followed the tall woman inside the coach. The door closed behind them. With a lurch, the gleaming vehicle rode on.

So this was how it felt to leave one's life behind. Scarlet shivered. There would be no turning back. A wince of disgust almost cracked the impassive mask she'd spent years perfecting under Werner and his friends' base attentions. Her sex felt sore, and she'd love nothing better than to wash his seed off her, but could do nothing about it for now except grit her teeth and wait. She was used to that.

A small glass lamp lit the interior of the cabin, which was the closest thing Scarlet had ever seen to a palace. Brocade seat covers, velvet partition walls, silk drapes embroidered with a blazon she couldn't recognize. Even the floor looked opulent. And her with a tattered cotton dress and muddy wooden shoes!

"Well, *kleiner Apfel*, this man seems to want a bite of you."

No one had ever called her that before. She didn't like the implications. Scarlet Heerlen was no one's "little apple". But the woman had been very kind to help her and Scarlet held her tongue. For now. "*Danke*," she replied in what little German she knew.

"You are most welcome," the woman said in nearly accentless Dutch, a small grin lifting the corner of her exquisite, berry-colored mouth. She had eyes like blue diamonds. "Do not ever let men try to control you, Scarlet."

Scarlet agreed with a nod. It'd been difficult so far with no one to help, no one to fall back on. The streets of Amsterdam weren't friendly to lone women.

"You may call me Lady Katrina." She smiled.

"Thank you very much, Lady Katrina."

"Do you have family?"

"No...no, Lady Katrina." She'd have to make the effort of using the woman's title.

"You have been alone all your life?"

A warning bell tolled in Scarlet's mind. Years on the streets, mostly by herself, had honed her senses to daggers. Giving details about one's life was never a safe thing to do.

After a long silence, Lady Katrina shook her head. "Do not worry. Nothing bad happens to those I value."

Unsure how to respond Scarlet tilted her head. Through the partly drawn curtains, the pale moon hid her face behind a thick cover of clouds, but Scarlet knew it was there, had always felt a special kinship to her oftentimes only source of nightly light. A stoical, silent friend. One that never deserted her, no matter what Scarlet had to do to survive, no matter how low she'd sunk to earn a few coins. "I don't want to be trouble."

"You are not trouble, *kleiner Apfel*. And I will pay you well. Unless you have something else…"

Lady Katrina had to know there was nothing else, but she must have been too well-bred to mention it, for which Scarlet was grateful. "How long will I work for you?"

As if the point-blank tone were new to her, the woman arched a dark eyebrow then nodded, maybe deciding she rather liked it. "Well, it all depends on his health, of course. But he is very ill."

Honest work for the first time in her life. Though Scarlet wanted to kiss the woman's feet, she'd never let her gratitude show. With as much impassiveness as she could muster, she nodded. "Do you live very far, Lady Katrina?"

A nod revealed the most beautiful earrings Scarlet had ever seen. Huge, tear-shaped rubies. "Quite. About a week's journey. Do you know Germany very well?" she asked, knowing full well Scarlet had not a clue, but again, showing too much courtesy to imply otherwise. Scarlet decided she liked Lady Katrina. For treating her as an equal, as a *person*.

"Not much. But I've always wanted to travel, see the countryside." Scarlet regretted right away sharing with a stranger such a personal thought and vowed to guard her soul better.

"You will be well served there, my dear, for the...*my* castle sits on an immense land, most of it forests and lakes."

Scarlet hadn't missed the hesitation when the woman said "my" castle. As though she weren't sure. But the lure of the countryside, its clean air and water, pushed away the nagging little voice in her head that had always served her so well. She'd become too distrustful in her twenty-odd years. Maybe it was time to finally let someone else lead for a while. At least until Scarlet would get to know her surroundings and what she could get from them. Then she'd leave and be on her own again but, this time, with some honest coins in her shoe and the countryside under her feet.

* * * * *

The journey to the lady's castle proved quite pleasant. The weather held nice for the entire eight days, the driver turned out to be a good imitator of people and accents, and Lady Katrina never tired of telling stories of travels and faraway lands. When they pulled onto the road leading to the castle, Scarlet couldn't keep the awe from slacking her jaw, rounding her eyes. Thick, strong oak trees guarded either side of the road as two neat rows of stoical sentinels. And the castle itself... Never had she seen such opulence, such serene strength.

Two massive towers, clearly older and rougher than the rest of the elegant affair, dwarfed the surrounding buildings. A moat, its water as green as pure jade, glittered at its base. Amid a thunderous beat of hooves, the coach rumbled onto the stone bridge leading to the raised portcullis, one that must have stood centuries past.

Scarlet sat beside the driver who regaled her of stories about barbarian invaders breaking their teeth upon the massive structure and of the galas and balls of years past.

Looking up at one of the two round towers, Scarlet thought she spotted a face at the only window—more like a slit—she could see. But when she blinked and looked again, the face was gone.

"Tell me, Frank, who lives in the tower there?" she asked, pointing up to her right.

A shadow crossed the weathered face. "The mistress may tell you. 'Tis not for me to say."

With a shrug, Scarlet let her gaze follow every corner of the castle, from moss-green gargoyles to gleaming oaken doors. This was a well-maintained gem of a home. Years of love and care had tended to the grounds she could spot through the interior gates. A rose garden the likes of which she'd never seen took an entire side of the walled garden beyond the enclosure. If she had any time to herself, she'd visit there first.

The coach lurched to a stop, horses fidgety and tired after such a long voyage. Scarlet nimbly jumped off the driver's seat, to Frank's pretend scowl, and landed silently on the cobbles. Lady Katrina did the same, opening the door herself and stepping down unaided. This was a woman who led her own life. Scarlet offered the tall woman a guarded nod.

Drawing near, Lady Katrina rested a hand over Scarlet's shoulder. "I will let Ute take care of you while I get a few things ready. When you are freshened, come see me in the library. We will discuss your employment then."

A gnarled old woman who must have been the Ute in question marched out of a door and took a straight line for Scarlet. Before she could say a word, the old woman brusquely jerked her thumb in the direction of a door and turned heel.

"Don't mind the old hen, she's as sweet as honey when you get to know her." Frank winked.

Scarlet had her doubts but followed the old woman across the courtyard. The whole time she felt observed, as though someone had eyes fixed on her alone. Without knowing why, she looked up to the east tower again but saw no one at the tiny window on this side. To hide her nervousness, she tossed an annoying red curl from her forehead and followed Ute into the kitchen.

Noises and smells greeted her, as did too many people to count or whom to remember the names. They seemed a friendly enough bunch save for Ute who grumbled and pushed the maids around.

"What's your name?" she asked suddenly, whirling on her heel and coming right up under Scarlet's nose.

"Scarlet." The short, simple reply seemed to please Ute for she nodded, a shadow of a grin appearing on her wrinkled face.

"Has the mistress told you what your work will be?"

Scarlet nodded. "Clean mostly and take care of an ill man. Her words."

Ute nodded, seemingly quite happy with the news. "We're so lucky Lady Katrina is taking such good care of her cousin. Came all the way here from the city too, she did. Good thing she was here on visit when it happened, when the master fell ill. Took charge of everything. She moved here within days to help care for him. Good woman, Lady Katrina."

Scarlet wasn't sure which city Ute meant but thought better than to ask.

"If you're going to take care of the master, then come here and get cleaned up, you smell like city pigs."

City pigs. Charming.

After washing the smell of "city pigs" from her with perfumed soap—a first in her life—Scarlet donned the clothes Ute had thrown at her over the swinging door of the lavatories. Gray dress, gray apron and gray underthings. Her copper hair must have stood out as though her head were on fire. Grinding her teeth, Scarlet came out of the lavatories to the approving nod of Ute and followed the old woman through the kitchen.

"Get a bite to eat on the run. You're already late."

In a whirlwind of unanswered questions, Scarlet wolfed down her food — which she was used to doing...when she had any. The library was in front of her before she knew she'd walked far enough to reach it. As much as she prided herself on never having become lost in a large city, this castle, with its part medieval portions meshed with more recent ones, proved to be a maze of corridors and stairs leading to labyrinthine halls and rooms.

Scarlet let out a gasp of shock when she entered the library.

Lady Katrina sat on a red velvet settee, her knees quite far apart from each other, and a broad-backed man with a ponytail knelt in between, enthusiastically lapping at her sex. Boots laced up to her knees gleamed like ink on either side of the man's head.

"Scarlet, my dear, how quick you are," Lady Katrina said as she toyed with the man's ponytail with a lacquered fingernail.

Emerging from between the lady's thighs, his lips glistening, the man in question stood. He must have enjoyed his task very much for his pleasure showed abundantly enough in his trousers.

"Where are my manners? Please meet my trusted friend and physician, Master Lothar," the lady said, stretching catlike.

Scarlet had to admit this could be one of the most handsome men she'd ever seen. Tall and muscled with large, square hands. He bowed, never letting his gaze break contact. "My pleasure."

Scarlet only nodded, her mind reeling with the concept that a lady of such quality would do these...things. It wasn't the idea per se, more the setting, with books, refinement and schooling surrounding them while they partook in carnal pleasure. A shiver snaked up her spine. She'd always associated carnal knowledge with pain, or at least discomfort and misery, with a lack of choice.

When he crossed the room, Scarlet tried to ignore the impressive bulge in the man's trousers and focused instead on the lady's face. Circling her like a vulture, Lothar drew near, extremely near. Heat from his body tickled the back of her neck when he passed behind her. A hint of female musk and perfume tickled Scarlet's nostrils. She gritted her teeth in alarm and excitement when he let a single finger trace the contour of her collar. Shivers followed in a tight wake. Blowing gently on the nape of her neck, Lothar planted himself right behind her, his torso and hips a hair away from her back. While he remained thus, almost touching her but not quite, his hands floated down along her arms and seized her wrists, which he brought back behind her. The whole while the lady watched, her cheeks flushed, obviously aroused herself.

Scarlet had to stifle a gasp when Master Lothar pressed her trapped hands against his stiffness. She could tell he was well-endowed, and by the way he let his breath stir strands of hair around her face and how he had run a gentle finger over her skin, Scarlet knew this had to be a spectacularly skilled man. And a dangerous one as well.

"I love your hair," he murmured, grasping both her wrists with a large hand. Another accent layered his speech. Austrian, perhaps? She'd heard that particular inflection before. His free hand came up behind her head and loosely fisted her curls. Scarlet fought the urge to pull against him and instead followed his backward movement. When her head rested completely on his chest, Master Lothar's hand released her wrists. His caress of her neck made Scarlet shiver.

And she who'd told Werner she wouldn't be no one's whore! The sobering thought tightened her mouth. She stared hard at Lady Katrina, hoping the message would get through.

"Do you want him to stop, Scarlet?" the lady asked, coming to her feet.

Scarlet sighed in relief. "Yes."

Though the word implied one thing, her breathlessness implied quite the contrary. How completely idiotic had she become in the span of a few moments? This place was provoking her dark humors.

Then suddenly a small, burning sting on her arm made her yelp. Whirling around and rubbing her biceps, Scarlet noticed Lothar had a small jewel-tipped needle in hand.

"What have you done to me?" Scarlet demanded, too late worrying about the edge in her voice.

Lothar didn't seem overly upset as he dropped the needle into a tiny vial he'd just pulled out of his vest pocket. The drop of blood on its tip swirled around and dissolved in the clear liquid.

"It is only a small test, Scarlet. To make sure it is safe for you to be near my cousin. I should have warned you. My apologies."

After a nod, Lothar slipped the bottle back in his vest. "Her blood is clean." Bowing, he took his leave without another word.

"The physician had to make sure no disease polluted your blood, so as not to infect my cousin. His health is already so fragile." She made a sad face. "No one here has passed the test in some time. Their blood is tainted, I am afraid. Something about living in these parts, perhaps. That is why we now must find someone who has never lived here. Only Lothar and I passed the test, being from another city. And now you."

Scarlet rubbed at her arm again. No blood had seeped through the cloth for which she was glad. Showing up for work bleeding hadn't been part of her plan to make a good first impression.

"Do you know how to read?" the lady asked, drawing near. She had the silver-ended cane in her hand, though she obviously had no need for it.

Still angry at being poked and prodded like cattle, Scarlet only managed a tight, "No."

"That is unfortunate. Your patient enjoys being read to. Let us meet him, then. I know he has seen you from his window."

"How much will I get paid?" Scarlet asked, regretting the question as soon as it left her mouth. Stupid girl.

After a long, withering glare, Lady Katrina's expression softened. "I forget what you had to go through in life just to survive." She brought the pommel of her cane up to Scarlet's chin and gently, slowly, ran it along her jaw. Scarlet stared through her mounting fear.

The lady leaned into Scarlet, their mouths an inch apart. "You have a strong will. I shall enjoy our association," she murmured before kissing Scarlet on the mouth.

As much as she tried to be shocked and revolted, Scarlet couldn't. The sheer sexuality and magnetism emanating from the tall woman almost pierced Scarlet's defenses. Almost. And when Lady Katrina straightened, Scarlet felt strangely bereft.

Such a strange place, this. Strange and dangerous.

Eager to break the spell, Scarlet clutched her hands behind her back and followed Lady Katrina up the stairs. An old man probably, ill and unable to read himself. Or a blind man, or perhaps one crippled in a hunt or battle. Scarlet didn't care if she'd be sloshing chamber pots around, as long as she received enough coins to make a new life for herself. *Elsewhere.*

Lady Katrina led the way deeper into the older portion of the castle. Scarlet recognized the different brickwork and mortar of the tower when they reached it. A small oil lamp blazed on a nearby table.

"Get the light," the lady said.

Scarlet did, holding the small lamp by its handle. A barred door took a good portion of the rounded wall. After digging under her tight midnight blue bodice, Lady Katrina pulled a brass key, which she inserted into the keyhole.

Strange way to an ill man's chambers.

"Here," the lady said, giving the key to Scarlet. "I keep the original. This one here is the only copy. If something happens to it while I am away…"

Scarlet could easily have picked the lock by the looks of it, but wouldn't tell the lady that. She put the key in her pocket. "Am I to be the only one to take care of him, then?"

"Yes. Aside from the physician and myself."

A thought occurred to Scarlet. "Who used to take care of him? Other servants here?"

Lady Katrina smiled. "The one who took care of him is…gone. It is hard work to care for an ill man and when he could no longer manage it, I found him easier work elsewhere. Now let us go meet my cousin."

When she opened the door, the small lamp's sputtering light flooded a staircase landing, and all Scarlet could see were steps twisting up. Narrow, steep steps. With no apparent effort, the lady climbed those steps at a brisk pace with Scarlet right on her heels.

A nagging suspicion slithered in Scarlet's mind. Why would the lady, with her obvious wealth and connections, want a mere street woman to care for her cousin? Why not a real maid or manservant? Where was that "other" gone to?

Trying not to let fear show through the stoic mask was hard. When she judged they'd gone almost to the top of the tower, a thick, cleated door barred further progress. A simple latch closed this one and no lock. When they opened it, a circular room the size of a small house gaped beyond.

Scarlet went in after the other woman, marveling at the size of the room, which went right up to the timbered ceiling. Two narrow slits, one on either side of the room, gave just enough light to make out pieces of furniture near the far wall. An expensive-looking rug covered most of the circular floor. Not a sound stirred the air. She'd expected smells of the sick and dying, but instead, a faint male perfume greeted her.

Along the wall near the door, a copper basin the size of a large barrel lying on its side gleamed softly in the faint light.

To her left, Lady Katrina took the lamp and put it on a nearby table. "Good day, cousin. I trust your health is good?"

No reply.

As much as she tried, Scarlet couldn't see a thing past the lamp's golden glow. Lumpy shadows here and there could have been the cousin in question but she couldn't be sure. There was a princely bed along the wall, with a mess of cushions and pillows. A table with two chairs, each at opposite ends. The inescapable chamber pot near the foot of the bed and a small dresser by the headboard. And that was the whole of this huge room's furniture.

"My cousin can be very quiet at times," the lady said, her mouth a tight line. Turning back to the elusive man, she added, "This is Scarlet, your new maid."

Scarlet had the distinct feeling the man in question was looking at her and not the lady. It was the same sensation she'd felt earlier when she'd first come into the courtyard. Not knowing where he was and what to call him, she just nodded at the shadows and crossed her hands behind her back. Fear was making her palms clammy.

"Come now, cousin, you do not want to scare away someone who will be so good to you."

Stifling a gasp, Scarlet noticed in a corner something her brain refused to assimilate. Then when she looked harder, it was gone. A trick of the light, no doubt. For a second, she'd seen a pair of glowing eyes, like those of animals in the darkness.

Chapter Three

✦

"It's time," a female voice said in the darkness.

Scarlet was instantly alert in her cot and fighting the urge to crouch in a defensive position. "Ute?"

The door to her room opened to let a single blade of light in. "Who else do you think is up at this ungodly hour?" Ute snapped, leaving her candle on Scarlet's dresser and closing the door back again.

Scarlet got out of bed without stretching and tiptoed to the washbasin. When she dipped her hands in it, Scarlet noticed the water had been perfumed. Good Ute. A grin the likes of which only the moon had seen spread on Scarlet's face. She quickly subdued it and washed herself though she'd had a bath the day before and was by no means dirty. Still, this was her first day at work and she wanted to make a good impression. She took particular care of her hands, which had always been grimy and caked with dirt under her fingernails. They had to be perfect today. She'd be serving a nobleman and had to show some good breeding.

When she entered, the kitchen was already a beehive of activity. Ute loudly berated one of the serving girls for having let "the master's food" grow cold.

"Master Lothar resides here as well?" Scarlet asked, hoping he didn't.

Ute rounded on her with fists on her hips. "I'm talking about the *true* master," she snarled, the poison in her tone surprising Scarlet. "Come," Ute went on, tugging Scarlet by a sleeve. "You make quick before this serving grows cold too." A withering glare at the serving girl added weight to the old woman's already menacing air.

Slowly, with an almost reverent air about her, Ute took a small vial from her pocket and let two drops sink into the master's food. Fanning it with her hand, she replaced the vial in her dress.

A faint scent came to her, tickled her memory. Scarlet wanted to ask but changed her mind. Questions weren't part of her duties.

As though the old woman had read her mind, she nodded gravely. "It's something the physician gave, it'll keep the master strong. Two drops, never less, never more. Something to do with a special thing...mi-ne-ral, I think." She struggled with the strange word.

Scarlet had never heard of it. She took the tray, balancing it expertly in one hand. "Is there a quicker way to his chamber?"

As if the question pleased Ute to the highest degree, she nodded. "Quick brain too, I'm glad to notice. Their blood may have been better than ours, but they didn't seem to have much in coin in their purse." Ute pointed to her temple with a gnarled index finger. "None of the others before you even thought of asking if there was a quicker way. And, yes, there is, a way us servants use. Come."

How many others had there been before her, exactly? Scarlet swallowed hard but kept her mouth shut.

Right turn at the kitchen, down a corridor with a blue carpet, up three steps and left into a low-hanging alcove. This time, Scarlet would remember this route. The door to the tower was there. The tray in one hand, she slipped the key out of her pocket and slid it smoothly in the keyhole. This thing would be a trifle to pick. Barely four or five rings inside the mechanism. Scarlet's practiced eye never missed a detail on any lock. There wasn't a one she couldn't pick.

"You've good hands from what I can see. So, what is it you used to do, girlie?"

"Tried my best not to starve," replied Scarlet while avoiding the astute old woman's eyes.

A soft chuckle warmed her heart. "Don't we all. Did the mistress tell you about the master's condition?"

Scarlet shook her head, knowing when to speak and when not to.

"Sun's his nemesis. Any kind of light, for that matter. His eyes are too pale to sustain any direct light. God knows he used to, out and about and as fit as a fiddle, back before his illness took over. He was always a tad different, mind you. But just you make sure to keep the lamp out of his face. Master Lothar said it could kill him. You hear?"

Killed by light. People were usually killed by darkness, or by not knowing how to handle it. Strange illness.

"I'll make sure the light is down low." She lowered the cap even farther on the lamp, shielding most of the light behind the copper plate.

"Good girl."

After the old woman had left, Scarlet took to the steps briskly, tray in one hand over her head, lamp clutched in her other, which she kept soft so the light wouldn't bounce around and make her misjudge a step. After she reached the cleated door, she noiselessly pushed it in and poked her head in the opening.

In the large bed lay her charge, long pale hair spilled onto dark pillows. He was much taller and wider of shoulder than she would've thought for a frail old man. Without a sound, she placed the lamp on the floor, padded to the table and deposited the tray there.

Through one of the narrow windows in the walls, a sliver of dawn light cut in at an angle. Despite the near darkness, she could spot something peculiar about the rug covering the portion of the room closer to the bed. A worn, narrow path in a semicircle went from one side of the room to the other. Like the curve of a bow.

Shrugging, Scarlet arranged the cutlery and teapot for her patient. She wasn't exactly sure how incapacitated he was, but she preferred to err on the side of caution. She depended on his good graces—and the lady's—to gather enough coins for her new life. Maybe she could even buy a small farm and grow—

A small metallic clink alerted her keen senses. She whirled around, one hand going reflexively for the fork.

"Servants usually *knock* before they enter my room."

His voice floated in from the gloom like the rustle of drapes in a breeze. In a corner, she spotted a tall, dark form slowly approaching. It came closer until she could make out a head and wide shoulders. He stepped into the sliver of dawn light with the eerie silence of a ghost ship gliding into port.

Scarlet tightened her fist around the fork as the man drew nearer. She could see very straight white hair that came down just above his square shoulders, through the long bangs a pale, high brow, white eyebrows, a long and narrow nose and…

Eyes the color of blood.

Scarlet swallowed discreetly, drawing on a life spent on the streets of Amsterdam to help keep her wits about her. Primal alarm twisted her insides. This was no time to show fear or doubt, for this man would sense it right away. She could recognize a predator when she spotted one, and this man was one.

So this was to be her patient. Not the frail old man she'd expected. In his thirties, if she'd have to guess, although his eyes were much, much too old for the rest of him, with skin so pale as to appear white and standing a good two hands above her. He wore a high-collared black tunic, which hugged his lean frame and came down to the floor. A row of buttons like a string of silver pearls went from his neck to between his feet.

Scarlet gritted her teeth, forced her face into an impassive mask. "I didn't want to disturb you." Lying came so easily to her.

"Are you going to stab me with my own cutlery?" His Dutch was much more accented than the lady's or even Lothar's. Rs rolled in the master's mouth.

"If you have wicked intentions toward me, yes, I'll stab you with whatever I have." Scarlet forced herself not to wince at her abruptness.

A row of pearly teeth flashed when he grinned. The smile was so fleeting she could have imagined the whole thing. "Fair warning," he replied. The velvet tunic rustled softly when he moved. Now that she could study his chest closely, the buttons holding the tunic together were in the image of a snarling wolf's face.

Scarlet slowly, cautiously, set the fork by the plate. "Your food, it's growing cold...Master...Sire. Sir."

His strange gaze scanned her from head to hem. Scarlet resisted the urge to squirm.

After a while, he cocked his head to the side, clearly gauging her. "My cousin really outdid herself this time. You almost sound real."

"Almost sound real?" she blurted out.

If her tone bothered him, he didn't let it show. Another small step brought him a mere hand from her. Though she was no short thing herself, she had to look up, way up, to meet his gaze. Her heart gave a great thud. There was something unnatural about his eyes. Apart from the color...

Sweat clammed her hands. Scarlet wanted to run away as fast as she could but couldn't break the strange moment of them facing each other. She should run. Right now. *Flee.* This was too much for a single day. If Lothar had elicited a reaction from her body, this man here took the prize. It was all she could do not to faint dead on the floor. By God, he was beautiful in a ghostlike, eerie way. And he was very, very dangerous.

"What's in it?"

"Ute prepared it, Master, I didn't. Smelled like eggs and ham, though." Her stomach used the silence to let its presence be heard.

A white eyebrow arched but he said nothing. Without warning, he leaned into her and kissed her.

Her first reaction was panic. Scarlet almost kneed him and ran. Almost.

This sort of thing had been done to her before. Men always seemed to think they could get away with it. Scarlet closed her eyes. It was all about control, she knew. This one was wrestling control away from her, using his intimidating appearance to frighten her into submission. Werner had tried to cow her as well, only it hadn't worked. And it wouldn't now.

Yet Scarlet couldn't remember any kiss being so…gentle. Not the bruising ordeal she was used to. Gentle as silk, his lips barely touched hers, only grazed from one corner of her mouth to the other. His breath stopped for a while then resumed. An ache the likes of which she'd never experienced before clutched at her belly, reduced her nipples to tiny throbbing hearts. How could a man she'd only just met produce such a reaction in her?

Heat like a fever flushed her cheeks. Raising her face to his, she let him kiss her more deeply, until his tongue tentatively brushed against the seal of her lips. A moan struggled up her throat, but she pushed it back down, refusing to yield to the mounting desire clawing at her, refusing to succumb to her flesh. Her instincts had kept her alive. She should listen to them now and flee while she still could. Scarlet, instead, raised her head higher. She could perhaps just let him kiss her, take her pleasure while she could, but not surrender the rest.

Within a matter of moments, Scarlet's flesh felt on fire. She was slipping fast.

Knowing it may open something she couldn't close back again, Scarlet yielded to the yearning, to the call of the flesh this man so easily raised. When he put a hand to her cheek, she let it rest against it, enjoying the way his palm provided warmth and soft support to her head. Hesitantly, she touched his white hair, marveling at the silky quality of it, then snaked a hand up his arm, around his neck. Scarlet pressed his head down against hers.

The man pressed his other hand against her chest, seemingly feeling for her heart, which thudded against her ribs with the rhythm of a mad drum. Long fingers traced the contour of her collar, parted the fabric in the middle, even managed to undo the first tiny button.

Her body reacted almost violently to his touch. Spasms tightened her sex, which was growing slicker by the second. Arching back into him, she allowed his gentle mouth access to her throat while his hand pulled the fabric of her bodice under a breast, exposing the aching nipple to air. And to his mouth.

Scarlet hissed a breath when he wrapped his lips around then suckled the nipple he'd just freed from its constraint. No man had ever bothered to pleasure her this way before. They usually just went ahead with their own pursuit.

He said something in German she couldn't understand. The sound of his velvet voice, deep yet soft, raised the fine hair on her arms. If he went further than kissing, she wasn't sure she'd object. May even help.

A metallic clink triggered an immediate reaction in her sharp-edged instincts. Scarlet pulled away several paces, hurriedly rearranging her dress before bumping against the copper bathtub occupying the wall near the door. The man just stood there, panting, then leaned against his end of the table for support. He stepped back from the sliver of dawn light, back into the shadows.

The door to the room opened wider. "Good morning, dear cousin Fredrick. I trust you are in capable hands."

Shame flushed Scarlet's cheeks. Refusing to give in to it, she stared stubbornly at the lady when she glided in the room, silver cane jauntily resting over a shoulder.

"Very capable hands, but that's why you hired her, wasn't it?" the man—Fredrick—sneered, coming back into the pale light and sitting at the table. He poured himself a cup of tea.

Stung more acutely than she should have, Scarlet noticed his hands shook. So did hers, for that matter. He threw a quick glance at her through his bangs and sat straighter. A collection of dull clinks accompanied his movements. With her gaze, she searched for its source.

Then the realization hit her. Everything about the room, the peculiar worn path on the rug, the table so distant from the rest of the furniture...it all hit her squarely in the chest.

He was in chains.

This was no sick man's room, but a cell.

A silver-colored manacle and lock bound the man's naked ankle, crusted with blood, with the other end of the long chain cemented directly into the wall behind the bed. She hadn't seen it when he'd been lying there, and hadn't heard it when he walked to the table. If she hadn't been so engrossed by his eerie beauty, his tender mouth...

Her instincts had failed her.

"Do not look so scared, Scarlet, my cousin may look...menacing, but he is properly restrained."

"I'm not scared, Lady Katrina. It's just...the chains..."

The lady looked annoyed for a split second before smiling sadly. "For his own safety, of course. Such is his illness."

Perhaps he suffered from an illness of the mind? Was prone to hurting himself or others? Something was obviously abnormal about his feverish, haunted gaze. Would he be dangerous to work around? She never made a habit of turning her back on anyone, but perhaps this man would require even more awareness. Still, to chain him?

Scarlet clenched her jaws harder. Hers wasn't the place to ask questions. If there was a chain around the man's ankle, it was because it needed to be there. All she wanted, all she cared for, was making enough coins to get out of there and start a new life far from Werner and his greedy clutches. Far from Lady Katrina and whatever dark secret she fostered. And—most importantly—far from this dangerously beautiful man with the feverish eyes and tender mouth.

* * * * *

Fredrick had been alive a long time. God knew he had. Too long, he thought sometimes. Yet he'd never met a woman like her. *Scarlet.* He remembered *her* name right away, unlike the others before. Not the usual sort his cousin brought back from the city to take care of him. His thoughts turned right back to Scarlet and his spirits were considerably lifted.

To say the woman had walked right into the room, so close he'd been able to touch her. It'd been such a long time since he'd tasted a real woman, and not his sadistic cousin. He hadn't been able to stop himself in time.

She hadn't recoiled despite his appearance, which unfailingly made people who weren't used to it uneasy. This required pluck. Instead, she'd welcomed his attentions, even manifested her own. Strange, spirited woman. If only she weren't in his cousin's employ, an ally to his own personal devil.

Fredrick watched the servant leave, pretending to be too engrossed with his breakfast—which was excellent and devoid of any suspect matter or smell—to notice. But he did notice. As did his cousin.

"What a succulent *kleiner Apfel* she is, do you not think?" Cousin said, leaning against the cane. "One just wants to take a bite, *nein?*"

Fredrick's first reaction was anger, which surprised him. Why did he care if his cousin was attracted to the young woman? She could have the servant. It's not as though she were relevant. Not as though she'd ever be his. Melancholy filled his heart. He pushed the emotion down, kept it from Cousin's cunning eyes.

"Why deny it? I would have enjoyed her as well," she replied, smiling widely. "Then again, maybe I *will*. Lothar is already enamored with her, may even invite her into our chambers."

At the mention of the vile man, Fredrick nearly lost his crackling composure, one he'd fought the last two years to attain. He fought the rage welling up inside him, fought the darker side of his soul as it struggled for control. It was his cousin's dearest wish to break him, make him lose control, let the beast within rip out of his soul.

"What do you want, Cousin? I'm eating."

The grin slid off her angular face. "Then you better enjoy it while you can, because it is that time of the month again. I shall be back tonight."

After she left, Fredrick finished his breakfast. He'd need his strength.

* * * * *

Fredrick had felt it for days. The moon was rising high in the sky, its face a perfect disk. A full moon.

And as with every full moon, his cousin's malicious game would begin. It usually went thus— His cousin would ask for his signature of the marriage and transfer deed. He'd say no, send her to Hell. Her thugs would show up. Then his world would become one of pain. Again. It'd been this way for the past two years, ever since he'd invited her for a short visit. She'd seduced him, drugged him with the help of her odious physician. Fredrick had awakened here, in the tower, and hadn't seen the sky since.

Scheming witch.

It wasn't the thought of her and that man-whore sleeping in his room, or her running his castle that disgusted him the most. For all her faults, his cousin was a clever businesswoman, albeit a ruthless one. It was what she intended to do with his people that sent his blood boiling. Because she was indeed such an astute trade-minded person, she wanted to split up his lands and sell them off, one bit at a time. Where would his people find work, which was so rare in these parts? Though the same von Innsbruck blood flowed in her veins, she felt no sense of allegiance whatsoever toward their land, the people depending on them.

He *did* feel an allegiance to his people and prided himself on knowing each one by first name and family history. No wonder, since he was both the ancestor who'd gathered the wealth in the first place, and the descendant who now owned it. Fredrick von Innsbruck the First. Only he knew his exact age — one hundred and twenty-two years — the last eighty-six or so in his present "form". Ever since that long ago night, in the forest, when he'd been attacked...left *different*.

As if the word alone had summoned the demon, she entered the room, looking more ravishing than ever. If demons were the image of the Devil himself, then Hell was peopled with beautiful creatures indeed. Beautiful and deadly.

"I am glad to have found a new plaything for you, Fredrick," she said, intruding upon his thoughts. "The next few months will be particularly enjoyable. For both of us, I think."

Three months. That was usually how long she kept her servants around. By that time, either they would develop pity for him and try to help, or they would turn into nasty little swines like the last one. Either way, they invariably ended up a nuisance to his cousin. And being a nuisance to that woman meant only one thing.

Scarlet would be no different. The thought that someone else was going to suffer and die because of him weighed on his soul. Yet giving in to Cousin would mean much worse —

poverty and misery for the hundreds who depended on the von Innsbrucks. And so Fredrick had to live with the fact he had, and would again, sacrifice a few to save many.

Feigning indifference, Fredrick shrugged as he emptied his cup of cold tea. Then, rising, he stood in the center of the room, waiting for the inevitable, like a beach for the tide.

She carried the cane in one hand and a five-arm candelabrum in the other. For her benefit, and that of her thugs, since Fredrick had no need for light.

"Why can you not admit what you cannot change?" she asked, coming so very close he could smell her. "Marry me, give me an heir. I would even let you live a while to see him or her prosper under my tutelage."

"Tutelage? You mean something like this?" Fredrick said, tapping his foot once so the chain would clink.

Cousin tut-tutted. "Of course not. Never my own flesh and blood. I would not do it to my future husband, either. Were it not for your special...abilities, I never would have chained you in my tower. I would have tied you to my bed."

Fredrick didn't join in her laughter. "It's *my* tower and *my* bed, in case you're forgetting your place."

The grin turned into an ugly scowl. "I know what you are," she snapped as she angrily struck the floor with the butt of the cane. "Do not try to hide it from me. I have known for years, Fredrick. Years. And I have watched you, studied you, until I could find a flaw in your armor — oh, it is hard to find — but there is one. Some day, Fredrick, I will find it, and when I do, I will slide a blade right into it."

Fredrick snorted in derision. "There is no flaw in my armor."

A sudden cramp made his lip twitch. Was it time already?

Cousin's eyes narrowed. She licked her lips. "Why do you fight it? I would not."

Fight it? As though he could.

Already, he could feel the first subtle changes in his body. Smells became sharper, so did sounds. His vision, already better than most, heightened. Then he heard them. Four pairs of feet climbing up the steps.

"You can feel them coming, can you not?" she asked, her nostrils flared with excitement. "What I would not do to taste you like this, right at this moment, to take you all in." Lust blazed behind her eyes. She let the silver butt of the cane rest against her thigh, slowly rubbing up and down.

The quick knock on the door sounded like thunderclap to Fredrick's acute senses. Four men spilled into the room in perfect silence, each with a hatchet handle in his hand. A revolting mixture of smells accompanied them. Onions, ale and mutton. Oil from one of the men's boots and tobacco from another's mouth. One of them had recently bled for Fredrick could smell the coppery tang he knew too well.

His cousin licked her ruby lips, teasing him with the sight of her tongue. "It is time to change your mind, dear cousin. Sign the deed and all of this will go away."

"Go to Hell."

She laughed. "You will not mind if I let you get there first?"

With a quick nod of her chin, she indicated the men could begin. After taking a few steps back, she set the candelabrum on her side of the table, sat on the chair and proceeded to pleasure herself with his cane.

Without emotions, the men fanned out on either side. He never had to wait long.

Fredrick undid the first few buttons on his tunic. The usual signal. Such a perverted dance this had become.

Fredrick sidestepped the first attack, snarling in triumph when his fist collided against one's face. Bones crunched satisfyingly under his knuckles. But the transformation was making it hard to control his limbs. He stumbled back, exploding suns of pain behind his eyelids, searing, blinding him. His expanding jaw cracked audibly, made him groan.

He swung with a throbbing fist, caught something. Then something swung at him, caught him. Fredrick tasted blood on his tongue. Bastards. His neck stretched impossibly wide as his shoulders popped out of their sockets. White-hot pokers singed him as his skin split over his elbows, his hands.

Images, horrible with clarity, flashed in front of him, like a mad monochromatic puppet show. *People fleeing in terror at the sight of him. Others brandishing crude weapons, spitting insults, setting fire to his refuge.* So long ago, too many memories.

He tried to shut them out, reel back from the visions of Hell and damnation. For this is how he felt, damned. In every way. Damned to Hell, damned to life. Damned to solitude and ostracism.

His whole body rang with grief. Fredrick took blind swipes of his rapidly changing hands but met only air. A cry of impotence and frustration ripped up his throat. Blood was blinding him. *His* blood, damn it!

After what felt an eternity, he collapsed onto one knee, panting, wheezing. Still, the men pounded on him. He was struck on a kneecap and felt it split, howled at the liquid fire spreading up his thigh. Another blow, and this one ruined his left hand, which he was using to cover his head.

The sound accompanying each blow sounded dull as a felt drum. In one last desperate charge, he managed to grab one by the throat, squeezed through the hail of blows falling on him. The man yelled in pain. The sound of gurgles forced Fredrick's eyes open. Through the blood trickling down into his eyes, he saw his victim hanging limply by the throat. Fredrick's hand, the one holding the lifeless form, had sprouted glistening dark claws, which dug into the man's flesh. A thin but powerful jet of blood squirted out rhythmically. Someone yelled. Man, woman, he could no longer tell.

Fredrick only had time to wince when one of the men hit him squarely on the mouth. He dropped the lifeless body, threw himself at this new tormentor. The chain shredded his flesh. Something popped in his ankle.

Now forced on all fours by the agony of the transformation and the men's relentless assault, Fredrick could do nothing but yelp with each strike. His vocal cords and most of the sinews holding his head tore apart, he heard every single one pop in his skull. Yet Fredrick knew the worst was still to come.

When his face began to change, his nose and mouth to elongate, his growing teeth to pierce and shred his gums, his eye sockets to separate, the blinding pain reduced him to a quivering heap on the floor. The men had stopped beating him. That or he could no longer feel the blows. Then complete silence.

Before the change completely took him and his human mind, he felt rather than sensed a presence by his side. Through a ruined mouth, which no longer functioned as a man's, Fredrick struggled to force words out, to show he was still in control.

"…kill you…"

Hellish pain made him roar. The howl escaping his mouth a sound no man could make.

Chapter Four

ജ

There was a beast after her. She heard it panting, growling. Strangely, a sweet smell accompanied it, tickled Scarlet's memory. She knew that smell. Out of breath, she ran down the tower staircase. Stones abraded her palms, which she kept against the walls to keep from falling. She'd always been a good runner. It'd kept her alive all these years. But the beast was gaining. It'd catch her soon. A clawed hand fell on Scarlet's shoulder. She screamed.

Scarlet snapped up in her bunk with the force of a breaking bowstring. Sweat clammed her hands. The smell of her nightmare, sweet, flowery scent, drifted away. Snarling a curse, she flopped back down and rolled over. A soft knock came to her door.

"Scarlet," Ute said before opening the door. "Are you all right, girl? Heard you scream all the way to the kitchen."

Scarlet slid out of bed and hurriedly donned her clothes. "I'm fine."

Keeping her gaze averted as she slid by Ute and through the doorway, Scarlet climbed up the steps to the kitchen. She'd never had many dreams, never seemed to have slept long enough *to* dream.

She knew the beast. Of that, she was sure.

"'Tis the master's bath today," Ute said before putting the cover back on the plate. "While you help him with breakfast, I'll have the lads bring the hot water to the tower. They'll leave it by the door downstairs because none of them's blood was good."

Lothar's test came back to Scarlet's mind. "The physician tested everyone?"

Ute nodded, pain shrouding her usually clear gaze. "Even me, who've cared for him for so long, wasn't pure enough to get inside the tower. But the lady spared no coin, let me tell you. She searched far and wide to find those with the good kind of blood so as not to infect the master. And then the physician tests them, to make sure."

"What happens when someone's blood isn't..." Scarlet stopped, unwilling to use the word "pure" but not knowing any other fitting term.

Ute's cheeks grew blotchy red. "The special brew in the vial turns green."

A wave of sympathy engulfed Scarlet for the anguish in the old woman's eyes made her look twice her age. Poor, loyal woman. Yet another thought clouded the first. What sort of flaw in one's blood could make it turn green?

Scarlet pushed the nagging suspicion aside and concentrated on the day's task. The thought of bringing all that water up the tower stairs didn't particularly please her. But she'd want a bath once in a while too, and surely the master did. She shook images of his naked body from her mind.

She was still fighting off visions of a naked Fredrick by the time she came to the tower. Her heart beat madly against her chest. She still wasn't sure if stealing hadn't been better than standing by while a man was kept chained to the wall.

Scarlet pushed the thought away. Not her place. She'd be gone soon, never return, no use getting in trouble.

Darkness greeted her when she unlocked the door. Letting her eyes adjust to it took only a few seconds. She'd always felt a kinship to darkness, to the night. She grabbed the small candle and put it on his tray.

The image of the master, his red eyes glowing softly, made her swallow hard. After climbing up the steps, she stopped and, this time, she knocked.

Some grumbled reply came to her through the thick door. She pushed against it with her hip. A smell permeated the whole place. Like musk, but sweeter.

A single beam of pale light hit the floor at an angle. Particles of dust floated around the room and danced in swirly patterns. Scarlet closed the door with her heel.

"I have your breakfast here, Master Fredrick," she said, for some reason feeling the need to whisper.

There was a strange stillness in the air, as though she'd just entered after a violent gust of wind had knocked everything over. Like a blanket settling down.

"Leave it on the table," his voice said from the deeper darkness across the circular room.

She did, keeping well outside the worn mark on the rug.

After she'd placed his cutlery and serviette by the plate and filled his cup with steaming water for his tea, Scarlet took a few steps back. Something wasn't quite right. She couldn't explain it.

"Is everything all right, Master Fredrick?"

"Why do you ask?" There was a point of irony in his voice.

"Are you too ill to come to the table? I could…"

She'd been about to offer him to put the tray on his bed. Could she, suspecting, *knowing* how dangerous he was? How dangerous and alluring and irresistible he was. She clearly remembered how little in control she'd felt when he'd kissed her.

"Take the tray to me, you mean?" he finished for her.

She hated the note of sarcasm in his tone, the mockery. Why did he make her feel this way for showing sympathy?

A faint sound announced he was moving. Scarlet fought the urge to back up against the door. Trepidation fluttered in her gut as a shadowy lump stood erect and approached the center of the room. Master Fredrick stopped right at the edge of light.

Scarlet's chin dropped. "What happened?"

A nasty bruise covered his temple, went over his left eye then blackened the bridge of his nose. His lower lip was split as well. His opened tunic revealed more bruises on his pale chest.

"I fell."

Derision dripped from his words. Scarlet grabbed her hands behind her back. "You fell hard. Can I bring you anything for the pain?"

He shook his head, dislodging strands of white hair from his delicate ears. He took a step closer, which drew the chain taut behind him. "Will you give me my bath today?"

"Pardon me? I don't think...it wasn't part—" Scarlet stammered. He was supposed to take his own bath, not with her around. Or this is what she'd thought. Him naked while she...

She'd seen naked men before. Too many, in fact. But they didn't matter. This felt different, for some reason. Did it mean *he* mattered? She threw a quick peek at the copper bathtub by the door.

He merely watched as she struggled to form a polite and coherent reply. As though amused, he crossed his arms and cocked his head to the side, waiting patiently. Feeling a fool, Scarlet gritted her teeth. "Of course, Master Fredrick. That's what I get paid for. Ute said she'd have the water waiting downstairs by the time you finish your breakfast." There.

She hadn't linked so many words in years.

He nodded. "I'm looking forward to a nice, hot bath."

The grin he bore looked more like a snarl than anything else and Scarlet balled fists at her sides to hide her uneasiness. Her excitement, as well.

Blood beat a liquid tempo in her ears as she tried not to imagine him naked. She failed miserably.

While he ate, she busied her mind on other matters, such as how she would give the man his bath without coming in contact with him.

"Why do you always tiptoe?" he asked, giving her a look through a section of bangs.

Scarlet started. "I don't tiptoe."

He nodded. "You do. Why?"

She didn't tiptoe. Did she? After a while, she just shrugged. "I don't want to make noise, I guess."

He stared a long while before he tipped his chin at her. "Frightened children tiptoe. But you're a woman. Are you frightened?"

A tiny sound from down below alerted her keen senses and saved her from answering. *Yes*, she admitted, *I'm frightened. Everything here is frightening.*

She looked at the doorway, even if she knew no one would be coming through it.

"You have good ears," Master Fredrick commented between mouthfuls. The man ate as though each bite were the most succulent he'd ever tasted.

"They keep me out of trouble," Scarlet replied without thinking. She clamped her mouth shut, frustrated at showing such openness to this man.

He lifted his head, sniffed once. "Can you smell this?"

Scarlet took in a slow breath through her nose, leaving her mouth partly opened so she could taste the air as well. Nothing at first, but then a very faint odor reached her. "Sage?"

"Close. Lavender. It's my bath."

Scarlet swallowed hard. With a nod, she left the room, ran down the steps, and emerged just as a pair of lads had deposited four buckets filled with steaming water and beside which a small wooden crate contained bottles, soaps and quilted linen. The smell of lavender was indeed very strong here.

She thanked the lads, took two of the buckets and brought them up the steps where she emptied them in the copper bathtub. It took her about ten trips to fill it. The whole while, Master Fredrick stared at her silently, as though gauging her, weighing her against some mental scale only he knew. Scarlet's cheeks felt flushed with the exertion and his scrutiny. Finally, puffing slightly, Scarlet emptied the last bucket, set it down by the door then put her fists on her hips. What now? The chain wasn't long enough.

"It has wheels," Fredrick offered, standing.

Scarlet checked underneath the bathtub. So it had. She barely needed to spare a look at the mechanism to know how it worked. She'd always been good at things like these, even if she couldn't even write her own name. Releasing the four foot-triggers, the bathtub was raised slightly off the floor. Quite ingenious.

Master Fredrick came to the end of his chain. "It took your predecessor a good hour to figure the wheels. It was very entertaining."

"I've always had a good eye for gears and…"

"And…?"

"Nothing," Scarlet replied, busily maneuvering the heavy contraption from against the wall.

"When I ask a question, I expect an answer," he said, his voice much deeper now.

She turned to look at him, noted the downward slant of his mouth. She groaned inwardly. "Locks," she said. "I've a good eye for locks."

He didn't push it.

Scarlet guided the bathtub farther into the room, onto the carpet, making sure no water was wasted. When she turned to gauge his reach, she gasped.

He wore nothing but a collection of nasty bruises and his chain.

Her reaction was amusing to Fredrick. Here was a woman obviously hardened by life, with senses almost as keen as his own, yet she gasped at his nudity. Even averted her eyes.

If her reaction was interesting, his own was proving embarrassing. Already his member was growing by increments the more she wrestled the bathtub into place, with sweat dampening her lips, making her hair clingy and frizzy. Fredrick took a step closer, hurting his already raw ankle. When it was close enough, he helped, pulling the bathtub closer to him and turned it so it faced the door. Had she done it on purpose, he wondered, presented the bathtub so he'd have his back to her while he bathed? For some irrational reason, he wanted to watch her while he took his bath. He wanted her to *watch him* take his bath.

Scarlet brought the wooden crate containing his things. His favorite lavender soap smelled strongly now—good old Ute. Scarlet stopped, looked at the chain on the floor then his arms, as though trying to gauge his reach.

She was already well inside it.

But Fredrick didn't let it show. Instead, he put the stops back on the wheels and stepped in. The water was still very hot, thanks to her quick work. He'd had baths weekly, but they'd been the cold sorts. He hadn't had hot water in his bath in over four months, since the maid before the last servant had left—had been *killed*.

And the same fate awaited this woman here as well. Averting his gaze, Fredrick sank in the bathtub and let out a long sigh of contentment.

Though he would be healed before nightfall, several bruises from his encounter of the night before still marred his pale skin. And he knew she'd noticed, felt glad, in fact, of the way she seemed upset by it.

"I need the soap," he said, reaching toward her.

She didn't even flinch. All the others before her, except for his manservant, had looked horrified at the prospect of coming so near. With a couple of cautious steps, she reached out and proffered the thick bar of soap. On purpose, he let his fingers graze hers. Goose bumps appeared on her neck and down her cleavage. His erection became even tighter.

She retreated, but not as far as she'd originally been. With an occasional glance her way, Fredrick lathered his chest then his legs. When he came to his ankle, he could tell she wanted to take a closer look. The lock beaded with water.

Fredrick hooked his leg over the rim, letting his foot dangle out.

With an inclination of her torso almost imperceptible except to him, she leaned closer. This was no idle curiosity. A professional was presently looking at his lock. He could tell she was mentally picking it just by the way she stared unblinkingly, her fingers twitching. So she'd been a thief at the least, perhaps even disguised as a paid escort. He'd seen them often enough—young women trained to pick their patrons' pockets just as efficiently as bed them. This last thought, with accompanying images of Scarlet with other men, sent a jolt of jealousy through him.

"What do you think?" he asked, masking his emotions with the stoic mask he'd perfected over the years.

"It's expensive. Custom-made. But it's strange though…" she stopped, as if she'd just spoken too much.

He nodded, patiently waiting. Time was something he had plenty of.

"It's made of *silver*," she said finally.

"No other lock you've seen is made of silver?" He knew the answer. No one would use such an expensive material to lock someone down. Unless said someone was able to break out of any type of metal. Except silver.

"No, never. It sure costs an arm." She smiled in a guarded, cautious way.

Costs an arm?

He grinned inwardly. Yet at the same time, his old, old mind began to consider the possibilities. The gears in his brain began turning. Could she pick *this* lock? he wondered. Would she? Surely she must have been afraid of his cousin and Lothar. Who wouldn't? Could he convince her to do this for him?

Fredrick von Innsbruck the First, the Second and the Third, all one and the same man, hadn't led a virtuous life. Far from it. But he had one quality. Patience. To be as old as he was, he'd needed to be patient, to let things come instead of chasing after them. And this woman, this prickly and edgy woman, would spot him a league away if he merely *thought* of chasing after her. She had the senses of a bird of prey. Fredrick licked his lips. Using Scarlet, the only decent person he'd met in the last several cold, lonely months, wouldn't be the highlight of his life. But whatever it took, he would do. She just *had* to pick the damned lock—otherwise, he'd die here. All he had to do now was convince her he wasn't dangerous...

Fredrick looked at her as Scarlet stood next to the bathtub, the crate in her hands, an expression he couldn't quite define on her angular face. She was so beautiful to him, not in the elegant ways of ladies of the court, or through sheer sexuality. Too thin for her height, she had rough, skinny hands and out-of-control hair. All the privations she must have endured showed well enough in her hard lines and dark eyes. She wouldn't have graced any artist's tableau. But to Fredrick, Scarlet was beautiful because she was *real*.

His cousin was wrong. Scarlet wasn't a small apple, but a woman. A resilient, bristly, beautiful woman.

Slowly so as not to startle her, Fredrick reached out, let his index finger brush against her wrist. Though he could tell she wanted to pull her hand away, she didn't. With eyes half closed, he traced the edge of her rough palm then each finger one at a time. A shiver shook her.

Fredrick let his other hand rest against the bathtub's rim—well in view. His member now bobbed almost to the surface between his bruised knees. He knew she could see it through the soapy water. This pleased him. Foolish pride. Through the fabric of her dress, her nipples hardened into garnets. Remembering the taste and silky quality of them, Fredrick let his hand travel up her sleeve, wet spots seeping into the gray cotton, and finally reached the collar. He ran his index finger slowly down along the simple trim of her cleavage and marveled at the willpower she displayed by staying perfectly immobile, though he could tell she wanted to run.

"How old are you, Scarlet?" he asked gently, knowing anything could trigger her defensive instincts.

She shrugged. "I'm not sure."

He guessed mid- to late twenties but it was hard to judge with someone who had lived such a hard life. She could have been eighteen for all he knew.

Instead of continuing down into her cleavage, something he wanted more than anything else at the moment, he turned his hand so his palm faced up and retraced his journey, only this time, he followed her too-thin neck, the sharp jaw and pointy chin. Lips like pink orchids glistened softly in the dim light. Such pretty, freckled skin for one so unrefined. He liked her nose, come to think of it. A sharp nose that ended in a slight downward curve. A strong nose. Yet he avoided looking into her eyes. He couldn't take the chance she'd see through his ruse.

To his complete shock and excitement, Scarlet reached out and touched his cheek. The rough finger traced his cheekbone then the bridge of his recently broken nose. It'd heal. It always did.

Bracing herself against the edge, she knelt by the bathtub. After pulling her sleeves up over the most sinewy forearms he'd seen on a woman, she took the square of quilted linen and rubbed it too hard against the bar of soap. As though checking for his approval—which she had, by God—Scarlet slowly slid her hand inside the washcloth. Fredrick had to bite down hard to keep his face impassive when she rubbed his shoulder, each one in turn then back again, then his arms. She took care not to press too hard around the many places where bruises marred his skin. The whole while, he looked at her hands, never her eyes. *Never look into her eyes.*

After she rinsed the washcloth, she repeated the process with the soap and came up behind his head. Using her fingers like a comb, she raked his hair back, sending tingles of pleasure down to his curled-in toes then ran the washcloth from his scalp to the ends of his hair. Heat from the water and her gentle ways made him sigh. When she was done with his hair, rinsing profusely and wringing out the excess water, she returned to his side and lathered the washcloth again. This time, Fredrick could readily guess her destination.

Slowly, without looking into his face once, Scarlet pressed the washcloth against his knee. Getting the hint, he pulled his foot out of the water and let it rest against the rim. She didn't hurt him once when she went around his swollen and raw ankle. How could a woman so obviously rough be so gentle? For the first time in his life, someone was washing him, washing his *feet*, for Pete's sake. He felt torn between guilt and pleasure, but he remained motionless, afraid to his core to break the spell.

With a muscle twitching at her jaw, Scarlet slid her linen-covered hand past his knee, down along the top of his thigh, before swerving inward. Fredrick stopped breathing.

He couldn't take much more of this!

But he had to. If he startled her, she'd never trust him again, and he'd be stuck here forever. Only she could help him now. Only she could open the damned lock. After—if—she opened the lock and set him free, he'd take care of things from there. And God help his cousin.

Ride it, he told his feverish body. *Don't let it ride you.*

Fredrick closed his eyes and let the hot water and this peculiar woman's ministrations take him to a place he'd forgotten existed. Peace.

He felt the washcloth going around his aching member then under between his cheeks, before coming back up again. His lower belly constricted when Scarlet spent too long washing him there, his balls constricted. Damn. He'd spill himself if she didn't stop.

"Scarlet..." he said, his tone a warning he prayed she would—wouldn't—listen.

She answered his prayer. With her eyes still downcast, she wrapped her hand around his shaft, soap squeezing out of her fist, and rubbed up and down, slowly but firmly. Fredrick nearly bit his tongue. A few other strokes would unmake him. Closing his eyes and holding on to the bath's rim with the strength of a drowning man, he heaved a deep sigh. Unrelenting, Scarlet pumped. His seed exploded out of him and into the washcloth. This woman could achieve in moments what others in the past had worked very hard to do. Two years chained in one's own tower probably helped too.

Opening his eyes, he sighed harder than he would've liked as Scarlet folded the washcloth and placed it in the wooden crate.

"There," she said, her voice barely above a whisper. "Good as new."

That mouth. God, he wanted so much more than her hands on him. He wanted that mouth, as well, everywhere. He forgot himself. Before she could step away, he snatched her wrist and pulled her down to him.

Scarlet's mouth tightened into a line. Her gaze grew cold. Cursing his stupidity, he released her. She backed away several paces.

"Forgive me," he said, his words no lie. "I haven't...it's been a while since a woman was this gentle with me."

Then he made his biggest and worst mistake. He looked up into her eyes.

Loneliness. Hurt. Years of distrust and hardships. It was all there in her coal-colored eyes.

The jolt hit him right in the chest, as acutely as if someone had struck him. Fredrick averted his eyes right away. Too late. His heart had recognized the feeling, although it'd never manifested itself in such a strong way.

Bury it, he told himself. *For you sanity, bury it.*

Chapter Five

❧

And to say she'd let him touch her. And she'd touched him. Yet the pain in his eyes after he'd let her wrist go wasn't faked. She could spot faked a league away.

She wondered how well-behaved she'd be after two years in a tower, chained to the wall, with nothing but a lowly servant for company. And the occasional visit from a...*cousin*.

Scarlet sat on the last step at the base of the stairwell. Bringing all that water up then down was hard. And she'd have to do it all again next week. She should ask Ute for help. At least have the lads bring the water up and leave it at the door.

Scarlet shivered in her wet dress, still quivered as a just-fired arrow with the slew of emotions pressing against her heart. Though she knew it'd been a mistake on her part, she'd enjoyed rubbing the master all over his pale, hard body. Her heart had beaten a wild arrhythmic tempo the whole while. Such a beautiful, strange man. And dangerous. There was something predatory about him. Not the overtly malevolent aura of men she'd come too close to, never that. No, Master Fredrick was, all in all, a goodhearted man. She'd no doubt. But deep underneath the stoic exterior, the alabaster mask, was something else. Something restless. Feral. Like a prowling beast.

Scarlet snorted a quick laugh. Where'd she gotten this silly notion? A beast indeed. He was no more a beast than she was.

Yawning with fatigue and spent adrenaline, Scarlet stretched and was about to push the door open when hurried steps stopped her. For some unexplainable reason, she froze in alarm. The steps went by the door, slowed. She held her breath. When the steps resumed, Scarlet let out a tiny slip of air through her nose.

Keeping the door tight against its hinges so it wouldn't creak—she was already learning the ways of this old castle—she chanced a quick peek in the corridor. A muscled back clad in a jade green doublet. Master Lothar was rounding the corner to the right, his ponytail briskly swinging between his shoulder blades.

Closing the door and locking it, Scarlet fought the urge to follow him. But contrary to what her instincts were telling her—screaming at her—she left the buckets where they were and silently crept down the corridor where she'd seen Lothar disappear. Across a square hall, a door she hadn't noticed before gaped wide.

Scarlet padded closer and looked inside. Darkness. Used to the darkness in more ways than she cared to explore right then, Scarlet quieted her mind and stepped inside the landing. Stairs going down. Nothing else. She followed these, keeping a hand against the wall for safeguard, and was about to turn around and curse her foolishness when a small sound caught her ears. Laughter?

Bolstered, she stepped down a couple more steps and stumbled when her foot came down even at the base of the staircase. A faint line of light filtered out from under a cleated door. Just like Master Fredrick's door. It must have been part of the old castle as well. A quick peek at the lock made Scarlet shake her head. Why did people bothered with such silly things? It'd never stop anyone worth stopping. It sure wouldn't stop her!

A man laughed again. Lothar. She recognized his deep voice. Knowing curiosity had killed many cats she knew of, Scarlet put her eye to the square keyhole.

A naked young woman Scarlet recognized as one of the milkmaids sat astride a strange contraption. It resembled a cross between the body of a horse and a barrel on its side with thick legs for support while thick-looking black leather covered the entire thing. An intricate mesh of ropes bound her hands behind her back, her ankles close to her buttocks and was looped around her neck. A large candelabrum cast golden light in the small room.

Scarlet put her hand to her mouth, instantly thinking the maid in distress. But a crooked grin spread on the young woman's face, which considerably lowered Scarlet's heartbeat. Out of sight, Lothar said something, and the maid giggled the way only young women could.

Scarlet couldn't remember ever giggling. She'd never had much reason to.

Somehow, the young woman managed to twist her bound body into a complete half circle so she faced the door behind which Scarlet hid. Scarlet shut her eyes hard. She should leave. But she knelt by the door and instead changed eyes.

Angry red lines under the black ropes slashed her skin. The maid leaned over and let her chin rest against the barrel, her behind sticking up in the air in a pair of half-moons separated by twin lengths of rope.

From somewhere to her right, Lothar appeared in Scarlet's thin line of sight. His torso was naked. A bottle glistened in his bejeweled hand. As much as Master Fredrick was athletic and sinewy, Lothar's body was all thick muscles.

Should Master Fredrick see her now, spying in on a private scene...

Scarlet felt her cheeks flushing. She was about to leave her post when Lothar reached out and caressed the maid's hair gently, slowly, as though he were appraising her for some future project only he knew.

A shiver raced up Scarlet's back. She'd never trust a man so completely as to let him bind her this way.

Circling the contraption, Lothar stopped behind the maid, leaned in between her cheeks, strands of his ponytail spilling over his shoulder. He licked her. A moan escaped the young woman. She twisted, despite the ropes hindering her movements, so she could look back at the man but gave up after a while. She closed her eyes.

While Lothar was giving the maid what appeared to be very satisfying attention, Scarlet clenched her teeth hard. Her sex ached as she watched, her mind quickly replacing Lothar with another man whose tongue she'd tasted and was hurting to taste again. Would Master Fredrick do this, tie her so he could pleasure her this way? Scarlet pressed her palms on either side of the keyhole. Sweat moistened her upper lip.

After a while of licking his partner, who writhed in obvious pleasure, Lothar grabbed the contraption's sides and spun it completely around. Scarlet hadn't noticed the wheels. Feeling guilty, thrilled, Scarlet had a full view of the woman's glistening cleft. A length of rope went down on either side of her lips, bound her tightly around the waist then came back up her lower back to secure her hands. Each of her large breasts were trapped independently with crisscrossing rope. Scarlet could only guess at the time required to do such intricate roping. The maid must have been there before Lothar. There was no way he'd had time to tie the maid so intricately before Scarlet arrived.

Murmuring something in the young woman's ear, Lothar brought the bottle neck to her lips and helped her take a few sips. He took a few as well, though his eyes never left the maid's face.

A sense of dread washed over Scarlet. She should leave. Now.

With one hand, Lothar undid his trouser flap and let it hang down over his thighs. His impressive member bobbed into view. Scarlet put her hand to her mouth.

Giggling again, the maid strained against her bonds toward the glistening member and flicked her tongue at it. A grin on his handsome face, Lothar approached and supported her chin while the young woman kissed and licked him. He played with the knot on her back. A look of euphoria spread over her face. Her eyes blinked a couple of times. She said something.

Then, as if she were suddenly very drunk, the young woman began to mumble incoherently, her mouth spread in a wide, confused grin. With a sheen of sweat now covering his muscled torso, Lothar took another long gulp from the bottle then walked out of Scarlet's sight.

Meanwhile, the young woman continued blabbering, at one time letting her head rest sideways against the "horse". Lothar came back. Still smiling, he grabbed the corner of the contraption and spun it a few times to the delight of its rider. The maid faced Scarlet again, for which she was glad. But as much as she told herself to leave, her forehead remained pressed against the door.

Raising his hand high above his shoulder, which corded his thick muscles, he brought it down hard and fast. The young woman's cry ended with a hiccupping laugh.

Scarlet put both hands to her mouth. What was he doing?

Lothar slapped the maid's backside several times. She could see redness on the exposed skin, yet the maid only seemed more aroused by the rough treatment.

A broad grin on his face, Lothar grabbed the maid by the ropes and slid her to him. Scarlet bit her lip when he caressed the round bottom offered him, the pair of half-moons bound with black silk thrust up in the air for his taking. He looked jubilant when he parted the young woman's cheeks wider with his thumbs, and looked even more so when he sank into the inviting flesh.

Heat seeped to Scarlet's own as she watched him slide all the way in then all the way out. A gasp of pleasure erupted from the maid. Lothar repeated the process, quicker, harder. Sweat slicked his chest, beaded on his skin. Though the handsome man proved enjoyable to watch, Scarlet closed her eyes and imagined someone else in his place. Someone gentler, taller, leaner. Someone with red eyes.

Throbbing pulled at her sex, and Scarlet had to squeeze her thighs together to keep from trying to rub herself. By God, she wanted to. Fredrick's pale member inside her was the most exciting, impious thought she'd ever had. And why not? She was a woman. She had needs. Many men had used her to fulfill theirs, leaving her yearning for the touch of a man such as Fredrick. But it was wrong. And it was dangerous.

Another cry of pleasure tore from the maid's throat. Lothar reached down and bunched a fist in the girl's long, dark hair. Scarlet cringed when he pulled his partner's head back sharply. She hissed a long "yes". Scarlet could tell the ropes were digging tighter in the girl's throat. A deep red line spread right under her jaw. How she would hide these, Scarlet could only guess.

While he kept his fist in her hair, Lothar guided his member back in the young woman. Only this time he stabbed so hard his ponytail dissolved around his muscled shoulders, and the young woman's knees left the pad. Then he pounded again. And again.

Scarlet could only watch in mute fascination and horror as he pounded and pounded an increasing tempo, which matched the girl's strangled cries. The "horse" creaked and groaned under the assault, but Lothar held it securely with his knees jammed against it. The young woman's face had turned an angry shade of red with veins clearly visible along her throat and temples.

Scarlet gasped in shock.

Lothar's sweaty face snapped up, and through tousled hair his gaze went directly to the door. He kissed the air in her direction.

Horrified, Scarlet jumped back, landed on her backside and scooted away against the far wall. Panting, with bile rising up her throat, she floundered to her feet and took the stairs two by two. Her heart beat a mad cadence as she ran back to the tower. And to say she'd imagined Fredrick...

Shame flushed her cheeks. Scarlet grabbed the nearest buckets, spilling water everywhere, and ran-walked as fast as she could.

Think of the coins, she told her swirling mind. *Think of the new life you'll be able to afford.* Though the price of her new life seemed to be climbing steadily. Scarlet shuddered at the thought.

How far would she be willing to go for those coins? How low could she sink?

As she made her way to her room, Scarlet fought the urge to check behind her every two steps. And to her shock, she realized she'd tiptoed the whole time.

Chapter Six

ဢ

Scarlet sighed as she counted her coins. She'd been working at Castle Innsbruck for a little over three weeks. Yet she hadn't near enough to leave, though Lady Katrina paid her well.

She stuffed them back in the old napkin and slid the tiny bundle inside the mattress. After making sure the puncture didn't show, Scarlet donned her uniform, slid her feet in the leather slippers Ute had given her and made her way to the kitchen.

After that bizarre day, back when she'd given the master his bath then watched Lothar brutalize a maid, Scarlet had made sure to revert to her old, guarded self. No more friendly overtures to the man in the chains, and she avoided the other the best she could. It'd worked for the last three weeks. For her sanity, she hoped it'd last.

The day was spent in a frenzy of chores, and since Lady Katrina had insisted on bringing the master his supper, it'd given Scarlet one less thing to do. Even if this one thing was both joy and torture. She shook her head to clear the carnal thoughts. He wasn't meant for her. She wasn't meant...well, she wasn't meant for anyone if she could have her say in it. Better to live alone than at the employ of others.

Scarlet realized night had fallen. Through a window, she spotted a clear full moon illuminating the rose garden below. Despite knowing she wasn't supposed to be out at night, Scarlet slipped out of a narrow door leading to the interior courtyard—a door she'd discovered quite by accident and which looked abandoned for several years—and emerged in the rose garden. Wind whistled a forlorn tune. Scarlet shivered in her uniform.

In the dim light, some of the roses seemed to glow pale blue and silver. Their scent wafted to Scarlet as she meandered along the narrow path of irregular slate tiles and soon she'd reached the corner where an old, dried fountain disappeared under a thick rosebush. She narrowed her eyes, trying to discern what color these could be. They looked too pale to be red but definitely too dark to be pink.

Melancholy stabbed at her heart. Sitting on a stone bench against the fountain's decrepit edge, Scarlet couldn't help but notice the mix of neglect and care that fought against one another in this garden. With a sigh, she lay along the bench with her arm bent under her head. Stars twinkled between strips of brown and purple clouds. Sounds from the kitchen wafted to her, discordant on air currents, and soon her eyelids began to drop. She fought at first, as she always did. Then she let go.

The wind had changed. It no longer blew dried leaves and twigs in twisters and instead had all but died. The clouds were gone as well. Scarlet sat on the bench and rubbed her hair back. She should cut it.

Looking up, she saw a crescent moon and thought it looked like a lopsided grin. Master Fredrick smiled this way — the one time she'd seen him do it. A sudden gust blew across the walled garden, shook the rosebushes enough some lost petals, which floated to the ground like blood-colored snowflakes.

A grating sound made Scarlet jump to her feet. Her gaze went to the gate where stood a tall, dark form. It entered the garden without sound, gliding, shrouded in darkness deeper than the night.

Scarlet wanted to say something but couldn't for the steel grip squeezing her throat. She backed a step, right into one of the orange rosebushes. Tiny thorns hooked in her uniform. Without looking back, she pulled the hem of her skirts free.

Pebbles crunched under the visitor's feet. As he drew nearer, pale hair and skin emerged into the bluish light. She recognized him at once, and her heart began to palpitate arrhythmically and her lips to ache for his.

"Master Fredrick? How did you…?"

His strange glowing eyes narrowed when he smiled. Such a beautiful thing. Scarlet smiled in return.

He stopped a few paces from her. The deep V of his parted tunic revealed his firm and fit figure and a thin, downward strip of platinum hair below his navel. The black velvet garment hid the rest. Desire for the eerily beautiful man flared in Scarlet. Sweet Mary, give me strength.

"Are you afraid of me?" Fredrick asked, taking one step toward her. He moved with the loose, restrained power of a predator at ease.

She'd never noticed before just how much taller than her he was. She barely reached his collarbone. But it was hard to judge a man's height when fifteen feet of chain weighed him down by the ankle. Guilt lowered her gaze. She backed into the bench. "Nothing frightens me anymore."

Her whisper barely passed her lips. Heat suffused her belly and breasts and thighs. She yearned for him with such intensity it scared her. Scarlet looked up into his angular face, at the straight and narrow nose, slightly flaring nostrils, the perfection of his slim mouth, and marveled that such beauty could also be so menacing.

Fredrick raised his long, pale hand and beckoned.

Scarlet was walking before her brain registered movement. With a sigh she pressed her forehead against his chest. His heart beat hard against her temple. A frisson fluttered along her spine when Fredrick, light fingers enlaced in her curls, leaned into her and kissed the base of her neck. She turned slightly, searched his mouth with hers and found it.

"You should leave while you can," he breathed into her mouth. Yet his actions belied his words when he pressed her into him and kissed her deeply.

With notions of decorum fading fast, Scarlet responded in kind, raising herself on the tips of her wooden shoes to meet his kiss then double it. His chest felt warm and hard under her hands, and she had to resist the urge to rake her nails down the length of him, instead caressing the pale skin with the pads of her fingers, softly, slowly. Fredrick shivered.

She snaked her hands on either side of his narrow waist inside the parted tunic. This time she couldn't resist a quick graze of her curled fingers. His reaction was immediate. Scarlet let out a small cry of surprise and excitement when Fredrick tugged the collar of her uniform past her shoulder and dove for the exposed flesh. Squeezing out of her sleeve, Scarlet freed a hand, which she used to pull his head down to her throat. Cold night air caressed her breast, tightened her nipple. He trapped it with his mouth, pulled until she breathed his name. He seemed to grow extra pairs of hands as he cupped her exposed breast, squeezed her tender nipple, raked her hair back from her face, yet at the same time, never releasing his tight embrace or ceasing his torturous caress. He hardened against her belly, the heat seeping through layers of fabric.

Scarlet throbbed and ached. Tossing aside the last shreds of modesty, she unbuttoned the rest of his long tunic with fingers that trembled with excitement.

"Turn around."

He grabbed her by the shoulders and whirled her around like a dancer would. The dress came loose around her when he expertly unlaced the back of it. It fell limply around her waist but she never had time to step out of it as Fredrick spun her back to face him and slid the garment down past her hips. He draped the bench with it.

"There," he said, guiding her back so she'd sit.

Scarlet sat on the bench, her back to the fountain, unsure what to do next. But when he crouched in front of her, parted her legs and knelt between them, she knew. His tunic spilled on either side of him like great black wings when he leaned forward and proceeded to assail her all the way down from throat to navel. Her breasts heaved sharply when his hands joined his mouth. His glowing gaze on her face the whole time, he kissed her lower belly then the inside of her thighs until his progress stopped just above her pulsating sex. The tip of his tongue poked out of a corner of his mouth, slid all the way along his upper lip before disappearing back inside. A flash of teeth heralded a sharp sting of pain when he bit her high between the legs. Instead of feeling scared, Scarlet spread her knees wider, kicked her shoes off so she could point her feet. Arching her back, she waited – prayed – for more.

And it came.

Using his thumbs, he spread her wide before giving her a lash of his burning tongue. Scarlet hissed. Her whole legs trembled under the strain of keeping them immobile.

Fredrick renewed his efforts, which she rewarded with increasingly louder moans of pleasure. Fire accompanied the wave that threatened to spill over her, and Scarlet gritted her teeth, braced her arms far and wide behind her. But he must have had other plans for when she arched, waiting for the climax to claim her, Fredrick stopped.

"Don't...please."

With a devilish grin, he returned to her bud, which throbbed demandingly, and brought her there again, only to abandon her the second she started to writhe with contentment. And he did this so many times, after a while Scarlet seriously considered throwing him down and assaulting him right there on the spot. But she didn't have to. For before she could voice her frustration, Fredrick knelt on the bench between her legs, scooped her up with one arm and sat her on his lap.

Their gazes fixed on each other, Fredrick angled the tip of his member right at the juncture of her lips, rubbed in a circular motion before sliding inside. Then he retreated, almost all the way out. A low groan escaped Scarlet.

"It's too late for you to leave now." He stabbed his hips upward.

Scarlet's cry reverberated in the walled garden. Her climax exploded out of her, left her quivering like a just-fired arrow. Welcoming Fredrick's ferocious lovemaking with encouraging groans and hip torsions, Scarlet let her head fall back, her spine bent into a deep curve.

The stone fountain abraded her palms. Through the tangled foliage, she spotted looming above her the upside-down head of a snarling white wolf with his fanged maw wide open. She yelped in shock, only to realize the head was made of stone. When a delightfully sharp thrust from Fredrick nearly made her bite her tongue, she straightened to look into his eyes.

She gasped.

Above her, snarling, was Fredrick…except it wasn't his human face looking down at her but the same wolf's head as in the fountain. Only this one wasn't made of stone. This one was real.

Scarlet woke with a scream struggling up her throat. She clamped both hands over her mouth. *Sweet, sweet Mary. What…?*

Her heart beat so fast she feared for a moment she would collapse under the strain. A breeze smarting with the first signs of autumn grazed her neck. Scarlet bolted upright and looked around. *A dream. Thank God.*

The rose garden was around her. The bench under her, the fountain behind her. No Fredrick. No snarling white wolf. She knuckled her eyes, trying to rub the last shred of dream away. And to add to her misery, her sex throbbed its unfulfilled needs at her. A thought crossed her turbulent mind. What if?

Scarlet reached over the fountain's edge and parted the tangled rosebush. Nothing. She pushed farther, leaning precariously over the decaying stone. Crushed thorns bit her flesh. But she overextended and slipped inside where she landed on her hands. Face to snout with a snarling lupine head. Most of its teeth were missing.

Scrambling back, Scarlet floundered to her feet. How could she have known a white marble wolf's head had once graced the fountain? She couldn't possibly have seen it through the thick rosebush. Despite the delectable nature of her dream—the first portion anyway—Scarlet couldn't shake the sadness choking her. Dreams were the only way she could ever know a man like Fredrick von Innsbruck.

The overwhelming feelings of sadness pervading the place chased her out of the garden. She closed the grate behind her.

Light far above caught her attention. It came from the tower, out of the master's room.

His cell, she mentally corrected herself.

Her heart sank. During the last weeks, she'd been distant with him, hadn't responded to any of his advances. And after a while, she'd seen the sparkle in his eyes die away. She hated herself for it. And now, in a perverse twist of nature, she had dreams about the man. Dreams that left her yearning for him in shameful ways.

Perhaps the Fredrick of her dream was right—she should leave while she still could. But leave for what? And to go where? She couldn't return to Amsterdam where Werner's connections and revenge would extend to every hole in the ground. She knew no one else but the folks here. And in a strange new way, Scarlet was starting to develop tiny roots to this place, despite what went on behind the stone façade. If she could only shake off the guilt.

To make her way back to the unused door Scarlet had to climb a set of dangerously worn stone steps that brought her close to the parapet near the tower. Scarlet squinted as she looked directly above her head, about fifty feet up. A strip of golden light pierced the dark wall of the tower. Too much light for a man who preferred darkness. As she pondered on this, she heard faint voices. Then what sounded like a howl. But the wind blew so strongly she could have been mistaken.

Shivering, Scarlet made her way back inside. Perhaps a cup of tea would do her good, would wash away the uneasiness.

As she stepped inside the warm kitchen, Scarlet spotted Ute in a corner giving a verbal lashing to a maid. Her! The same Lothar had… Scarlet hadn't seen her in a while. A wool vest covered the maid's shoulders and the deep red lines that would undoubtedly still show. Scarlet averted her gaze. Picking at the dried skin on her knuckles, Scarlet waited until Ute had finished with the maid.

The old woman muttered a curse before sitting at the table. "How's the master tonight?" She sounded tired and older.

"The lady brought him his supper tonight. They had affairs to discuss she said." Scarlet took a breath, meant to speak but checked herself in time.

"What?"

No use trying to fool the shrewd woman. "Well…he's not as ill as I thought he'd be. Has he always been…like this?"

"Come with me," Ute said, her voice uncharacteristically soft.

Scarlet followed her into the dining hall where the hustle and bustle of servants preparing the castle for the next day would nullify any eavesdropping. Scarlet sat on a chair by the old woman. Ute pulled out the vial of tonic and absentmindedly toyed with it.

Again, the barely remembered flowery smell wafted to Scarlet, the one from her dream. An image of a tall plant with clusters of violet-blue flowers at its tip appeared in Scarlet's mind. Then she remembered. Werner had once forced Scarlet to steal some from the apothecary across the city.

"Wolfsbane."

"What, my girl?" Ute asked.

Scarlet clamped her mouth shut. "Nothing, I just remembered something."

Good God. This is what they put in Master Fredrick's food? Wolfsbane was an extremely virulent poison when taken in large quantities. In small doses, as in Fredrick's case, maybe it would make even someone his size controllable, docile. But could it also kill him in the long run? What did she know? She was no physician. An utter pig, Lothar was still a physician.

Ute closed her eyes briefly and smiled. "Master Fredrick's always been different," she said. Scarlet forced her mind to clear.

"The white hair, the pale skin and his eyes. It's a condition his family is known for. Some of his ancestors had it too. But it never bothered him none. Always on the go, he was. Could be seen here and there, hunting with our men, fishing with the lads from the village. But he has a temper. Takes it from his father before him. The wicked fits he can throw. The noble families walk on eggs whenever they come around. Ever since—" Ute stopped, reminiscing with her eyes half closed, then chuckled. "After the master caught a visiting duke having a go at one of the maids who just wanted to be left alone, he threw him out on his arse. The sight."

Scarlet could tell Ute loved her master. And to hear the description, she would've appreciated such a man as well. Yet she couldn't reconcile the one she'd seen in the tower. He looked neither healthy nor pleasant, although he'd been very gentle in his attentions toward her. She felt herself blush.

Ute smiled widely. "Ah, but don't go fancying him, girlie, you'll only end up hurtin'. He's not a noble per se, but just as good. He's a *Langraf*. That's what they call landholders in our country. Answers directly to the king."

"I wasn't fancying him," Scarlet replied too quickly. She'd spent the last three weeks trying to convince herself of this, failing with increasing misery. She more than fancied him. She spent entire nights dreaming of his pale hands on her, his lips pressed against hers.

Ute put a gnarled hand over her shoulder. "Tell me how he looked. It's been so long since I've been allowed up there."

"I know about the physician's test…but still…" Scarlet shook her head then lowered her voice. "I'm sure Master Fredrick would like the company."

"*Nein, nein.* Oh no, that'd kill him!" Ute replied, as though the mere thought gave her an attack of the humors. "Only those the physician cleared may see him. Like you, dear girl. The physician's been very clear about that. Otherwise, we could give the master diseases he can't fight, ill as he is. Even a cold would kill him."

So this is why they kept him locked up in the tower. Scarlet understood now. She had no doubt the man was ill, but it wasn't only from his sun affliction. It was the wolfsbane that caused him to look constantly feverish and sluggish. Yet Fredrick still looked menacing enough take on three men his size.

What was going on? Scarlet was so tired from a long day of chores she couldn't even think straight. What if he was mentally unstable and the wolfsbane was the only brew that kept him manageable? Ute had just told her he had a temper. What if the chains were there to protect Fredrick? The lady had said so. Maybe the willful man wouldn't listen to the physician and insisted on going out, where the sun would roast his fair skin, blind his strange eyes? Yet the chain bothered Scarlet night and day. There had to be a way to keep him safe without resorting to such drastic measures.

"There's something I've been meaning to ask you," Scarlet began. "I wonder if the chains aren't—"

"My dear, I was just looking for you," a man said forcefully from the doorway.

Scarlet turned toward the voice, where Lothar stood leaning against the doorjamb. Shiny and smooth, his hair was pulled back into a perfect ponytail. He beckoned to her with a finger.

Ute's face remained mostly expressionless, though Scarlet could detect a slight trace of animosity. Trying to hide her panic, Scarlet stood and followed him.

"The lady requires your assistance," he said, giving her a penetrating look. He had a small bag in his hands.

He was taking her to the tower. She knew it in her heart. But he was taking the long route, not the one used by the servants. Maybe he didn't know of it. Though he was impossibly alluring and elegant, especially this evening dressed all in jade green velvet, Scarlet couldn't quell the warning bells tolling in her gut, couldn't cleanse her mind of the images he'd put there. Sick bastard. Sick, dangerous bastard. Surely the lady had him in sight, her being shrewd and all, and knew what sort of man her friend was. Scarlet could have thrown Lothar farther than she could trust him, yet despite her mistrust, she had to believe in the lady's good judgment regarding her own cousin. She wouldn't let anything bad happen to Fredrick.

When they'd turned into a deserted corridor, Scarlet reacted too slowly and Lothar was able to grab her by an arm and pull her to him.

"Succulent little thing," he murmured, aiming a kiss at her but only getting a cheek after Scarlet turned her head away.

He grinned, nodding. "Pardon my enthusiasm, Scarlet. But the mere sight of you unmakes me."

She shivered. His hand was gentle when he cupped her backside. "The things I want to do to you…"

She could well imagine what sort of things. Perverted man.

"Lady Katrina is waiting, Master Lothar," Scarlet said, trying to keep her tone even though her heart was beating a mad tempo. Everything in her body was telling her to knee him where it counts and run like the Devil was after her. Which wouldn't have been so far from the truth.

"Yes, of course, she is waiting." Lothar kissed her on the forehead then pulled away.

When they rounded the last corner, Scarlet spotted the lady pacing in front of the tower door.

As soon as they were within arm's reach, she took the bag from Lothar's hands and shoved it into Scarlet's. "My dear cousin has fallen off his bed again." Her eyes were hard. "Poor helpless man. See to him, would you, Scarlet?"

Scarlet threw a sidelong look at Lothar. Wasn't he a physician? Why ask a mere servant?

"My dear, I don't treat such trifle cases. I'm sure your ministrations will be just perfect."

Trifle? How could he call Master Fredrick's state a trifle when the lady looked beside herself with worry?

"The physician has done his part and now you must do yours." The lady narrowed her eyes in Lothar's direction. He shrugged, looked ready to say something but clamped his mouth shut before storming off.

Drawing near, Lady Katrina placed a hot hand over Scarlet's shoulder. "Lothar said he found him on the floor, but I..." she faltered, seemed lost for words. "The physician can sometimes be a very driven man. Be careful around him, Scarlet."

Scarlet nodded.

"Please, do be quick. My cousin needs you." Then Lady Katrina was off, the hem of her midnight blue dress fretting about her ankles as if a beast struggled within its folds.

With horrid images dancing in her head, Scarlet rushed up the steps, not bothering to check if anyone would follow her or not. Had he injured himself severely? she wondered. And Ute who'd asked only now how the master was doing. Scarlet hoped no one would blame her. What if they did?

She stormed into the room. A lone oil lamp, probably left by Lothar or the lady, lit the sorry scene before her. The bag slipped from her hands.

Pure chaos. Upturned furniture, ripped cushions, shredded black velvet littered the floor. As though something had exploded out of the tunic. And on the floor in the middle of a pool of blood, Fredrick, naked, lying on his front. The white of his hair was streaked with crimson.

"Good Heaven..."

She'd seen enough beatings in her life to recognize one. This man hadn't fallen off anything. He'd been beaten. Savagely.

Which brought her back to the last time she'd seen him bruised. Almost four weeks ago. Tonight was ten times worse.

Torn between being quick and being careful, Scarlet rushed to his side and knelt.

"Master Fredrick," she murmured, placing a hand over his shoulder. So hot. That fever again.

His vein fluttered at his neck, so he lived still, of that she was sure. But he didn't respond to any of her urgings. What if he died? The thought of the beautiful man dying in her arms horrified her. Looking around in mounting panic, Scarlet meant to call for help but thought better of it. What if they thought it'd been her doing? What if someone came, someone not entitled, and gave some illness to the wounded man, finished off Master Fredrick? What if it was *Lothar* who answered her call?

No, she'd have to rely purely on herself. The story of her life.

She'd need to drag the inert man to his bed if she hoped to be able to bandage him. She couldn't very well leave him on the stone floor where he'd catch his death.

Though her throat was squeezed painfully tight, she gathered her wits about her and grabbed the coverlet from the bed, folded it in half and tucked it under him. After she grabbed the corners near his head, she crouched down low and tugged him to his bed. He was *much* heavier than he looked, despite his lean figure. It took all her strength and a good while to hoist him onto the mattress. Good Heaven! He was heavy.

Finally, she had him resting on his back, in his bed, with the now-bloodied coverlet under him so she'd at least save the sheets and mattress. Remembering the bag, she untied it and inside found several rolls of bandages and some ointment, which reeked to high Heaven.

There was some water left in the washbasin so Scarlet proceeded in wiping blood off the man as best she could. She'd done it enough times for her female friends, those more unfortunate than herself who'd fallen prey to nasty patrons. As a mere thief for Werner, she was afforded at least some security.

Strangely, for all the blood covering him, there weren't that many wounds to find. Bruises were plentiful and swollen, especially on his face, where one of his eyes was crusted shut. He had cuts and scrapes as though he'd been pulled backward through a rosebush—these abounded, but other than that, no really deep gash that could explain the blood loss. Unless it wasn't his own. His ankle though, was severely torn, with some hard, whitish tissue showing through the ruined skin. Scarlet bandaged it nice and wide so the cotton wouldn't roll under the manacle. When she did so, she took a closer look at the lock, for purely vain reasons. She'd been thinking about this lock. It wouldn't prove too much of a challenge. All she'd need…

Scarlet stopped herself. It wasn't her place.

To give herself something to do while she tried not to mentally pick the tempting lock, she went looking for the silver buttons of his tunic. She wasn't exactly sure how many there were, but after she'd dug around under the bed, the table and lifted every corner of the carpet, she had a handful and figured that had to be it. Most of them glistened crimson, filling with blood the tiny wolves' mouths. She shivered.

Coming back to the bed, she rinsed the buttons and set them noiselessly on the small dresser. Scarlet sat on the edge of the mattress.

The sight of him drew a stake in her heart. She knew what it felt like to be powerless, overwhelmed by the odds and an unfair situation. She'd bled too, as he did now. And she knew just whom to blame. Lothar. It was all his doing. Coward. Why didn't the lady do anything? She had the power, the status to have him thrown out of Castle Innsbruck. Why keep him around? Scarlet's shoulders dropped.

Because she's scared.

Fear had that effect on women, made them keep men around even when they shouldn't, despite knowing they were the worst sorts of characters. When women were afraid, they froze. Scarlet knew too well. Poor Lady Katrina, to be so powerful yet ultimately as helpless as any other woman confronted with a man she couldn't refuse.

"Why would the sick bastard do this?"

"Because he can."

Scarlet leapt cleanly off the bed, both hands raised to fend off blows. Her wits quickly came back to her and she lowered her hands, staring into the man's strange eyes.

"I'm sorry I rocked the bed," she offered, trying to force her hands from reaching out to him. Though her heart felt no such limitation. She'd always had a weak spot for the underdog. And underdog he was, but only because of the chain around his ankle, otherwise, she'd no doubt he could take very good care of himself. Still, to see him this way, bleeding, naked…

Naked.

Sweet Mary.

She hurriedly pulled what portion of sheet she could from under him and hid his lower body with it. While she fussed with the ends of the sheet, Fredrick only stared at her with his good eye. When she was done, she clutched her hands behind her back, shifting uncertainly from one foot to the other.

"Are you thirsty? Hungry perhaps? I could go—"

He squeezed his eye tightly as though to shut her up. She did. A master at appreciating facial expressions, she'd learned early in her life how to read people. And this man wanted *silence*.

Poking his chained foot from under the sheet, exposing his lean and well-formed thigh, he raised it slightly to check on his bandaged ankle. "You've done this before."

She nodded, torn between her judgment, which was telling her to stay well away from his reach, and her heart, which clamored that she wrap her arms around his shoulders and hold him tight.

"You've wasted your time and skill then," he went on, the red eye never leaving her face. "I'll be back this way in four weeks."

A strong gust buffeted the tiny flame in her heart. "What do you mean?"

Anger flashed across his face, but was quickly replaced with something that melted her insides. Anguish. He looked away.

Never let your guard down, show fear or doubt or guilt. Never let anyone close.

The mantra she'd chanted to herself since she was a little girl couldn't help her now. It hadn't helped her in the last weeks either as she tried to ignore the budding feeling in her heart.

It was all too late, Scarlet realized—she'd already let her guard down.

Chapter Seven

ഐ

Fredrick would have shaken his head. There was no deflating this girl. To look at her now, standing straight as a poker, well inside his reach, one would think there was no danger being near him, that perhaps this woman felt no fear. She did, of course, he could smell it faintly, though not the overpowering stench of the others before her.

And he'd never noticed before how beautiful she was, with a mane of unruly copper curls and the darkest eyes. Of course, he'd noticed her enough to kiss her and try to use her—a lot of good that did him—but he hadn't yet taken the time to really *look* at her. She'd been working for him what, a moon now? An ache in his chest flared, an old ache, one he thought long gone. Fredrick pushed it down below the surface. Only pain there. Nothing else.

Anyway, he was too old for her by at least eighty-five years. The thought made him grin, which triggered a scree of painful spasms along his sides and neck. That bitch of a cousin. He'd rip her heart out if he ever had the chance. But he forced the murderous thoughts away and concentrated on Scarlet and trying to win her over once again. He'd been so rash to grab her wrist, and he'd cursed his stupidity many times in the last month. She'd been so distant. So guarded. Now he had to climb that same hill all over again. And it would undoubtedly be steeper than the last time.

"How's the rose garden? Has someone been taking care of it?"

She blushed beet red. "The rose garden...? Ah, yes. Someone must take very good care of it. It's very beautiful."

Her strange attitude piqued his curiosity. Why would she blush so completely when all he asked about was the state of his garden? Nonetheless, pride swelled his heart. He'd worked damn hard on that garden. It was even older than he was. "Good. Are there any orange roses left? Near the corner, beside the fountain?"

With her cheeks still rosy, Scarlet nodded. "Most are in full bloom now. Did you plant it all?"

"Almost," Fredrick replied, trying to hide a stitch of pain when he fiddled behind him to adjust a pillow. She drew near and did it for him but retreated right away. "But the orange ones are my favorites. It took me a while to learn how to handle them. They have very prickly personalities." He tried not to smile. "They remind me of you."

"They do?"

Was she blushing again? She *was*.

Fredrick wanted to pat himself on the back and at the same time, he'd like nothing more than give his backside a good kick. He was shamelessly tricking the only decent person he'd come in contact with in the past several months. It would seem his cousin had exacerbated some traits he would've preferred remained dormant. God, he hated himself right then.

"You should leave while you can, Scarlet," he let out under his breath. "This is no place for the likes of you."

He winced inwardly. Fredrick couldn't remember ever showing such candor to anyone. What was wrong with him? Since when had he begun to speak openly about…well, anything? Lying didn't come easily around her. Using Scarlet wasn't going the way he'd planned, not at all. She wasn't supposed to be this…decent, this likable. *Bury it*, he told himself for the tenth time this day.

"The likes of me?" she replied, those two dark gems for eyes flashing in anger.

Before he could say another word, she marched to the door and left. The sting her departure elicited surprised him. She'd obviously misunderstood him. He'd only meant…

Why should he care? After—if—he succeeded in convincing her to pick his lock, he'd owe her his life and would make sure she had enough coins to make a new life for herself. But then she'd leave. For what woman in her right mind would stay around here, around *him*?

The thought of not seeing her again brought with it such a pang of sadness that Fredrick had to press his hand against his chest. He'd been there too long and couldn't think straight.

Moments later, he felt a presence in the stairs but heard nothing. Scarlet. Only she could be so stealthy. He watched as she maneuvered the doorway balancing a plate in one hand and a teapot in the other. Balance, stability and strength. All rolled into a very thorny but lovely package.

Scarlet crossed the circular room and set her things on his side of the table. She stood clearly inside the semicircle worn in the rug.

So strange, he was already getting used to her tiptoeing right inside his reach, though he couldn't guess why she did it, knowing he could easily overpower her, hurt her. As he'd told her, tiptoeing was for frightened children. She was no child. But clearly, she was frightened. Yet she managed to dredge courage out of herself and face him every day. And if this was the only thing he knew about her, it'd still be enough. Scarlet had a good soul.

"Here, have some tea. It always helps me when…the heat will help you."

Outside a night bird threw a shrill note. He looked up at the cleft in the wall, which was supposedly someone's idea of a window. It was barely wide enough for his face. A sigh struggled up his chest. He forced it down.

"You're obviously Dutch. Where are you from?" The question made him cringe. He shouldn't ask questions, shouldn't let her become more…more than what, exactly?

"Amsterdam."

Short and to the point. He was beginning to like this woman a bit much.

"What were you doing before she hired you?" Thieving, he knew it as surely as he knew the moon was round. But what else? He wasn't sure why he wanted to know, but he did. Foolish male pride, no doubt.

Scarlet shrugged. The mask was lowered again, hiding her feelings, guarding her soul.

"Were you a whore or a thief? Or both?" Shame at being so rude to her made him even angrier with himself. Yet images of her bedding other men angered him beyond caution. He *had* to know.

"You sure have a strange way to show gratitude, *Master*," she replied evenly, though he could tell he'd upset her.

She poured a cup of tea and set it on the table. Coming to the head of his bed, she piled pillows under him. Calluses marked her palms and knuckles. Her touch, both rough and gentle, triggered an awareness he could've done without. The way she'd bathed him a few weeks back stabbed at his brain with merciless clarity. His shaft remembered too. But every week afterward had been different. She'd stood by while he bathed, not looking at him, an expression he couldn't read on her face.

She was proving to be a tough nut to crack. But he was desperate and patient. Not a good combination when he came to think of it.

When she raised the cup to his lips, the heat emanating from it indeed did him good. "My thanks," he muttered after taking a small sip.

"Where did all the blood come from? I haven't seen any wound on you deep enough for this," she asked, pointing to the dark stain on the stone floor.

He froze with his lips against the cup. She must have noticed his reaction for she arched a copper eyebrow.

"The blood isn't mine."

Again, frankness. Fredrick wanted to roll his eyes but it hurt too much. Already his body was healing, closing cuts, smoothing down bruises. His swollen eye had begun to open again. He knew the extent of his condition's healing capability for having tested it repeatedly, especially over the past two years with his cousin's sadistic tactics. She used to come up to him only on full moons, and then a couple of times a month. Recently, she'd taken to tormenting him every chance she had. The hated bitch.

There had been times when he'd transformed out of rage. But never in the tower, much to his cousin's chagrin. That had been before, long ago, back when he had no self-control. He did now. He'd get out eventually, and when he did...God help them.

Only this moon, someone *had* noticed the incongruous amount of blood given the state of his body. Too smart this woman. But he could never tell her why he had the ability to heal so fast. She wouldn't understand. She would think him a freak, a monstrous aberration.

"Whose is it then?"

Questions! Had she no sense? Anger bubbled dangerously close to the surface. Coming here, asking questions, remaining where he could touch her. *Touch her.* God, how he wanted to! To again feel her lean body against his, her lips on his.

"Aren't you afraid of me? I could kill you with one hand."

A guarded smile lifted a corner of her exquisite mouth. "If you wanted me dead, I would be. Here, have a biscuit. The cooks had them cooling on the rack."

I'm trying to warn her, and she's offering me a biscuit!

The sight of her smile—no beaming grin but a smile nonetheless—felt as though a choir of angelic voices had just struck a crystal-clear note. The pathetic imagery left him depressed and cross.

Who was using whom now? He felt a puppet in a tangle of strings because of her.

Feeling moodier by the second, Fredrick took one of the offered biscuits and slowly bit into it. Warm butter seeped onto his tongue. By God, they were good. Fredrick gobbled up two in a row then took his time with the third. With the steaming tea and the succulent biscuits in his belly, he did indeed feel much better, contrary to his regular meals, which always left him with a thick tongue and a headache. So Lothar hadn't had access to *this* food.

Fredrick's brow darkened at the thought of Lothar and his "medicine". When he got free, he'd begin with Lothar. Oh, and he'd make it last too.

Scarlet sat on the edge of the bed, looking at him while he ate. Though he didn't care at first, her continued scrutiny began to make him uncomfortable, pulled him out of his satisfying mental imagery of revenge. Was she staring because of his pale skin, his white hair? Did she think him a freak? He could deal with curiosity. It wasn't everyday someone met a man who towered over the rest by a good head, one with white skin and hair. One with red eyes. Even before his attack, as a child, he'd suffered under strangers' stares or worse, the barely veiled pity.

He needed no one's pity.

"Leave," he snarled. "Now!"

The look of pain on her face as she stepped away from the bed tore at his chest, made him wince. She gathered the remnants of his meal and left without another word.

He'd have no chance now convincing her to help him. Fredrick snarled and threw the cup she'd left behind against the far wall. He'd failed. In another month or two, his cousin would grow tired of Scarlet and begin searching for another unfortunate, another orphan. Another disposable.

And it was all his fault.

Chapter Eight

❧

Tears welled in her eyes. Even now, more than a fortnight later, Fredrick's words still hurt. Angrily she wiped the tears away. Why should she care what he said? All she wanted was her money so she could make another life for herself. Never mind the enticing lock at his ankle, a lock she itched to pick.

"Are you all right there, Scarlet?" Frank asked, his riding crop ever-present in his hand. His weathered face looked tight with worry.

As much as she enjoyed being around the old driver, today, with the clouds and implacable wind tearing at her face and the weight pulling at her heart, she didn't want company. "I'm fine. Just a bit tired." The interior courtyard was deserted. No one in his or her right mind would be out on such a day.

Through the metal gate, she could spot the rosebushes fretting in the wind that managed to reach the walled enclosure. Bright spots of orange caught her eye. His favorites, he'd said. Right before yelling at her to leave. She gave a good shake to the rug she'd just beaten.

Frank looked past her at the rose garden. "I've been the one caring for them ever since. I do what I can, but I don't have the master's skill. Nor his patience."

She stopped wrestling with the rug. "The roses?"

He nodded. "They're old," he said. "Very old." A grin lifted the old man's mouth. "Master Fredrick got you working ragged, hasn't he? He was always harder on himself than others, though."

"What was he like, before his...illness?" She'd realized by now no illness was keeping him in the tower. Something else did, much darker, much more sinister.

Frank snorted in disgust. "Illness, my eye."

Shocked, Scarlet leaned into the old man, keeping the rug stretched on the line as barrier against potential onlookers. "What do you mean? I saw him. He's all flushed and feverish." Beaten and bloodied and half-poisoned as well. But this, she left unsaid. Guilt was gnawing at her on a daily basis now, and haunted her nights too. She was part of the dark affair, willingly kept her mouth shut even though she could smell the lie for what it was. All because of coins. What did this make of her?

"I'd be this way too if I were stuck in that place for two years. He hasn't come out once since they put him there. And no one here's managed to pass that damn test recently...except those the lady hires from away." He threw her an oblique glance. One she avoided.

Two years. Good Heaven. Scarlet hadn't even thought to ask. Her guilt flared. And he hadn't come out once? Her anger at his harsh words subsided in the face of his greater plight. She wouldn't know what she'd become if she were confined to a tower for two years. No wonder he'd lost his temper.

"You've known him for a while? Since he was a boy?"

Frank's face hardened and he looked at her a long while before he spoke. "Not since he was a boy. I doubt anyone has." A shadow crossed the old face. "Master Fredrick's different, Scarlet. Has a dark streak in him. Once in a while he's..." He stopped, shook his head sadly. "But he's a good man. Never forget that, no matter what happens."

Master Fredrick's different.

She could tell. And he wasn't the only strange thing in these parts either. There was Lothar and his sick ways, the Lady Katrina who let it all happen—then there were the beatings, seemingly at regular intervals...

Scarlet had never seen someone heal so fast from such vicious beatings. Merely a day after she'd found him naked, bleeding on the floor, he was completely healed, with not a scratch on him.

Fredrick von Innsbruck was more than just "different". Though she wasn't exactly sure *what* he was.

* * * * *

Later that night, when it was time to bring the master his last meal of the day, Scarlet took a longer time to prepare herself. She'd try to talk to him tonight, maybe even have a closer look at the blasted lock. The danger of such a line of thinking made her tight and twitchy. What if the lady surprised her? Wouldn't she be thrilled to have a servant she'd saved from certain death meddle in her affairs. What if Lothar caught her tinkering his patient's lock? Her fear of him had her nearly paralyzed.

No matter. Her mind was made. Scarlet had often taken chances. Tonight, she would again. And a big one at that.

She took a bath, tried her damnedest to make *something* of her hair then reported to the kitchen just as Ute was pulling the vial of tonic from her vest. A jolt of shame pricked Scarlet's heart. Ute probably didn't even know what she was putting in her master's food. Only devious characters would know — crooks and thieves and murderers. People like her.

"Good evening, Scarlet," she said as she ceremoniously put two drops of the stuff onto the pork chops. "The master's favorite," she added fondly.

Without looking down at the tray, Scarlet took it to the tower door and unlocked it. She was about to enter when someone put a hand on the door and closed it in front of her.

"Just a moment of your time, my dear," Lothar said very close to her ear. A stray strand of his long hair tickled her cheek.

Scarlet gripped the tray tighter. The disgust she felt for him must have shown plainly enough. She forced a blank expression. "I'm very busy, Master Lothar."

"I think I have fallen in love with you, my dear," he said, leaning against the door and crossing his arms. The deep blue of his doublet accentuated his hazel eyes and luscious lips.

Any other woman would've thrown herself at his feet. And Scarlet was sure it happened often enough. But the wicked things this man did…the maid bound and straddling that odious contraption…and even the Lady Katrina, such a strong woman, cowed by fear because of Lothar. But what made Scarlet's jaw harden was what Lothar did—continued to do—to Fredrick. Some things could never be forgiven. This was one of them.

"You torture me, Scarlet," Lothar said, running his tongue behind his teeth. "Perhaps I could invite you to my chambers tonight? Would you come?"

The mere thought horrified her. "Master Lothar," she replied, needing all her aplomb to not kick him in the shins and run. "I'm flattered, but I don't think Lady Katrina would like this very much. Please, I must do my work."

"So dedicated," he replied, moving away but watching her like a hawk would a mouse. "Do not make me beg. I hate begging…when I am the one doing it."

Scarlet stared stubbornly at the ground while the man turned away. "Oh, one last thing," he said, looking back over his shoulder. His gathered hair glistened like a golden-brown snake. "Don't become too attached to dying men. In my trade, we have to learn this lesson quickly. I wouldn't want you to get hurt."

A jolt of fear jabbed her heart. *Dying men.* She nodded. When he left, she stayed at the base of the stairs, trying to calm her nerves. There could be no plainer warning. What had she gotten herself into? Yet inaction was proving more difficult than taunting good fortune with a sharp stick as she was about to do tonight.

Scarlet's plan had crystallized by the time she got to the top of the darkened stairs. She knocked twice and waited.

"Come in," came the gruff reply.

"Your meal, Master Fredrick," Scarlet said, putting the tray on the table.

Avoiding her gaze, he sat at his end of the table and planted his palms on the tabletop when Scarlet drew near and flapped the serviette above his lap. It looked as though he was struggling to keep his hands on the table.

Scarlet looked back at the door, took a deep breath and said, "The pork may be a bit underdone tonight."

As though something had poked him in the backside, he started and looked up at her. "What did you say?"

Would she hear it if someone sneaked up the steps? Had her guilt shown plainly on her face when Lothar had seen her? What if he wanted to check on his "patient" and caught her at it? It was a chance she was willing to take.

Scarlet looked at the door again then back at him. "The pork," she replied, straightening, "I think it's a bit…underdone."

His red eyes were fixed on her for so long Scarlet thought she'd melt. Finally, a small nod confirmed he'd taken her hint.

"Then I'll avoid the pork."

Fredrick wasn't ill. It was Lothar's "tonic" — wolfsbane, a poison — that was responsible for the constant fever, the dullness of his gaze. She'd seen poisoned people before, unfortunately knew something of it herself. As much as she'd enjoyed cursing Werner for his bad influence, Scarlet was more than happy now to have recognized the signs.

If this is what it was.

Perhaps she would kill him by depriving his body of the "tonic". What if it was a genuine remedy? Although she doubted it very much, what if she were wrong and it wasn't wolfsbane Lothar was giving Fredrick? Scarlet closed her eyes briefly. She had to do something. She couldn't be part of it anymore. She *wouldn't*.

While she wrestled with her conscience, Fredrick cut his food with deliberate care, brought it in small bits to his well-formed mouth and chewed slowly, carefully. He took a sip of wine, his eyes never leaving hers. When he brought the glass down, his lips glistened.

Watching him eat was entrancing. She swallowed hard. To Hell with self-doubts. She was going to assist this man and Heaven help her if she failed. And Heaven help *them* if she succeeded.

"Oh, you dropped a piece of bread," Scarlet said, kneeling by the foot of his chair.

She felt him tense when she wrapped her hand around his ankle. Only one look would suffice. A push lock, two tiny directional bolts and an armored front to prevent it from being smashed open. Pricey and custom-fitted as well. A challenge, but not impossible. She'd need a pick and a pair of long-nosed pliers. Some twine.

Scarlet straightened. "There, no trouble at all."

Her sudden movement blew out the tiny candle.

The moon cast bluish light that barely poked in the room, and Scarlet realized she could only see about a foot in front of her, despite her excellent night vision. But she knew Fredrick could see *very* well in the dark. His eyes were two glowing embers.

"Darkness doesn't frighten you?" His voice was like velvet on her skin.

She shook her head. "It's always been my friend. My protector."

"To protect you against what?"

She felt the heat of his hand but not his touch. He must have put it very close, yet didn't make contact. A shiver rippled up her spine.

"Why don't you sit?"

Scarlet sat in the chair opposite his.

"So, against what does darkness protect you?"

"Those who wanted to hurt me."

"Did the darkness always protect you?"

"No. Sometimes they found me anyway. But I gave them a run for their money."

Fredrick blinked in the darkness, the glowing orbs disappearing for a split second. A flash of teeth revealed he was grinning. "I'm glad to hear it."

Scarlet smiled the first true smile in what felt like ages. No guarded thing, either, but a true smile that conveyed the happiness, the comfort she felt now. Like she'd always been here, conversing in the shadows with this strange man. As though she *belonged* here. Despite her best effort, the smile slid off her face. She belonged here no more than she did anywhere. She'd be gone soon, and she wouldn't see Fredrick von Innsbruck again.

But she sure wouldn't leave before trying to help!

He must have seen her change of expression for he leaned forward and put a hand over hers. The heat emanating from his palm felt good to her chilled hands. She let him gently run an index finger over the small bone at her wrist.

The simple touch was liberation to her soul. The terrible guilt gnawing at her lessened. She didn't know this man. But she didn't *need* to. She recognized wickedness when she saw it, and this castle was host to the most sordid affair she'd seen. And she wouldn't be part of it anymore.

"Why are you doing this?" he whispered.

"Because it's wrong...all of this," she snarled, pointing with her chin at the whole room, "is wrong and I won't be..." She cursed under her breath. "Look," she said quickly before she changed her mind, "I'm a thief and a liar, so I can't judge. But I'm not *that* bad."

By now, her eyes had accustomed to the near darkness and she saw Fredrick lower his chin, as though fighting an internal battle. Scarlet put her other hand over his, and squeezed it tightly. "I'm not the only one who thinks it's wrong either. Frank thinks so too, and Ute would if she knew…if she'd seen…"

Without thinking, Scarlet pushed her chair back and came around his side of the table. Fear of being discovered made the whole thing even more urgent, left her heart beating so hard it hurt.

Fredrick didn't look up as she wrapped her arms around his head and pulled him to her chest nor did he try to stop her when she slowly ran her fingers through his hair, slicked back the silky white locks.

Scarlet's heart beat madly against her ribs, and she knew Fredrick could hear it well with his ear right against it. For the first time in her life, she followed her heart, even if her instincts were clamoring that she leave this dangerous place and never look back. She let her hand fall to his shoulder then to his throat. The whole while he felt rigid, tense.

"You must…" Fredrick began, faltered. "She'll do to you what she did to all the others."

Instead of replying, Scarlet undid the first silver button.

He balled his fists on the table. But he didn't move.

Another button came undone in her fingers. Outside the shrill song of a night bird pierced the silence. A third button. With her ears buzzing with fright and excitement, Scarlet slipped her hand inside the tunic, gently, slowly, grazed the skin with the pads of her fingers. Her dream came back to her. She pushed the dreadful image of the snarling wolf's head out of her mind. Fredrick was a man and she a woman, both with very human needs.

A strange sound accompanied her progress. She realized with shock it was coming from Fredrick's mouth. He was grinding his teeth. His tiny nipple tightened when she circled it with her index finger.

"*Scarlet*." Her name was a warning.

She unbuttoned him down to his waist and parted the lapels of his tunic. Despite the gloom, she could make out the contrast of black fabric against pale skin. His breathing became quick and shallow. Scarlet snaked her hand lower along his abdomen and gasped when he grabbed her wrist. She wasn't quite sure how he did it — one moment she was standing beside him, his head against her chest and the next she was straddling him as he avidly gorged on her throat. His hands shook as he pulled the rest of his tunic apart.

Scarlet moaned as she tugged the lace holding the collar of her dress and created a V of flesh into which Fredrick quickly dove. While he pulled her bodice open, she hoisted herself up from his lap, her hand feverishly searching under her. His ember-hot cock emerged from underneath layers of twisted fabric.

"Scarlet," Fredrick murmured, this time her name not a warning but a plea.

The thrill of their forbidden actions slicked her sex, and she was more than ready for him when she guided his member into her. As she was about to descend onto him, Fredrick grabbed her hips and tilted his pelvis upward. A hiss of pleasure escaped her when the smooth shaft glided in effortlessly, rubbing along her sensitive pearl. When she bore down with all her weight, the feeling of fullness made her groan.

She was used to men taking their pleasure and leaving it at that. So Scarlet gasped in surprise when Fredrick snaked a hand under her to stroke her bud with his thumb. A tiny ripple heralded the wave that hit her lower belly. Cramping her cheek muscles hard, she arched, not caring what she must have looked like, until her back connected with the table.

As he thrust into her with a frenzy that both delighted and shocked her, Fredrick trapped one of her nipples with his lips and sucked hard. At the same time, his thumb, now wet from her juices, rubbed upward over her burning bud, which produced a jolt that shook her. Scarlet cried out. And when a wave unlike anything she'd felt before unfurled—a flag catching a strong gust—she snarled his name.

Standing, Fredrick pumped hard and fast now, his hands clutched at her thighs, his mouth ravaging her breasts and throat. Scarlet let herself fall back against the table but held on against the edge to keep from moving under Fredrick's assault.

Another wave hit her. This time, Scarlet didn't care if she woke the dead. A long, plaintive cry that started in her belly tore up her throat. Fredrick gathered her in his arms and pulled her to him. When he stumbled back down in his chair, Scarlet thought he was going to pierce her womb for the force with which his member drove in. Panting hard now, Fredrick pulled almost all the way out. As Scarlet was about to protest, he thrust back in.

"Scarlet!" he snarled in her ear as a great tremor shook him.

Knowing he'd spilled himself, she cradled his head against her chest until both their breaths had returned to normal rhythms. Sweat slicked her chest and thighs while her nether lips throbbed contentedly. Scarlet smiled in the darkness.

After a while, she meant to pull up from him but he held her. "I must leave."

"Yes, you must. I want you to pack your bags and leave tonight." He spoke urgently. His arms encircled her shoulders and squeezed tightly. "It's dangerous here. Especially now."

"Especially now what?"

Fredrick let out a great sigh. "She'll know."

"Lady Katrina?"

"Don't call her that," Fredrick snapped as he let Scarlet off his lap. "She's no lady. But she's smart. She'll notice the difference. So I want you gone by dawn, Scarlet. Do you understand?"

"It's not her, it's Lothar. He's the one behind it all—"

"Dawn, Scarlet. Please."

Without him in her, she felt bereft and empty, despite the happy throb in her sex. Scarlet rearranged her dress and hair. But she suspected he was right, that his cousin would notice. She'd have to be extra careful. Extra *sneaky*. Scarlet sighed. Unfortunately, she was good at that.

After grabbing her hand in his, he kissed her palm and let it go. "Tomorrow, if you're still here, I'll tell my cousin I don't want you anymore. That you're a lousy servant."

She knew his words were meant to sting, make her leave Innsbruck. It wouldn't work. She had a plan. And maybe, maybe, it'd work.

"I have to leave for now," she said, rushing for the door. "But I'll be back."

"Scarlet, tonight is…"

The last sight she had of him was Fredrick leaning his head dejectedly against the table.

Once outside, the draft cooled her cheeks. She could pretend bravery, pretend she had a plan so Fredrick would feel better. She *had* a plan, but it was a foolish one at best. What if she failed? She'd never be able to face him again, knowing he'd still be chained, at the mercy of God knew what Lothar was doing. Filthy bastard. She hoped Fredrick got his hands on him.

Scarlet forced calm into her mind.

No. This had to be about business, not feelings. She couldn't let her affection for Fredrick get in the way.

She'd go find the tools she'd need and pick Fredrick's lock. She was good at it. With any luck, she'd do it quickly and get out of this place. What he wished to do once he was freed surely didn't include her. What did she have to offer a man like him?

When she reached the door down the stairs, Scarlet slipped her hand in her pocket to get her key.

It wasn't there.

Rummaging through her many pockets, she turned up nothing. Where could her key have been? In the room upstairs? Surely not, she would've heard it falling. Perhaps when she knelt by the chair? Or when she was with Fredrick? No, her pocket was much too deep. Plus, her comb was still there and so the key should be too.

Fredrick? Had he stolen her key? But it wouldn't open the lock to his manacle. It made no sense at all. She'd met no one else after using it to enter the tower.

Lothar.

Oh, the tricky… Anger boiled in Scarlet's veins. She'd seen his type before, the backstabbing, scheming sort. Well, he judged her wrong if he thought she'd go to his chambers and beg for her key. She'd go straight to the lady and ask for hers, plead for her forgiveness at having lost her own key. Better this than crawl into that man's bed.

But what if the lady was in on the whole affair? Scarlet closed the door, but it wouldn't stay closed and creaked ajar. She cursed. They'd notice right away it wasn't locked and come looking for her. No way she could find what she needed to pick his lock, get back here, do it then help him out. And do it all before either Lothar or the lady would know the tower was unlocked. If not them, then any good-intentioned servant would bring it to their attention. An uproar would ensue. Scarlet raked her hair back.

No way out of this one. She'd have to go to the lady and ask for her key, invent some story as to where her own key was. Scarlet decided against it right away. Stick to the truth as much as possible. Those made the best lies.

After a quick trip to her room to wash up and change uniform, Scarlet went in search of the lady's apartments. Finding them proved easy enough, though she'd never been there before. Fear twisting her insides, she knocked on the door, waited a while then knocked again. *Like waiting to enter the lair of the beast.*

"Enter," she heard the lady say.

Scarlet did, pushing against the thickly carved door. A rosette of walnut and maple in the shape of a wolf's head took a good portion of the upper panel. Rubies for eyes gleamed like fire when she passed it. It reminded her of her dream.

Something snapped in place in Scarlet's mind. Another piece of the puzzle. The problem was—she had no idea what the picture represented.

"Lady Katrina, I'm sorry to pester you at such a time."

"You never pester me," the lady replied as she came out from behind a three-paneled screen. A sleeveless silk robe of the darkest red crossed in front was tightly cinched at her waist with a cord. Yet she still wore those long black boots that came up mid-thigh.

"It's my key, Lady Katrina…" *Stick to as much of the truth.*

A small smile lifted the corner of the lady's exquisite mouth. She drew near, toyed with one of Scarlet's curls. "Your key?"

"It's gone." She stared at the floor, pulled her wits together. "I think someone took it."

"Oh my. Please take a seat and tell me about it."

Avoiding the penetrating gaze, Scarlet nervously followed the lady deeper into her apartments. She sat on the very corner of the chair the woman pointed at and crossed her sweaty hands over her lap. They made dark prints on her uniform. Scarlet hoped the lady wouldn't notice.

The place wasn't as opulent as she would've expected. It was almost masculine. Deep colors, simple, though well-made furniture.

"Have a drink," the lady said, offering one of the already-poured glasses from the low table in front of her. She took the other one and sipped at it.

Torn between fear for herself and horror at the cost of her failure, Scarlet tried her best to appear normal and took the offered glass. She only dipped her lips in it, not entirely sure she should even come in contact with the stuff. But what else could she do? She absolutely had to get her hands on that key, otherwise Fredrick would remain in his cell and she, well, she'd probably end up at the bottom of the moat. A shiver slithered up her spine.

"And how was it?" the lady asked, a wide grin on her face.

"It's very good, my lady…"

A glint Scarlet had never seen before appeared in the woman's pale eyes. She shook her head. "No, no, I meant Fredrick. How was it *with Fredrick*?"

A wave of dread flowed out from her chest to her entire being. Before she could formulate a denial, a tiny sting began at her lips. Across from her, the lady leaned back against her chair and let one of her long legs rest slightly to the side, revealing a sculpted thigh of the palest ivory.

"The key, Lady Katrina?" Scarlet asked, struggling with the last word but knowing she had to pretend. For Fredrick's sake, she had to push on. She coughed, tried to clear her throat. She noticed her hands shook. She put the glass down on the table where it clinked and broke. "I'm…sorry."

Everything started to spin. She put a hand to her head.

"Your key, my dear, is here," the lady said.

"But if you want it back, you will have to earn it," Lothar said from behind the screen. He was holding something in front of him. There, at the end of its short black cord, dangled her key.

Horror made Scarlet leap to her feet. But she stumbled and collapsed on the chaise again.

The lady rushed forward, reached out to steady Scarlet. "Careful, *kleiner Apfel*, we would not want you to injure yourself."

"You tricked me," Scarlet managed to snarl, or she hoped she did. Conniving bastards, both of them. And she thought Lothar was the lying swine. The lady too. Not that it was a big surprise. Stupid girl. "You knew about what happened to him."

"Your judgment really was clouded, my dear," Katrina said, shaking her head. "And here I thought you were a smart little thing. Of course, I knew about Fredrick's 'accidents'. I was there. Every time. And I enjoyed it too. But not as much as I'll enjoy it tonight."

Scarlet wanted to stand but couldn't put pressure on her legs without them buckling. Fear and horror and self-disgust tightened her throat. She'd escaped Werner only to fall into worse hands.

"Think of poor Fredrick, all alone in his tower, with no one to bring him food," Lady Katrina said, a wide smile spreading on her face.

"I hear starvation is the worst of deaths," Lothar went on.

"Why?" Scarlet wanted to demand, but only managing to croak the word.

A shrug lifted the lady's square shoulders. "People do nasty things to one another. Some do it for greed, others lust. I do it for both."

When Lothar approached and leaned over her, his loose hair trickled down on either side of his handsome, detestable face. Scarlet wanted to push him away but what they'd given her must have dulled her brain and her body for she could barely lift a hand. She snarled a curse when he bent down and kissed her. His tongue felt pointy and rough on her lips. Sounds became muffled then the lights dimmed. Fear choked Scarlet. A visceral, familiar fear.

An image of the milkmaid, bound and clearly drunk danced in her fogging mind.

What had she done?

Chapter Nine

✥

Fredrick sat up in his bed, staring at the ceiling. Her smell still floated around him in thin swirls. Sometimes he'd catch one and inhale deeply. Then it'd be gone. Just like her.

How long had it been since he'd lain with a woman, a real woman? He couldn't even remember. His member felt heavy, comfortably so. Fredrick allowed himself a small grin. And she hadn't tiptoed the entire time.

She'd pick his lock. He knew she would. The stubborn little thing wouldn't listen, which caused a deep tear in his heart. On the one side, he wanted her gone from Innsbruck where danger lurked around every corner. But there was a small, shameful part of him that hoped she'd come back as she'd said.

Excitement tightened his chest. *Control yourself*, he chanted in his head. There were a lot of "ifs" and "maybes" in the whole thing. *If* Scarlet decided to help him, *if* she could find the things she needed, *maybe* she could free him. *If* she could do it without his cousin's knowledge, then *maybe* he'd have a chance to "surprise" them.

He relished the thought of finally wrapping his hands around her neck.

But for now, he had to be patient. And wait.

It must have been around midnight outside, though he couldn't see the sky. He missed it so much. During the day, through the narrow windows, he could spot only a tiny section of it because of the thick rafters jutting out of the masonry above. If he stood a certain way, he could look down into the courtyard, as he'd done the day Scarlet had arrived. Her coppery hair had been the brightest thing he'd seen in a while.

Someone opened the door to the tower. The air shifted around him. Was it her already? Shameful hope flared in his chest at the thought of Scarlet coming back for him, even if he'd told her to leave, even if she should already *be* gone. Noise accompanied the entrance. More than one pair of feet climbed the steps. Not Scarlet then. His heart sank. Yet at the same time, he reminded himself, how much better it was this way, that Scarlet would be safer if she never came back at all. Fredrick crossed his arms and stared at the door. This was highly unusual for Cousin to come torment him at this time of the night. She usually was much too busy for him.

The door opened and in came Cousin, looking as though she'd just been crowned queen. Then Lothar followed. Fredrick jumped to his feet with the force of a broken bowline.

The man had Scarlet in his arms. She was giggling and moaning, her head lolling left and right. An iron fist squeezed Fredrick's throat. Scarlet wasn't the type of woman who *giggled*.

Not trusting his voice, he came to the end of his chain and stared hard at his cousin. He could tell she was gauging his reaction. If he showed the tiniest uneasiness, the faintest weakness, she'd smell it with the accuracy of a predator. So he kept his face stoic, his eyes cold. But inside, he was boiling.

"I bring you a gift," she said. A silk robe barely done in front left little to his imagination. She held the cane in her hand.

"I want nothing from you," he snapped.

Lothar deposited Scarlet's feet on the floor where she stumbled groggily, her eyes glazed and vacant. She searched the room with her gaze then settled on Fredrick. A flash of recognition passed over her confused expression but was gone the next moment. A blade sliced Fredrick's heart. She leaned against the wall for support.

Cousin went to Scarlet, ran a finger over the other woman's lips. "Such a pretty *kleiner Apfel* you are."

111

Scarlet beamed, nuzzling her head on the taller woman's shoulder.

"We shall play a game, yes?" Katrina asked.

Scarlet nodded.

Fredrick's heart sank to the bottom of his feet.

While she encircled Scarlet's shoulders with an arm, his cousin motioned to Lothar. Displaying incredible strength, the man grabbed the "visitor" side of the heavy table and effortlessly dragged it farther away until Fredrick couldn't reach it any longer. The physician's thick shoulders strained the fabric of his exquisitely tailored silk tunic and reminded Fredrick that should things go wrong, he'd do well to dispatch him first. *And keep Cousin for last.*

"As much as I admire your imagination, Cousin, I'm bored and tired. Why don't you—"

"Shut up, before I do it for you," snarled Lothar. Usually wearing a smug expression, Lothar looked extremely displeased. Fredrick would've wanted very much to know what had caused his displeasure, just so he could taunt the man into making a mistake. Like coming too near.

Cousin tut-tutted. "There, there. No need for this. It is such an exciting moment, we do not want to spoil it with you two acting like peasants. Do we, little one?" she added for Scarlet's benefit.

A shake of her copper head was her only coherent answer.

"There, Scarlet, lie down right here," Cousin said, guiding the stumbling young woman to the table Lothar had moved.

Fredrick kept an impassive front while Scarlet laid on the table with her legs dangling over the edge, and he had to physically wrestle his mouth from twisting in disgust when his cousin menacingly circled the table.

"Do you like this, Scarlet?" she asked, her hand going to the other woman's chin and gently tracing the curve of her neck.

Scarlet's head lolled side to side.

"Oh, but you will. Lothar is very skilled."

Fredrick balled fists at his side. If he had doubts as to what was going to happen, he didn't anymore. "Why do you do this?" he asked, knowing he sounded...defeated.

One of her perfectly trimmed eyebrows arched. "Because it will bring us all pleasure." To add weight to her words, she expertly undid Scarlet's bodice with her free hand and left the gray fabric wide open over the pale chest. "And do not think she will not enjoy it. She will. Eventually."

Bending down, his cousin kissed Scarlet on the mouth, and Fredrick hissed a silent curse when the younger woman tried futilely to bat the offending touch away.

Behind them, Lothar unbuttoned his tunic before draping it on the rim of the bathtub. Beneath his long, loose hair, his chest swelled thick with muscles.

"Undress her," his cousin said to Lothar.

Deliberately slow, the man stood at the end of the table, between Scarlet's knees, and slid her closer so he could untie the rest of her garment.

A shiver raced up Fredrick's back. The man was gentle so far. But Fredrick had tasted Lothar's attention too many times to be fooled. He was a brute, a sadistic monster. And he was standing between Scarlet's knees while Fredrick impotently watched.

But he could stop it all, couldn't he? All he had to do was tell Cousin what she wanted to hear. Yet could he do this, endanger the fate of so many for a single one? His people would lose everything. And he'd forfeit his life and that of Scarlet's as well, no doubt about it.

Fredrick threw a murderous glare at Lothar who seemed to enjoy it very much for he gave a sharp little tug on Scarlet's dress. The sound of tearing jolted Fredrick's raw nerves.

"There's no need for that," Fredrick said, fighting with each breath to keep his anger hidden.

When Scarlet lay completely naked, except for worn stockings, Katrina bent over and flicked her tongue at an erect nipple.

Fredrick kept telling himself that as long as they didn't hurt Scarlet, he could take their game, as though such detail would make the whole thing more tolerable. How he despised himself right then. And how he *hated* Katrina. Fredrick realized with shock he'd just referred to his cousin by name. She'd already scored a hit without her knowing.

Lothar stood immobile between Scarlet's knees, his arms crossed over his chest. His impressive member strained his jade green trousers, yet he looked in complete control of himself, occasionally looking at Fredrick.

"Where should we start?" Katrina asked, tapping her chin with the butt of the cane. Her face brightened. "I know, with me." She laughed. "Let me demonstrate what Lothar will do to your charming partner in crime."

His face must have registered something for she laughed at Fredrick. "Of course I knew. I knew all along she would try. Although I *was* wondering if she would do it for the challenge of her trade or out of pity for you. Which is it?"

Fredrick closed his heart to her poisonous words. *If only I could break free of this*, he thought as he looked down at his foot. Through his bangs, he glanced up at his cousin while she lay down on the table by Scarlet's side. A bead of sweat snaked down his spine and lost itself in the fabric of his tunic.

With a peek his way, Katrina rested her head on the table and parted her knees so Lothar could stand between them. Roughly grabbing her by the crook of the hips, he pulled her closer to him while he crouched down.

"First, he will use his tongue," Katrina said as she closed her eyes and allowed her lover full access of her flesh.

He did not need telling twice. With a snarl he dove in, raising her hips off the table in his ardor. The sound of Lothar's mouth and tongue against Katrina's sex made

Fredrick curl his lip, and when she arched her back and hissed, he squeezed his eyes shut.

"Oh no, cousin," Katrina snapped, staring at Fredrick despite the obvious wave of pleasure hitting her. "You will look or else I will let Lothar have her right now whichever way he wants."

As though she knew someone spoke of her, Scarlet mumbled incoherently and nearly rolled off the table. Only Lothar's quick reflex kept her in place as he grabbed her knee and pinned it down with his hand.

Perhaps it was the way Lothar's fingers dug in the pale skin or how Scarlet, despite her state, managed to recognize the fiend's touch and tried to evade it, but something stirred in Fredrick, detached itself from his heart. Like a plaster cast crackling off something that it had hidden from view, protected from touch, for a very long time. He felt lighter, younger than he'd ever felt. And he felt angrier. In all his long life, he'd never known such deep-seated rage. And when he stalked at the end of his chain, his hands curling inward into trembling fists, he could swear Katrina looked alarmed. Lothar stood.

"Keep your hands off her."

The air seemed to congeal around the room. One of the candles sputtered and died.

Lothar smacked Scarlet's thigh. "Or...?"

"Or I'll rip your throat out," Fredrick growled through his teeth. A subtle shift in the air heralded the change—a change he couldn't afford right then. He needed to stay lucid. He wouldn't be able to help if he changed. Not that he could do much if he didn't.

"You'll rip my throat out, will you?" The physician took a threatening step toward Fredrick. His muscled neck corded.

"Enough!" Katrina snapped, giving her lover a sharp crack on the arm with the cane. "She is not for you yet."

He didn't even look back. Both men stared at each other for a long time before Lothar finally retreated. An ugly smile pulled his lips to one side.

"*Yet*," he said.

Fredrick cursed. "Take my chain off, and I'll show you what *I* have for you."

"You men are so brutish. Come, Lothar, let us continue our demonstration before Fredrick forgets who is next and where his motivation lies."

She chuckled when Lothar brusquely flipped her on her stomach, legs dangling down on either side of him. Stretching her cheeks with his thumbs, he resumed his gorging with renewed zeal, and soon, Katrina was fisting the cane and pointing her feet.

"And after his tongue," she said through clenched teeth, "Lothar will use his cock to fill Scarlet's delightful sheath." She humphed when her lover put her words into action. "*Mmm. You know exactly how that feels, do you not, Fredrick?*"

Lothar's shoulders and pectorals strained when he grabbed the woman's hips and pounded into her, which caused a rippling effect in his unbound hair. The table scraped the floor.

While the pair went at it, Fredrick stared at Scarlet, hoping she was too stupefied with drugs to notice what went on. Or to hear Katrina's warning.

Wet sounds accompanied Lothar's furious assault while Katrina moaned his name, her hair spilling over her face and brushing the table.

"But maybe Lothar will want to sink into her other sheath. I am sure it has been visited before. You should meet the man for whom she used to work. Sordid even by my standards. I did her an immense favor."

A flare of rage wafted up his chest, tightened his throat. Fredrick would love nothing better than to wrap his hands around that man's throat. He could well imagine the sort of things he'd done to Scarlet. Concern for her welfare threatened to cloud his judgment. If he lost control for one second, Katrina would see it. And if she saw how much he cared for Scarlet, there'd be no end to this.

"Hard, my love, like you do it best," his cousin said, looking back over her shoulder.

After he pulled out of her, Lothar pressed the tip of his member high along her cleft and sank all the way into her ass. A ragged cry escaped Katrina. Before he could go on, she bucked back and pulled away. "Do not spill yourself yet. You still have another to satisfy." Sweat covered her back and thighs. Deep red handprints marred her pale flesh on either side of her pelvis. "Now," she went on, looking at Fredrick and standing, "on to our affairs."

Hope left Fredrick, fell to a thousand jagged shards around his feet. He had no way out of this one. If he told his cousin to go to Hell, she'd drag Scarlet there instead of him. If he acquiesced to Katrina's demand, everything was lost, but Scarlet might be spared. Yet what else could he do? Let them do to her what he'd just witnessed? Fredrick doubted he could live with that sort of guilt. He carried enough as it was, he didn't need the extra weight of having caused such debased torment to the one person who'd shown him so much kindness. It was enough he'd let it happen to others…the thought of Scarlet's days ending in a shallow grave somewhere on his land repulsed him to the highest degree. She'd become precious to him in the span of a few weeks. Like he'd found an overlooked treasure and would guard it jealously. He felt a kinship with the wounded young woman, for she too had lived her life constantly looking over her shoulder, her soul concealed, her heart guarded. Pain had visited her often, as it had him. His soul called to hers, his body ached for hers, and his heart…it stopped for a full second every time she entered the room. Those were real, what mattered. She liked him, even a little, for she wouldn't have allowed him near if she hadn't. And he wasn't about to betray her heart. Nor his.

Katrina circled the table and stood at one end. She caressed Scarlet's fiery hair with a shaking hand. Female musk reached Fredrick's sensitive nostrils and he cringed in disgust. He couldn't believe von Innsbruck blood filled those foul veins.

"Sign the deed."

Despair muted Fredrick.

Katrina nodded to a grinning Lothar who stood between Scarlet's legs.

"No!"

Fredrick's growl froze everyone, even Scarlet.

"No?" Katrina asked, crossing her arms. "No, what? You do not want Lothar to taste what you have already tasted yourself? I never knew you were so selfish."

At this, a look of white-hot hatred flashed in Lothar's hazel eyes as he looked from Scarlet to Fredrick then back again. He angrily pulled himself back in and buttoned his trousers. But Katrina didn't seem to notice the danger lurking in her lover's face as she sat on a corner of the table. Her hand still stroked Scarlet's curls. "Should we stop, then? Is this what you want, Fredrick?"

Fredrick forced his mind to clear. All Katrina wanted was to break him. He'd assisted, impotent, to this sort of thing before. To much worse, in fact. If he betrayed his feelings, his cousin would recognize it for what it was, and Fredrick doubted even giving in to Katrina would save Scarlet. Not if she knew she could use his love against him.

Love.

The word shocked him. He hadn't even thought of it in so long, if ever. Throughout his long life, there hadn't been many women and definitely no one like Scarlet. She brought out defensive feelings he didn't know he had. Impotent rage flared, and he feared for a second he'd lost control. But no, the change didn't come.

Yet Katrina still must have sensed the subtle shift for she stared at him long, her pale, icy eyes narrowing to slits. A grin pulled her lips to one side. She slid off the table and stood between Scarlet's knees. After a quick kiss for Lothar, she indicated the other end of the table.

"I shall take this end. Meanwhile, while we have Fredrick's undivided attention," she stopped, rested the cane against the table before caressing Scarlet's outstretched knees. "You fuck her mouth."

At Katrina's command, Lothar smiled widely.

Fredrick would've taken a step but was prevented by the chain cutting at his ankle. "No."

But the man didn't listen and circled the table, stopping near Scarlet's head. She turned to look at him, a confused expression on her face while he reached for the twin rows of buttons on his trousers.

"Cousin, there's no need for this," Fredrick said, the warning in his voice plain as salt on a wound.

"Why not? She would enjoy it."

With Lothar looming threateningly over Scarlet, a deep sigh swelled Fredrick's chest. He'd lost. Might as well finish it all right now. "Stop it."

Katrina froze, motioned for Lothar to do the same. "Only you can stop it, Fredrick. But are you really willing to?"

Fredrick nodded curtly.

"I do not think you mean it," she replied. "Lothar."

Cradling Scarlet's chin in his large hand and turning it to the side, the man leaned over her.

The sight drove a knife in Fredrick's heart. He couldn't even bring himself to look anymore. "I'm telling you. Stop it."

He realized too late his tone wasn't what his cousin wanted. "You are *telling* me?" Katrina demanded.

Lothar grinned. He undid two buttons on his trousers. Scarlet mumbled something as she pressed her hand against the man's muscled belly.

"For Christ's sake, Katrina, stop it!"

"You think you can order me?" she snarled, spreading Scarlet's trembling knees even wider apart. "You will have to beg me, Fredrick. *Beg* me."

Fredrick fisted his hair. "She has nothing to do with us," he began then gritted his teeth when two more of Lothar's buttons came undone. The mere thought of this man's cock in Scarlet sickened Fredrick. "Leave her alone, you filthy swine!"

The force of Fredrick's voice froze Lothar. His expression changed from excitement to malice. He reached down and pinched one of Scarlet's nipples. A little cry escaped her.

"*Katrina,*" snarled Fredrick.

"Enough," Katrina said. Lothar reluctantly released Scarlet's chin. "You were saying, dear cousin?"

"I'll do it," Fredrick replied softly, hoping the whole sickening affair would just go away.

"I said you would have to beg."

Fredrick gritted his teeth. The hated bitch. "Please," he said, putting emphasis on the word. "Stop tormenting Scarlet."

She grinned, motioned to the floor in front of Fredrick. "*Beg.*"

Keeping his gaze locked with the woman's, Fredrick slowly went down onto one knee then onto the other. There, kneeling, he took a great sigh through his dilated nostrils. *Fight it down,* he told himself when he thought he could feel the first signs of transformation. *Control it.* But he couldn't control the tears welling up his eyes. "Please, Katrina, I beg you, stop tormenting Scarlet."

"I don't know about you," Lothar said, "but he's not convincing me."

Katrina nodded. "I agree."

Panic and bile rising in his throat, Fredrick said, "Please, stop it. I'm begging you."

"I loath hurting her, Fredrick, believe me. I rather like my little apple. But I do not think you understand how…resolute I can be. So," she said as she retrieved the cane, poising its handle right over Scarlet's belly and waited. "Convince me."

Fear and horror filled Fredrick's gut. "Katrina," he snarled, unable to keep the tremor from his voice. Silent sobs of rage choked him. "Please, please don't do it."

The silver butt rubbed against Scarlet's skin, threateningly lower and lower.

As though his soul had been ripped apart, Fredrick let out a long, anguished growl. "I'm begging you, please! Katrina! No!"

She straightened, leaned the cane across Scarlet's thighs. She shook her head a couple of times. "He actually did it."

Lothar sniggered while he rubbed back Scarlet's hair with one hand. "I am still not convinced he means it."

A look of surprise, of shock tightened Katrina's face. "You do mean it. You would beg for a *servant*?"

Though he said nothing, Fredrick knew his tearing eyes told the whole truth. Instead of feeling ashamed of it, he marveled at the strength it'd given him, the renewed hope he could somehow turn this situation into something good. Yes, he would beg for a servant. He would beg and grovel for Scarlet. He'd *kill* for her as well and if there was a God, if there was a shred of good fortune lying about, something he was definitely beginning to doubt, he'd get his hands on Katrina. She'd be the one going to Hell.

"Have you finally seen the light, Fredrick?" Katrina asked, coming closer to him than she'd ever been…while he could do something about it anyway. She never shied away from rubbing herself against him or performing the vilest act on him while he was drugged and unable to wring her neck for it. "Have you finally seen that we would be a perfect match, you and I? That our heir would take the family name to new heights? Well...*my* heir, anyway." She winked.

He couldn't even talk for the fear twisting his insides. Fredrick nodded.

"And are you prepared to do what is necessary?"

"Whatever is needed to stop this. You won, Katrina," he murmured.

"Very well," she said after a while. "Give her something to wake her," she added for Lothar's benefit.

The man looked as though someone had just demanded for both his hands. He buttoned his trousers back up. Throwing a venomous glance at Fredrick and Katrina, he went to his tunic, rummaged in it and produced a small vial. Keeping Scarlet's head immobile with a hand much too rough for Fredrick's taste, he let a single drop into her mouth.

"She should feel better in a short while," Katrina offered, uncharacteristically showing a soft expression, even patting Scarlet's thigh.

Utterly spent, Fredrick sat on his heels, raked shaking hands through his hair and closed his eyes. He felt as though the weight of the world had been lifted off his shoulders. Although he knew he'd pay for it later. Pay with his life. But dying would be easy compared to the guilt of having caused Scarlet pain. He could hardly stomach the thought. Katrina would've killed her. No doubt about it.

"Poor *kleiner Apfel*," Katrina murmured. "So young. So foolish."

Dread seeped into Fredrick's heart. He stood slowly, his gaze riveted to his cousin's face, searching for...he wasn't sure what.

After sitting on the table and letting her legs dangle, Katrina shook her head. "You two think you had me fooled? That I had not noticed?"

"There's nothing to notice. I just don't want someone else's death on my conscience."

"God knows your conscience never bothered you before," she snorted derisively. "I am talking about you having a soft spot for my *kleiner Apfel* and she having one for you in return."

Something broke in Fredrick's heart. Breathing harder, he shook his head. "She doesn't—"

"Oh please, you insult me. Did you think I would not see that special glow in her eyes?" Katrina demanded, clearly irked. "I was hoping she would liven things up for you, but still."

"Don't make her sound like a whore." Fredrick knew she may be a thief, but Scarlet was no whore, even if his cousin made her sound this way. Actually, of everyone in this room, he'd no doubt Scarlet surpassed them all in virtue and honesty.

"So territorial."

A look of deep frustration flashed in Lothar's hazel eyes. He looked down at Scarlet and shook his head. "So you've fallen in love with a monster. Such a waste." His face tightened into an odd combination of disappointment and cold fury.

By God, Fredrick thought, repulsed beyond words. *He's jealous.*

While they talked, Lothar kept brushing back Scarlet's hair. Her eyes had lost the confused glaze. Something else now shone in her dark gaze—awareness. And fear. Fredrick's heart squeezed at the thought. Perhaps she should've remained drugged. At least she wouldn't have heard all of this.

"Let's end this. I told you I'd do what you want. Just give me the damn deed so I can sign it."

Katrina shrugged. "Although I enjoy watching you beg— and believe me I did—I do not think I will let you keep her. I love winning too much."

He pointed an accusing finger at her. "Keep your end so I can sign away every damn pebble on this land. *You won*. Don't you like the sound of that? You waited damn long to hear it, haven't you? Well, Katrina, you won. I yield!"

Anger was rising. Old, seething rage. He couldn't hold it down forever. And Scarlet, who was awakening, her knees coming tighter together as if she were cold. Or ashamed.

A lift of her ruby lips showed gleaming white teeth. Katrina spread her knees farther apart, which parted the robe she wore, revealed herself to him though he wanted nothing to do with her. She inserted a lacquered finger, hummed some soft tune to herself, as though pondering her next move. She'd always been devilishly good at chess.

"I like the sound of it. 'I yield.' But you know me, I do not enjoy just winning. What I like best is breaking my opponent, utterly crushing him."

A vicious grin spread on Lothar's face. When Scarlet turned to face him and started to recoil, he grabbed her hair and pulled her so she knelt on the table. "She's awake now," he said to Katrina.

"We agreed on your terms. I'll sign everything to you."

Fredrick sounded desperate and he knew it. But the sight of Scarlet, clearly frightened and close to tears drove all other thoughts away. His anger bubbled even closer to the surface. He breathed harder, felt his nostrils dilate. Just a little while longer. Just until Katrina let Scarlet go. *God, please, give me strength*, he prayed for the first time in his life, needing to ask help from the divine.

"Yes, you would. I can see it." She sighed. "But it will no longer be enough."

"What do you mean?" he snarled through clenched teeth. It was gaining—the rage within. The beast.

"I mean I want to see you grovel at my feet, begging me to stop while Lothar gives your little thief his special attention. You have been dreaming of it, have you not?" she asked of her companion.

A look of sadistic pleasure crossed Lothar's face. He forced Scarlet back so she faced him, and kissed her hard. The skin of her lips looked red when he pulled away. She still looked too weak to fight him off. Not as though she'd much chance, given his stature.

Fredrick knew he'd lost. He'd been tricked again by this demon. Only this time, he wasn't the only one who'd suffer. And this, more than anything Lothar or Katrina's thugs could have done to him, broke what little resolve he still managed to cling to. He felt it breaking as though something physical had just fallen and crashed on the stone floor. Smells became more acute while his vision sharpened. His hands hurt when they began to curl in with his swelling knuckles.

"Katrina, you lying bitch!" Fredrick roared.

He collapsed back onto his knees, though this time, he wasn't begging. He was changing.

Chapter Ten

ଛ

A cry of pain escaped her when Lothar fisted her hair. "I can't wait to hear you scream," he murmured in her ear.

His fingers were rough as they searched her, invaded her. Scarlet tried to squeeze her knees tighter but couldn't quite yet control her body. Tendrils like smoke still clouded her vision, slowed her mind. Her head throbbed.

When Fredrick roared, Scarlet froze to watch him. Something was wrong with him, in the way he knelt on all fours, his spine clearly visible through the long velvet tunic. When he looked up, she gasped. His eyes were completely bloodshot.

"Did you think you could win against me?" Lady Katrina demanded. She sat near Scarlet's knees, pleasuring herself with her hand. "Did you, for one second, actually trust me?"

For reply, Fredrick roared again, though this time, the sound couldn't possibly have come from his throat. No human could make such a sound. A high-pitched wail laced with a raw, feral growl. The sound a predator would make. It triggered an instinctive reaction in Scarlet, as if the primal cry had awakened parts of her brain long dormant. A fear-induced thrill rushed through her veins. Scarlet shivered. Even Lothar seemed transfixed with the transformation, and he stopped pawing at her.

Scarlet heard what she hoped wasn't bones crunching but knew was when Fredrick arched his head back, his face contorted by pain. Bloody cuts appeared along his neck, at the corners of his mouth, as though something was pushing out of him from inside.

"You lied," he snarled, obviously having difficulty speaking.

"Do not act like such a bloody virgin," the lady snapped. To Scarlet's shock, she saw the woman insert the butt of the cane in her, thrusting in and out with abandon.

A violent jolt shook Fredrick. "Let her...go." The last word sounded like a growl.

Scarlet's heart squeezed in pain at his plight. Whatever was happening to him must have been agonizing. Blood dripped from his nose and into his mouth. His hands had curled in on themselves and split over the knuckles.

"What's happening?" she managed to ask, though her tongue was thick, her throat dry.

At the sound of her voice, Fredrick's blood-glazed eyes locked with hers. Time seemed to stop.

For a split second, Scarlet could see the man within, still struggling for control. She could see clearly through the heart of the man, could see his soul through those predatory eyes and knew he was still Fredrick—only for some reason, was becoming different. The old driver's words filtered into her shocked brain.

"*Master Fredrick's different, Scarlet,*" Frank had said. "*Has a dark streak in him. Once in a while, he's...*" Then Frank had stopped, had shaken his head sadly. "*But he's a good man. Never forget that, no matter what happens.*"

Fredrick squeezed his eyes shut, breaking the connection. Scarlet's guts twisted.

A series of muffled snaps from Fredrick's body forced Scarlet to cover her ears. He floundered up onto his knees, ripped his tunic opened to reveal a chest hideously...different. Ribs stood out prominently while his abdomen was caved in. Body hair, which she'd never seen on him except in a couple of places, grew thick and long, covered every part of him she could see.

"Sweet Mary," she heard herself say over and over.

When his face began to elongate around the mouth, his eyes to widen, the back of his skull to become more pointed, the lady turned back to Scarlet and grinned viciously.

"This is the part I enjoy best. When the last shred of man breaks down."

"What do you…oh, Fredrick," Scarlet murmured.

Bile seeped up her throat when Fredrick's jaw clearly popped under the strain. The sound almost made her faint. Fangs the size of her baby fingers sprouted from shredding, bleeding gums. She meant to turn away.

"Watch it," hissed Lothar as he pulled her hair so she faced the horrible spectacle of Fredrick changing into…she wasn't sure she could contain the thought.

Then every tiny detail of the past month or so came back to her.

The silver chain around his ankle, most of the decorative pieces, the buttons on his tunic, and the rosette carved in the lady's bedchamber doors. All bearing the same image. The head of a white wolf. And how badly he'd looked after the full moon, so pale and drawn. The need to have him nearly sedated at all times. Using wolfsbane, no less. His illness Frank and Ute had mentioned. Especially Frank. He must have known.

Landgraf Fredrick von Innsbruck was a *werewolf*.

But these were tales told to children to frighten them. Surely, no such being existed? The notion spun in her head. Yet there was no denying what happened to him now. And to say she'd come close to him, had *touched* him. Horrified, she looked on as Fredrick's transformation became more complete.

"See the power you have over him?" Lothar whispered in Scarlet's ear.

She tried to look away again. This wasn't her doing. Whatever was happening to Fredrick wasn't because or for her. Was it?

"She broke him because of you," Lothar went on, nibbling at her neck. She tried pushing his face away but he bit her on the forearm. "You were his only weakness. As you are mine."

Weakness? Then Scarlet understood. His cousin must have wanted something from him, which he'd refused for the past two years. The lady must have used her, his only contact to the outside world, to force him. But what had triggered Fredrick's change?

As though reading her mind, Lothar cupped her chin and forced her to look up into his hazel eyes. For the first time since she'd met the man, he looked sincere, even solemn. "See what happens when you let a little worm like you into your heart? You lose *control*."

"Into his heart?" Scarlet asked, shocked at the deep tone of her voice. Strength was returning to her body, to her mind. And with it, a fury she didn't know was there.

Fredrick was going through this horrible transformation because he'd let her into his heart. Because he cared for her?

He howled before slumping pitifully to his side, his whole body quivering with a series of massive spasms. The pain must have been unbearable.

Fear-induced energy fizzed in her veins, tightened her muscles and cleared her mind of the last spiderwebs. She'd seen too much pain in her life—too damn much.

The lady hissed a curse of pleasure as she continued with the cane. "Do you not wish you could taste him just the way he is now, not quite the beast, with the man still visible inside? I would give anything to have him savage me right this instant."

Lothar, who was fisting Scarlet's hair with both hands, released one so he could reach over and grab at the lady's. She arched back, her eyes closed, while he twisted the black mane around his fist.

There'd be no other chance.

Scarlet bucked as hard as she could. Caught off guard, Lothar stumbled back, but he still managed to hold her hair and Scarlet was forced back with him. When her backside slid off the table and her weight completely rested against the man's chest, Scarlet planted her feet against the table's edge and pushed with all her might.

The table tilted forward and took the lady with it, and both toppled noisily deeper inside the room. Right beside Fredrick.

A strangled yelp tore from Lady Katrina as her cousin closed a twisted hand over her ankle and dragged her to him.

Scarlet too yelled when Lothar spun her around and punched her in the belly. She bent in half, gagging.

"Help me!" the lady cried as she struggled against Fredrick's grip.

While Scarlet collapsed on all fours and struggled to keep from vomiting, Lothar stalked to Fredrick's chair, picked the massive thing up as if it weighed nothing, and lifted it high over his head.

"No!" Scarlet screamed.

The chair came down.

Fredrick howled when it crashed over his back and head. Splinters showered him and the lady. Fredrick grew very still. Scarlet squeezed her eyes shut against the sight of his unmoving, battered body, and for the first time in many years, she let the tears come freely. Lothar used the silence and eerie calm to drag the woman out of harm's way and dump her unceremoniously to the floor beside Scarlet.

"Get the men," the lady snarled, saliva dribbling down her chin. "Tell them to bring the chains."

"Get them yourself. I have what I wanted."

Lothar grinned as he came over, picked Scarlet up by an arm and hoisted her to her knees. As much as she tried to punch, scratch and otherwise hurt him, he was even stronger than Werner and only shook her for her effort. "I'll enjoy this spirit a bit more later when we have a bit of privacy. But not now."

His knuckles accompanied her into oblivion.

* * * * *

Scarlet's world exploded into tiny, bursting suns. She felt rough stone against her cheek. Somewhere, she heard something whimper.

Fredrick.

Struggling up to her knees, she spotted him still down, but at least moving a bit. Tears flowed down her cheeks. Blood filled her mouth. The door clattered against the wall. People coming in. The smell of sweat and ale and onions, all of which she'd learn to associate with pain and cruelty. Only this time, they weren't there for her. But for the man who cared for her.

"Make him pay. And do not stop until I tell you to," the lady said from somewhere behind her. Her voice was so calm, so cold, it sliced through Scarlet's very soul.

Turning, she spotted the woman leaning against the wall. The maniacal glint in her eyes would have made anyone cross himself twice. Four men, each carrying a length of chain, stood around her, and each looked more brutish than the other. Scarlet knew the type.

She was still trying to clear her mind when Lothar grabbed her hair and pulled hard. "You're coming with me while she's having fun with him."

She couldn't leave him, she had to help! He was still lying on his side, blood matting his white hair...*fur*. Scarlet meant to break away from Lothar but couldn't.

Giving her a sharp tug upward, he snarled, "Let's go."

As she was dragged backward to the door, Fredrick struggled to lift his head and stare at her. In this split second connection, with a fragile thread linking them both, she put all her heart and soul into, she prayed, what would be a flash of light in his darkening horizon. With some good fortune, he'd understand.

She'd be back for him.

Still naked, Scarlet was forced to leave the room, leave Fredrick behind to face this horrible woman and her thugs. Ghastly images gnawed at her soul. The things they'd do to him…

But her own immediate fate, which wasn't much better than Fredrick's, forced Scarlet to calm her nerves and try to think clearly. Lothar was much stronger than she was, so there was no way for her to overpower him. She'd have to outsmart the man if she stood a chance of getting away.

Yet fear crept up her spine with the tingly march of a thousand spiders when he wrapped his arm around her neck in a headlock and forced her in half so she wouldn't be a nuisance. They went down the steps this way.

"I've never had to resort to this. Women, in general, come with me quite happily. But you're not just any woman, are you, Scarlet?" Lothar took a deep breath. "No, you're not."

After he wrapped a large hand over her mouth and jaw, he opened the door at the base of the tower, looked both ways then shuffled down the corridor with her barely touching the ground for his arm around her. When they came to the door she'd discovered the other day, panic nearly shredded what little control she still had over herself. An image of the horrible "horse" contraption and the maid bound to it flashed in Scarlet's mind. Instinct kicked in and she began to flail with all she had.

Grunting with the effort, Lothar pushed her against the wall, pinning her with his body while he fished inside his trousers and pulled a small key. He wrestled open the door with growing excitement showing on his handsome face. "I can't wait to sink myself into your tight little arse. I'll fuck you until you scream for me to stop. Then I'll fuck you until you can't scream anymore."

He didn't even stop to retrieve his key and left it in the keyhole. Darkness enveloped them when he opened the door. Lothar pushed her in. Her arms windmilling, Scarlet just managed not to fall down the steps. He caught her by the throat and forced her down the staircase backward, thereby quashing any attempt she could've made to escape. It was all she could do not to kill herself as it was. When they reached the base of the stairs, he kept guiding her backward, still with his hand tightly around her throat. Stars popped around her vision. Scarlet feared she would collapse from fear and pain and lack of air. But she had to remain strong. Fredrick depended on her.

This gave her strength. She gritted her teeth when Lothar pushed in the door to his…she didn't know what to call this room, but when she spotted the contraption, all gleaming black leather, Scarlet's mind clouded over in panic. The multi-branched candelabrum illuminated the room with pitiless clarity. On a table she hadn't seen previously, a row of glistening metal tools, then a collection of riding crops, whips, other things she knew not the meaning. Bottles lined neatly on a shelf. The smell of sweat. Dark dots on the stone floor. Blood?

A shriek pierced the silence. Scarlet realized with shock it'd been her voice.

He silenced her with his fist.

Scarlet backpedaled, hit the "horse", which spun crazily around, and could only groan when Lothar trapped her between his body and the contraption. He pushed his pelvis hard against hers, crushing the sensitive skin.

"Scarlet," he sighed, grinning a lopsided grin which would have made rows of women swoon.

Only to her, it symbolized the ugliest, trickiest and basest thing to which a man could sink. To be so beautiful on the outside, yet wicked and malevolent through the core. And someone like Fredrick, who no doubt had often felt the icy tongue of gossip because of his physical difference. Yet inside, what better man was there? He was willing to die for her—a nobody. A thief. And die horribly too.

A strange calm took over Scarlet. As though waiting for something she didn't know would happen—or when. Or *if* it would happen at all. Yet this peculiar peace brought lucidity as sharp as a razor's blade. Scarlet took in a long breath. Control. She'd win against Lothar by remaining in control.

He slid his hand down her belly, gently slipped a finger inside. "I knew you liked me, even a little bit," he murmured, running his tongue up and down her neck, then lower.

She gasped when he caught a nipple between his teeth and smiled up at her. Intensifying the pressure, he watched her like a hawk. Scarlet balled her fists to keep from crying out, knowing the sight of others' pain excited this sort of man. Instead, she forced a smile.

"Climb on it," he said, grabbing her by the armpits and hoisting her astride the "horse" as if she weighed nothing.

Feeling exposed and vulnerable, Scarlet straddled the thing. *Control*, she told herself.

Beaming now, Lothar took a step back. "Bend forward, with your arms behind you." He slid her stockings off skillfully, like someone who had done this many times before, then went to the table while she lowered her chest onto the contraption. Lothar came back as she was bringing her naked feet closer to her backside, resting them on the sort of ledge made for that purpose, she surmised.

Lothar grabbed the end of the "horse" and spun it around so Scarlet faced away. She didn't like him standing behind her this way but could do nothing. "Put your hands back."

She closed her eyes and wrapped her arms under the belly of the wooden horse. "I can't. I'll fall."

Control, she told herself again, her internal voice becoming calmer. Harder.

He chuckled. She kept her eyes closed, didn't look back when she felt his hand against her cheek. He slapped her, hard. The clack resounded in the small, bare room. "Falling will be the last of your worries, Scarlet. Now put your hands back."

Since she'd closed her eyes and blocked out light from the candles, her mind felt more at ease. An image flashed in her mind—a bleeding Fredrick, on all fours, yet still managing to find the inner strength to meet her gaze. Lothar—that odious man—standing above with a chair poised over his head.

Grabbing the "horse" flanks with all her might, Scarlet kicked out with both feet. Lothar let out a satisfying humph of air when her feet connected, and she heard him crash back against the candelabrum, bringing it down. He howled in pain. Hot wax everywhere, no doubt.

Instant, familiar darkness fell on the room. Within a second, Scarlet was off the thing and across the room. Behind her, Lothar's yelp of pain turned into a guttural growl of frustration. Scarlet didn't wait around to see if he could see as well as she in the darkness and bolted for the door. She turned left, took a couple of tentative paces then the first step connected against her toes. Cursing profusely, Lothar crashed about in the room before spilling out into the dark corridor.

Two by two, Scarlet silently rushed up the stairs, not missing a single step, and charged up the last few. Growling with pain and fear and adrenaline, she gripped the door, spun around it then shouldered it shut. Her hands were quick but shaking as she turned the key twice, a split second before a thunderous crash hit the other side.

"Open the door, or I swear I'll skin you alive," Lothar snarled through the thick door.

Now shaking violently, Scarlet threw the key as far as she could. Let the bastard try to get it back!

Sweat slicked her hands, the insides of her thighs. Shivering, barefoot on the cold stone, she ran toward the newer part of the castle and was just reaching the passage reserved for servants when she realized she was naked. But each moment lost going to her room and getting dressed was one more Fredrick had to endure at the hands of his tormentors.

And naked she was when she burst into the crowded kitchen, screaming for help at the top of her lungs. Some just stood around, stupefied. Ute was quick to make her appearance and rapidly took charge. Pre-dawn light barely poked rays through the kitchen windows.

"Calm down, girl, I can't hear a word," the old woman said as she gripped Scarlet's shoulder in a surprisingly strong gnarled hand.

"It's Master Fredrick, they're killing him!" Scarlet yelled, unable or unwilling to bring herself to talk.

Ute paled to chalk. "What?"

"Master Fredrick, he's up there, and there are four men beating him with chains, I saw them. Please," Scarlet snarled, pulling her arm out of Ute's hand. "We have to help him."

"We will," Frank said from the doorway. "Should've dealt with the greedy witch the first day she got here instead of convincing myself everything was rosy."

Sharing the older man's guilt, Scarlet knuckled tears of relief from her cheeks. As Frank was calling to the kitchen lads to go fetch every man they crossed, Ute retrieved an overcoat hanging on a hook and slipped it on Scarlet.

"What men?" Ute demanded. She was clearly not getting it as completely as Frank, though she did appear back her usual stern self, only now she looked incandescent with anger. "*Whose* men?"

"Katrina's, they're her men. And Fredrick, they beat him when he refuses to…" she stopped, unsure. What did Katrina want, anyway? "She wants something from him, and that's why she's been keeping him locked up, until he gives it over to her." Scarlet told a shocked crowd what she knew in as few words as she could. They were losing precious seconds.

"I'll bring the tonic for the master, just in case," said Ute.

"No," Scarlet snapped with more force than she intended. "It's how the physician was keeping the master quiet. It's wolfsbane...a poison, Ute."

Crushing guilt crossed the woman's wrinkled face. She put a hand to her mouth and formed the word "no". Not a sound came out.

Scarlet crossed her arms to ward off cold as nerves were finally catching on. "I'm sorry."

The lads burst back in with more men than she'd ever seen in a kitchen. Each looked burlier and angrier than the next.

"Come on," Frank said, elbowing his way through. His riding crop cleaved a path in front of him, though he never raised it once. The menacing glint in his gaze would've split a log. Yet guilt is what blazed brightest.

Scarlet ran to the front of the small crowd, more like a mob with every passing moment, and balled both fists when they reached the tower door and spotted one man standing guard.

"How could you turn on the master this way, you traitor?" Frank yelled from twenty paces away. "How could you?!"

Perhaps it was the old man's tone of voice, or the mob on his heels. Whatever it was, the would-be guard turned tail and ran the other way. A pair of Frank's men caught him before he could turn the corner. Scarlet didn't know nor cared what happened to him. He could roast to death tied to a post under the sun for all she cared.

Frank's charge stopped when he pulled on the door and found that it was locked. "Bust it down."

"That will take too long," Scarlet snapped as she bent closer to the opening. "I need something sharp." Without turning her eyes away from the lock, mentally picking it, she reached back and waited until someone had found "something sharp".

"Here, girl, make it quick," Frank said as he placed something in her hand. "I've already waited too damn long. What a fool I've been."

Scarlet sighed when she brought a finishing nail up to the lock. Better than nothing.

With more speed than she'd ever used for picking at a lock, Scarlet twisted the thin nail into the keyhole and tried to find the lever which would spring the bolt. First try!

The door clicked half a second before Frank crossed the doorway. "Damn, it's dark in here."

A lamp came through the group and made its way to the old man's hand. "Only you three," he said to some men after a pointed look at Scarlet. "The rest wait here. Place a lad with good ears halfway up but he's not to enter the master's room until I say so. Is that clear?"

Collective agreement was voiced.

Passing him nimbly, Scarlet took the steps as fast as she could. The soles of her feet burned against the icy stones, but her heart hurt much more with the image of Fredrick dancing in front of her. What if he was dead? She'd never forgive herself. Neither would anyone coming up the stairs behind her.

Scarlet was wondering how to approach the situation when a long, plaintive cry echoed around the circular staircase.

Yelling something that could as well have been in another language, she charged up the last steps and shouldered the door.

Then Scarlet screamed.

Chapter Eleven

ജ

Pain.

In each limb, in his mouth, inside his brain. Like burning water being poured into his skull.

He tried to think but couldn't seem to form a coherent thought, as though parts of his brain weren't functioning properly. He meant to talk, only his mouth wouldn't move the way it should. Fear crept into his numb body.

Voices. He couldn't recognize any of them. The same word over and over. His name? Many times his name. Harsh words of which he couldn't understand the meaning were flung at him. He could smell though. Everything and everyone. So many smells here. Bad smells. Like hurt, evil, death. One of the smells became stronger, until it filled his nostrils. *Blood.* His own.

* * * * *

Warmth touched his cheek. The other rested against something cold and hard. He tried to open his eyes but couldn't. So he concentrated instead on sounds and smells. These were different. Friendly, somehow. And voices again, but gentler, some so soft he had to pay close attention to hear them.

The smell of something special but forgotten floated close to his face. This one particular scent chased away every other. Fredrick didn't mind. He liked this smell. It reminded him of summer and flowers. Someone had once mistaken it for sage.

Lavender!

The lavender smell came closer, filled his nostrils. He heard his voice say something but couldn't understand his own words. What strange tongue was this?

Then pain hit again. This time though, it came from within and wasn't inflicted from without.

* * * * *

"Fredrick."

His name emerged from so far away it might as well have drifted in across some foggy marsh.

At the sound of this voice, all he could get was a color. Red — the fiery golden red of copper gleaming under the sun. Then something tugged at his ankle and he groaned.

"I'm sorry," he heard the voice say. A woman's voice. One he knew.

"Scarlet?" His mouth could barely work. His teeth felt loose.

"Hold still, Master, the girl's almost done," a man said.

An older voice, a man's. Fredrick's heart swelled at the memories flooding his brain. Through a supreme feat of will, he opened his eyes. Two silver-haired persons stood on either side of him. He lay on the floor, with cold stone hurting his back and head. Near his feet, a redhead bent close to his aching ankle.

And in the corner, being watched over by two very angry-looking men, a black-haired woman knelt with her hands behind her back. A nasty bruise covered her throat and part of her chin. As though someone had punched her *and* tried to strangle her.

He wouldn't mind doing both.

"I'm almost done," the redhead said.

Fredrick's mind cleared at once. "Scarlet?"

She turned to him a bruised face and a bloodied nose, but smiling eyes as well. He heard his sigh of relief even if his ears buzzed painfully. "What happened to you?" Then it came back to him. "Where's Lothar?" he snarled, meaning to raise his head.

"He's gone, the sneaky bastard," an old woman said. "Now, you need to lie still and wait 'til she's done, Master."

"Ute, it's been so long. And Frank..." Words caught in his throat. So much time had been stolen from him. Anger welled up in his chest.

That bitch kneeling in the corner — it was all her doing.

A faint click broke the dark chain of his thoughts. He looked down at a beaming Scarlet as she brandished an empty manacle and wide-open lock.

For the first time in a long time, Fredrick could move his foot without the painful ache caused by the chain. With the help of Ute and Frank, he sat up.

Utter mayhem surrounded him. His tunic hung in tatters and barely covered him. Two men lay on the floor, one looking dead, the other even more so. Their blood had followed the grout between stones and coursed right out of the doorway. He'd have this room walled in as soon as he could.

His gaze settled onto Scarlet again and a tentative smile found her lips. Reaching out with a shaking hand, he motioned for her to come closer.

"Come," Frank said, getting to his feet with an assortment of joint creaks, "we have this to take care of."

The "this" in question smiled viciously when the men guarding her each grabbed hold of an arm and pulled.

"Do not think you have the last word, Fredrick," Katrina said, her voice strangely calm. "Lothar is already out of your reach, and soon, I will be."

"Stay your tongue before I cut it out," Ute snapped. She leveled her index finger at the lady and shook it. "Tricked us into helping you, kept the master chained like a beast in his own tower. There's a special Hell for the likes of you."

141

As everyone but Scarlet trooped out of the room, Frank having told his men to remove the "deadwood", Scarlet sat on her heels by Fredrick's side.

"You sure do look bad."

"You look like an angel to me."

Scarlet seemed ill at ease. "Don't say that, Master. I'm no angel. Can you move?"

Master? The word stung.

Then he realized she could probably remember the last time she'd been in this room, with Katrina at one end of the table and Lothar at the other. As though Scarlet knew he was thinking about it, she blushed violently.

"They drugged you. I've been through it enough times to know there's nothing you could've done." His voice sounded raw. His throat hurt.

She avoided his gaze while she fiddled with the blood-encrusted lock. "I could've fought a little harder, used my brain a little sooner."

He shook his head. "They tricked *me*, Scarlet, when I'm thrice their age. Do you want to know how?" He cupped her chin and angled her face toward his. "Because they're both beautiful and charming and conniving backbiters. I let Katrina use her guiles on me, just as she did on everyone else. She knew I spent most of my time here alone and played to that, convinced me to visit with them in the city. She's always been devilishly good at chess and positioned her pieces very well. I didn't realize she was poisoning me until it was too late."

Anger flashed in Scarlet's dark gaze. God help those who ever crossed her. "They poisoned you before…this?"

He nodded. "Despite my better judgment, I invited them for a week, and one night, I wasn't feeling well. Luckily, Lothar was a physician and gave me something for the headache." Fredrick laughed in derision.

"I woke up here, chained to the wall. We always suspect the ones who are different, or sinister. We never see it coming from those who look like those two."

Scarlet snorted. "I should've seen it coming, even from good-looking folk."

"You're being too hard on yourself."

Reaching out, he let his hand rest over her forearm and marveled at the heat that transferred to him. He already felt better. Before he could put into words every crazy thought swirling into his head, a soft knock came to the door.

Frank poked his head in. "How 'bout we get you out of here and into your own rooms, Master. Ute's already after the staff to rip every piece of fabric out of your chambers...so it's *clean* for you. Had to talk the woman out of asking for a priest to perform an exorcism." A sparkle of smile danced in his eyes when he looked at Scarlet then back at Fredrick.

"Good idea," Fredrick replied, meaning to stand up.

His gesture must have triggered something in both Frank and Scarlet for each gasped and reached out to stop him. Affection for his people—and love for Scarlet—swelled his chest. If this sensation could be with him forever, he wouldn't mind living another hundred and twenty years.

"Now just you wait a moment, Master, Scarlet and I'll help you down now that you're...back."

A shadow passed over Scarlet's eyes. Fredrick tried to ignore the jab of pain this caused. She'd seen him change. It was his only clear memory of this night, before he became the beast. She'd been kneeling on the table, with Lothar holding her still, while Fredrick changed into...a monster. She'd discovered in the worst possible manner something for which he would've spent years preparing her. No one should be exposed to such horrible experience without warning.

And Fredrick discovered he hated Katrina the most because of this—she'd stolen his chance to explain to Scarlet what he was, to slowly disclose his darker side so as not to scare her away. As it was now, he was surprised to see her still there and willing to be near. He closed his eyes.

"Is everything all right, Master Fredrick?" Scarlet asked.

How to tell her? How to share what was burning a path right through his heart when she'd seen what sort of beast he could become? His newfound elation burst like a fragile soap bubble. But at least she was safe now, if forever out of his reach.

"I'm tired, that's all," he replied, forcing his expression to remain stoic when he looked at her, at the way candlelight created fiery gold sparkles in her hair.

As he drew near, Frank's face seemed to sag. Wise old man.

"Let's get out of this place," the old driver said as he snaked an arm under Fredrick's.

With Scarlet holding him on one side and Frank the other, Fredrick got to his feet. Everything spun for a few crazy seconds then got back to normal. He'd be healed within the day. Still, the first few hours were always the worst.

"Nice and steady," Frank muttered as they maneuvered their three bodies in the doorway then down the uneven steps.

Surprisingly, no one was waiting for them when they reached the main floor, for which Fredrick was very happy. No use allowing everyone to see a bleeding and barefoot master in a tattered tunic. They only met a couple of obviously relieved servants on their way to his chambers and when he spotted the door with the carving he'd commissioned so long ago, a lump squeezed his throat. He was home.

"I want to walk."

Tentatively, with Scarlet and Frank hovering like two vigilant birds of prey, Fredrick opened the double doors to smells of freshly stewed lavender flowers and a very large opened window. He went to it first, slowly, then gaining momentum as the first few rays of dawn poked in between the pulled curtains. He roughly pushed them back at arm's length.

A sliver of sun crested over mountains to the south. Tears rolled down his cheeks.

A faint click indicated the doors had been closed. Hoping she'd still be there, he turned. His fresh-smelling chambers, just now vented and cleaned, with crisp linen embroidered from his grandmother's own hands and lush cushions he'd acquired on his travels east, felt as empty and cold as the stone cell in which he'd been forced to spend the last two years.

Scarlet was gone.

* * * * *

Guilt was gnawing at her heart with the unrelenting energy of a rat. Scarlet would've gone to her room and hid there the rest of her life if it hadn't been for Frank's orders that she follow him to the kitchen "right this instant".

With her heart in her throat, she followed him there and had to suffer through a crowd of people asking questions, demanding answers or just venting their impotent rage. All of which they had a right. Her guilt flared.

After Frank shooed everyone away, he poured two cups of steaming broth and sat by her on the bench.

"They're just very sad, my girl, it's not your fault."

"Yes, it is," she snapped back, surprised at the anger in her voice. She stubbornly looked into her mug and didn't meet the old man's gaze.

"We were all lied to—"

She shook her head. "It took me a month to do something. And I was right there... I could see."

Fredrick in chains, being savagely beaten, blood everywhere, and her too damn afraid to do anything.

"It took *me* two years," he replied gently.

"You didn't know how it was," Scarlet countered, not about to let someone else shoulder the blame for her. For the first time in her life, someone had needed her and she'd done nothing for too long. Doing something too late was as bad as doing nothing at all.

"I could've gone there and demand to see him. But I didn't want to take the chance I'd make the master sick. My blood wasn't good enough, according to them." Frank looked so much older right then, and worn to the bones.

She knew the feeling. Scarlet felt worn, weary, guilty. She felt *dirty*.

"For what it's worth, I've known the master all my life, and I've never seen him looking so…happy — and so damn sad at the same time."

Scarlet chanced a peek at the old man.

"He's not a monster, he's just different," Frank offered gently, his liver-spotted hand reaching out and covering hers.

Tears welled up her eyes. The man didn't understand!

"Don't you think I'd like nothing better than stay here and be around him, even if I just get to change his chamber pot — " she raised a hand to silence Frank when he seemed about to voice an argument. "I love him. I've never loved anyone, not even myself!" The words flowed out of her in a torrent — a dam had been breached and couldn't be repaired. "I know he's just different. He didn't choose to be what he is now. He's not a monster. I am. I chose to lie and to steal and be a whore to men who didn't deserve my spit — "

Scarlet clamped her mouth shut. She'd said too much. Frank may have been nodding in understanding but she'd seen the difference when she'd said the last few words. She was a liar, a thief and a whore.

And now she'd be a coward as well.

For Scarlet would run away again, run from what she couldn't deal with, as she'd done all her life. She'd run away because she didn't know if she could stay around Fredrick and take the chance he'd grow tired of her, or feel as though his debt of gratitude were repaid. He wouldn't cast her aside, she knew his heart too much. But he'd become distant, polite. And while she grew old and wrinkled, he'd remain fit and firm and would find another woman to please his eyes. She couldn't even contain the thought.

Scarlet was standing in her room by the time she realized she'd moved. Tears stopped flowing from her eyes. With her sleeve, she rubbed her face. She needed to wash the stench of Lothar off her before she got sick.

As she scrubbed new life into her battered body, her head began to clear as well. A thought filtered in her mind, threaded itself into a string of neat images, clearer than she'd had in several weeks. She'd been so focused before coming to Innsbruck Castle. Everything had been simple. Steal for Werner. Stay one step ahead of him. Survive. For a while, it'd all become muddled, confused by emotions she didn't know how to handle, and people she couldn't bear hurting. Scarlet closed her eyes.

It was becoming clear once again. She knew what had to be done.

Then she could leave in peace, knowing she'd left behind something good.

Chapter Twelve

Șꝋ

Scarlet clutched the overcoat around her shivering frame. Night owned the drafty castle. Her nipples were hard and aching against the thick fabric. Her nudity under the overcoat made her twitchy, nervous. But she was resolute.

She padded along corridors, darkness her ally and protector once again. A thin ray of bluish light drifted in through the high-cut window. A cloudless sky tonight, with a moon nearly full.

Smoothing her wet, freshly washed hair away from her face, she rounded the corner and stopped in front of the thick double doors. Even in the gloom, the wolf's head grinned at her. She grinned back.

Putting her ear to the panel, she waited a long time to make sure Fredrick was asleep. She couldn't hear a thing. With a thin strip of metal she'd scrounged from the farrier early in the evening, Scarlet noiselessly picked the lock. It only took her a moment for this one was obviously for show rather than security. Scarlet opened the door and slipped inside.

The curtains had been pulled all the way back to reveal a wide window through which the moon spilled its blue light onto lush carpets of faraway places. She liked the room much better now that its genuine owner was back.

A faint whimper caught her ears.

Fredrick, facing away from her, tossed in the bed before flopping onto his back. One of his arms rested over his eyes, as if he were trying to fend off something that meant him harm. His foot stuck out from underneath the sheets. Scarlet's heart broke. Probably some remnants of having spent the last two years chained by the ankle.

Her heart in her throat, Scarlet unbuttoned her long cloak and let it drop. A soft rustle accompanied it to the floor. The breeze coming in from the window carried with it the first hint of fall and pebbled her skin and breasts. Excitement helped too.

When she stood over Fredrick, admiring how sleep softened his angular features, Scarlet almost lost her pluck.

She *had* to do this.

It wasn't as though it'd be terrible. A grin pulled at her lips. On the contrary, this would be very pleasant indeed. Probably the most beautiful thing in her life, something she'd cherish in the years of solitude to come.

Ribbons of his white hair weaved intricate patterns over the crumpled pillows. Scarlet longed to touch it, sink her face in it. A shiver shook him. He mumbled something.

Scarlet circled the bed and cautiously climbed in beside Fredrick. Careful not to wake him abruptly, she let her hand rest slowly and gently over his chest while she nestled in closer. Despite her best effort, he woke with a start and a curse.

Scarlet raised her face to his so he could right away see who troubled his sleep.

His expression went from deep rage to disbelief then wonderment in the span of a moment.

"Scarlet?" he asked, clearly unsure.

She rested her head on his heaving chest. "I'm cold."

Despite the gloom, she could tell her visit was making him very, very happy.

He put his hot hand over the back of her head as he drew in a long sigh. "Scarlet."

No one had ever said her name just quite as he had, simply, yet imbued with warmth and the deepest respect, and bearing a man's hopes. She liked the sound of her name in his mouth, liked the way he rolled the R in the back of his throat.

While he caressed her head, she traced the curves of his ribs and lean muscles, drawing circles and serpentine shapes on skin which had suffered so terribly and which, if she succeeded, would be flushed with pleasure this night.

The effect her fingers had made her grin. Rising on an elbow, she brushed her lips along his flank. Yielding to the temptation, Scarlet trapped a nipple between her lips. A gentle tug made him hiss a breath. Images of them both in the throes of passion nearly jostled Scarlet from the path she'd chosen. This was to be his night, her gift to him. She couldn't afford to let herself lose control. With her hand, with her mouth, she teased and nibbled and kissed Fredrick up and down his sinewy chest. He shivered violently.

"I'll close the window," she offered before he could argue. She needed the break or she'd completely forget what she intended.

Scarlet was pulling the drapes in when Fredrick came up behind her, encircled her waist with shaking hands, brushed gentle lips against her shoulders. The fine hair all along her arms rose in waves. She felt exposed, standing near the large window opened to the midnight sky and the swollen moon above. Below the stone balcony, a portion of the rose garden poked out of the darkness. She closed her eyes, remembering how they smelled.

"Leave them," he murmured in her ear as he pried her fingers off the curtains.

But she couldn't let go and instead used the drapes to keep herself from falling back against him. Scarlet fisted a panel on either side of her and threw her head back.

Fredrick's hands were gentle as he followed each curve up and down along her sides. His member pressed in the small of her back. So hot.

"How I love every inch of you," he breathed before raking his fingers up from hips to breasts. She felt like the string of a harp only he knew how to play.

A deep sigh of contentment escaped Scarlet. She pushed the rest down, all these emotions threatening her judgment. No time for anything else tonight but pleasure. His.

When he bent down over her and planted a passionate kiss on her mouth, Scarlet couldn't suppress a moan. She spun around and pressed her whole front against his.

With the radiance of the moon fully in his face, his strange eyes glowed. He closed them briefly. "This must be a dream."

Scarlet allowed herself a grin before she pulled his face to hers for a deep kiss. Fredrick was panting hard when she was done with him. "Not a dream."

"It's been so damn long, Scarlet...I think I've forgotten how." He chuckled as he cupped her backside and squeezed.

"You seemed to remember when you first met me," Scarlet replied with a grin she couldn't suppress.

"Ah, but I couldn't control myself then. I just had to see if you tasted as good as you looked."

Scarlet wrapped both her hands in his white hair—almost pale blue in the moonlight—and took a long whiff of it. Lavender and male musk. "And...? Did I taste as good as I looked?"

"You did."

With more force than she intended, Scarlet pulled him down to her by the fistfuls of hair and rubbed her face in it, let it get in her mouth, in her nose. She wanted him inside every possible way. Her vigor must have triggered something in him for he grunted and forced her arms out wide.

"Grab the drapes again," he whispered.

While she did, he went down on one knee and crushed her belly to his ravenous mouth. She chewed her cheek as Fredrick licked, nibbled and bit his way across her abdomen, before capturing her breasts. But she wanted more. Scarlet spread her feet wider, on either side of his knees, hoping—knowing—he'd get the hint. He did.

Fisting the fabric hard, Scarlet tilted her pelvis forward to allow Fredrick access to her engorged bud. His mouth was gentle at first then harder, until he was nearly lifting her off the floor. His bristly chin felt delightfully rough against her sensitive skin. With his thumbs, he spread her wide.

Out of the deepest recess of her core, a tiny ripple broke the surface, grew in intensity, unfurled as a flag over her belly and sex then hit with the violence of a thunderclap. Spasms tightened her muscles and she knew she was pulling on the drapes too hard, yet didn't care. Scarlet moaned loudly.

Spurred on, Fredrick inserted a finger while continuing his assault on her pulsing bud. Throwing all decorum to the wind, Scarlet spread her legs wide and arched back, letting her whole weight hang on the drapes. The sound of ripping forced her eyes open. But as she felt herself falling back, a pair of impossibly fast arms caught her, eased her down onto the carpets.

With her writhing on her back, arms still splayed out wide, Fredrick pressed his face between her thighs so he could continue his feast. Wet sounds mixed with deep rumblings from his chest excited Scarlet into a twisting frenzy. With a groan of pleasure, she grabbed his head with her wide-opened hands and thrust her pelvis up onto his face, hoping his tongue would go deep, his fingers would crush her flesh. Another wave hit. Scarlet screamed.

By his hair, she pulled him up over her face, kissed a trail down under him until she reached his glistening member. With him straddling her face, Scarlet sank his cock into her mouth. She could tell how excited he was just by the thrusting motion he fought valiantly to suppress. Such nonsense. With her hands on his backside, she pressed him in deeper, took his silky member as deep as it'd go, not caring if a gag reflex tickled the back of her throat.

"Scarlet..."

She knew what troubled him. He was about to spill himself.

Not that often but still too many times, this had been forced on her by men she didn't care for, men she would've killed in their sleep. But tonight, she meant to sheathe Fredrick into her mouth while he spilled his seed. She'd take it all in gladly, lovingly.

When she felt him about to pull out, Scarlet trapped him over her mouth by locking her arms around his waist and her lips firmly in place.

"Scarlet…" he warned, giving a gentle but firm tug back.

But she wouldn't let go. To show her consent of his essence, Scarlet drew her head back before sliding his member all the way in again.

Shaking violently, Fredrick collapsed onto his elbows. Tiny pulsations at the base of his cock announced his released pleasure. Scarlet moaned in satisfaction as it slid into her effortlessly. Working her jaw around, she made sure to not waste any of this precious man's liquid silk.

Scooting out from under him, Scarlet let him collapse on his front, panting, his back slicked with sweat, his pale backside round and firm and so inviting.

As she knelt between his thighs, Scarlet let her hands roam freely over Fredrick's skin. Such a glorious body. Long and lean and fit. Her tongue soon followed suit. Each curve and recess was explored. Moans of pleasure assured her she was doing good work. But a deeper need began to make itself increasingly more pressing. She wanted—needed—Fredrick in her, needed to feel his flesh sheathed in hers, their two bodies connected, forming one.

Without speaking, Scarlet pulled on his shoulder and had him roll onto his back. Moonlight spilled herself on his magnificent figure. So much so Scarlet sat on her heels between his shins and took a moment to remember him this way. She wanted to burn the image into her mind, brand it in her soul, so she'd never forget Fredrick von Innsbruck.

"You're so beautiful," he murmured as he crossed his hands behind his head.

Even though he'd recently had his pleasure, his member didn't seem to relent and boldly pointed up. Fredrick looked down at himself and grinned. Manly pride. Scarlet laughed.

Perhaps the sound triggered something in him. Scarlet never had time to ponder as he sat up, wrapped his arms around her then laid back down with her on top. There he feasted on her breasts until Scarlet thought she'd melt all over him. There was no more dallying. She wanted him now. Before she was forced to leave.

When she reached down for his member, Fredrick froze and looked up into her eyes, his own searching, as if he could see right through her soul. Avoiding his intent gaze, Scarlet clutched the base of his cock and squeezed hard. *There, sir, focus on this.* Feeling powerful when he squeezed his eyes tightly and rolled his head side to side, Scarlet raised herself over him then waited.

This had to be special. This had to last her a lifetime.

Fredrick opened his eyes.

Slick with her juices and his saliva, his member glided in effortlessly, despite its thick girth and her tight fit. A hiss left him. She soon echoed him with one of her own. Even better than their forbidden encounter in the tower. Fredrick tried to thrust his hips up, but she raised herself higher than his reach. He groaned his frustration.

But she didn't move.

Despite his fingers digging in her thighs, urging her to rock in cadence with him. Despite his face becoming increasingly tight with frustration. She wouldn't move.

Scarlet sat immobile, her gaze fixed to his. This was about control. And he'd been deprived of it for so long. Scarlet felt his agony, the old anger clawing its way to the surface. This was her gift to him. More than mere mating. She would give him back control.

With a snarl, Fredrick grabbed her waist with one arm while he twisted onto his side then down on his front, trapping her underneath with his greater weight. Staring down at Scarlet, Fredrick stabbed his flesh into hers. The force of his thrust pushed her up by several fingers. Scarlet clawed at his back when he anchored his elbows over her shoulders to keep her from moving up. He stabbed into her again. This time Scarlet didn't move. A cry of shock and pleasure ripped through her. After planting her heels firmly on either side of his hips, she spread herself wide, pulled and clawed at her own flesh so he'd have better access. His shaft crushed her bud, rubbed mercilessly all the way up, then after a short reprieve while he pulled out, he sank all the way back in again, with fire hot on the heels of his rock-hard cock.

"Again," she growled through her teeth, bucking up against him when he pulled back almost all the way out.

But he didn't. He was taking control.

Fredrick stared at her while he remained poised, the tip of his member just barely inside her, just enough to part the throbbing folds and tease her burning pearl. Then he pulled out and sat on his heels.

"Come to me," he said, his voice barely above a growl.

Scarlet sat up then climbed onto her knees. It was all she could do not to grind her sex onto one of her own heels! It was throbbing painfully, demandingly. It needed to be filled.

With hands both firm and gentle, Fredrick grabbed her shoulders and aimed her at the window. Then he pressed against the back of her neck until she'd taken the hint and gone down onto her hands and knees. Juices slicked her thighs. A whimper escaped her. She wanted him. Now.

But Fredrick was taking his time. First, he merely caressed her back and cheeks. Then he spread them wider with his thumbs, before giving her engorged lips a tongue-lashing which made her hiss. But he wouldn't grace her with his cock, wouldn't sheathe himself into her oh-so-ready flesh.

Fredrick's tongue was bringing her passion even higher, satiating her, and she found she could wait a while longer before he thrust himself back in again. When the first tiny ripple began to tingle along her cleft and straight up to her navel, Scarlet arched her backside up and forced her spine into a deep downward curve. Demandingly parting her cheeks with hands close to being rough, Fredrick pushed his tongue into her.

"Yesss," Scarlet whispered. She looked up at the moon, at the shadows and dark pits on its surface.

Then Fredrick entered her.

Brutally. An incoherent cry tore up her throat. She was forced down onto her chest under the violence of his thrusts. Yet she wouldn't have changed a thing in the world. Scarlet twisted her head to watch him so deeply gripped in the throes of lust. His eyes were heavenward, staring at the moon out the window. The red of them glowed faintly. A sheen of sweat covered his chest where corded muscles rippled under the white skin.

Biting her knuckles because she didn't know how else to vent her pleasure, Scarlet turned toward the window and again welcomed Fredrick's assault. Each thrust soon brought with it a burning sensation, which spread through her whole body. She wouldn't be able to endure much longer. Her knees and elbows were raw.

Fredrick emitted a long cry when he finally reached his climax and finished in an arrhythmic series of shaking thrusts. Wheezing, he leaned over her and kissed the nape of her neck.

"Thank you," he breathed in her ear.

She meant to thank him as well, but couldn't find her voice. Already, with pleasure receding to pleasant aches, what she had to do loomed over her. Scarlet closed her eyes when he picked her up and carried her to the bed where he gently deposited her. Fredrick lay down by her side, nestled her against his chest.

"Promise me you'll be there when I wake."

There was such intensity in his voice it broke her heart. Scarlet pretended to be asleep. She could tell him she'd be there come morning, just so he'd sleep peacefully for a change. Scarlet Heerlen was a good liar. But not tonight. Not to Fredrick.

He didn't push it and instead pulled the sheet over her shoulders and tucked it under her elbow. Soon, his breathing became deeper, more regular.

Silent sobs twisted her guts. This would be the hardest thing she'd ever had to do.

Chapter Thirteen

ဢ

Wind picked her hair and threw it about her face when Scarlet stopped just beyond the moat and turned for a last look at the closest thing she'd known to a home.

She closed her eyes to fully appreciate the journey before her, for today was special—the first hours of the day, the first day of the week, the first week of her new life. Hopefully, it'd be a better one.

So low, she felt as though she could touch it, the moon seemed swelled with tears. Gritting her teeth against her own, Scarlet clutched the cloak tighter and took to the woods. Dawn would be approaching fast, offering a bit of light to show her the way. Already the sky paled from black to brown and purple. She'd stay within sight of the road, but wouldn't walk directly on it in case she met someone. Anyone.

That Lothar had escaped a so richly deserved justice didn't bother her so much as knowing he could be anywhere. Though she doubted he'd lurk around Innsbruck for fear of being recognized and dragged back to the master to face an array of charges, all of which meant the noose. Surely the man knew what Fredrick would do should he find him on his land. No, she told herself while looking back, what she should mind now were the usual difficulties facing a lone woman traveling by night. A mirthless grin pulled her lips. Typical.

She stumbled on a root and caught a young tree just in time. In her pocket, her coins tinkled. She'd never had so many. The lady might have been a demon, but she'd kept her word and paid Scarlet handsomely every seventh day. Though she probably intended to get her coins back by getting rid of Scarlet at the first opportunity as she'd done with the other servants before. Scarlet shivered. She'd come close this time, very close.

Wind whistled plaintively among the ancient trees. Lichen hung in long tatters from limbs as thick as her middle. Smells of moist foliage laced the overpowering scent of earth and made her want to dig through it with her hands. Somewhere a night bird cried its ethereal song.

Fredrick owned a magnificent land.

The image of Fredrick sleeping peacefully after their lovemaking warmed her heart. But it brought tears to her eyes just the same. Just as well, for there wouldn't have been anything for her there. Nothing but heartache. He was a werewolf—a *werewolf*—and would live for a very long time while she'd grow old and die long before he would. And, he'd be better with a lady of his status and not some street woman to cause gossip and bring contempt to his name.

Scarlet walked until midday, rested for a few hours during the afternoon then resumed walking after sunset. All she'd had to eat that day was a couple of apples left over from the harvests she'd plucked along the way. These were probably Fredrick's orchards. Unless she'd already left his land. Monday had come and gone relatively quickly, except now, at night, a time reminding her acutely of him.

A long shiver presently shook her and she pulled the cloak tighter. A strong gust brought with it traces of autumn. Smells were becoming sharper, the air colder. Leaves had begun to fall.

Scarlet looked up at the patches of night sky she could see through the branches. The moon was already beginning to rise above the thinning canopy of leaves. It must have been close to midnight. Scarlet pulled the overcoat tighter. She'd walked for a fair time already and didn't feel tired. Not bad.

Scarlet grinned to herself as she fisted the coins. They weighed nicely in her hand, not the usual guilt-ridden weight dragging her down. No, this time, these honest coins weighed just the right weight. Scarlet sighed.

She'd be a street woman no more. No more pilfering rich patrons, breaking into merchants' homes, picking locks on places not meant for her. She'd lead a normal, honest life from now on.

She stumbled again. The road to her right, so flat and *meant* for walking looked so inviting. Perhaps she could...

No. Just in case.

She'd no idea what lay to the south, didn't even know how long until the next village or town. Would she stop at the first and find work? Not likely, come to think of it, as she wanted to put as much distance between Innsbruck and her as possible. After a few days, or maybe when she got to a large town. Scarlet figured she'd decide when she got there. She'd get that feeling of "home" hopefully, and she'd settle there. Maybe work on a farm at first, or as a servant. She still didn't have enough coins to get her own place or anything else for that matter. But she had *some* and only this counted. Fredrick would understand in time. It was breaking her heart, but he'd find someone worthy of him. It was better this way.

She blinked a few times. It took a full two seconds for Scarlet to recognize the pain radiating along her neck. She'd been struck behind the head. Stars fizzed around the edges of her vision.

"I was wondering when you'd get restless and leave."

The back of her head felt hot and tight. And it tingled. Whirling around despite the nausea creeping up her throat, Scarlet stumbled back several paces.

A wide, disbelieving grin stretched Lothar's face. A small broken branch hung in his hand. "You have one hard head, Scarlet."

Something hot dribbled down the back of her neck then between her shoulder blades. Hot waves tightened her scalp.

After she reached behind her head to rub the hurt, Scarlet's fingers came back bloodied. "You...you..."

"Now, now, be polite," he said, the grin slipping off his handsome face. He cast the branch aside, took a step forward.

Instincts kicked in.

Scarlet spun on her heels and tore through a thick cluster of bushes. She heard Lothar's heavy breathing behind her and hoped the man was only strong and not fast as well. Scarlet didn't make it far.

"Come here!" Lothar snarled, closing a hand over the back of her collar.

Both her legs flew out in front of her. She fell heavily amid a tangle of coat and limbs.

Lothar was on her before she could roll away. While he straddled her lower back, he pulled her head up by a fistful of hair. Something sharp and cold slid across her throat. Scarlet froze, recognizing the distinct feel of steel held with intent and precision.

"I know you don't believe me, but I never intended to hurt you," he whispered through both their disheveled hair. "Though I will if you make me."

Fear tightened her throat, churned her stomach. She feared being sick. A subtle nod from her and the blade lifted. The back of her head burned where she'd been hit. Scarlet squeezed tears out of her eyes. She was born in a gutter and would end in one. Maybe she wasn't meant to have a good, honest life. Maybe she'd done too much ill in her life, had soured what chances she had by not responding to Fredrick's plight soon enough. Was this God's punishment? The coins in her pocket might not have been as honest as she'd hoped, given the kind of work which had generated them.

Her dreams, her future. She'd come so close.

Lothar stood, hoisting her up against him by the fistful of hair he still held in an implacable grip. "I have just the place for us," he announced before forcing her forward. "It's not that far, but secluded enough. You'll have the liberty of screaming obscenities at me all you want."

Scarlet forced him out of her mind and tried to focus on her whereabouts should she find the strength to escape him. Such good fortune she doubted she'd have, and Scarlet realized the window of opportunity was getting narrower with each stumbling step she took deeper into the woods. But as soon as thoughts of escaping surfaced, his dire warning cut in. He was physically stronger and had a weapon while she was half his girth and had nothing with which to defend herself. All was lost.

As they proceeded down a gentle decline, trees became more massive and closer together. The night was dark even for her. Scarlet wondered for a second if Fredrick had gone looking for her when he'd woken in the morning. Perhaps he had known she would leave and had asked just in case. Answering him had proven beyond her strength. What he must think of her now.

"Thinking of your prince?" Lothar said, his tone surprisingly soft. "Forget him. You never would have made a dent in his armor. It took Katrina months just to get him to be civil with her, and she's a mistress at seduction. Although I *can* understand — and do share — your lust for him."

Heat rose to her cheeks. For a man to take pleasure from another unwilling man implied such wickedness, such a bestial nature, Scarlet nearly vomited at the thought of what awaited her. When she meant to struggle against him, Lothar shook her.

"Remember what I said."

Her scalp burned, and Scarlet wrapped both her hands over his to alleviate the tension on her hair.

He chortled. "Ever the practical one."

They had walked for a few hours, by her estimation, when through a break in the clouds, Scarlet spotted a dilapidated hunting lodge, its maladjusted planks giving the whole affair a sad air. It looked as though a giant had tried to sit on the tiny shack. As she drew nearer, she saw that a Dutch door, both halves closed, presented the only opening in the construction. No chimney or windows—only one way in or out. Scarlet's heart sank.

Lothar pushed her onward but when she faltered, he pressed himself into her, pinning her against the door before he opened it and let it swing completely in. A tiny twister of dead leaves rolled at her feet when she stepped past the threshold.

"Ladies first," he said, giving her a slight push in the back that nudged her a couple of steps inside the one-room lodge.

Scarlet flattened herself against the far wall, keeping her back to it and Lothar well in view. While he turned his back to her and dug through the pockets of his cloak, Scarlet eyed the door. Barely four steps. Could she do it?

"If you move even one foot, that will make me very angry," he said, quashing her budding hopes. "And you don't want me angry."

A spark flew out from his cupped hands, and a tiny oil lamp Scarlet hadn't seen hanging in the corner came to life. Amber light chased shadows up to the timbered ceiling.

Lothar turned and leaned back against the wall. The lamp beside his head reflected in his wavy light brown hair. How could a man be gifted with such outward beauty yet foster such a vile soul? He could have had all the women he wanted. Why her?

His jade green tunic gleamed like snakeskin when he crossed his arms. "What now, Scarlet? I can hardly think when you're near. So you tell me what will happen now."

"Please, Master Lothar. Let me go. I won't tell anyone I saw you." Her tongue felt thick when she spoke.

At the farthest edge of her hearing range, Scarlet thought she heard the high-pitched neigh of a horse. But when it came again, she realized it must have been the wind whistling through the door.

Lothar's laugh was almost good-natured when he shook his head at her. "You're just unflappable. You won't tell on me, indeed." He laughed again, which only deepened Scarlet's misery. He slid the knife under his belt behind his back. "Well, in exchange, I won't tell on *you*."

"What do you mean?" she blurted out, fearing right away the triumphant glint in his eyes.

"Firstly, I won't tell you helped torture von Innsbruck for weeks before you did a damn thing about it." Lothar uncrossed his arms then took a step sideways, blocking the door with his body. "Then I won't tell how you let Katrina fuck you while beloved Fredrick watched, chained like the beast he is."

Scarlet recoiled when Lothar pretended to rush for her. He grinned then resumed his slow pacing in front of the door. "And I won't tell a *soul* how you watched me fuck that maid until she was blue with lust. I always wondered if you were watching because you enjoyed the sight of me ramming my cock into such a lovely person, or if you were imagining yourself in her place." He winked. "Personally, I was pretending it was you. So I guess we're evenly wicked."

Shame silenced her. For all his deviousness, Lothar's words rang with truth. She did help Fredrick too late. She did let Katrina and this loathsome man do things to her. That she hardly could have fought either of them off given her drugged state was no excuse. She should have seen it coming. And finally, watching Lothar shove himself into the happily writhing maid *had* excited Scarlet. Though not because she was the least bit inclined to pretend it was Lothar and she. But worse, she had, for a split second, imagined it was Fredrick doing it to her, vigorously thrusting himself into her while she was bound to that strange contraption. She lowered her gaze.

"Don't be so hard on yourself, if I trusted you ever so slightly, I'd let you do it to me. But I don't trust anyone." The smile crystallized at the edges of his elegant, hateful mouth. "I lost the ability to trust a long time ago."

Scarlet pressed her back harder against the wall. Instincts told her he was about to pounce.

He did.

She pushed herself off the wall with a yelp, barely managed to evade his greedy clutches, before slamming against the opposite wall.

He grinned widely, clearly enjoying himself very much. The strain in his trousers confirmed this. Lothar widened his stance, looking like a draft horse ready to draw a hoe.

With a snarl he charged her, but this time, he kept his arms out wide should she decide to slip beneath his reach. It was all quite unnecessary for Scarlet remained rooted to the spot, fear having immobilized her as surely as Fredrick's chain had him. A strangled gasp escaped her when Lothar bunched her cloak and ripped it off her shoulders.

Her neck burned where the fabric chafed her skin. Scarlet squeezed her eyes shut when he slammed her back against the wall and pinned her there with his chest. Wedging a thigh between hers, Lothar had her nearly suspended against the wall.

"What's wrong, Scarlet? No more fight in you?" he demanded while his hand trapped a breast through her dress. She couldn't bear to look at him. He sounded angry.

The wind whistled through the door again. Scarlet swore it sounded like a woman screaming. Then the wail intensified, until she knew this was no wind. It was her. And she couldn't stop.

Despite Lothar's brutal handling and his repeated command that she "show some spirit" and at least try to fight him off, all Scarlet could do was scream.

Chapter Fourteen

ॐ

When he woke, Fredrick knew she was gone. He could feel it as acutely as a missing limb. Even before he rolled onto his side to find the other half of the bed cold and empty, he knew she was gone. Indeed, Fredrick had known even while he was asking her the night before. She might have been a thief, but she was a poor liar. And the ache in his heart surprised him by its intensity and rawness.

Unable to face anyone—even himself—Fredrick closed his eyes again and let oblivion swallow his soul.

* * * * *

Later on that day, he woke and noticed someone had closed the drapes for the evening. His hand reached out over the other side of the bed before he could stop himself. For a split second, he had forgotten yet again that Scarlet was gone. Would the ache never leave him?

He was too old for her anyway, he kept telling himself as he dressed, refusing to wash her scent off him. It was all he had left of Scarlet. He'd be damned if he'd lose this too. At least for today, he'd keep her with him this way.

Once dressed, wearing trousers and a shirt for the first time in so long, Fredrick felt more like himself. A small sound alerted his keen senses a split second before someone knocked at his door.

"Yes," he called, enjoying how his voice didn't echo off stone walls but was instead soaked up by the tapestries hung around his chambers. Every little uplifting detail mattered on this day.

Ute poked her head in, her wrinkled face tight with worry and something else which poked his heart. "It's not my place, but you should eat something today, Master."

Fredrick pretended levity. "You're right, young madam, and please tell me you've brought with you an assortment of your fine cooking." She'd always enjoyed his taking a more formal tone with her.

Her smile didn't convince him. She nodded as she stepped inside the room, a tray piled high with mouth-watering foods. A crystal carafe throned in its center where a crimson liquid gently sloshed around with her brusque gait. Avoiding his gaze, she set the tray down on a small table by the window then took a step back. Ute still hadn't raised her gaze to him.

Cursing Katrina again for causing his people such grief, Fredrick crossed the room and wrapped his arms around the old woman's tiny frame. She briefly tried to push him away but let go and buried her face in his chest.

"How I've failed you, young Master... I'll never forgive myself..."

While he held her, Fredrick tried to let go of his hatred for his cousin but discovered he couldn't. He could no more forgive Katrina than he could forget Scarlet.

After Ute's sobs quieted to silent tears, Fredrick took the serviette from the tray and dabbed her eyes and nose. "You've nothing to hold against yourself."

"I should've known, Master Fredrick. I should've been more careful, asked more questions—but my blood, they said it wasn't good enough...and I didn't want to make it worse..."

"And then an accident would've happened to you too, just as it did for old Nikolaus," Fredrick replied. "He tried to help. She killed him for it."

"Nikolaus? But I thought...everyone thought he'd had an attack of the heart." She looked ready to cry again.

Fredrick shook his head. "Katrina killed him. Poisoned him, the poor man, because he'd started to ask too many questions."

When Ute didn't seem to find the strength to speak, Fredrick went on. "Since she's barely an Innsbruck and can never get her claws into my affairs, she wanted a heir from me, one she could manipulate. She wanted to sell everything, cast you all out in the snow with nothing. I couldn't let that happen."

"But she hurt you, all that time. The— I should go in there and wring her scrawny neck."

A chuckle managed to lift Fredrick's spirit. Ute. "I'd like nothing better myself. But I want people to know what she did. I want them all to know."

"I'll tend to you myself, I swear on my mother's grave, you'll never be without anything again," Ute replied with as much force as he'd come to expect from her.

Fredrick smiled through his own, very personal grief. "Now what did you bring me today?"

Ute chanced a quick peek at his bed, noticed the disarray and strewn cushions. A small grin played on her face. "No wonder I couldn't find the girl all day," she said, tut-tutting. "Whenever she's ready, I need her in the kitchen. Work's piling up."

Fredrick felt as though Ute had dragged a razor across his chest. "She's gone." It was all he managed to say.

To her credit, the old woman seemed to understand right away. "So sad. She was just the kind of girl I needed around here. I'm so sorry, Master Fredrick, I know she meant—"

Though he didn't mean to be brusque, Fredrick raised his hand to stay the rest of Ute's words. He didn't need to hear any more of this. "That'll be all, Ute. My thanks."

The door unexpectedly opened. A red-faced Frank burst in, his riding crop in a white-knuckled fist. "She's gone!"

Fredrick had to take a deep breath to remind himself how good it was to be interrupted again. He'd spent the last two years hoping—praying—for someone to come unexpectedly through his door. "I know, Frank. She left at dawn."

Frank paled so completely Fredrick extended his hand to steady the older man. "But... that's impossible, I checked on her just today, around midday." He shook his head. "Then you've let her go freely? After all she's done... I...I'm sorry for saying so, Master Fredrick, but I think you made a mistake."

Anger flared in Fredrick's chest. He stared hard at Frank. "Scarlet was never a prisoner in my house, Frank."

"Scarlet? She's gone, as well? I thought, well, we *all* thought she was in here with you."

Dread twisted his guts as intensely as bad wine. "What do you mean?" he asked, fighting a losing battle with self-control. His fingers curled in on themselves in trembling fists.

Frank opened his mouth to speak, snapped it closed then shook his head. "Oh, dear God. Master Fredrick, the lady is gone. *Lady Katrina*. She's gone. Both guards were found dead. I think she lured them in when they gave her supper—"

Fredrick could hear nothing more. His blood pounded in his ears, filled his head with liquid drumbeat. How stupid could those men have been? Couldn't they see how dangerous she was? Then he remembered he too, had once fallen for her charms. Rage filled him.

"When?" he snarled through his teeth.

Ute took a step back, clearly frightened.

Frank, knowing Fredrick's dark secret, appeared calmer, though much paler. "As I said, it couldn't have been this morning, I went by and she was still there. So I'd say she's been gone only a short while. And she took a horse..."

"What else did she take?" Fredrick roared "The family heirlooms? Half the Godforsaken castle?"

A sharp jolt of pain bent him at the waist. It flared along his shoulders and neck, up his face, down his shaking legs. His hands trembled violently. There'd always been danger in his anger. He should've known and tried to remain calm.

"Get out!" he snarled, leaning against the wall for support.

Ute meant to help him but Frank—good old friend— pulled her back, told her something about fetching drinks before closing the door in her startled face.

His belly constricted painfully now, and a grunt escaped him. Katrina. Gone.

"Is it too late?" Frank put his face directly in Fredrick's sight.

Unable to speak, Fredrick only nodded. Already, he could feel his heart pumping madly against his ribs, which strained against the unnatural stress placed on them by his transformation.

"Then there isn't much time." The old man wrenched the door open and tugged Fredrick by the front of his shirt.

As fast as he could, knowing each second was precious and could mean life and death for anyone caught too close to him after he changed, Fredrick stumbled after Frank. Down the corridor, through an archway he couldn't remember being there, out some door he'd forgotten, they ran as fast as either of them could. When his legs began to warp into something other than human anatomy, Fredrick slowed down. He was wheezing by now, emitting guttural snarls, which shamed him. He was such a monstrous freak. No wonder Scarlet had left. Pain doubled in his heart, his head.

"Sweet Jesus, there's no more time."

Fredrick humphed then collapsed on all fours. Convulsions racked his body. Tears appeared over the skin of his arms, his thighs. He moaned. God, the pain!

Fresh air caressed his bristling cheeks. Fredrick looked up in time to see Frank opening a fence leading to a wide expanse of green the likes of which Fredrick hadn't seen in a long time.

Smells of animals and earth assailed his nostrils. He breathed in deeply.

"Find her, Master!" Frank pleaded as he wrapped his hands around Fredrick's distending face, forcing eye-to-eye contact. "Find Katrina before she finds Scarlet."

Dear Lord. Of course, she'd go after Scarlet.

The old man's words had the effect of a stone thrown in a pond. Ripples of understanding reached Fredrick's fading consciousness until all he could think about, all he could cling to, was Scarlet's face. He howled when fangs shredded out of his gums, talons of his fingers. Creaks and crunches of breaking bones and snapping tendons echoed in his ears. Or at least, he thought he heard them. A veil of red descended on his mind, narrowed his awareness to a knife's edge. Though he could smell the minutest odor, see the faintest detail, hear the softest sound, Fredrick's mind couldn't grasp much more than a simple concept.

He had to find Scarlet before Katrina did. She was on horse, Scarlet on foot, and despite the few hours she had on his cousin, it wouldn't matter.

Must find Scarlet.

The smell of another being very close by occupied him for a while, but some instinct told him it wasn't important. Dirt flew behind him when he clawed past the opened fence and out into a field.

Must find…

He was forgetting what it was he should be finding. His brain couldn't seem to grasp the abstract concept. Moist earth gave way to rocks then the soft, quiet beings that swayed with the breeze. Trees—those were called trees, damn it. Everything was getting so muddled. A stew of sounds and scents assaulted him, made him lose his track.

Red. A being he'd come to associate with red. No harm should come to this being.

Run. Hurry. Find.

A scent caught his attention. The smell of fear.

He veered sharply back onto the hard surface that resembled a dried river. *Road?* Light began to dim. How long had he been running? Smells became stronger, more humid. He stopped once or twice to lift his head to the breeze. Then he caught it again.

The thrill of the hunt filled his heart. He'd long wanted to catch this particular prey. And its fear was only making him more agitated.

A faint sound floated in from up ahead. He stopped to hear better, turning his head this way and that. Growling in glee, he resumed his hunt, this time devouring the ground under him. He was close. Very close.

The sound accentuated, drowned every other. More than one being? No matter. His teeth ached for the feel of his prey's flesh. A large being with a thundering gait flicked once or twice some distance ahead. By the time he caught up for a better look, light had left behind the dark and quiet shapes that swayed with the wind.

He stopped, knowing he'd caught up with his prey. And he howled.

He could tell the beings heard him, could smell their fear on currents of air left behind them. Following one such thread, he lengthened his pace, doubled his cadence. Unnaturally fast, he caught up to them just as they were rounding a corner of the flat and rough surface.

A shiny hindquarter pumped wildly a few paces in front, and on it, another being. This was the source of the stench. This was the one who was afraid the most.

Giving one mighty push, he leaped, front members out in front of him, claws retracted for his prey wasn't the larger being, but the smaller one. The sudden weight pushed the hindquarter farther to the side than it could go. A shrill sound accompanied its fall. And when it fell, he was there, waiting.

The large being landed on the smaller one, who screamed with pain. While he circled their struggling forms, a wave of calm from somewhere deep within engulfed him.

Terrible agony accompanied the strange stillness, until sounds and smells and his eyesight had changed, dimmed, but been replaced with a higher level of consciousness.

Fredrick climbed to his feet, shaking violently. The horse he'd tackled was already getting back on its feet. It shook its head with barely contained fright. A shrill neigh pierced the night. Katrina was also getting back on her feet, though Fredrick could tell she was injured. She still had his cane in her hand.

"Stay away, Fredrick," she snarled, waving the cane like a sword. She was an adept swordswoman, and he remained in place for the time being, until his body had completely transformed back into a man's, and he could fully savor his revenge. Blood trickled from her lips as she limped back a couple of paces. The cane still pointed directly at him. Now that he felt in full control, Fredrick took a step forward.

"You think you can best me?" A wide swipe of the cane added emphasis to her words.

Fredrick took another step. "I don't intend to *best* you."

Another swipe, this one aimed higher, directly at his head. Fredrick caught it in midair. Staring at her the whole time, he forced the cane down at waist-level before giving it a sharp twist. Katrina lost her grip on it. Fredrick brought the butt of the cane to his face. "I don't think I'll be using it again." He tossed it behind him.

"You won't dare come near me. Lothar is still out there. And he'll find you. He'll find *her*, you know that. She put a spell on all of us, it would seem."

"What do you mean?" Fredrick asked warily.

She choked back a mirthless laugh. "I know you find it hard to believe that I would be capable of it, but I loved your young friend. And so does Lothar. He will never stop looking for her. You will not be able to protect Scarlet. Not against him. Only I can control Lothar."

Fredrick shook his head. "People like you and he aren't capable of love. And leave Lothar to me. He'll pay. As you will."

The menace lurking behind his words made Katrina's eyes flare wide. She turned and ran. Two long strides were all it took for Fredrick to close his hand on her arm.

Instead of trying to fight him off, she turned and plastered herself against him. Her lips found his.

"I have been wanting this for so long," she murmured against his cheek. Her hand raked a path against his side. "Give me an heir, and I will call him off her. You can still save her, Fredrick."

He shook his head. "You can't have an heir any more than I can."

She looked up into his eyes, understanding slowly turning her face into a hideous mask. "You cannot produce a heir? You are *barren*? How...how long have you known?" Katrina's upper lip curled up with disgust and frustration.

"The future heirs in my seed left when my humanity did, a long time ago."

"And you never told me!"

Flecks of spit hit his face. He wiped it with his sleeve. "So you could kill me before my next breath?" Fredrick sneered. "You think you're the only lying, deceitful Innsbruck in this family?"

"The years I wasted on you..." she faltered. Then suddenly a flash of metal appeared out of nowhere.

Fredrick pushed her at arm's length. Too late. A burning sting in his flank made him look down.

"My God, Fredrick, how can you be so old yet so naïve?" Katrina snarled, pulling the slender dagger out of his flesh. She grinned devilishly.

Before Fredrick could register the extent of his injury, he reached out, gripped Katrina by the throat and pulled her close. When she tried to stab him again, he seized the knife by the blade, slicing his palm deeply, and wrenched it from her. Her mouth opened soundlessly as he gripped ever tighter, his other hand soon joining the first.

"You've caused enough suffering to those around you."

Fredrick pressed her to his chest while he kept both hands wrapped around her neck. She'd kept him chained for two years, had killed an old friend and twisted his people's loyal nature into something ugly she could use for her depraved motives. She'd violated him, had allowed others to do so as well. She'd beaten him, starved him, had poisoned him down into a feverish shell of himself. It was this greedy demon who'd caused him to lose the only woman he ever could have loved.

He'd lost everything because of Katrina and her fiendish charlatan Lothar. But above all, what kept his muscles mercilessly corded against her weakening struggle was one single deed. Her terrible mistake had been to hurt Scarlet.

"You've caused pain to the last person, my cousin," he murmured when she slumped against his chest, her legs buckling. "This stops here and now."

He lowered her to the ground, gently laid her lifeless form against the damp grass. Fredrick was straightening when he heard it for the first time. The faint sound barely registered in his brain.

A scream. Silence. Then another.

Chapter Fifteen

ॐ

Scarlet fought for each breath as Lothar cruelly bruised her face and throat with his teeth, his whole mouth. His hand did even more ravagement as he tore at the hem of her dress. The sound of ripping fabric pierced the split-second silence between her screams. Before she could formulate the thought, her hands clawed at his face. She kicked, arched, pulled his hair, bit him back.

He seemed to be pleased by her newfound energy and snarled a laugh every time she managed a good hit into him. But as much as she tried, she was no match against his sheer brute strength.

He kept saying her name while he wrapped his arm around her, managed to pull her dress high enough behind her thighs for him to access her backside. His hand was sickeningly gentle when he found her skin and caressed her. Scarlet shrieked in rage and panic. Lothar shook his head as if in disbelief. "Good God, Scarlet, I've never had to fight for a woman before. Why can't you—?"

Craning her neck, Scarlet sank her teeth in his throat. A good chunk of flesh followed when Lothar shook her off. Blood dribbled down his chest. He looked down in surprise. "What...?"

Scarlet managed to free a hand from under his tight bear hug. She used her palm like a hammer and drove it on the bridge of his nose. Lothar pressed his face very close to her neck so she couldn't hit him again. "I'm starting to think you don't like me very much...maybe I should—"

An explosion deafened her, drowned Lothar's next words. The upper part of the Dutch door literally disintegrated inward, hinges and ironwork twisting under a tremendous force.

A white form soared at Lothar and took him down. The wind created by the white blur buffeted the room and extinguished the oil lamp. But before the light died, an image was seared in the back of her eyes.

A lupine form, not quite erect but not on all fours either, heralded by a fanged maw, had Lothar in a bear hug.

She murmured his name, disbelieving. *Fredrick.*

Darkness descended on Scarlet. A terrible crash was heard. A series of yelps and groans then a loud thump made her blindly stumble back toward the corner of the hut. Something trapped her foot. Her cloak. She retrieved it without really knowing why. As her eyes adjusted to the darkness, she could make out two large forms wrestling about on the floor then spilling out into the night.

She rushed out right after them. Outside, the low moon lit a terrible scene. Lothar was standing with his back to her, holding in a headlock what could only be Fredrick. White fur was streaked with large inky spots. The sound of snapping jaws clacked loudly. Then Fredrick gave a mighty shove and Lothar went flying back.

He rolled once, twice then stood. The knife gleamed in his hand. "Come here," he spat, crouching. "I've been waiting a long time for this."

The wolflike creature—Fredrick, she kept reminding herself—crouched also before he sprang up high, front paws extended, claws gleaming dangerously. A blur was all Scarlet could see when the two collided.

Fredrick leaped back with a sharp yelp. A new cut dribbled along his chest. He lowered his head the way dogs do when assessing a new situation. He scanned the area then his glowing gaze settled on Scarlet and for a split second, she saw him. The man was indeed inside, looking out of this not-quite-wolf creature. Fredrick, risking his life for hers. Again.

While Lothar continued taunting Fredrick, having utterly dismissed her, Scarlet crept closer until she stood a few paces directly behind him. The cloak fell from her hand.

Keeping her gaze fixed on Fredrick's, she sensed the tension in his body in the way he crouched slightly lower, spread his hind legs and dug his claws in a bit deeper.

Time stopped for Scarlet. A lifetime of words couldn't have been any clearer than this split second, this clarity illuminating her heart to its most guarded recesses. And if she was allowed to live to a ripe old age, she'd remember this single moment as the one time when everything felt right. Fredrick's haunted but resolute eyes shining out through the face of a beast and the untold words she could plainly see there were all she needed. It was all she *wanted*.

When Fredrick charged, Scarlet was ready.

Lothar sidestepped the attack. But not quite far enough. Fredrick slashed once, twice, and caught the man on the shoulder. A cry of pain escaped Lothar. Twinkling like a jewel, the dagger flew out of his hand. It landed only a few feet from Scarlet who readily picked it up. The handle felt worn smooth in her steady grip. Wrapping her other palm over the protruding pommel, she raised her hands high and waited.

But both men went rolling in a tangle of limbs, furred and clothed. Fredrick tore at Lothar's garment, shredding the tunic as if it were thin gauze, and reduced the exposed skin to rags of flesh. With a strangled curse, Lothar kicked and pummeled his attacker, landing one crippling blow on Fredrick's nose. He used his incredible strength to roll on top of Fredrick. The blood of each intermixed with the other as they grappled and exchanged blows. Save for the occasional grunt, the terrible violence was eerily quiet.

When Lothar cocked his fist back for a vicious blow, Scarlet was already in place. With both feet planted wide, she brought the blade down with as much force as she could muster. It sank deep in Lothar's back but stopped abruptly. A gasp escaped her when she sliced her palm along the protruding portion of blade.

She recoiled when he turned to her, his handsome face twisted with pain and rage.

"Why?" he snarled, reaching back.

The word had barely left Lothar's mouth when Fredrick snapped his head around and sank his fangs into the other's neck. Dark blood spurted out to stain his chest and shoulders. He clawed back, trying vainly to disengage Fredrick's maw from his throat.

Scarlet shut her eyes and turned away as Fredrick tore out the man's flesh in great chunks. Sounds of clacking jaws and tearing tissue made her twitch.

"Fredrick, please, it's over."

Silence answered her. A low moan—a *human* moan—made her look at the sky. Good God, Lothar was still alive.

Movement from behind her triggered a primal sense of alarm. But this quickly passed when she remembered how human he'd looked while she searched his gaze. This was Fredrick. A man. Not a monster.

She looked back to find him gingerly approaching her. His nose twitched as he sniffed the air. Blood dribbled from his fanged snout. One paw in front of the other, like an overly muscled wolf with a chest too big for the rest of him, Fredrick drew near.

Streaks of what looked like black ink covered his head and back and flanks, and Scarlet knew some of it had to be his. Her heart swelled with relief and sadness and shame. She'd left and he'd come after her. And the price had been this.

Scarlet reached out slowly, offered the back of her bleeding hand to him. His fur was surprisingly soft when he pushed his great head underneath her palm. Heat transferred from him to her then back to him. A complete circle. When he collapsed on his side with a great humph, Scarlet retrieved her cloak and draped it over him then knelt and cradled his head on her lap, offering silent support as his body was racked by convulsions that made him whimper.

Horrible, muffled crunches were heard under his flesh as his frame was adjusting itself once more to that of a man. Scarlet ran her hand over his head, feeling his skull change shape. Soon, fur had slipped back into the tightening pores over his face and body, until only his white hair remained, streaked with blood she prayed wasn't all his. With a last violent spasm, Fredrick rolled onto his side and curled in on himself. He was wheezing.

Scarlet adjusted the cloak so it'd cover the most skin possible. A hand emerged from underneath the garment and reached out tentatively. She grasped it, shocked at the deathly coolness of it.

"My thanks," he murmured, his mouth quivering with restrained pain.

He was offering thanks to her when she should be the one lavishing praise on his head. She'd come so close. Scarlet chanced a peek back at Lothar, who lay on his front, his poor mangled form rising ever-so-slightly with each labored breath, his once-luxurious, golden-brown hair a mess of bloody clumps. She knew he didn't have long. It'd almost be a mercy to finish him off now. But there had been enough violence already.

Keeping an eye out for Lothar, in case he rose from near-death in some unnatural feat of willpower, Scarlet silently caressed Fredrick's head until his breathing had slowed to a more regular rhythm. Her right hand was dribbling blood and so she kept it in a tight fist.

Scarlet looked up. The nearly full moon was low in the sky, and appeared ready to sink among the trees. How her life had changed in such a short time. Only the night before she was sharing Fredrick's bed, when tonight, she'd been captured, rescued and now was needed again.

"We need to get moving," Fredrick said, clutching at his side while struggling to sit.

"Can't we wait a little bit? You're still too hurt to walk."

"I can't be seen this way."

While he sat on his heels, Scarlet realized he was right. He couldn't be seen this way, bloodied all over, naked except for her too-small cloak. She offered her arm when he meant to stand, which he took without meeting her gaze.

"Don't be ashamed for needing my help," she offered softly.

"It's not for needing your help that I'm ashamed…it's for exposing you to all this." His sweeping gesture encompassed himself, Lothar, the demolished door and everything else around them.

"Nothing here happened without good reason. I owe you my life."

His tight grin pulled his bleeding lips. "Good, I hate being in debt." He turned toward Lothar, his expression hardening. "Let me finish this before we leave."

Scarlet held his arm. "No, please, let's just leave. He'll meet his end when it's meant to happen."

Fredrick stared at prone form for a long time, as though gauging the man's condition.

"He's as good as dead," Scarlet said as she put her hand over Fredrick's arm. "Please."

She couldn't stomach the idea of Fredrick slicing a dying man's throat, even if the man in question was Lothar.

As she wrapped her cloak around his narrow waist and secured it with a tight knot, Fredrick stared down at her then raised a hand to touch her cheek. But he looked at it, at the blood-encrusted and broken fingernails, and let it drop by his side with a disgusted curve to his lip.

Scarlet looked back only once as they made their way toward the road. Between trees, she could still see Lothar's form lying where he'd fallen, his face in the dirt. She tried to feel sorry for the man but couldn't.

Turning back toward what lay ahead, she walked by Fredrick's side, occasionally glancing up at his face. He looked displeased to the highest degree.

Scarlet pulled her dress tighter over her chest. "How did it happen?"

He must have known what she meant for he stared at her a long time before replying. "A rabid man attacked me while I was on a hunting trip in the north. I never saw him until it was too late. He had fangs coming out of his mouth, it was horrible. I didn't know it then, but he was changing. We fought, and I managed to wound him before he threw me down and tried to rip my throat open. The only thing that saved me was the sound of my hunting party looking for me. The horn must have scared him for he just left. There was blood everywhere, mine and his."

"Did you...*change* right away?"

Fredrick shook his head. "Not until the next full moon. I didn't know what was wrong with me, I had no idea…"

Her heart swelled at his obvious grief. "It must have been terrifying, not knowing what was happening to you."

She could just imagine the panic, the sheer terror she'd feel at changing into something so dreadful. Not knowing if she'd change back, if she'd stay the beast forever, locked in her own body, looking out through eyes both foreign and known—it must have been terrible. Scarlet squeezed his forearm.

"It wasn't as terrifying as changing *back* and not knowing where I'd been or where I was. And the whole time wondering what I'd done." Fredrick stared at her intently. "While I'm *it*, I don't recognize anyone nor can I tell ally from foe. I could attack a friend and not know it."

Scarlet shook her head. "You recognized me, I could see it in your eyes. It was you."

"But I don't *remember*," he growled, his hand balling into a fist. "How can I trust myself when I can't remember?"

Scarlet forced herself not to wince at the pain in her arm when he squeezed it. "I trust you," she said.

He must have realized he was holding on too tight because he grimaced and released her arm.

They kept the road to their left as they walked back toward Innsbruck. The whole time, Fredrick maintained a rigid expression, occasionally glancing at her when he thought she wasn't looking.

A small rustling sound caused her to raise both hands protectively. Fredrick froze by her side. Extending his arm in front of her, he tilted his head up, inhaled deeply then turned away.

A form moved out from between trees to their right and approached.

Scarlet let out a great sigh as Frank emerged from the gloom with an expression of intense relief on his old face.

"Praise the Lord, I'm glad you're both all right. I have fresh horses waiting a bit farther down the road. We have to hurry." Scarlet realized Fredrick still had his arm extended protectively in front, even if he were hardly in any condition to defend her. Scarlet's heart swelled nonetheless. His first instinct had been to offer protection. She looked up into his face, noted the resolve etched deep. Her love flared into a tiny sun that warmed her heart. The old distrust, which had clung to her with such tenacity, couldn't keep her soul from reaching out to this man. She loved him, and he, in turn, seemed to feel *something* for her. Otherwise, he wouldn't be there, bleeding and hurt.

Frank left, one last concerned glance for Fredrick. A jingle of harnesses heralded his return and he emerged on the road with the reins to four horses in his fist. "I sent the lads down to the village, so that should give us time."

With some difficulty, but his look barring any offer of help, Fredrick mounted a horse, and after Frank and Scarlet followed suit, the trio kicked their mounts into a brisk trot.

Scarlet spent the time looking over her shoulder, afraid someone would spot them. Their good fortune held, and they didn't have to share the road but once, forcing them into the woods until the wagon had passed. With harvest time over, the roads were quiet.

By the time they came in view of the moat the following evening, with the moon profiling the castle in bluish tones, Fredrick leaned against his horse's neck. "Just give me a moment."

Her heart in her throat, for his pain must have been unbearable after such a long ride, Scarlet stopped herself from trying to help Fredrick. His pride had suffered enough.

Frank meant to take Fredrick's reins but he pulled out of reach. Nodding, the old man led them around the castle and over a narrow bridge on the moat. A goat bleated a tremulous greeting as they crossed the field. A simple wooden door appeared as they rounded the corner of a small annex. She couldn't even tell to which part of the castle it led. They left the horses there, Frank and Scarlet exchanging a worried look while Fredrick did his best to dismount gracefully.

"You need to rest, Master. It's only a night away," Frank commented somberly as he pushed the door in with his shoulder.

"What is?" asked Scarlet.

Frank closed the door behind them. A brass oil lamp hung just inside the doorway. He grabbed it.

"The full moon," Fredrick said, taking his arm from around Scarlet's shoulders and leaning against the wall. The cloak tied at his waist was soaked in blood where the skin touched. A gash in his flank oozed thickly. He looked down at himself and snarled a curse. "She managed to hurt me one last time."

"Where can I send the lads to retrieve her?" Frank asked, not looking overly concerned about the lady's fate.

"Let the animals have her. She'll at least do good in death if she never did in life." Fredrick raked a hand in his hair.

Frank nodded. "And him?"

"Same."

After putting a long hand over the old man's shoulder, Fredrick threw an oblique glance at Scarlet, lowered his gaze then walked away.

Scarlet must not have done a good job hiding the hurt for Frank drew close and wrapped his arm around her. "Come, let's get you cleaned up. And Ute has been asking about you without pause. I don't think the woman breathes."

Looking back once where Fredrick was disappearing around a corner, Scarlet felt as though someone had just doused her with glacial water. Perhaps he'd saved her to repay his debt and not because of any other reason. And she *had* left his bed already once—ran away like a thief, in fact—and maybe Fredrick was loath to suffer the same treatment twice.

It was just as well, Scarlet thought as she tried to keep the lump in her throat from rising. For where could a union such as theirs ever hope to go? She was a street woman, an orphan without coin or name. And she was *mortal*.

Chapter Sixteen

❧

All that blood.

It was dripping down her front, between her breasts, down past her navel. Fredrick took a step away from her.

"Scarlet…my God."

She stood with her arms outstretched toward him, but he couldn't move. Looking down at his hands, he gasped. Covered in blood.

"What have I done?" he asked, his voice breaking.

Fredrick snapped up in his bed. He was so happy to wake up that he flopped back down and rubbed the sheets on either side of him. What a horrible dream.

His hand reached outward but encountered nothing. No one.

Scarlet should be here. She belonged here. But he couldn't have let her come into his room last night, not with the way he'd looked, bleeding, angry and half-coherent. She'd seen enough without being exposed to that as well. After a long, hot bath though, he'd regretted not having invited her. Not only because his flesh hungered for hers, but also because he'd wanted to explain everything.

And still did.

Fredrick rummaged around the room, found his best trousers and shirt, took care of his hair for the first time in…he couldn't remember the last time he pulled a comb through his hair instead of just his fingers, and slipped into supple leather boots that came high over his calves. A quick check in the mirror made him wince. He looked gaunt and even paler than usual, if that were at all possible. And his side still bled. Not the image he wanted to present her. But she'd have to take him the way he was. Monster and all.

Fredrick von Innsbruck was going to ask this woman to accept him the way he was, and he would ask only once. If Scarlet refused — and God knew there were plenty of reasons to — then he'd make his peace with living under the same roof as her, even if her heart would be forever closed to him.

Fredrick found Ute in the kitchen. She must have known why he was there for she pointed to the window.

The door clattered against the wall when he stepped into the pale dawn light. Tendrils of fog still clung to glistening grass blades. On second thought, he whirled around and made for the rose garden instead.

His heart leaped with joy when he saw them beyond the gate. He pushed the grate in and slipped inside. Jogging to the end of the garden, Fredrick let his hand touch every bush he could reach. In the corner, some of his favorites still clung to their stems, petals browned a bit by the night's cold but looking exactly as he remembered them. He deftly broke one coral-colored rose high under its head so there wouldn't be any thorns. Its subtle smell made him smile. Just like Scarlet.

Fredrick ignored the many curious stares of servants out and about as he marched through the small field, jumped the fence then jogged down to the lake, which served as moat to his castle. Scarlet wasn't near the water's edge. Nor was she sitting on the bench he'd built many years ago. Looking around, Fredrick felt panic rise in his throat like bad wine. What if she'd gone? Again.

A faint scent caressed his nostrils. He sighed in relief. Lavender.

He walked farther away from the castle. A sharp bend in the lake's edge created a little creek of sorts. He'd played there as a boy, catching crayfish among the rocks...

"No time for this," he snarled under his breath.

He was about to bare his soul to someone in a way he'd never done before. No time for reminiscing about when he was a boy. That was his other life, back before—back when he hadn't a care in the world.

Fredrick took a deep breath. He'd ask once. He'd accept whatever answer she gave him, even if it tore his heart out. He crested over a small hill overlooking the place where the lake became a river and where the forest was claiming back its territory.

Then he saw her. And his resolve failed.

But before he could turn away and reconsider, Scarlet stood from the rock on which she sat and waved at him. Ears too damn good. A low moan escaped him.

His legs mechanically took him down the grassy slope. A stitch at his side made him look down. Blood had seeped through the bandage and shirt. But too little blood was there. Any other man would still be in bed recuperating. Any other man might have bled to death. Another reminder of his dark nature. By the time he came up to Scarlet, who looked as pale and drawn as he did, Fredrick could think of nothing to say to this woman. The rose cradled in his palm felt cool and moist. He looked down at it.

"We must talk, Fredrick," she began, stopped then tucked a wayward strand behind her ear. Her hand was bandaged.

His heart filled with dread just as his belly tightened with yearning, but he fought both down. He brought the rose up and offered it to her. "It's a bit bruised, I fear."

With a smile she took it. "It's beautiful. My thanks."

Fredrick fought the urge to gather her up in his arms and never let go. But he couldn't let his emotions overwhelm her. Or him.

She wore her servant uniform, and Fredrick surmised she'd at least spend the day at Innsbruck. If nothing else, he still had a few hours.

Her dark gaze settled on his face, tracing it as though she were seeing it for the first time. Or the last. "I've always wanted to see the world, ever since I was very little," she said, turning toward the lake. "There's so much to see out there."

She didn't see Fredrick press a hand against his chest, looking down for a moment before putting on a stoic front. No use trying to convince her to stay now, not with what she was telling him. He knew what was coming. Fredrick could almost hear it. *I'm sorry, Fredrick, but I can't live like this. Your changing into this thing every moon would be too much. I'm afraid. I'm afraid of you.*

Scarlet turned back toward him. "Everything that's happened here... It made me realize something. What I've seen —"

"Just say it." Fredrick regretted his sharp tone, but at the same time was unable to spend another second waiting for her to say she was leaving.

She looked like a woman ready to throw herself into a lake, knowing she didn't swim. "I'd like to stay here, if I could. The people here are nice to me. I'd sure work for my keep though, and Ute already —"

Fredrick drowned the rest of her sentence with his mouth. He wrapped his arms around her shoulders and held her until she grunted in protest.

"I can't...breathe."

He released her a little but didn't let go. He'd been ready to collapse into a heap on the ground and now, now he could see himself flying with the birds! Fredrick buried his face in her frizzy hair. "Scarlet, *Scarlet...*" he repeated under his breath.

Her wiry arms held him tightly, which burned his wounded side. It was his turn to grunt.

"Oh, I'm so sorry," Scarlet said, retreating to arm's length and looking down at the spot of blood on his shirt.

"It's nothing, just a little hole," Fredrick replied, unable to keep the foolish grin from spreading wide. He hadn't smiled this way in a long, long time.

When Scarlet cupped his face with her hands, which were delightfully rough and gentle at the same time, and pulled him to her, Fredrick closed his eyes and let joy fill his heart. If he lost everything else tomorrow, he'd have this moment.

Their mouths connected. And when they did, when her lips pressed tenderly against his, Fredrick felt the tension of the past two years shed from his shoulders as if someone had lifted off him a heavy, wet cloak.

"Scarlet," he murmured against her lips.

Their kiss became more passionate. As they clutched at each other's clothes, their breathing accelerated. Fredrick kept murmuring her name. He couldn't stop nor did he want to. Ever.

He gathered her coppery hair in his hands and inhaled deeply. Scarlet chuckled. This had to be the most beautiful sound he'd ever heard. When he cupped her backside and squeezed her hard against him, the grin slid off her face. Lust blazed behind her dark eyes.

"I want you," she whispered, dropping the rose and pulling at the lapels of his shirt.

"Oh, but you can have me!"

He tried to do it gently, he really did, but he ended up pulling too hard on the ribbon holding her collar together and it broke. The small ripping sound froze him. Had he scared her? His doubts returned tenfold. He couldn't be trusted to control himself, not when he'd shown time and time again how his temper kept surfacing at the least opportune moment. Scarlet was too precious. She deserved better.

As he was about to pull away, Scarlet grabbed him by a fistful of linen collar. Without a word, her gaze unwavering against his, she unlaced his shirt down to his navel. The breeze caressed his bare chest. She finished with a quick jerk. His shirt hung loosely on his shoulders, partly out of his trousers, partly in.

"I told you, Fredrick. I *trust* you. You don't scare me. I've seen true evil. I can spot it a league away. And you're not it."

He fell on her with the vigor and despair of a man drowning. His hands on her skin, his mouth over hers, their clothes in twisted lumps over their bodies. They were naked before they hit the ground. Wet grass clung in tiny raspy tongues to their legs and backs. Gray dawn light gave everything a pale quality. Except for her hair, which stood out like a flame in darkness.

His side hurt and bled again, and he noticed her hand did as well. Scarlet shrugged. "I've had worse."

And he could tell. Anger flared in his heart again. He wouldn't mind going to Amsterdam and ripping apart whoever had abused her all these years. Actually, he resolved to do just that. The budding plan quickly flew out of his mind when she rolled over him and straddled his middle. Her freckled breasts pebbled with goose bumps, the nipples hard and pointing sharply up.

She looked down at him, her face an unreadable mask. "I want to love you always."

Now is the time to show your true worth, von Innsbruck, he told himself. *Only once, no matter her answer.* Fredrick looked up and held her gaze. "Would you take my name?"

Scarlet raised an eyebrow, clearly not understanding.

"My name, Scarlet, would you accept it as your own?"

Understanding dawned on her in blushing increments. Tears welled her eyes. "I'm a street woman. I have nothing to bring your name. What will your people say?"

Fredrick let his hands run up her flanks and trapped both nipples between his thumb and index fingers. She sucked in a sharp breath. "Those who know you will think me a lucky man," he said, pinching a bit harder. "And those who know me will keep their mouths shut."

When she said nothing, Fredrick dropped the matter. Only once, and he'd asked it. With the implications of such a request, Scarlet deserved time to think about it, even if every second, to him, would feel like an eternity walking on broken glass.

"Sit higher," he said, releasing her nipples to grab at her thighs.

Scarlet bit her lip as she scooted up higher over his chest. Her knee pressed against his bleeding side but he didn't care. Her orchid-colored flesh glistened invitingly only a few inches from his face. She moaned in pleasure when he used his thumbs to part the folds and gave one wide lap all the way up.

"Again?"

She nodded emphatically.

Fredrick obliged, this time putting more force into it. The thin lips stretched taut against his tongue while her tiny pearl emerged from its shell. He lapped again. Scarlet's thighs cramped noticeably on either side of his head.

"Again?" he asked, teasing her bud with the tip of his tongue.

A quick, frustrated nod answered him.

"Say it."

"Again."

Another flick. "Again what?"

"Lick me," she snarled.

"You mean like this?" Fredrick parted the folds as wide as he dared and slightly up, exposing her sex like a ripe fruit to his hungry mouth.

His tongue ached from the strain but he wouldn't have stopped for all the gold in the world. He lashed, lapped, thrust, flicked her swollen bud until she began to shake. And when he was rewarded by her gushing pleasure, Fredrick felt as though his whole life had been spent in a dark cave until this moment.

Fire rippled out from her bud to her belly. Scarlet couldn't keep the cry of pleasure tightening her throat from reverberating in their small patch of paradise. She clamped a hand over her mouth, bit her knuckles. After such a wave of pleasure, she needed a short reprieve and crawled back down over Fredrick, settling on him. She saw him wince.

"Have I hurt you?"

He shrugged, looking down at his side. "I can't seem to heal as quickly as usual. But it should be gone in a few days."

She noticed the blood and gasped. She meant to put her hand to it but he brusquely seized it and kept it away. "Don't put it near. You're bleeding too. I don't want to…"

Scarlet waited for him to say it, but he didn't. "You mean make me like you?"

He nodded. A faraway look glazed his blood-colored eyes. "*Infect* is a better word."

"It's not a disease," Scarlet began, letting her hand run down his belly to his lance-straight member. He stopped breathing for a few seconds as she stroked him.

"It *is* a disease."

"Not to me." Another long stroke up his shaft then down again. He shivered.

If she could only make him see! He wasn't a monster to her. He was a man. A man she loved. She would take his name in an instant, only this would mean growing old and dying in his arms. She'd much rather…

She'd much rather what? Go through the agonizing transformation every moon, suffer his Hell when his body twisted and bent into something not meant for it? Could she do it?

Scarlet looked down at him, his pale skin and white hair, the thin mouth so gentle, the way dawn made him almost a ghost. Something must have shown on her face for his expression turned horrified.

"No, Scarlet, don't even think about it."

"I want to be with you," she countered. "Always."

"And you will. I'll love you every day of your life and cherish you—"

"Until I die?"

Fredrick looked away. "When I chased after you and that sick bastard, after I caught him and made him pay for touching you, it was the first time that I wasn't alone after…"

"After you changed back into a man?" Her heart swelled with compassion. How lonely it must have been all these years. How frightening, to wake up alone from such a traumatic experience. And with practically no memories of it.

He nodded. "You have no idea how good it felt to have someone by my side. To have you by my side."

Scarlet pulled herself up on her hands and backed over his thighs. His member glistened invitingly. Licking her lips, her gaze on his face the whole time, she took the tip of it into her mouth.

A violent shiver shook him. Scarlet used her mouth and her hands to bring him almost to the edge. She knew it was cruel but she had no argument as strong as this one. She loved him too much for half measures. She pulled away and sat on her heels. "Make me like you, Fredrick."

Terror flared his eyes. "What? No!"

"Yes, make me like you. I want to be with you always, not die in your arms."

He pushed away from her and knelt, his member heavy between his thighs. "I'd never curse anyone, especially you to a life like mine."

"But you'd curse me to a lonely death?" she said, coming closer and cupping his face in her hands. "I've never had anything good in my life, until I met you. And I sure won't lose you now."

Fredrick squeezed his eyes shut and let his forehead rest against hers. "What you're asking of me, Scarlet...think about it. The pain, the shame. And it's dangerous. If you ever come close to people, either they'll hunt you down and kill you, or you'll hurt them without meaning to. There's nothing but grief and loneliness. It's a *curse*, Scarlet!"

How could she make him understand? Her love for him transcended her mortal coil. She didn't just want to love him as man and wife, she wanted to understand him, share with him everything, every shred of her soul, every breath, every day of joy and pain and boring things like the weather. She wanted to be with him in every possible way.

"Fredrick," she began, hoping her humble words would be up to the task. "All I have is you. All I *want* is you. Please, don't let me grow old and die alone. I've been alone too long."

He took a deep breath. His mouth opened but no words came out. He grew still, his gaze lost in the distance somewhere over her head. Her insides began to churn when she feared he'd deny her request. So she *would* die in his arms. This, to her, was the real curse.

Slowly, Fredrick reached to his flank and began unwrapping the bandage. Tears welled his eyes when he looked down at her.

Her salvation couldn't have been sweeter. Scarlet undid her own bandage around her hand and exposed the gash in her palm. She flexed it wide and hissed when the wound reopened. Blood trickled from it down past her wrist. She offered her hand to Fredrick, who took it as though it were the most fragile thing in the world.

"Think about what you're asking me to do," he began, faltered. "You'll be just like me. A monster."

For reply, she pressed her hand against his bleeding flank and held it there. Her blood seeped onto his wound while his own essence soaked her skin. Wet heat transferred from him to her then back to him. A complete circle. A long sigh escaped him. Joy and sadness and a slew of emotions flashed in his eyes.

"I'll take your name, and I'll take your fate as well."

"Scarlet von Innsbruck," he said, clearly relishing the taste. "The best picker of locks."

When he kissed her, Scarlet sensed a difference in him. As though he were no longer afraid to break her, or scare her away. His hand was gentle but demanding when he wrapped it around her breast and pulled it to his mouth. She arched back, his arm around her waist to keep from falling. She'd finally broken through the layers of isolation and distrust around him. She'd picked the lock at his ankle just as she had the one around his heart.

"Scarlet," he growled as he sucked one nipple after the other.

She still couldn't get used to this man saying her name in so many different ways. In his mouth, her name was like a warning, a plea, a sigh, or like just now, an expression of pure joy.

A gasp escaped her when Fredrick pushed her down on her back and lay on top of her. The wiry muscles at his shoulders corded when he backed down, parted her thighs with his elbows and dove at her with an energy that left her panting. His mouth was rough as he gorged on her, his fingers stretching her wide, slipping inside both her sheaths. He brought her knees up over her chest while he kept one palm pressed against her cleft, his middle finger curled in and rubbing fiercely. Soon, her sensitive bud began to burn.

Scarlet meant to open her knees wider but Fredrick held her securely with his arm wrapped around her legs, his own knees on either side of her hips. As though she'd unleashed him, he knelt triumphantly behind her raised legs, his angular face hard but his eyes loving. A snarl curled his lips as he slipped his fingers deeper, searching, probing. Claiming.

Scarlet closed her eyes when a wall of pleasure hit. Fire burned in expanding rings and although she wanted to spread wide, open herself to him, she couldn't move her legs. Twisting, she grabbed at blades of grass above her head.

"Fredrick," she moaned, not caring if she sounded less than honorable.

As she came in his hand, he grabbed her in the crook of a hip and flipped her on her knees. Another cry of pleasure left her when he parted her cheeks wide and used his whole palm to rub her slicked cleft. With his other, he reached under and captured a breast, which he reduced to a throbbing mound of flesh with his forceful fingers.

Bending under the weight, she sprawled on her belly with a great humph. She meant to climb back up on her knees, to better savor his thrilling ardor. She'd no idea he could be so...feral.

"No," he growled, putting a flat hand between her shoulder blades and pressing her back against the ground. With his knees, he spread her legs wide apart. Blades of wet grass tickled her exposed flesh.

A finger entered her. Then another. She gritted her teeth when a soft breeze caressed her nether hole. The hot, wet band of his tongue passed over and produced the sharpest pleasure yet. While he thrust with his fingers, he made slow and leisurely passes of his tongue. Scarlet felt another wave coming. Tilting her backside up against his face, she buried hers in the grass, wrapped her arms over her head. She was almost there.

Then everything stopped. When she looked back over her shoulder, she noticed the blood dribbling down from his flank to his hip. But it was his eyes that stopped her heart. Entirely bloodshot. He was changing!

Scarlet emitted an excited, panicked squeal as Fredrick bore down on her, pulled her up against his poised cock. She came right as he stabbed in. Pleasure exploded out of her. His name came out twisted when she snarled it. His brutal thrusts shook Scarlet, lifted her knees off the ground, bounced her small breasts. Yet as much as his transformation had frightened her at first, she could tell it wasn't complete. He was still the man, only imbued with a feral spirit that left her breathless.

Fire radiated outward from her engorged sex. She cried out as her pleasure deepened, flowed through her as though her blood were quicksilver. She wanted him to assail her, wanted him to prove to her he didn't think she was too fragile to take his love. Scarlet turned to look at him, lost in his own pleasure.

"Hold my hands," she said, bending her arms behind her and letting her cheek rest against the ground.

He slowed for a few seconds, his eyes focusing on her. With a smile as ferocious as it was loving, he gathered her wrists in one hand and continued pounding himself into her.

Scarlet bit her lip against the onslaught. Never had she taken pleasure from being powerless. But this was different. She trusted Fredrick.

After a particularly violent shove that made him snarl incoherently, they both slumped against the ground, him on top of her, his weight a comfortable protection. Sweat bonded them from knees to neck.

"My love," he murmured through her disheveled hair. "My one love."

After a while, he rolled off her. Snuggling up against his side, she wrapped an arm over his heaving chest and looked up at the brightening sky.

Sometime later she felt him tense.

She rose on an elbow. "What is troubling you?"

"Now that we're both...the same, we'll have to take certain precautions."

"If you're afraid that we'll get with child, I could always go to the chemist. I've accompanied other women, I know how it works." She'd accompanied them to the barber surgeon as well, a much worse place, but hoped it wouldn't come to this.

Fredrick turned to look at her. Anguish flashed in his gaze. "We'll never be *able* to produce a child, Scarlet. I'm sorry...my seed has long been barren."

Relief flooded through her, though she fought to keep it from showing in case it hurt him. "Then we'll lavish attention to the children around us. What sort of precautions, then?"

"With both of us changing on the same night, I doubt we could be close to each other, in case one would attack the other. I'll have Frank prepare a comfortable place for you to change. I used to do that the first few years."

A special room for her to change into a werewolf. Scarlet tried to picture what it would look like and couldn't. "How did Frank learn about you?"

"Years ago, while the change loomed near, I made the mistake of coming too close to a town. I must have made somewhat of a racket for people laid chase to me, they were unrelenting, and I was too arrogant to know better. At one point while I was still a man, but barely, they cornered me near the top of a ravine. All I remember, all I could process in my mind was the wind in my face as I jumped into the river below."

When Scarlet gasped, Fredrick stopped and laid a reassuring hand on her belly. "I came to lying beside a fire, with a young lad watching over me like a hawk."

"Frank."

He nodded. "He'd been fishing by the river, he explained, and saw me floating by, still in wolf form. As he was tugging me in, I began to change back. The shock he must have had."

Rising over his chest, she planted a kiss on his cheek. "I'm sure glad he didn't finish you off like those rabid people who chased you."

"They weren't rabid, just afraid. It's something we'll both have to deal with now." Fredrick yawned wide.

She liked how the word "both" sounded. "We will."

His smile brought warmth to her soul. She could spend eternity like this, snuggled in the grass, safe in his arms.

"What now?"

"We wait," he replied, kissing her forehead. "But this time, I'm not waiting alone."

She agreed with a nod, stretched far to her left and came back with the rose in hand.

He looked at it, smiled and sighed deeply. His eyelids lowered in increments. "Promise me you'll be there when I wake."

"Always."

BAIN'S WOLF

ঌ

Trademarks Acknowledgement

The author acknowledges the trademarked status and trademark owners of the following wordmarks mentioned in this work of fiction:

Bronco: Ford Motor Company Corporation

David Clark H10-56 Headset: David Clark Company Inc.

De Havilland Otter DHC-3: Bombardier Corporation

G.I. Joe: Hasbro Inc.

Gore-Tex: W. L. Gore & Associates Corporation

Indiglo: Timex Corporation

Lego: Kirkbi AG Corporation

Sorel: Sorel Corporation

Styrofoam: Dow Chemical Company

Toyota: Toyota Motor Corporation

Velcro: Velcro Industries B.V. Limited

Chapter One

ℰꙮ

"Please buckle your seat belts, gentlemen, we're about to take off," Erica said as she finished her pre-takeoff checks.

After making one last note on her kneeboard, she pulled down the zipper to her jacket and shifted in her seat. She should change the sheepskin again for it kept bunching up in her lower back.

Thanks to her brand-new, top-of-the-line, noise-reduction David Clark HC10-56 headset—a cool three hundred dollars—the engine's roar sounded muffled and faraway. Her best investment yet. After transmitting in the blind, she broadcasted her intentions to take off.

With a grin and a wink over her shoulder for her six passengers, Erica gunned the engine, pulling the yoke steadily closer over her lap until the vibrations faded and her floatplane took off from Whitehorse, Yukon, and began the flight for Blackstone, two hundred miles north and east.

Shortly after getting airborne, she switched frequency and promptly checked-in with Edmonton Center and using her best "pilot voice", she radioed the tower.

"Edmonton Center, good day, this is Floater zero one off Lake Laberge at two zero one zero Zulu, en route Blackstone at six thousand five hundred feet."

"Floater zero one, Edmonton Center, thanks, good day," the radio crackled back at her.

There were advantages to flying in the High North. A pilot had much more latitude when came time to check-in and out of airspace and since pretty much everyone was on a first-name basis, flying hadn't become bogged down in red tape and decorum. But with the increasing influx of visitors, things were bound to change.

When the plane reached cruising altitude and speed, she checked back to see how her passengers were doing. She wasn't exactly renowned for her finesse with the yoke. But if someone paid her well enough, she could land her floatplane in a wading pool! Her brothers always teased her about her flying skills. Jealous.

She'd never flown this route before. Hunters who usually chartered her went to other game preserves like Keno or Elsa but not ever Blackstone. Even though she'd lived her entire life in the Yukon, she hadn't even known there was *anything* around that lake until they'd contacted her the week prior.

Well, anything but furry friends with lots of claws and sharp teeth. I hope they know what they're doing, these guys.

For the amount of US dollars they were paying her, she'd fly them to the North Pole! They were going halfway there anyway. Speaking of money, she was willing to bet—had she had any to spare—they'd be calling her back within forty-eight hours, begging for her to return them to civilization. She'd seen it happen so often, city folks trying to get their lungs full of nice clean air, their eyes full of nice clean sky, but ending up feeling trapped or bored and missing the noise of other people. She didn't mind silence. Some just couldn't take it.

She felt a presence over her shoulder and turned to find one of her passengers—Thomson, the group's mouthpiece—smiling down at her with his too bright, perfect teeth amid his tan-in-a-can complexion. He reminded her of a news anchor.

"Yes?" she asked as she pulled one side of her headset down to her jaw so she could listen to both radio and passenger at once. "Everything all right?"

"Everything is great, Miss Bain. You sure can take off fast." He chuckled. "How long until we land at Miner's Point?"

"Miner's Point? I'm taking you to *Blackstone*."

He appeared confused for a second, shook his head then crouched by her seat. "No, no, we're going to Miner's Point, just like the fax I sent you last week."

There was no way in hell she could've made that sort of mistake. The guy was changing his destination on her *during* the flight? *Shit.*

"I'm so sorry, Miss Bain," Thomson went on, shaking his head and pursing his lips. "I don't know...argh, I must have put down the wrong place, do you want to bet? We were looking at Blackstone first but changed plans at the last minute. I bet I put in the old place instead! What are we going to do now?"

Kick your sorry butt, she meant to say, but instead took a deep breath, gritted her teeth and whipped out her map. *The customer is always right*, she chanted in her head. *Doesn't make him smart though.*

A quick check revealed Miner's Point wouldn't take more fuel. In fact, instead of flying two hundred miles north and east, she'd be going north and west, but for the same distance. Great. Now she'd have to change her whole flight plan and log it in all over again. *Damn, damn, damn.*

"Okay," she said at length after she let him marinate in his idiocy for a minute or two. "I'll fly you up to Miner's Point, but you have to realize this is a big deal for me. For safety reasons, I'm not supposed to change flight plans halfway. What if something goes wrong and they can't find us?"

A flicker of triumph pulled at his tanned cheek. "Of course. I understand perfectly and I apologize again, Miss Bain. We're just all very keen to finally get some vacation time, you know. That's very nice of you to do this for us. So, any idea when we'll land then?"

After a quick check to her watch, she looked back to him and caught Thomson staring down the zipper of her nylon sports jacket. He quickly snapped his gaze back to her face. She got that a lot. Most passengers weren't expecting a freckle-faced, perma-grin, thirty-two-year-old woman to be their bush pilot *du jour.*

"About three and a half hours. We should be there shortly after two o'clock."

He nodded and returned to his seat. He didn't buckle up. Erica wanted to point to the sign—bright yellow with black letters, the supposed sharpest contrast the human eye could pick up—but gave up. He obviously was a man used to getting his way—hadn't he just gotten it?—and even if she wouldn't let anyone buffalo her around, she disliked arguing. If he wanted to become a meat missile should things go wrong, then so be it.

His "rich city slicker dressed as a hunter" look made her want to laugh. So obvious. Everything was just too *perfect*, right out of an outdoors magazine. From Gore-Tex anorak to Sorel hunting boots. He could afford it though. If someone smelled like money, it had to be Thomson. His friends too, although they seemed to look up to him. She wondered what sort of game they were going to hunt with the impressive arsenal they'd brought with them. Aluminum boxes and expensive-looking rifle cases had looked so incongruous against her all-metal, no-frills single-engine Otter. With the six of them and all that fancy-looking gear, she'd pushed her aircraft to its maximum payload. But they paid well and on time so she didn't care what they were going to hunt in their private lodge.

Little boys in their secret clubhouse.

Erica kept herself busy as they flew over the Nordenskiold Wetland Area. To her right, the MacKenzie Mountains resembled a piece of crumpled blue leather below the tungsten gray sky. Nightfall would come quickly this day. Already September was bringing more rain and shorter days. She loved fall and grinned at the thought of taking a few days off next week to go hiking with friends.

Since starting out on her own in the charter air business, Erica couldn't remember the last time she'd had a full week off all to herself. In seven years. She should take Gabe up on his offer and let the protective older brother join in the fun. *Her* company. Erica grinned at the thought of him taking orders from her. Ah, sweet revenge.

At five to two, she was doing her overfly to assess wind strength and direction and guesstimating the best angle of approach to Miner's Point Lake. According to Thomson's coordinates—which she hoped he'd relayed to her correctly this time—she had to bring them to a spot near the northern tip of the lake.

Ah, there it is. Whew.

The wooden pier didn't do justice to the flicker of mansion she saw up the embankment. Despite the cover of trees, she saw a large black roof and a timber house large enough to be an inn. And they had *two* rigid-hull inflatable boats. Not just one RIB but two. At ten thousand apiece! These guys definitely had *money*. Too bad they couldn't read a damned map or fill out a simple form!

With her typical lack of elegance, she banked tightly, reduced speed, dropped to a couple hundred feet and slammed her plane down hard on the smooth surface of the lake. While she kept a steel grip on the yoke, the floats shook violently as though she rolled over rocks. The fuselage quivered. She brought them right along the pier, cut the engine and flung the headset over the control column.

After she'd powered everything down, Erica squeezed out of her seat with a big "aren't I good?" grin for her pale-faced passengers then lightly jumped down to the pier. Before she could reach it, the cargo doors burst open.

"Lord, Miss Bain, I thought my teeth would fall out," laughed Thomson. He gestured behind him with a thumb and rolled his eyes.

One of his friends, a tall and lanky fellow with a bald spot so distinct it looked shaved, stumbled out and barreled down the pier where he bent over and vomited in the gravel path leading up to the house.

Erica managed not to grin only because the next passenger, dressed in camouflage fatigues, jumped out and landed with a great thud a foot from her. In her catalog of people, she'd put him under "bully". He stared down at her, his porcine gaze sliding down her front before coming back up.

Yeah, bud, a chick flew your butt up North. Live with the times.

He didn't say a word as he unlocked and swung the cargo doors wide and started pulling stuff out. Despite his gruff attitude, he seemed overly careful with the luggage.

The pair of British hunters came next, both looking pale but not as near as Baldy. One of them sucked on his bottom lip in just the way pipe smokers tended to do. Erica's sixth and last passenger emerged with a big smile on his face. His yellow-tinted shooting glasses made his pale eyes look acid green.

"Now *that* was a landing, Mrs. Pilot!" he said, stepping off the plane with much more grace than the one before. He went to Bully and both took care of the luggage.

"You will join us for coffee, won't you, Miss Bain? It's the least we can do for messing up your flight plan this way," Thomson asked with a paternal pat on her arm she tried to ignore. Partly succeeded. Fraternizing with clientele had never been good for any business. Plus, he gave her the willies with his fake tan and teeth. She'd rather have coffee with a family of bears...but she *did* need to use their bathroom.

"I'm sorry, gotta get back up before three. Nightfall comes quickly around here. But I'd like to use your bathroom, if I could?"

"Of course, Miss Bain. No problem at all."

"Here, let me help." She grabbed one of the black nylon bags and meant to lift it but it remained firmly on the pier. What the hell was in there?

Thomson hurriedly pulled the straps from her hands. "That's okay, Al will take care of it. You're not our bellboy."

Renaming Bully "Big Al" in her head, Erica shrugged and followed the cigar-smelling man up the path and couldn't contain her "whew" of surprise when she saw the lodge.

"Some hotels I know aren't even as big as this."

"Isn't it nice?" Thomson replied with a proud grin. "A small African country would fit in it, don't you think?" He laughed at his own joke.

That had to be the rudest thing she'd hear all week—despite working alongside male bush pilots and being the younger sister to two overly protective, macho older brothers. That said a lot.

After he opened the thick door, the interior proved to be just as opulent as the exterior with gleaming dark wood walls and floors. Animal heads lined the walls, their glassy eyes staring vacantly. A table with hoofed paws for legs and a huge ivory tusk caught her attention. Poachers? Great.

"It's down the hall to your right. Last door. I had a man bring the RIBs up to the lodge earlier in the week to get the electricity and water going."

So they really had meant to come here all along and not Blackstone. Good thing she was a flexible pilot, otherwise they would've had no vacation at all and flown back to Whitehorse. Erica was rounding the corner of the hall when she collided with a man's chest. She gasped and jumped back.

Must be the guy who came up by himself. How had he managed to pilot both RIBs at once? Ah, probably piloted one and towed the other.

"Sorry, miss," said the man. He made Bully look like a cheerleader. A thick blond beard obscured his facial features. He didn't move as she squeezed around him and peeked inside the last door. The bathroom was luxurious and well-appointed. She did her business with a mix of relief and anxiety. She'd locked the door first thing but still...

Creepy hunters with creepy animal heads on the wall with creepy fake teeth...horror movies start this way. The only thing missing was a big guy with a hockey mask and a machete.

Back outside, she saw Yellow Glasses rushing up the path holding something. He put both hands in his pockets and smiled as he came up to her. "Thank you for the lift, see you later."

She turned to watch him as the fine hair rose on the back of her neck. Just as she was heading back toward the lake, by the corner of her eye she caught him throwing a quick peek over his shoulder.

Thomson was waiting for her when she neared the pier. He grinned and shook her hand in his bear paw. "So, we'll see you next Sunday, around noon?"

Erica nodded. She looked up at the sky and winced. Dark clouds were forming up north. She'd better be quick. "Yep. Everything all right with the lodge? Don't need me to pick something up for you?"

Thomson shook his head. "Everything went perfectly. Take care. We'll see you Sunday next week."

"See you."

Too bad she wouldn't have time to follow the beautiful Yukon River from the hunters' lodge right down to Dawson and instead would have to fly directly over the preserve again. Trees as far as the eye could see. Bo—ring.

Her pre-flight routine completed, she adjusted her chinos and jacket before remaining stuck in the same position for the next three hours and looked behind as she took off and left her seven rich hunters for a week of...who knew what.

She never asked clients the purpose of their trip to the Yukon. She had no qualms about anything or anybody as long as they looked legal. Her only rule was simple to follow—no animal parts whatsoever would get in her plane unless the kills had been cleaned, enveloped in triple-layer plastic wrap and put in portable Styrofoam iceboxes. Otherwise the smell would stay with her for weeks, despite some serious scrubbing. Things were changing though. When she first started her company and its catchy slogan *"Get There Now"* seven years before, she flew mostly hunters, whereas nowadays, she had a mixed bag of nature lovers, governmental officials—

A faint smell tickled her nose. She looked back in the cabin but saw nothing out of the ordinary. Had someone smoked in her plane, despite the clear interdiction sign?

Oh right, I have to radio my new flight plan.

When a strip of smoke, very, very faint but quite noticeable in her Otter's small cockpit, started to drift out of the floorboard below the seat next to her, she immediately switched on her radio to relay her position in case something happened. She wasn't anywhere near where she was supposed to be. Nothing. Changing frequencies didn't help either, everything was dead. To add to her to predicament, blinding blades of sun stabbed between the dark clouds right in her eyes.

Erica cursed as she hurriedly pulled her manual out and ran her finger on the plasticized tabs. "Electrical Malfunction and-or Smoke in Cockpit".

Good enough for me.

While she followed the checklist's procedures, smoke rose in thickening tendrils until she started to cough. She'd just finished flicking off every electric system and would have to do things manually from then on. Bleary-eyed, she yanked the map from the clip above her head and scanned the region, looking for any suitable landing spot.

Come on, come on.

Because turning around meant more wasted time and fuel than just continuing south, she dismissed returning to the hunters' lodge and the two closest lakes. Plus, there had to be *something* around so she could contact Dawson City and report her emergency. It wouldn't do her any good to land on some deserted lake and be stuck there for days while they looked for her. As the options were quickly rejected, her list of potential landing spots dwindled to two. Beaverbrook or the weather station.

With her heart in her throat, Erica banked south and west, hoping she'd have time to land before she passed out from the fumes or lost situational awareness. She had minutes, tops. Pushing against her window, she pressed her face as close as she could and gulped a few breaths. Sweat clammed her hands, which slid against the yoke's vinyl cover. No altitude, no speed, no fuel gauge. No nothing.

"Shit," she snarled. Punching the control panel—as good as it felt—didn't fix her problem.

She was going to have to land that thing on visuals alone. That meant daylight. Or what was left of it. There wouldn't be time to reach Beaverbrook. The weather station would have to do. At least they had a radio there.

Smoke stinging her eyes, her throat raw from coughing, Erica flew over the last stretch of skinny spruce forest before she spotted the Yukon river, a thin silver ribbon in her teary eyes. Her hopes flared when the weather station's white sphere gleamed in the setting sun. She just might make it!

Pulling all the stops, Erica side-slipped her plane so it'd go down at an angle and not nose first—she didn't need more speed, just less altitude—knowing that the tiniest wave would make her floats catch and flip her over as though she'd tried to land in pudding. While keeping the station dead front and center, she used all her skills to drop nice and level, her nose slightly to the left.

"Steady, steadyyyy," she snarled through clenched teeth.

Using yoke, pedals and throttle as an orchestra conductor would, Erica managed to bring her floatplane into a gentle right roll. Heat had begun to rise in the cockpit. She smelled burned plastic. The acrid smoke stung her eyes.

Despite trying to touch down with one float first, she slammed both at once. A violent shock rocked her forward against the five-point harness, which dug in her shoulders and made her cringe.

"Argh, shit!"

But she didn't flip over as she'd feared and instead kept going toward the station farther along the river. With her cheek against the tilted window so she could see where she was going, Erica fought against the uneven surface of the river and wrestled her floatplane toward the opposite bank, where she hooted in triumph when the pier came into view.

Coughing hard, she opened the door and scooted sideways while keeping the plane in the right direction with only one hand. The smoke was getting bad. She could barely see. She cut the engine, unbuckled her harness — being stuck in a smoky airplane would kill her more surely than slamming against the controls — made double sure everything was switched off even if there was no electricity going through and pocketed the ignition key. At the speed she was going, she'd reach the pier without problem — which might in itself *be* a problem.

Too fast.

Way too fast.

A thud announced she'd bumped against either the pier or the embankment. Erica was projected sideways against the door, which gaped all the way out under her. With a gasp, she tumbled out of the cockpit and fell in a heap onto a regular and hard surface. *The pier then. Good.*

"Damn," she snarled between bouts of cough.

She had to put out the fire immediately or she'd lose her plane, her job and her entire fleet — one whole, entire single-engine de Havilland Otter DHC-3. She'd worked so hard even for that one aircraft...she couldn't lose it all for a simple electrical malfunction. She couldn't go back to "the guys" with her tail tucked between her legs and let everyone think owning and operating a charter company was too much for her…a *woman*.

Braving the smoke again, she braced the door with her shoulder as she reached over her seat with her eyes closed, her lips tightly pressed, and palmed the area where the handheld extinguisher was clipped. Finally, she closed her hand over it and yanked it out.

Stars fizzed around the edges of her vision. A gag reflex forced her back, stumbling, collapsing on all fours. She heard the thud of the extinguisher when she dropped it and feared for a second it'd roll over and into the water.

"Step back," said a male voice somewhere behind her.

Despite not seeing a damned thing, Erica crawled a bit sideways. She was going to cough out a lung! Her throat felt raw, her face burned.

The "*shhhht*" of the extinguisher announced he knew enough to catch the fire quickly before it ate through everything. Good man.

After a while, the "*shhhht*" sputtered and stopped. By that time, Erica was coughing a bit less and could see through the haze of tears. She sat on her heels and pressed her palms to her eyes. She heard him pull both passenger and cargo doors wide. So he knew he had to vent it out. Her savior! She'd buy him a beer at the first opportunity.

"The fire's out," he announced, the thump of a heavy tread growing as he neared her. All she could see were old-fashioned brown leather mountaineering boots. A strong hand pulled her up by an arm as if she weighed nothing more than a coffee pot.

"Thanks, bud," she said, coughing.

"Breathe slowly," he urged, his rich voice filling her ear when he leaned into her. He put a hand flat on the small of her back. "Slowly."

Erica did, gagging and coughing by fits, but after a while, managed to breathe somewhat normally. Heat from his hand transferred through her jacket. When she looked up at his face, she forgot to cough for a good five seconds.

A face such as his she'd never seen in person. Women had giggling fits and girls sighed at slumber parties over faces like his. His golden-brown hair was just wavy enough, his eyebrows just arched enough, his nose straight and aristocratic, his mouth…good grief his *mouth*!

There was something on the side of his face but she couldn't see for the angle. He narrowed his hazel eyes at her and said something.

Snap out of it.

"Excuse me?"

"I asked if you were all right," he repeated, clearly annoyed. His mouth was tight.

"Yeah," Erica replied, patting herself down and coughing again. "Ouch."

She looked down at her right hand to see that she'd burned it while searching for the extinguisher. Red, raw-looking welts covered her knuckles.

Grabbing her hand and bringing it higher so he could see, his scowl deepened. "We have to take care of that. Burns infect easily. Can you walk?"

She nodded then blew on her hand.

"Stop that. You're going to make it worse." He whirled around and marched off the pier without even checking back to see if she *could* walk.

Um.

Erica followed slowly, casting one last glance at her sad-looking plane as it bobbed along the pier. She noticed he'd tied it to the mooring ring. *So all this and foresight too!*

Up ahead, the station gleamed with the timid sun's dying rays. A large building in the middle where smoke rose out of a chimney resembled an old army barracks, while the smaller annexes on either side — half-cylinders on their sides really —

were made of corrugated metal. An old, battered gray Toyota truck with mean-looking radial mudders was parked nearby.

The steep incline to the station made her pant like crazy and she started to cough again. Her eyes welled up. She knuckled them away and followed the broad V-shaped back as he climbed up toward the main building. The cargo pants underlined his amazingly tight and nice butt while the parted fleece jacket beat his waist on either side of him with each forceful step.

She reached him just as he leaped up the few metal stairs to the covered front door. White paint flaked around the doorjamb, showing the station's age. Her hand burned. Cringing, she followed the man inside and down a dimly lit corridor. It must indeed have been an old army barrack for she could still see placards underneath several coats of institutional beige paint depicting a crown and maple leaf design.

"In here," he called from farther down the hall. A neon light sputtered on in a room to the right.

The smell of disinfectant made her wince as she stepped inside the large room occupied mostly by…*stuff*. Weather watching equipment, obviously, though she couldn't recognize a single thing besides the computer by the window.

"Take your jacket off and sit."

Talkative.

His back was to her when she sat on the lone chair in the room and put her hand on the table by the computer mouse. Even ambient air burned against her raw skin. While she gingerly removed her jacket, Erica fought the grimace down. She didn't mind other people's blood or protruding bones — as she'd seen several times growing up with her two hockey-playing brothers and their multitude of handsome male friends — but she didn't enjoy it so much when it was her own.

The man joined her by the computer with a white metal first-aid kit in his hands. She'd never seen a kit so well stocked. Some stuff, she didn't even know what it was for.

He crouched in front of her. Under the neon's unforgiving light, she finally saw what had caught her eye earlier. Good thing she wasn't squeamish. A nasty scar ran down the man's temple and cheek then curved under his jaw. The thing was as wide as one of her fingers. Whatever injury had caused it must have hurt like nobody's business. It was a wonder his face was still attached to his skull.

Erica returned his stare without blinking. She knew he'd seen her looking at his scar and intuitively felt he was gauging her reaction, perhaps searching for something only he knew. So she made sure her face remained unchanged. She hated making people uncomfortable. Her brothers had milked that soft streak in her for all it was worth. Good thing she didn't hold grudges.

Without a word, he tipped a bottle of disinfectant—the amber-colored one, the kind that burned—into a gauze compress then applied it to her knuckles. Despite her best effort, she cringed.

"You're supposed to tell me it's going to sting," she said through a tight smile.

"You knew it would."

"True."

He looked up for a second, seemed to consider something then returned to his work. The way he was cleaning her wound with practiced, economical movements let Erica know he'd done this before.

"You must have passed your first-aid course with straight 'A's, bud. You're good at this."

"I've had a lot of practice, unfortunately," he replied as he tightened the gauze bandage around her wrist. His fingers felt so hot against her skin.

When he cut the white adhesive tape with his teeth, Erica couldn't look at anything else but his mouth. Not too full, not too slim, with just the right curve to it. Perfect for kissing.

Whew. Down girl. With a face like his, he has girlfriends in every city from here to Argentina.

"Thanks."

He nodded as he put his things back in the first-aid kit. Erica wondered why the man's hands were shaking.

"Was it a bear?" she asked, pointing at her own cheek.

"Wolf."

"Big wolf."

A sardonic half-smile tugged at the corner of his mouth. "*Very* big."

She offered her injured right hand before switching to her left one. "I'm Erica Bain."

And I'm in trouble, Lothar thought. "Miss Bain. Lothar."

He shook her lean, strong hand just long enough to feel the heat seeping into his palm. He hurriedly released it and stood. With much more deliberation than necessary, he returned the first-aid kit to the cabinet and used the few seconds to clear his mind.

The grinning, pale-eyed, freckle-faced brunette made him want to stare well beyond the boundaries of propriety. He'd seen women in his long life, some of them exquisite beauties, but none quite like her, with a mix of exuberance and candor he found positively charming. As in "deadly cobra about to strike" charming. Exactly what he'd thought after she said her name…he *was* in trouble.

Forcing his mind to clear of her image, Lothar spun on his heel and crossed his muscular arms, knowing he might either intimidate or scare her. Either way, he made sure she saw him as he was…a dangerous man.

For the life of him, she merely leaned back and smiled. "Thanks again, bud...er, Lothar. You probably saved my plane. Would you mind if I used your radio to call Dawson City? I'll need parts."

Bud? No one had ever called him that. He wasn't sure he liked it. But since it came from her...

Lothar shook his head. It shouldn't, *didn't*, matter that it came from her.

Relieved to have something to do other than look at the attractive, wiry woman, Lothar nodded and left the room. He heard her soft tread behind him and caught a whiff of her healthy, fresh scent. Shampoo and mint. After he flicked the light switch hard enough to break it, the neon buzzed for a few seconds then blinked on. His radio was behind a desk in a corner not nearly big enough for two people. He hoped she knew how to work that particular model so he wouldn't have to be near when she used it. Proximity to the woman was already ranking high on his list of things to avoid.

He crossed the room, switched on the radio and tuned to the right frequency but not quickly enough to finish before she drew near. While he held the mike in one hand, he tried to squeeze out of the enclosed space at the same time as she tried to wedge in sideways, which resulted in her becoming trapped between the desk and his hip. Her backside a perfect height and shape against his hip, she "*oops-ed*" and tried to turn around but became tangled in the mike's coiled wire. Lust flared like a bad fever.

Could the woman be more oblivious?

"Sorry."

Lothar sighed while he passed the wire over her head then around her shoulder. Her face turned to his and for a split second their gazes met and held.

In that split second he drank in her obvious beauty, but more than this, he basked in the warm glow of her kind eyes through which shone a healthy and vibrant soul. All of which he wasn't.

"Here," Lothar snapped, breaking the spell and shoving the mike in her left hand.

It was with great relief that he went to wait by the door. *Breathe*, he commanded to himself.

No way to get rid of her that night. Even *he* wasn't callous enough to kick her out...although he used to be. While long-buried memories surfaced, Lothar's fists became tighter.

He hadn't thought about this in a while, about Sister Jane's obstinate claim that there was good in all men. She'd been kinder to him than he'd ever deserved, but she'd also been wrong. Some men hadn't a speck of good in them. Like him.

Now in an increasingly darker mood, Lothar waited while she relayed her situation to Dawson City and hoped someone would be there first thing in the morning to get her off his hands. He abhorred people like her, the happy-go-lucky optimists who bumbled through life without a care in the world, generally causing trouble everywhere they went. And that beatific grin...it grated on his nerves already.

When she flicked the radio off and stood to look at him—with that smile on her face still—her T-shirt molded her fine figure, the lean arms and graceful wrists. She was so pleasing, corresponded so much to his ideal of beauty that he allowed himself the rare luxury of admiring a woman.

His hands began to tingle with his mounting desire. Lothar thought he'd have to literally run out and chop some wood right then and there. Punishing physical labor had always worked with his sometimes hard-to-control temper, had always managed to burn off the extra energy, leaving him too exhausted to feel anything. Most of the times, it was the only way he could maintain the ironclad control he imposed on himself.

And unforgiving self-discipline meant the difference between living as a man and merely surviving as a beast.

Speaking of which, he heard her stomach growl from where he stood. Her embarrassed cough didn't quite cover the sound. Great. He'd have to feed her as well.

"Come with me," he said as he about-faced and strode back down the corridor toward the two-room apartment he occupied.

The Spartan common room with a tiny kitchen along the far wall and a dining room, living room combination that faced onto the river looked even plainer when she followed him in. He filled to capacity the cast iron woodstove in the corner just so he could do something with himself.

"I'm sorry to invade your space, Lothar," she began, shrugged then fell silent.

"I'm sure you didn't set fire to your own plane."

She laughed.

It'd been a while since someone had laughed at something he said. The sound was like the first warm rays of spring thawing frozen pine needles. And he loathed himself for it.

"Look, I've had a hard day, so just help yourself, okay."

Lothar ignored her look of awkwardness as he dug a blanket and a pillow out of the trunk that also served as a coffee table and dropped them on the couch along the window.

And to say he used to live in the opulence of Austria's aristocracy, surrounded by beauty and excess of all kinds, with beautiful women — and some men — circling him like vultures. The thought made him scowl.

"Keep your clothes on, it starts to get cold by the window in the fall."

"You're going to bed at six thirty?" she asked incredulously.

With a nod for the stunned woman, Lothar crossed the kitchen to his bedroom beyond, closing the door behind him.

Once in the safety — and isolation — of his darkened room, he took his first real breath since the woman had shown up in her smoking plane.

He'd never been so disturbed by the sight of a cute woman before. He'd had his share. But that one had literally fallen out of the sky and onto his lap and Lothar didn't know just what to do with all that positive energy. She exuded such vivacity.

With a snarl, he kicked his boots off and lay on his bed with his hands behind his head, his feet crossed at the ankles. Sounds from the kitchen reached him. Kitchen sounds, dishes, cutlery, the creaky drawer he should've fixed that day, the fridge opening and closing. The sounds of *life*.

It'd been so long since he'd had someone in his house. In fact, Erica — *don't call her by her first name, for Pete's sake* — was the second person to stand in his home. The first had been the man he'd replaced nine years earlier.

After a short moment of quiet, he started to hear sounds again, this time of her cleaning up and washing the dishes. Smells of toast and coffee tickled his nose. Saliva pooled under his tongue. He hadn't eaten since noon.

Another sort of hunger began to pull at him as well, one he'd worked hard and long to push down, to control. Carnal hunger. The woman awakened in him something with which he used to use to hurt others, just as it'd once been done to him. Lothar tried to ignore the stirring of his cock as it stiffened with images of Erica, of her lean and fit body, her calloused hands. His palms itched at the memory of her warm skin. She smelled so good.

A growl of frustration left him. He yanked the blanket over him, clothes and all, and rolled to his side. Still, visions of her followed implacably until he thought he'd have to go chop wood *right then* to alleviate the tension.

The worst of it was that he wouldn't get to rest before the full moon on Monday night, time during which every ounce of energy made the difference between mere torture and hellish agony. A time when Lothar Kessler became as monstrous outside as he was inside.

Chapter Two

ຮວ

After she'd used the bathroom, which was spotless and entirely white, she came back to the living room and lay on the couch, all her clothes still on as he'd said—as though she'd remove a single sock in a strange man's home—Erica couldn't help but wonder at Buddy's odd behavior. He acted as if he were afraid of her or something. A man built like him! Speaking of which, she would stop calling him "bud". He didn't look like a "bud" kind of guy. "Lothar" suited him too well. She wondered what nationality that was. She'd never heard it before. Neither had she seen a man so stunning.

It was too bad she hadn't had the opportunity to admire his body for more than a few minutes. But what little she'd seen had been enough to make her start fanning herself. Mentally of course.

She sucked food from between her teeth with a curl to her lips. Man, she wanted to brush her teeth almost bad enough to go back to the plane and get her overnight bag. But it must be cold outside.

Nah. She'd get it in the morning.

* * * * *

Erica woke with a start. After a few clueless seconds, she recognized her surroundings and grimaced when her hand began to sting. Sitting up, she realized she was alone. She checked her watch.

"Whew, five thirty. I overslept."

She'd always been an early riser. The door to Lothar's bedroom was ajar and she could spot an empty bed, impeccably made, beyond. After grabbing a muffin from the cupboard, she pulled on her running shoes and ran a hand through her hair. Not that it'd change anything. The thing had long ago broken her spirit.

When she stepped outside in the cool September fog, the sound of wood chopping reverberated around the still forest and river. A loon cried then took flight. Shivering, Erica made her way down by the water to inspect her plane and retrieve her overnight bag for the glorious toothbrush inside. She'd once gotten stuck without an overnight bag…she'd never repeated that icky mistake. Three days in the same clothes, no toothbrush, no nothing. Aside from the acrid smell of fire retardant and burned plastic, the damage wasn't nearly as bad as she'd initially feared. In fact, for all the smoke there'd been in the cockpit, she couldn't find more than a burned breaker in the circuit panel.

"That's it?" she murmured. Then something caught her attention. Some wires looked twisted behind the panel. She couldn't remember seeing wires stick out that way before and squeezed behind the front seat to investigate.

"What is *that*?"

A bunch of wires dangled from behind the panel. One of them had obviously shorted. No wonder it'd begun to smoke. Damn. The entire thing could've fried within minutes. She'd been lucky to make it as far as she had. Erica tried to remember the last time she'd had her plane serviced. Surely the mechanic wouldn't have made such a blatant mistake. Man, heads were going to roll when she returned to Whitehorse!

After making sure everything was secure, Erica returned to the station and brushed her teeth before pulling on fresh, clean clothes. *Ahh.*

The sound of someone—Lothar, evidently—chopping wood hadn't stopped. How much wood would he chop in one go? What an uncommon name, when she thought about it.

And he did speak with the faintest accent, as if his R's wanted to roll at the back of his throat. Sexy.

Dressed in jeans, T-shirt and jacket, she grabbed a pair of water bottles and followed the sound until she rounded the corner of one of the annexes. If he'd hidden his body the night before, he sure showed it this morning. Erica stifled the moronic grin rising to her lips.

Lothar had his back to her while he stood with both feet wide on a fallen tree where he'd cut a deep wedge to split it into logs. As she watched, he brought the axe down with such force that he not only separated the wedge but also cleaved a two-foot portion right off the trunk. She felt her jaw drop and remain so for a while before she consciously closed it.

He wore his mountaineering boots, a pair of threadbare jeans and a T-shirt that hugged his broad back in all the right places. Sweat literally steamed off his back and shoulders, which were wide and thick. Every time he brought the axe up over his head, skin would show underneath his T-shirt, giving Erica a glorious view of his tapered waist, and each time he brought the axe down, his back and legs would stiffen, making the muscles ripple and swell.

Sexual energy spiked in her body, right down to her toes. She hadn't been this breathless since high school, back when she had a pathetic crush on the school's hockey team captain. The guy had looked so good in a hockey jersey. Steven had always ignored her—she'd been such a geek back then—which was fortunate since he'd become a jerk and wife-beater. She hadn't seen him in a couple of years.

As much as Steven had been cute, he hadn't been as, well, *delicious* as Lothar. Even now, despite Steven's unofficial tag of "Cutest Guy in Miles", he barely registered on the cuteness scale while the weatherman was off the chart.

More like Weathergod.

Serious heat wafted out of her jacket. She zipped it down.

At the faint sound, Lothar whirled around, the axe poised in his hands, a dark look in his eyes. For a split second, Erica could only stare at him, the water bottles forgotten. He looked feral. A predator. Shivers snaked down her spine. Her situation suddenly scared her. There she was, a lone woman in a strange man's home, miles away from the nearest...*anything*. If he decided to do something nasty to her, there wouldn't be a thing to stop him, herself included. Not against a man with his physique.

To give herself some countenance, she sloshed the bottles in a pendulum and approached. "I figured you'd be thirsty. Good grief, buddy, did you chop it all this morning?"

Jeez, don't call him buddy.

Two other tree trunks lay beyond him, severed in equal lengths of about two feet. Some had even been quartered. It kind of resembled a lumber carnage when she thought of it. A tree massacre.

Lothar looked back and shrugged. "Like I said, it gets cold up here."

She proffered one of the bottles, which he took with his intent gaze still fixed on her. Even if common sense and instincts were screaming at her to back away gently, not make eye contact and adopt a fetal position, she stayed put and watched him twist the cap off and take a long swallow. His Adam's apple bobbed appetizingly.

With her heart sinking, she noticed other scars on either side of his throat, as though something big had chewed on him. What sort of animal had made such damage?

"It's not polite to stare," he said after a while.

He'd been peeking at her over the bottle. Oops. She smiled. "You're right, I'm sorry. I was just trying to imagine a wolf big enough to do this. It was a wolf, you said?"

He nodded.

"Not a bear."

He shook his head.

"Could it have been a grizzly bear wearing a wolf fur coat maybe?"

Lothar's mouth quivered. Was that a smile? She wanted to pat herself on the back. *So he can smile like the rest of us.*

"It was a wolf, believe me," he replied, draining the last of his water. He eyed hers but didn't say anything.

"Here," she said, giving it to him, "you deserve it more than I do."

His fingers brushed against hers when he took the bottle. The touch sent a jolt of energy right to her chest. Erica had to literally remind herself to breathe. And she knew he'd noticed her reaction too, much to her mortification. Just by the way his gaze lingered on hers long past any standards of etiquette.

Is that it, sexual tension?

Lothar continued his visual examination while she did the same. *Someone should say something.*

With obvious effort, he broke the spell, looked down at the bottle in his hands and cleared his throat. "You should radio Dawson to see if they can still send the parts you need. There's bad weather coming down from the north. It should hit later on today. I gave them the report earlier this morning but I don't know what they'll decide flying wise." He put the bottle on one of the diced tree trunks and grabbed the axe. "You can't stay here much longer."

Erica's heart twitched. Of course, she couldn't stay…it wouldn't be proper, now would it? She'd no intention of staying more than she needed to.

After a quick peek northward where indeed some strips of dark clouds were massing over the MacKenzie Mountains, she nodded. "Good idea."

As she went back to the house, she resisted the urge to look behind to see if he was watching her but couldn't stop the mental trip down Sexual Tension Avenue.

I wonder if he's watching. I can't look back…it's so uncool and needy. I'm cool and I don't need anything. That's it. I won't look back.

Is he watching me?

When she rounded the corner of the building, she threw a quick peek his way. He was watching!

Feeling buoyed and quite gauche about her excitement over such a simple thing as a look, she radioed Dawson City her situation report. After a bit of a wait, she got through. The news wasn't good.

"You're going to have to wait at least another twenty-four hours," said Sam, the extra-vinegar dispatcher. "There's a storm gathering north of Keno and I'm not sending anyone up until it clears."

Erica rolled her eyes. She could *so* fly if she had the parts. Wussies. "It's not for another few hours, from what the meteorologist said, why can't they take off now right quick before the storm hits?"

"I'm not risking someone's life just because you don't want to stay another day at the station." The jerk sounded pleased. She'd always hated him. The only person she could think of who she really, honestly disliked. "So is he as charming as when he comes down to town?"

The moron kept the button on his mike pressed down so she'd hear his laugh.

"Who?"

"Kessler, the weather guy."

Weather*god*, she mentally corrected.

"There's nothing wrong with him. What are you blabbering about, bud?"

Whew, where had the sudden protective feelings come from? Lothar could defend himself, she was sure of it. With those arms…and legs and that nice butt.

Hey.

229

"He broke a guy's legs this summer. Apparently, he doesn't take jokes. Anyway, I've got to go. Have a great time with Mr. Personality. Over and out."

"Jerk," she muttered as she switched off.

"So it's not just me who thinks so."

Erica spun around. Lothar stood leaning against the jamb, both bottles in one hand.

"Sam's always been an ass, pardon my French."

"Ass is not French."

Laughing, she nodded. "I knew someone was going to throw it back at me some day. So did you get the part about the delay?"

Lothar nodded. "I didn't know they would keep traffic down so long in advance." He cocked his head to one side, as though considering something. "Do you always laugh when people are rude to you?"

He peeled his muscled frame from the wall and entered the suddenly small room. His threadbare jeans had holes in them, one strategically placed high on a thigh. She tried not to look. Complete failure.

Erica shrugged while he drew near enough for her to touch him if she stretched an arm out. Definitely inside "The Zone".

"I don't pick at small stuff and just let people think what they want. I prefer to laugh it off."

"Just laugh it off? Sometimes I almost envy people like you, with not a care in the world, the optimists, the wide-eyed idealists."

His words stung her a bit. "There's nothing wrong with a bit of happiness once in a while, bud. You should try it some time."

He looked angry and sad at the same time. His hazel eyes nailed her right to the spot. *Oh this one has suffered in life.* She could tell. He knew all about pain, this man.

"I tried," he murmured, "but it didn't work."

"Work at what? Taking the pain away?"

When his mouth landed on hers, Erica's first reaction was shock. Weren't animal instincts supposed to come in two varieties—fight or flight? Then why did hers only manage to dredge "whew" and "oh my"?

Not moving a muscle, Erica watched him pull away as abruptly as if some giant rubber band had snapped him back. Horror and shock filled his eyes. He stepped away, said something, cleared his throat and tried again. "You better get a shower now. When storms hit, power always goes out."

He'd kissed her. A *stranger* had kissed her. And she'd let him!

Stuff like that only happened to others, never to her. She'd had boyfriends since high school and—excluding the one-time occurrence of sex on a quad—nothing as remotely exciting as this had ever occurred. The sensation of his gorgeous lips on hers lingered for several seconds. The man could *kiss*.

Lust blazed in sharp pulsations down in her pussy. She wanted him now more than ever. Ever?

I only met him yesterday. Um.

Things went fast when a girl knew what she wanted. And she wanted Lothar the Sexy and Cynical Meteorologist.

Erica rushed for the shower so he wouldn't be stuck without hot water. A towel had already been set on the washing machine across the room. When water hit her in a burning hail, she felt the knots between her shoulder blades loosen. Only for a while though as she kept her bandaged hand over the shower curtain. Good thing she was five-nine. She quickly washed and cut the water to save some for him. Toweled dry, she slipped her clothes back on, retrieved her overnight bag with the previous day's dirty clothes and headed outside to wash them as best she could in the river.

With a power outage looming, she didn't want to waste precious water and electricity doing laundry.

Now this is roughing it.

Using the bar of soap from her toiletries bag, she crouched by the water's edge and sloshed her clothes around one-handed, gave up soon afterward then wrung at least three full drops out of them. Her bandaged hand bothered her. She wondered if she could take the gauze wraps off. When she stood, she noticed how dark the sky had suddenly become. For once, Sam had been right about something. Didn't that suck!

She was closing the door behind her and turning toward the hall when she caught Lothar exiting the bathroom barefooted and only wearing his jeans. He'd obviously just stepped out of the shower himself and had his wet hair loose over his shoulders and chest. It was much longer than she'd expected and came down in a shiny golden-brown cascade over his pectorals. In her book, there was nothing on Earth sexier than a man just out of the shower, especially one looking as magnificent as him. Lothar had the power of a horse, the thick, loose muscles playing under his gleaming skin, yet the supple grace of a man much slimmer.

And enough scars to make his chest a map of lines.

Good grief. What are those?

Three long and wide gashes encircled his waist as if some beast had hugged him then pulled out, tilling his flesh to shreds. And another one, vicious-looking down his left shoulder. Claw marks. Those were all claw marks.

For the first time in her life, Erica couldn't think of something funny to say to alleviate the tension. What could someone say to *that*?

Lothar gauged her reaction. Surprisingly, she'd been looking down appreciatively at the rest of him and only appeared to notice the scars on her way back up. There was no pity in her eyes, for which he was eternally grateful. He hated pity above everything else on his long list of things he abhorred.

"It's almost noon, are you hungry?" He sure was. For *her*.

But he didn't dare show it in case she felt the same and things started happening. He didn't trust himself yet, not with a woman such as her. Sure, he satiated his lust with a paid companion once in a while when he went down to Whitehorse. But that was different. He knew they could handle him. They had experience with certain *tastes*. That Erica might have some such experience too titillated and frightened him enough to rush past her and make sure their arms didn't touch. He still couldn't believe he'd actually kissed her. And that she hadn't slapped him in return! She should have. It would've put him right back on the safe path.

While he dug the clothes dryer from behind the woodstove and folded it down in front of the comfortable heat, a roll of thunder rumbled in the distance. They had an hour of power at most. This just compounded the mess he was in...first, he'd be stuck with someone for another day, one day closer to the full moon on Monday night. Second, what if they couldn't fly her the parts she needed before then? What if she was still at the station when... Lothar refused to even entertain the thought.

As much as he'd wanted her to lose the beatific grin, now that she looked subdued and awkward, he wished she'd smile again.

"Here," he said, turning to her and pointing at the dryer. "Lay them out here. It'll be dry within the hour."

Erica nodded, silently padded to the woodstove and proceeded to lay her wet clothes on the grill. When it came to her underthings, a flush rose to her cheeks. How could a woman as frank and down-to-earth as her be shy to show her panties? He grinned when she wasn't looking.

"I'll go put something on."

Armed with a double layer of T-shirt and sweater, Lothar felt much better equipped to handle his rising desire. *It's a cast iron chastity belt I need.* Those awful things. And they *had* existed. The things women had had to wear back in the Middle Ages. He should know. He'd been there, born right in the middle of it in 1335.

While he sorted out the supplies they'd need to wait out the dark, she pulled out utensils and cutlery from the rack on the counter. Every time they came within proximity of each other, one would abruptly change direction and find something else to do. It infuriated him to have so little control over his own responses. Already his cock pressed against the button fly. He hoped to hell she wouldn't notice.

The water began to boil on the stove. Lothar dumped the pasta in and stirred with all the concentration he could dredge from his scattered mind. Erica stood next to him and offered her plate for him to fill. The symbolic gesture caused a stitch of gratification he quickly subdued.

"I'm starving," Erica said with a deep, unladylike sniff. She plopped down on the chair and waited until he'd sat as well.

After their simple meal of buttered pasta, toast and tea was finished, Lothar was in a sweat trying to keep his mind out of the gutter. Her lips glistened with the butter while tiny sounds from her mouth elicited the sharpest twinges of pleasure he'd felt since…

Think of something else.

He knew she felt something too for she'd stopped looking at him and fidgeted in her chair. In the course of his long years, he'd known enough women to recognize the precursors, even if modern females were much more unpredictable and determined, both of which he loved. If he hadn't been trailing a long chain of guilt behind him, he'd enjoy modern women every chance he got. They'd become so strong, independent and clear-minded. He'd love nothing better than to sample as many as he could. Except that since his "curse" shortly after he'd turned thirty-eight, he hadn't been able to fully savor a woman's embrace without the beast trying to claw out of his soul. A hell tailored just for him. If he'd been capable of believing in anything spiritual, Lothar could well imagine the devil slapping his thigh over that one. A punishment fitting the crime. Crimes, *plural*.

A sudden thunderclap made Erica start. A split second later, darkness fell around the house. With the thick cover of clouds, noon felt like evening. Comfortably dark, quiet and intimate.

Frighteningly so.

He could power up the generator right then and stave off the vision-inducing darkness. Already, images of her naked form plagued him. But if the power stayed down for a long time, they'd need the fuel for later. He lit some candles on the counter and brought one to their table. The trembling glow cast copper shadows in her hair, which didn't help his resolve at all.

"That was quick," she laughed, looking at the ceiling. "It always does that?"

Lothar nodded, not trusting his voice. He couldn't yield to the temptation. But he knew he was slipping fast.

"You know," she said after a while. She was toying with the base of her glass, probably not having the faintest clue how erotic it was to him. "This reminds me of summer camp. Did you ever go to one?"

"We didn't have them where I'm from." *Keep it platonic.*

"I was thinking about that this morning. 'Lothar' isn't very common here. Well, you're the only one, I wager. Where is it from?"

"I'm originally from a small village in Austria, near Vienna. But I lost my German accent a long time ago when I immigrated to the States." *Back in 1872.*

"Austria? You're far from home." She shook her head. "I don't want to argue, but your accent is still there, especially when you pronounce your R's. They roll at the back of your throat." She stopped abruptly, scratched her neck and looked away. "So what brought you up here?"

"Greed."

She laughed. The most beautiful sound in the world. It cut right through his carapace. "There hasn't been gold up here in quite a while!"

Verdammt!

How his mother tongue came back quickly in times of stress!

Dammit! He'd practically let it slip. His true age and why he appeared in his late thirties when he was over six hundred years old. After Sister Jane's death in 1899, more than a hundred years ago, he hadn't told anyone about his *condition*. Trust was required. And that virtue had long ago been twisted out of him.

"That's what they told me when I got here." Lothar forced a fake smile.

She studied him for a while, as if trying to decide if he were lying, playing with her or being acerbic again.

She shouldn't look at him for so long, not with those eyes like shards of ice, those adorable freckles that made it look as though someone had used a toothbrush and sprayed terra cotta paint on her nose and cheeks.

"Look, Miss Bain," he started, words floating out of his brain when she grinned widely at him. Such nice teeth. Would her mouth feel as soft as it looked? It did, since he'd already tasted it. He wanted so much more than a mere sip.

"Please, call me Erica. No, *you* look," she countered, getting to her feet. "You don't owe me a thing. I'm the one eating your food and taking all the hot water. If you want to keep some things to yourself, that's more than normal. I was just trying to make conversation."

With that she put her glass and utensils on her plate and went to the counter to wash them.

Lothar watched her fine figure from behind, the way her dark wavy hair brushed just past her shoulders, how the small of her back bent inward in a pronounced curve as she leaned against the counter. His most favorite part on the female anatomy, he could—and had done so—spend hours admiring a woman's back.

Whereas most men seemed to enjoy breasts most of all, Lothar took infinite pleasure gazing at the curve of a woman's lower back, the distinct, or not so, camber of her waist, those delectable dimples on either side of the spine. Some of the backs he'd embraced had been proud or nimble, delicate or broad. Back in his native medieval Austria, he'd loved quite a selection of backs. Strong ones, plump ones, delicate ones. And what he enjoyed most, what brought him to the edge in the blink of an eye was to watch the small of a woman's back arching with her rounded bottom up toward him in a voluptuous offering.

Lothar's gaze slid lower, at the way Erica's jeans enfolded her slim behind. He knew other men would find it too subtle, not curvy enough. Fools. All a man—or so-inclined woman—had to do was encourage a slight curve to the spine, apply pressure at just the right point for any bottom to become a most splendid, curvaceous gift. Looking at her again, Lothar could tell exactly where that spot would be for her, about a hand's breadth below the waistline. Heat tingled his palms.

Fight it. Don't let it win.

He closed his eyes but couldn't sever the vision. His member stiffened until it hurt. He knew he'd lost the battle. The devil was rubbing his hands.

Lothar stood.

Chapter Three

ഔ

Erica felt the heat of his hand long before he actually touched her. The skin on the small of her back tingled when his hand came down to rest there, flat and immobile against her. Heat suffused her entire body. Um.

His presence filled the room, dimmed everything else. She didn't turn around to look into his handsome face in case she broke the spell. A frisson spread out from where he had put his hand to the rest of her back. Shockingly, she had to resist the urge to curve her butt up and push against him. Where had he learned *that*!

"I tried," he murmured behind her.

"Tried to do what?"

"Keep my hands to myself."

"Well, I'm glad you didn't. If I had any courage, I would've started things myself."

"You shouldn't—"

"Shh," Erica cut him off. "Like I said, you owe me nothing."

Thunder rumbled closer and shook the windows when it hit. Rain ticked slowly at first, until a veritable deluge slammed against the side of the building.

While she kept her hands clutched around the sink's edge, Lothar slowly, reverently, moved up along her spine, his long fingers tracing each shoulder blade before moving her hair out of the way. His mouth, so soft and burning hot, landed butterfly-light on her shoulder. Through the T-shirt's thin cotton knit, his lips raised goose bumps when he trailed them up to her neck, below her ear. She sighed in contentment.

"No need to talk, okay?" he asked between kisses.

"Fine by me."

A soft chuckle rolled in his chest. Down her arm his hand went. As if he knew exactly where each muscle was attached, he traced them lightly with his middle finger, spent a while circling the crook of her elbow before sliding down her wrist. He circled the small bone there as if it were a clitoris. She couldn't help the gasp of thrill this simple touch elicited.

While he planted his other hand by hers on the counter, he kissed her neck for a long while, as though he meant to spend the night doing so. Desire tightened her pussy. This was good, so good.

Lothar's teeth raked against the curl of her ear, producing instant and sharp satisfaction. She loved when men kissed her ears. He must have known for he lingered there, nibbling softly, kissing, flicking the tip of his tongue at the sensitive lobe until a long shiver raced over her entire body. She felt as if her skin were on fire.

He changed sides then, lavished attention on her other ear while his hand slowly cupped her opposite butt cheek. A light squeeze made her smile. Such a muscled man to be so gentle. Erica closed her eyes and let her head loll back against him when he drew near, and allowed her shoulders to come to rest directly on his wide chest.

Outside, the rain pounded with increasing ferocity against the building while flashes of lightning illuminated the inside right into his bedroom. His hair spilled over his shoulder and along hers when he leaned over and kissed her throat. Burning lips traced a circuitous pattern over her skin. He was the best—hands down—kisser she'd ever been with. No one came even close. And he hadn't even touched her mouth yet.

Reaching behind her, Erica clasped his strong thigh and squeezed. At once, he seized her wrists, pulling them back and slightly up and made her feel pleasantly trapped. The pressure of his mouth accentuated against her throat. She moaned.

Her eyes flared wide when Lothar pressed her hands against his crotch. The size of that thing! She smiled.

Abandoning her wrists—which didn't compel her one bit to relinquish his impressive erection—Lothar encircled her waist and ran his hands slowly up over her T-shirt until they rested under her breasts. They swelled out with each sharp breath. She was so horny she could chew his clothes right off!

Each at a time, Lothar cupped her breasts and raised them slightly, weighed them, rubbed his thumbs against the sides with the soft touch of a bird's wing and when he angled his fingers so her stiff nipples came to rest in the crook of his index and middle fingers, Erica let out a long sigh. While Lothar kissed her neck, he squeezed his fingers together, creating intense, blazing gratification. With her palms still cupped around his crotch, Erica pushed her backside against her hands to create even more pressure. A sharp intake of air announced Lothar must have liked that.

One of his hands abandoned her breast—she could've cried—so he could snake it under her T-shirt then slid back up again to its former location. This time, the contact of skin against skin rounded her mouth in a perfect O. When he began to pull her T-shirt up around her sides, she didn't need telling twice. Up her hands went, as high as a bad guy in a Western movie!

Lothar skillfully slipped it up over her head and let it rest on the counter. Hands back behind her, she pressed them around his button fly as he pulled his sweater and T-shirt off simultaneously. His muscled front felt hot and hard against her back. After he'd pulled his tops off, Lothar sandwiched her against the counter. His breathing was quick and shallow.

When he wedged a thigh between hers, Erica raised herself on the tip of her toes. Lothar wasn't uncommonly tall, perhaps six, six-one, but he had long legs for his height. Her behind fitted so well right below his crotch that she swore she heard the deeply rewarding "click" of two pieces of Lego snapping together.

The analogy felt right somehow. She *had* "clicked" with him right away.

With more urgency, Lothar grabbed her hips and squeezed hard but softened his grip immediately and twisted so she'd turn around. His hair cascaded over his shoulders in a shiny curtain that resembled burnished gold in the candlelight. A feral light danced in his eyes.

Erica angled her chin invitingly and watched him lick his lips before pressing them to hers.

Fireworks!

When she meant to rub his rock-solid flank, Lothar abruptly pulled away to stare down at his feet. "I don't like to be touched there."

She nodded. "What about here?" She wrapped the imposing bulge on his jeans with a hand.

A lascivious grin answered her. He dove back in, sucked in each of her breaths while his parted lips grazed hers. Behind her back, she felt his skilled fingers unclasp her bra—one-handed too! The white cotton straps loosened, the cups slackened like the sheets on a sailboat losing its wind. Lothar stopped kissing her so he could slowly guide one shoulder strap down her arm with his index finger then the other, but he didn't try to uncover her breasts, as though he were keeping that for last. Excitement tightened her nipples, which showed prominently against the thin layer of fabric.

Gradually, Lothar lowered a cup, denuded her breast, her nipple. He did the same for the other. While he watched, Erica heard his breathing stop for a while then resume with a long, drawn-out inhalation.

"You are so—"

Erica put her fingers to his lips. "Shhh. No talking, remember?"

A bright flash of lightning illuminated his hazel eyes and for a second the intensity of his gaze frightened her. Thunder clapped, it would seem, right over the house.

Lothar kissed her deeply, his tongue flicked out, brushed her upper lip and retreated before she could suck it into her mouth. He did that again until she was pushing her face hard against his to try to trap the agile organ. When she met a row of teeth, she realized he was grinning wide. While his hands squeezed and rolled her nipples, Erica kissed him on the neck. Freshly shaven—so smooth. She kissed lower. Lothar froze when she kissed him on his scarred shoulder. She could tell he wasn't terribly comfortable with the notion of her kissing the ruined skin. As though she cared about that!

Softly, she grazed the healthy skin right beside the scar then came back over it, not staying, back and forth, a little longer each time. Then his other side, starting with the shoulder then his defined pectoral. Erica flicked her tongue at the tiny nipples, smiled when they tightened. Lower she went, trailing kisses down over his belly, coming closer and closer to the belt of scars around his sides. Erica was licking his smooth skin when Lothar squeezed her nipples hard enough to make her gasp. She straightened.

"I said *no.*"

Without waiting for her to reply, Lothar kissed her nipples, licked and sucked them until Erica was arching back slightly over the sink and grabbing at the counter behind her so she wouldn't topple over. His agile tongue flicked, whipped, circled, his lips pressed, sucked, and his hands—oh those hands—grabbed her hips and pulled her against him. The combined pleasure created a sharp twitch down to her pussy. She moaned.

He must have understood the signs for Lothar fisted the waist of her jeans and tugged her behind him as he marched for his bedroom.

"Wait, wait," she protested. Prying his fingers off her jeans, she rushed to her overnight bag, rummaged around for her toiletries pouch and brandished a wrinkled condom foil. She must have had the thing there for a year.

Grinning like a loon, she ran back to him, clamped his hand back over her jeans and gave him an enthusiastic twin thumbs-up.

Lothar rolled his eyes and kept going, towing her behind him. Lightning lit up his V-shaped back. Scars there too, of course. With one that looked very much like a stab wound. So many scars on the same body. Had he wrestled naked with an entire pack of wolves or what?

When he stopped, spun and wrapped his powerful arms around her shoulders, they tumbled onto the bed, which creaked under their combined weight. She humphed when he rolled on top, but kept going and ended underneath her. She would've preferred he stayed over her and press her into the mattress.

After straddling him and tossing the condom onto the nightstand, Erica winked as she backed down, mouth and hands busy over his chest—she skipped the ribs region—then directly on his lower belly. Intact, surprisingly enough.

One by one, she flicked the buttons, watching Lothar's expression tightening with each one. When the last button slipped out, Erica parted the jeans and rained kisses on the newly exposed skin. It was darker without the candles but the occasional lightning strike provided enough light to let her know she was looking at one hell of a gorgeous man. He raised his hips so she could remove his jeans and underwear. Like a coil, his cock sprang out of the tight boxer briefs and stood proudly between her hands.

Erica knew her expression betrayed the awe she felt. As far as cocks went, this one was not only thick and long but smooth and perfectly symmetrical. *Wow* was the only word she could think of. And it wasn't an overly eloquent one.

With a soft growl of excitement and territorial delight, she fisted him with her good hand. More than half of it still poked out over her fist. *Can't let that go to waste, can I?* With her mouth, she covered the exposed portion and flicked her tongue underneath. Lothar arched back against the mattress and closed his eyes.

Keeping the skin down, she pulled upward with her mouth, sank around his shaft before sucking back up again. A grimace—she hoped of pleasure—twisted his handsome features. Fists like blocks of pink stone grabbed the sheets over his head. Striated muscles swelled along his chest and sides. Erica continued what was obviously something special for him. Down her hands went, up her mouth pulled.

His fingers snaked in her hair and forced her face away from his burning cock. "Enough," he panted.

With her bum hand, she pushed her jeans down around her hips. Without a word, Lothar stood beside the bed and pulled her jeans off by the hems. After a few twists, both pants and panties slipped down her legs. His nakedness haloed by the flickering candlelight from the next room, he stood immobile, looking down at her until the weight of his gaze triggered a fever over her skin. He picked up her foot by the ankle and brought it up to his lips. The guy had some grip! Hot kisses all over the top of her foot created an array of delightful sensations to zing up her leg.

Okay, no man has ever kissed my feet before. My feet!

Lothar picked up her other leg and gripped both by the ankles, his face hidden behind her feet. So large were his hands that his fingers connected around her ankles like manacles, strong, unyielding. Slowly, he began to pull them apart, his face becoming visible by increments, his muscled neck, his wide chest, the shoulders bulging.

Erica watched in mute awe as he emerged from behind her legs. A lightning strike revealed his expression—raw, intense, gourmand. Wider he pulled her straight legs. Shoulders' width—wider still until he held her ankles at arm's length. Too bad she wasn't more flexible. The broad V of her parted legs underlined his waist and from her supine position, it looked as though his thick cock was already inside her.

His gaze always on her face, Lothar kissed the inside of an ankle, higher along her leg, the sensitive skin behind her knee, the inside of her thigh. Erica's breaths grew labored with his progress. She'd never been made to feel so completely desirable. He was bringing the woman out of her.

Lothar crouched between her raised legs, his powerful arms straight out and up so he could keep his iron grip around her ankles. His chin dipped toward the junction of her legs, his mouth parted. The heat of his breath touched her but his mouth didn't.

Oh the tease.

Erica moaned impulsively. She hadn't even come yet! But she knew she would. With a lover as skilled as he, she predicted for herself the best sex in her life.

Staring at her unblinkingly, he curled his tongue and ran it corner to corner over his upper lip. Erica nearly crimped her legs around his neck to force him down on her. This was more than sex…it was a phenomenon.

Her sex quivered. The thought of that tongue on her…*ahh.*

Finally putting her out of her misery, he brushed her swollen lips once. Only once. It was enough.

Sharp stabs of arousal preceded one serious heat wave down between her legs. *Whew.*

With the excitement, she forgot to keep her legs straight and her knees buckled. Lothar shook his head and increased the force around her ankles. Blood had long ago stopped flowing to her feet. Like she cared!

Working her abdominals to the burning point, Erica locked her knees and made damn sure her legs remained straight out in a wide V.

Tongue leading, Lothar sank against her pussy. Without the usual fumble and make sure it's the right place, his tongue immediately parted her lips, skimmed the length of her entry and flicked her clit with the practiced ease of a connoisseur. No *"am I there, honey?"* Lothar knew what he was doing.

Only the top of his face projected over her mons, illuminated irregularly with lightning strikes, revealing his ardent eyes still fixedly on her face while his mouth worked against her pussy. With a mix of trepidation and eagerness, she felt her folds become slicker with her honey. A powerful suck on her engorged clit triggered a spasm deep in her channel. Without warning, Erica climaxed.

She arched back. A long sigh escaped her. Then another.

With his mouth alone, never releasing her ankles, Lothar brought her repeatedly over the edge only to relent at the precise second where pleasure gave way to soreness. Like a dancer dipping his partner low enough to make her heart race but not enough to scare her.

Lothar kissed the insides of her thighs for a time and she knew he was waiting for the swelling to go down, the sensitivity to diffuse so he could feast on her again. She wondered how many times he could make her come with his mouth alone?

She stopped counting after four.

Erica was arching and clawing at the sheets above her head — pillows long tossed below the edge — by the time Lothar released her ankles. Her feet tingled when circulation renewed.

Whew.

Aroused as never before, Erica hurriedly rolled onto her front and climbed to her hands and knees while he ripped the condom wrapper and slipped the thing on. She wondered for a second if it'd fit. Although she was on the Pill and so damn turned on, the mere lack of latex wouldn't stop her from throwing herself at Lothar.

When he drew near, he tried to push so she'd roll onto her side but she widened her knees and looked back. "No, I want it this way."

A sharp shake of his head indicated his strong opposition to it. "I could hurt you that way."

That had to be a first...a man who didn't want to do it from behind...?

Reluctantly, she rolled onto her back and scooted down so he could fit between her legs. His latex-sheathed cock hanging heavy over his thighs, he leaned over her, his elbows digging deeply on either side of her shoulders.

"Are you sure about this?"

Erica nodded hard enough to dislocate her neck.

Closing his eyes, Lothar let her guide his member into her, where he entered gently by small increments so her channel could stretch to accommodate his thick girth. Good grief, he was huge!

Like a sword sliding into its sheath, the smooth and hot shaft glided, retreated to collect more of her wetness and sank deeper. She could tell the condom was a tight fit as there were none of the usual wrinkles and creases. When his belly touched hers, Erica sighed and wrapped her legs around his waist. Big, almost too much so, he finally sank in completely. A silly sense of pride swelled her chest. Lothar was the best-endowed lover she'd had so far.

His first push was deliberate, as though he were still testing the fit. Erica was afraid to lose her edge so she bucked against him hard. Exhilaration stopped her breath when his cock pushed against the edge of her channel. So she did it again, rocked her hips fast and abruptly to recapture the instant.

Staring down at her, his eyes narrowed, his upper lip twitched. His next push wasn't so gentle. A loud moan left her as she writhed beneath him. *Yes. That's it.*

Lothar slammed his hips forward. With a cry of pain-pleasure, Erica skipped every step and crashed directly to full-blown climax. Fire burned in rings around her cleft.

As she grunted in regret, Lothar wrapped her in his arms and rolled onto his back so she'd straddle him. She'd enjoyed having the weight of him pressing down on her. He was holding himself in check for some reason. She wondered why any man would hold back during sex. Oh well, he wanted her to mount him. So be it. There were worse things in life, right!

Erica sat up, using the headboard as an anchor—her hand burned like hell but she didn't care right then—and gyrated over him, tried to recapture the bliss of a few seconds past. While he seized her waist and pushed his hips underneath her, Erica began to bounce, slowly at first, leisurely then added speed and force as tiny shivers of pleasure tightened the back of her cleft. In a crescendo, her sighs changed to little cries of satisfaction. He was so big, so strong, so hot.

With her arms wrapped over her head, she rolled upward and drove back down hard, adding a twist of the hip, a squeeze of her pussy. Lothar's eyes were closed. He was biting his lip.

More intense now, she pulled out completely before ramming herself over him again and again. Now *that* opened his eyes.

"*Erica*," he snarled, his hands clutched around her waist. His tone was a definite warning.

For a second she wondered what it'd feel like to be taken hard by a man such as him. With the pistons he had for thighs, Erica had no doubt the ride would be epic.

As she rocked over him and sweat clammed them both, connected them, she felt herself coming closer now, a few thrusts away. She bit down as the next orgasm tightened her pussy around his shaft, tingled up to her breasts, before swelling over her in a fiery wave. Lothar echoed her moan when she started panting hard.

After a sharp buck, Erica groaned, spilling her pleasure. Tiny pulsations around the base of his cock announced he'd come too. Together? *Another first.*

Panting, Erica lay on top of him, still encased one inside the other. For some reason she couldn't explain—*and now isn't the time to start digging at that scab*—she knew their union could've been more passionate. If only Lothar hadn't held back. Afraid to hurt her, he'd said. Come on, her, the tomboy! She wasn't made of lace. She could take him.

He gently ran his hands over her back, up and down. After a while, she sat up and caught his expression before he put the impassive mask back on. He looked so *sad*.

"Are you okay?"

Lothar tapped her hip lightly and began to roll over, which gave her half a second to scramble off him. Without a word, he put the box of tissue between them and pulled the condom off.

Erica sat beside him against the edge of the bed. She squirmed while the last throbs of orgasm faded. *Should I say something?*

He looked at her then down at his feet. "Did I hurt you?"

"Nah. I'm all for wild monkey sex." Erica's chuckle died in her throat when he twisted around to look at her fully.

"Be careful what you wish for." He didn't look sad anymore.

His cock was still as stiff as before they'd had sex. He avoided her gaze as he stood, retrieved the wad of tissue and went into the kitchen to dispose of it.

"Are you thirsty?"

"No, thanks."

By candlelight, Erica watched him down an entire bottle of water, his hair spilling back behind his shoulders in a shiny cascade. The golden glow hit his throat, chest and belly while casting the rest of him in twisting shadows. His butt was just as delicious naked as it'd looked clad in denim. The fact that he was still hard bothered her. Hadn't she given him pleasure? She knew he'd come.

"Not that you owe me anything, but did I say something dumb? I'm known for that."

Without looking at her, Lothar closed his eyes. "You have to leave tomorrow, Erica. It's not safe for you here."

A sense of alarm tingled down her spine. She crossed her arms and leaned against the doorjamb to his bedroom. "Why are you so sad?"

"I'm not sad."

She shrugged. *Yeah, buddy, whatever you say.* Although she didn't call him "buddy" to his face. She doubted he'd like that. "You're, well, you're *big* but you didn't hurt me, if that's what bothers you."

Lothar hissed something in what she supposed was German before throwing the empty bottle across the room where it thudded repeatedly against furniture and walls before spinning on the floor.

Temper, temper.

"I see," she said.

He seemed surprised when he looked at her. "And what, exactly, do you see?"

"You have a temper. That's what scares you." Erika snorted a laugh. "We all hold back, you think you're the only one keeping yourself on a tight leash?"

His silence answered her more directly than anything he could've said.

"Okay, I'll start. Right now, I'm holding back because I'd like to chat and laugh and play cards with you. But I know you wouldn't like that so I shut up—well, mostly—and keep it inside."

"It's not the same thing," Lothar began, looked at the ceiling before leaning back against the counter and crossing his ankles. "It's really not the same thing, believe me."

Erica watched his cock still proudly affirming its prowess. Desire began to throb low in her belly. She wanted him again, but for real this time.

"Why isn't it the same? You're a person like I'm a person, like any other Joe out there. We're all doing the best we can. Sometimes we mess up."

"You sound like someone I used to know. She said the same thing—that we're all doing what we can with what we have. Some of us don't work that way. *I* don't work that way."

"So how long will you beat yourself over the head for whatever you think you did?"

"Some things take longer to punish than others."

"Like what?"

"*Verdammt*, Erica, would you just drop it!"

"Yeah, sure, but I don't think it's going to drop *you*."

Lothar didn't move other than turning his head toward her. That was enough. She'd gone too far too fast. Angry didn't begin to describe what he looked like. Alarms pinged in her. Um.

"You like to have the last word, don't you?" he demanded, rounding on her and taking a threatening step. "You think you have me all figured out, that I'm just some poor broken thing who needs to be fixed. Well, you can't *fix* me! There are too many pieces and they're all jagged, Erica, any one of them could cut you."

"I wasn't trying to f—"

She tried not to flinch when Lothar stalked up to her and grabbed her by the shoulders. His fingers dug in her flesh, his mouth landed on hers in a bruising kiss. Lothar slammed her against the wall and kept her there with his hips, stealing her "humph" with his mouth. Alarm and thrill fought for control.

While she snaked her hands in his lustrous hair and fisted it, he left her mouth so he could bite her neck and shoulders. One of his hands clasped her mons, claiming her, his fingers slipping inside. The sharp thrust upward caught her by surprise. Gritting her teeth, she fisted his rock-hard cock, angled it downward and pumped him as hard as she could. He growled deep in his chest.

Erica wasn't sure how he managed it but the next moment she was facing the wall with Lothar's hand wrapped around the back of her neck to keep her cheek against it. When he parted her butt cheek with his other hand and licked her cleft, she let out a yelp of surprise and pleasure. His face and mouth were all over her backside, on her pussy. Sharp climax rose in a swell. Lothar replaced his tongue with fingers so he could spread her honey around her lips. With her hip clutched in his hand, he pulled back toward him so her butt would stick out. A loud clack resounded in the room before a stinging heat radiated all over her ass. He'd slapped her butt!

"Hey!"

Before she could protest further, Lothar released her neck so he could part both cheeks wide. She gritted her teeth for she knew what was coming.

His belly had already made contact with her backside by the time she realized he'd sunk in. Erica gasped at the intense sensation of his member stretching her sex. Right before rapture enveloped her in a quivering cocoon. Orgasmic shivers raced down her back as Lothar slammed into her repeatedly, each thrust more forceful than the one preceding it.

Her sharp moans punctuated the surges of thrill. She was going to come. Hard.

In a merciless piston-like movement, he pushed into her. If she'd wondered what it'd be like to be taken hard by a man such as him, she now knew. It was exhilarating, scary and incredible all at once. Erica had to plant her palms on either side of her shoulders to keep from knocking against the wall under his brutal thrusts. *Oh my…*

Lothar's hands dug in her hips to the point of pain. A mighty shove crushed her against the wall. She nearly blacked out from the intensity of the heights to which he'd taken her. A long moan escaped her.

Just as brusquely as he'd penetrated her, he pulled out.

"What…"

As she was rolling against the wall to look at him, her vision still popping with tiny bursts of light, she spotted him sprinting for the lobby where he wrenched the front door wide and sent it clattering against the wall. Rain hit the lobby floor in thick ropes.

"Lothar!"

She went after him, her sex still throbbing demandingly. He'd left her right on the edge.

"Where are you going?" she yelled into the dark, stormy afternoon.

Rain lashed her face and shoulders as she ventured out onto the first step. She couldn't see him for the sheets of rain whipping her. Cold to the bone, she rushed back inside and hurriedly pulled her clothes back on. What was wrong with him? Was he hurt? Torn between primal fear and compassion, she grabbed her blanket from the sofa, the flashlight he'd put on the counter earlier and rushed outside.

Wind and the torrential downpour made it nearly impossible to see more than ten feet in front. Stumbling on the uneven ground, Erica circled the main building, couldn't see him anywhere and started to jog around the next when she heard a muffled "*TWAK*".

No, he's not…chopping wood?

Blanket rolled under her arm, she kept the beam of light right at her feet so he wouldn't see it before she saw him. Around the corner, she flicked it off. Lothar was there, wielding the axe with such ferocity it split the trunk almost in half. He raised it again and with a growl she could only describe as savage, he brought it down. The axe dug deep in the wood and remained stuck. Lothar's furious tugs didn't succeed in pulling it free. He roared in fury, ripped the axe out and threw it into the woods beyond. It twirled end over end before disappearing within the swaying trees.

Now that he no longer had an axe in his hands, Erica felt braver about approaching. She wanted to help, sure, but she didn't want him to cleave her skull in half before he realized it was she.

He must not have heard or seen her for he didn't turn around, only sank to his knees, his hands gripping the trunk like a man drowning. Wet hair hung in ribbons along his spine and down by his face. His ears jutted out in between flattened locks. There was something peculiar about his back, the way bones protruded sharply. But as she approached, she realized it must have been the poor light making unexpected shadows.

Whatever he's fighting, it's poisoning him from the inside.

The way his back was curved and his shoulders twitched, she knew he was crying. The blanket spread out wide like a matador, Erica crept forward and gently let it settle over him. He didn't acknowledge her. Although his shoulders stopped jerking.

Erica didn't know how long she stayed there, bent over him with the blanket wrapped around his back while a September rainstorm battered them. All she knew was that for once she had to just shut up.

Chapter Four

ᔓ

He'd come so close.

Lothar squeezed his eyes shut. He'd begun to *change*, right there while he was inside her. His knuckles had begun to ache, the skin to tingle. The beast had begun to claw at his soul to be let out.

Over the centuries, he'd changed often enough — because of the moon or out of a sudden surge in his emotional response — to recognize the early signs. Fully enjoying a woman without it triggering the transformation was forever beyond him. He'd had to restrain himself to pleasuring Erica for as long as she could take it while he drank her ecstasy, trying to forget that she received a mere sliver of his skill, of his passion. He was capable of so much more! This condition wasn't a mere curse or disease but his own personal hell, tailored just for him, and punished him by that which he'd sinned. The irony was cruel indeed.

Burning tears mixed with the cold rain. It bled into his mouth while the storm pummeled his bent back, his shaking arms. Lothar cringed when his mind conjured up memories of long ago, back when he was a boy working hard for a crumb of his father's affection. One spring day, when the county physician had come to their little mountain village for his yearly visit, he'd seemed to set his sights right away on Lothar and even offered him to become an apprentice. His parents had been quite glad to "settle" their third and burdensome son.

"*I need someone with a strong back*," he'd said. How true he'd been. Only not in the sense twelve-year-old Lothar had expected.

Under the physician's insidious cruelty—never outright violence, no, that would've been too easy to fight—Lothar had grown to be callous, ruthless and a sadistic monster. Just like his "master".

Feeling sorry for himself had worked for a while afterward. Hell, it'd worked until he'd met Sister Jane at the turn of the twentieth century. Her tough love approach had drawn him out—kicking and screaming—of his shell. Perhaps because there was no carnal hunger involved, she was able to put her obstinate finger right on his wound. Lothar could never tell. She'd loved him unconditionally, without question, for the whole twenty-seven years they had known each other. The devil knew how she could've passed judgment on him. The things he'd done…

After self-pity had come blame. He'd blamed his former lover Katrina for pulling him down into her schemes, for turning him into an even worse brute. But she'd only been the flame while he'd been and continued to be a keg of black powder. Then he'd blamed the physician for twisting Lothar's affection and craving for attention into something ugly, for introducing him to things no boy should know. For despoiling his youth and desecrating his trust.

No amount of blame had made him forget what he'd done to one woman. Scarlet. Like a spark, she'd come into his life and let him see something beyond the edge of the hole he'd dug for himself. But Lothar hadn't been able to stomach that another man would have her and not him. He had *so* ached for her, to possess her…even by force. Love was what he'd called it at the time. Misguided, warped, but love. Wasn't it? He kept repeating to himself how he'd only wanted to have her, not hurt her, while he lay agonizing after Fredrick— another Lothar had deeply wronged—had left him for dead, facedown in the dirt. A fitting end that never came. For with the full moon two nights after their violent battle, Lothar had changed into the beast and healed from his grisly wounds.

A subtle movement brought him reeling back to present times. The blanket felt heavy and comforting around his shoulders, yet not near as soothing as Erica's arm holding it there. She hadn't moved since putting it on him. She was waiting, waiting for him.

A slap of wind shook her, he felt her arm stiffen to keep her balance. She could easily have returned to the house and waited inside—with a cup of tea for him even, if that calmed her conscience. Instead, she chose to be outside where the cold rain and wind whipped them like wet towels. He owed her nothing, she'd said, but neither did she. Why would she put herself through this for a stranger? As much as he tried to rationale the situation, in a selfish way, her presence *did* ease his misery and Lothar was glad she offered it.

He raised his head to look at her. Though the rain lashed at her face and hair and stamped her clothes to her body, Erica held his gaze and smiled.

Without a word, Lothar stood slowly, the blanket falling from one shoulder, which Erica was quick to cover again. He didn't deserve someone like her. Not many men he knew deserved an Erica Bain.

They trudged back to the main building where she pulled and held the door for him. Lothar's shame burned his cheeks. He offered a murmured "thanks" to her before stepping inside the warm living room. Shivers threatened to dislodge his teeth. With a rattling sigh, he sank into a chair, still unable to meet her gaze. He heard her come and go across the kitchen, putting more logs inside the stove, pulling things out of cabinets.

Lothar opened his eyes to realize he must have dozed off, sitting up for a steaming cup landed in front of him.

"The cup is hot, watch out," Erica said as she sat across from him and delicately sipped at her cup.

The strong tea felt good against his lips. He forced himself to swallow the searing liquid, hoping it'd burn away the taste of ashes from his mouth. It did. She must have put half a cup of sugar in there.

He looked up into her gaze and prayed he'd see disgust there, fear, resentment, anything. It'd make things so much easier if she hated him.

He should've known it wouldn't be so. He doubted the woman was even capable of hatred.

A grin played at the corner of her mouth. She indicated the tea with her chin. "Too sweet?"

"It's perfect. Thank you."

"No problem. Although my mom says I cost her a fortune in sugar when I lived at home."

Lothar caught himself pondering what a home with her in it would feel like. Safe no doubt. And cheerful too. Disgusted and annoyed with feelings he shouldn't even harbor, he wrapped his palms over the cup and willingly let it burn him until he could think of nothing else but the searing tea.

"So...er, what's wrong with your plane?" he asked, sighing as he removed his hands from around the cup and took a sip.

She looked angry for the first time since she'd landed — literally — on him the day before. So Erica Bain *was* capable of anger. And judging by the lethal glint in her pale gaze, mercy on the one at the other end of it!

"Someone is going to get spanked for this, lemme tell you. I found pulled-out wires behind the circuit-breaker panel. Can you believe that? Someone didn't connect them properly and they came loose. I'm still wondering how it could have happened."

"Is it something a mechanic could've done?"

She shrugged. "I don't know. I sure didn't mess around with it. I'm still shocked I made it as far as here."

"Where were you coming from again?"

"Some rich guys' lodge about fifty miles north and west of here. If you take the Yukon River and head north, you'll get there. You should've seen the setup they had."

Lothar's spine tingled. He leaned forward, his head cocked. Something bothered him. "If it's a problem that degenerated quickly, how did you make it up there from Whitehorse in the first place?"

Erica opened her mouth to speak, closed it then tried again. "Well...I don't know."

"So it happened at the lodge..."

She shook her head. "I was there barely ten minutes. Even if I've never heard of it, maybe accidents like that happen. Maybe it's a fault with that particular aircraft design...?" She didn't look convinced. De Havilland's Otters were bush pilots' favorite, a real workhorse. The thing could take off and land anywhere, anytime.

"Maybe it wasn't an accident."

Her laugh didn't sound as easy as he'd come to expect. "What do you mean? I'm such a charming woman, everyone likes me!"

"You *are* charming," he replied before his brain could stop the silly remark. He saw her blush deeply and allowed himself the rare luxury of enjoying a woman's reaction to his words, something he used to do with great delight. "But did you leave your plane unattended when you were up there?" Lothar didn't like the sound of that malfunction. What sort of game did those men hunt anyway?

She shook her head. "I was with my plane the entire time...oh but yeah, that's right, I did use their bathroom. Five minutes though, that's not enough time."

"It's plenty when you've planned it beforehand and you know what you're doing."

A strange new sensation settled in his chest. Protectiveness.

He'd never had *that* before. It felt strange, similar to fear but with an added edge of cold fury underneath, a streak of determination to shield something, someone, with his own body if need be. He felt *protective* of Erica Bain. How could that be? He'd never felt protective of anyone except Sister Jane, and even then, she hadn't been the kind to let herself be protected.

Erica was different. She could obviously take care of herself, owned her own company, regularly flew over the rugged High North, was in the constant company of men most probably. She was intelligent, funny and beautiful.

The exact combination that made her off-limit to someone like him.

When she stopped talking and only stared at her empty cup, Lothar realized the rain had abated. The battery-operated clock indicated five p.m. yet he felt as if he'd been up two days straight. He should get some rest for Monday night. But before he could relax, he had to make sure Erica left the station.

"I doubt they'll be able to fly tomorrow, the fog will stay for at least half the day." She agreed with a nod. Lothar couldn't bear the worry he saw on her face. He wished he could comfort her as she'd done him. Comforting someone? Another new concept.

Resolve hardened his fists. She had to leave the station no matter what. He knew what to do.

"I'll drive you down to Dawson tomorrow," he announced before draining his cup. The syrupy last drops clung to the bottom like crystallized sap.

"It's at least a three-hour drive!" she replied, shaking her head. "It's much too far. I could wait until they can fly the parts over…?"

She looked as though she would've wanted that very much.

"No. You have to leave tomorrow. I have *plans*."

* * * * *

260

Erica hadn't slept well. She kept tossing and turning, probably waking Lothar every time. Because the blanket was soaked, she'd slept in his bed beside him. He'd had his back to her the entire night.

Her heart swelled. Why had she expected him to act like a lover? They'd just had friendly sex. More than friendly near the end but sex nonetheless. It's not as if they'd been seeing each other for a long time. Erica tried to remember if she'd ever slept with a man after knowing him less than a day.

Nope.

And without a condom too, when he'd taken her up against the wall. His forceful handling still triggered shivers down her back when she thought about it. *Whew.*

Usually, a second or third date would get a guy a kiss, more if they'd been nice and polite and hadn't looked at her funny when she revealed what she did for a living.

But she'd slept in a strange man's bed—after having the best sex ever—the day after she'd met him. On the other hand, she did feel a connection with Lothar, enjoyed spending time with him, as crazy as it sounded. The guy was obviously—if one based such judgment on the fact he'd made toothpicks out of a complete tree while stark naked in a rainstorm—trying to work things out in his head. It didn't faze her. At least with him it showed he had issues. So she knew what to expect. Or at least to expect *something*.

What plans did he have, she wondered. Why did she have to leave Sunday? Why not the day after? Or the week after… She wanted to stay a lot longer than was polite to do so.

The buzz of the fridge started again. Lights blinked on in the living room. Power. Yay!

She rolled onto her back and let her arm flop where Lothar should have been. *Where he should be right now.*

He'd gotten up and dressed at four that morning. Erica had half expected to hear the axe whacking at some logs. Instead, she heard the buzz of the radio when he'd communicated the day's weather report to Dawson. She knew he was right, there'd be no way in hell Sam was going to push the envelope for her and send someone.

A breaker and some wires, man, that's all I need!

Sam was such a Jerk. Capital J.

After she slipped on the clothes that had dried in front of the woodstove, stiff as cardboard and itchy, she slapped peanut butter on a slice of bread, drank some tea from the still-burning enamel kettle and did her morning ablutions with ice-cold water. The taste of toothpaste made her feel much better.

When she found him outside, fiddling under the hood of his truck — his divine butt stretching the cargo pants tight — she stopped to watch the show. She should've brought popcorn. Hell, she should've brought a bunch of girlfriends *and* popcorn!

The sting of his slap on her own behind made her flush. She may not admit it to anyone but she kind of hadn't minded. Well, okay, she'd enjoyed it. There.

"I still think it's not safe to take to the roads after that deluge yesterday," she remarked as she drew near.

"Didn't you land your plane on a river with half of you sticking out the door?" He straightened to look at her.

"Well, *I* am a professional, kids," she replied as she rubbed her nails on her chest.

"And I'm a professional driver."

"You are? Wow. Racing, you mean? Rallies?"

"Nothing like that, let's just say I've been driving for a long time."

A flicker of smile pulled his decadent lips to one side. In spite of the nasty scar — or perhaps because of it — he was positively the cutest man she'd ever seen. A wonder she'd never heard of him before. Whitehorse was maybe too big and too far, but Dawson? She'd been there plenty of times and yet had never heard a peep about the hunk living a few hours away…by his own self. Were women suddenly blind and stupid around these parts?

Too bad for them. And good for me!

"How old are you anyway?" she blurted out before checking with her brain. She had to stop doing that, especially around him.

He looked about to answer but stopped himself. "Older than you think."

"Yeah? Try me, I'm good at this." She tapped an index finger against her chin. "I'd say upper thirties, maybe forty. Max. So?"

"Close enough." He closed the hood and wiped his hands on a rag.

"Guys' rags are always red. Why?"

His laugh startled her. It must have taken him by surprise as well for Lothar quieted, wiped his hands meticulously— good thing he had only ten fingers—and stared at her.

"I wish I would've met you earlier. Much earlier."

"Says the guy who wants to kick me out of his house."

The sparkle died from his eyes. "Let's go, I want to be there when the airport garage opens."

"A three and a half hours drive before, oh—" she checked her watch "—nine o'clock? Like two hours from now? That poor old thing won't make it."

When she checked inside, she noticed he'd already packed for the road. The guy never slept? She gathered her stuff, the blown breaker and her jacket before climbing into the rumbling truck. Lothar looked good behind a wheel. He'd put his fleece over a gray turtleneck, which he kept unrolled. She wondered if he was trying to hide his scarred throat. All that shiny hair was back in a golden-brown ponytail behind him. She liked it better loose.

With a last check her way, he shifted the truck into gear and a loud whoop escaped her. Yippee!

A great lurch sent her rocking in her seat. She tightened the seat belt and grabbed the "holy shit" handle in a death grip. Despite the burns on her hand, she held that thing as if her life depended on it. It probably did. If she lacked finesse with a plane, the guy was a total maniac with his truck. A wonder the thing had lasted so long.

Steering with confidence and quite a bit of aggression, Lothar maneuvered the big truck down a path she hadn't seen earlier that led deeper into the forest. They passed the downed trees—his therapy couch—and Erica wondered for a second if he'd found his axe.

Across a small brook, down a gentle ravine, Erica kept an eye for the road and one for him. He looked...*free*, as bizarre as it sounded. Gaining momentum for a steep climb coming up, he leaned forward and narrowed his eyes.

"Hang on."

She did. When they reached Dawson, they'd have to use a crowbar to pry her fingers off the handle!

The engine roared when he gunned it, twisted the wheel at just the precise angle needed for traction but without sending the truck into the deep underbrush. Rocks scraped the bottom with an awful noise. Erica cringed. So this was how it felt like to fly with her. Um. She'd remember that.

Rattling like beans in a can, Erica and Lothar leaned sideways when the truck climbed higher on one side than the other.

"You sure you don't want me to wait at your place? I'll be very quiet," she said through her teeth.

Lothar threw a quick glance her way. "You're not afraid, are you?"

"Pfft! Of course not." Ha.

After an hour, if Lothar were to have asked that question again, she would've spilled her pathetic guts all over the dashboard. She was *terrified*.

While the road narrowed until branches scraped on either side, a fine mist began to fall. The wipers were on, creating a rhythmic, hypnotizing whirr. Erica put her palm to her forehead. She wasn't feeling too good right then. A violent jolt rocked her forward then back in her seat.

Gulp. *Uh-oh.*

"Not in the truck," Lothar said as he hurriedly rolled the wheel one-handed and hung on his own "holy shit" handle. They cleared the roughest section yet and emerged onto a wider road. No, not *emerged*, they *blasted out* onto the highway.

A smooth surface, good grief! She'd never been so glad to see packed gravel!

She nodded weakly as she put both hands on the dashboard. The bandages were wrinkled from holding on for dear life. She made a fist to keep them tight.

"How's your hand?"

"It stings a bit."

Thankfully, he pulled over and stopped the truck. Erica closed her eyes to better appreciate the lack of movement. It'd been close. How humiliating would it have been if she'd lost her breakfast in the guy's truck? A bush pilot with motion sickness. Funny.

He got out, retrieved something from the tailgate and circled the truck. She smiled at him when he opened and held the door with his hip. Erica couldn't help it, she liked him more and more, which meant he'd have to suffer more and more of her silly grins.

When he was done rubbing his fingers with a wet towelette, he shook his hands to air dry them. "Let me see."

She showed him her hand. Lothar undid the bandages and turned her hand over and back. He had that doctor look again.

"Did you pick at it?"

"Jeez, you sound like a doctor. No, I didn't pick at it. I only go for scabs, not raw flesh."

His nose crinkled. "Everyone picks."

While he applied fresh gauze, she kept her gaze on his face. Not even five seconds later she was horny as hell. Lothar was bent over her hand, like a suitor about to kiss it, so he couldn't see her other hand snaking past his shoulder and fingering the smooth ponytail. He visibly tensed when her fingers raked through his hair.

"You don't like it?"

"That's not the point. I can't work this way," he replied tightly.

She saw what he meant when he straightened and looked down at himself where his pants bulged below the belt.

Erica wiggled her eyebrows. "Good thing you're done then."

His grin would've powered a small city. Pushing away on the dashboard the miniature version of the first-aid kit he had at home, Lothar parted her knees so he could stand between and planted a passionate kiss on her mouth. She held on to his fleece collar and leaned back to force him harder against her. With the truck's height, his crotch aligned perfectly with hers. All she needed to do was spread wide.

With much more passion than the night prior — well, before he took her against the wall — Lothar tugged her T-shirt out of her chinos and readily went for her breasts. She helped him undo her pants and twisted one leg out of the shoe and underwear. His fingers were demanding when he began to rub her pussy. She was already so wet. A sharp little cry left her as Lothar simultaneously pinched her nipple and stroked her clit. Her hands in his hair and making a big mess of his shiny ponytail, Erica scooted closer to the edge of the seat and pushed his head against her chest. Oh and perceptive too! Good man.

With a snarl, he yanked her T-shirt up, her bra cup down and clamped his lips on her breast.

"*Ohhh.*" She didn't even try to keep it in. Her voice grew proportionally louder with Lothar's vigorous sucking.

And here I thought I wasn't a Scream Queen.

He pulled away to look at her. "Condom?"

"I don't have one. You?"

He shook his head then looked as though he wanted to pull away. It hadn't seemed to bother him the night before when he'd taken her standing. Neither had she, for that matter.

"I don't think so," Erica said as she fisted the front of his fleece jacket to keep him from leaving. "I'm on the Pill, it's okay."

Hazel eyes narrowed for a second, he looked as if he needed a bit of convincing.

She could do that.

Reaching down between her legs, she wrapped a hand over his tented crotch and stroked him. Good grief he was big.

With a muttered curse, Lothar dove back in and managed to bring her closer to an orgasm than she'd ever been with only a guy's mouth on her breast. *He is gooood.*

She felt his other hand snake around her butt and drag her closer still. Never pulling his mouth from her nipple, Lothar relinquished her pussy so he could undo his pants and his hazel gaze riveted to hers, he curled his spine and scooped her up with his hips. The tip of his cock rubbed hard against her bud and triggered instant ecstasy but when he continued to push, thrust up in one precise and controlled shove, Erica couldn't keep the cry inside.

Lothar drowned it with his mouth. While he held on to the edge of the truck's cabin with one hand, he kept her waist tightly cinched with his other, easily able to wrap it all the way around. Her channel stretched impossibly wide around his thick shaft with a slight burn at her entrance that only served to accentuate the next wave. She was coming again and fast.

As with her last orgasm, Lothar sucked it out of her mouth, bit her lips. Her hand slipped against the dashboard and she would've fallen over backward had he not crushed her to him with his arm. Of their own volition, her legs wrapped with a great spasm around his waist. She forced herself not to dig her heels in his sides for his scars. But she wanted to!

"Lothar," she cried out, amazed she'd moan a guy's name this way. No shame.

When she groaned his name again, he pulled his face from over her shoulder and stared at her. The irises grew larger, darker, his nostrils flared. A marked curve pulled his upper lip. Growling—literally *growling*—he gave a great push upward that sent her arching back with uncontrollable rapture. Tiny jets of fire announced he'd come as well.

Erica panted hard as she rode the multi-layered wave. Her eyes closed, she couldn't see Lothar but felt him press his face against her chest and remain there, puffing against her white T-shirt. The heat of his breath startled her. It was *hot*. Then his breathing slowed, his arm around her waist slackened. After a time, she felt him straighten.

"Whew," Erica sighed as she opened her eyes. "My, that was…that was…*whew*."

His ponytail had dissolved around his shoulders. After he pulled out of her and fished around the glove compartment, he gave her a thick wad of napkins, keeping some for himself. She only noticed then that he was bleeding from the mouth.

"Hey, what's wrong?"

Lothar hurriedly retrieved the first-aid box, put it under his arm, turned around and dabbed his mouth before heaving his member back in his pants. *Dammit.* Erica tried to wipe his semen from her while simultaneously kicking her foot back in the underwear, pant leg and shoe. And not doing a very good job at it either.

"What's wrong? Lemme see."

Finally, after wrestling herself back in some semblance of order, she jumped out of the truck and joined Lothar as he stomped back around toward the driver side. Her hand on his elbow froze him.

"Did you bite yourself? What happened?"

"I'm fine," he replied tersely. His gaze softened then he nodded. "I'll be fine now. Just got carried away."

"Well, I'll say," Erica replied with a wide grin. "Your poor old truck!"

A roll of his eyes told her he'd be all right.

Chapter Five

୫୬

He'd been about to change again, right there in the middle of lovemaking. Lothar knew Erica had seen his eyes change. Her expression had told him so. Already his fangs had begun to grow, despite his desperate efforts to keep them in check.

Amazingly, the beast had receded by itself. And he wondered what had caused it to. Was it because of Erica and how different — *alive* — she made him feel? Could it be that with her, he didn't experience any of the gut-wrenching fear and suspicion that she'd eventually try to control him?

While he held her in his arms, with her body pushing up against his so he'd take her more deeply, Lothar had felt more energized than he'd been in a long time.

For one moment, one shining, lightning-quick moment, Lothar had forgotten about his curse. Erica's passionate embrace and her calling his name had pushed the darkness back for the lifespan of a spark. He'd reached orgasm without any of the usual guilt or pain involved and this for the first time in…ever?

Even back with Katrina, his former flame, he'd never been able to achieve climax without the added layers of power and pain. His body would reach it without problem, but in his mind… He'd always known something was missing.

Not so with Erica.

Her heart was pure and true and colored her partiality — he wouldn't be disillusioned enough to call it affection — for him with a vibrant palette of colors. With her, Lothar had allowed himself to experience the moment, an instant of untainted ecstasy, a flash of joy both physical and emotional. It'd been *exquisite.*

A stolen glance at her revealed the satisfied half smile lifting her mouth. He too pleasantly tingled all over.

Erica stifled a laugh.

He realized with shock he *wanted* to know what she thought, what had amused her.

"What?"

"Tell me how come there aren't any women lined up from Whitehorse to here waiting for a date with you?"

"A date with me?"

By the corner of his eye, he saw her turn to him. "You're gorgeous. So how come I don't have to fight through hordes of females to get at you?"

Lothar knew and had always known he was pleasing to the eye—that had been his "tutor's" reason for noticing and bringing him back to the city. Growing up tall and strong, much taller than most in his time even if he wasn't unnaturally so by twenty-first century standards, had earned him many compliments and even more attentions. There had been soirées spent pleasuring rows of women, anyone he chose, until he couldn't remember whom he'd already embraced and who remained to be. After his fight with von Innsbruck, the one that had left him scarred, Lothar had thought his looks considerably diminished. Not so in Erica's eyes, it would seem. This pleased him greatly.

"I doubt 'hordes of females' would go after a man like me," is all he said.

She mumbled about there being something in the water that made women dumb and blind. Lothar couldn't keep the grin off his face.

The intimacy of the truck ended too soon as signs for Dawson City started popping up at regular intervals. There was also more traffic on the road. Definitely no place for the kind of encounter they'd had earlier. He caught himself wishing to spend more time with Erica.

As in the rest of the Yukon, wilderness gave way to city in the blink of an eye. First, black spruce as far as the eye could see then the city limits right afterward. It reminded Lothar of Europe in a way, this lack of suburban transition.

"I'm starving," Erica announced suddenly. "Could we stop at The Greasy Spoon?"

"The 'greasy' spoon?"

She laughed. "It's more accurate than its real name."

He had to admit she was right. The few times he'd stopped at that restaurant hadn't particularly pleased his Viennese palate. Although his collar had lost much of its former starch after spending a little over a hundred years in the High North, moving from place to place, he still enjoyed a fine meal once in a while, with some sweet German wine and chamber music. That required flying down to Vancouver, the closest city large enough to satisfy his occasional thirst for delicacies…or a sudden bout of nostalgia.

Puffing his cheeks, Lothar rolled down his window. An unexpected hot flash had just reminded him how close the full moon was. Only one night left. After he checked his nails for the telltale discoloration and finding none thus far, he gripped the steering wheel harder. It always came. First, there'd be a slight purplish tint to his fingernails, then his gums would start to ache, after would come the sensation of his teeth becoming loose. As a physician, he'd come to study the subtlest precursors of the change and noted them carefully so he could better predict how long he had until the beast ripped out of him. For sometimes the moon wasn't yet high in the sky that he'd change. Depending on the weather, if there was a thick cover of clouds or not, he'd transform early or late. He'd discovered moonlight affected him more than the actual full moon. But his body would always show the same signs in a remarkably accurate sequence, no matter the weather or atmospheric changes.

Lothar drove into Dawson City just as his gums indeed began to ache. He tried not to show the discomfort so Erica wouldn't ask questions. He knew she had a bag of them tucked away somewhere.

A quaint main street, flanked on either side with tourist-oriented little shops ranging from general stores — *three* of them — to eating places like The Golden Spoon aka "The Greasy Spoon", stretched for a couple of corners before the wilderness reclaimed its dominion. He remembered back in the early 1900s saloons and brothels had lined the street. How things had changed.

Lothar parked the truck in front of The Golden Spoon and cut the engine. Beside him, Erica was unbuckling her seat belt.

"My treat," she said, "it's the least I can do."

"Are you sure you want to be seen with 'Mr. Personality'?"

"Absolutely."

His ego swelled to dangerous proportions at the way she let the single word drop.

She leaped out of the truck, closed the door with a resolute bang and waited by the front bumper for him to join her. Lothar was already uncomfortable with the many stares he usually generated but with Erica's presence, it was getting ridiculous. After he pulled the door and held it for her, Erica strode inside the restaurant and gave a brisk shake of her head as greeting to the owner.

Johanna hurried down the length of the counter to greet Erica, the sparkle of a good bit of gossip already shining in her dark eyes when she spotted Lothar. She grinned widely as she handed two menus over the counter. Several heads swiveled toward the entrance, inspected the newcomers then returned to their dining. The restaurant's rustic décor was trying hard to recapture the Gold Rush days. It was close but needed some tweaking. For starters, it was missing can-can girls.

"It's been a while, love," Jo said to Erica. Her gaze flickered to Lothar.

He nodded but didn't return her smile. She'd never smiled at him before, only looked at him like a squirrel would a bear.

Or a wolf.

Erica nodded enthusiastically. "What? Two months, I'd say? My plane broke down, did you hear?"

Lothar snorted mentally. Of course she'd heard, as had half the population in the Yukon.

A table cleared just to their left and Erica marched for it with the determination of a Roman soldier. He had to admire her hermetic composure. She didn't seem to care people were watching them over their coffee mugs nor did she turn to look at a couple who glanced her way a bit too long to be mere acquaintances. The man did anyway, as for the woman, she looked because her companion did. Lothar recognized the baseball-cap-wearing man as one of the bouncers working at the Midnight Sun, the only bar for miles on end. Lothar had gone there twice, both visits had ended with the same result. He'd been challenged to step outside by overconfident drunkards, which he'd refused to do, causing the exact thing he'd wished to avoid in the first place. He hadn't gone back again.

When Lothar sat across from her, the vinyl seat squeaked plaintively. Definitely not Gold Rush epoch.

"I'm so hungry, I could eat lettuce," Erica announced with a big grin. Her eyes scanned left to right quickly as she perused the twenty-four-hour menu where everything came with a side of fries. Even fries.

Lothar looked at how her lips moved when she read the items on the menu. A sudden pang of arousal made him shift in the vinyl seat, which squeaked in protest again.

"Aren't those seats fun?" she said without lifting her gaze. She wiggled so her seat would answer his.

So unladylike. But then again, she wasn't a lady was she? No, he thought as he traced her jaw with his gaze. She was all woman. With a cough, he concentrated on his menu and stopped mentally peeling the clothes off her back. His stiffening cock already throbbed enough as it was.

Erica knew people stared at her but she'd be damned if she would let it show. Lothar ordered a hamburger and fries so she skipped breakfast fares as well and went for a club sandwich, extra mayo. Her brothers had always teased her about her stainless steel stomach. Both Lothar and she asked for iced tea. That pleased her somehow, that they'd share simple things this way.

Good grief. Steven.

How could she have had a crush on him?

Erica surreptitiously leaned to her left so she could look past Lothar's wide shoulder at a couple sitting a few tables down. Steven—hockey captain and high school crush—sat facing her. He didn't ignore her this time. How shocking! But his wife hadn't either and turned her perfectly coiffed platinum head around, either to check out Lothar or to see who her husband was nodding at. Erica smiled. Wife didn't.

Oops.

In spite of her, Erica couldn't help comparing Steven with Lothar. Even if there wasn't anything in common between the two men. Still, she perversely enjoyed it for the few seconds it lasted and that was that.

As much as Lothar was all long hair, compact muscles and chiseled, aristocratic features, Steven was the baseball-cap-wearing sports guy working in a bar. Cute, sure, but nothing more. Not that there was anything wrong with it, only that baseball caps on grown men, sitting in restaurants on top of things, kind of left her cold. His eyes were smaller than she remembered and meaner too. But he *was* a wife beater, according to rampant rumors. She believed them all. About him anyway.

When Jo put their plates down, Lothar managed a tight "thank you" that looked as though it'd hurt him. Erica had an attack of the giggles. Poor guy.

When he started to eat, she couldn't get over his manners. He must have been the only patron with his paper napkin on his lap!

Between fries, she wiped her mouth, ran her tongue over her teeth to make sure there was nothing embarrassing and smiled with her mouth closed. "Like I said, '*greasy* spoon'."

She gave him a conspiratorial wink that seemed to make him uncomfortable for he shifted in his seat again. The resulting squeak made her want to laugh but for his sake, she didn't.

"How long have you been working at the station?"

He diligently wiped his mouth then replaced the napkin on his lap. "Nine years."

"Where were you before? In the Yukon?"

A strange look came over his face, like he wanted to say something but couldn't bring himself to. Odd.

"It's my first tour as meteorologist. Before that I was working as a medical aide for a charitable organization."

"Ahh, *that's* why you're so good at this." She did a "Royal Wave" with her bandaged hand.

She couldn't quite picture him doing that sort of work. He didn't really have bedside manners. Although he had bedside *skills*. Har har.

"How long have you been flying?"

For a second, she realized he was changing the subject and doing it rather abruptly but she went with him. If the guy didn't want to talk about his past, then she had to respect that.

"I've been my own boss for seven years. It took that long to get enough money to buy my plane. I used to work for a small charter airline before that."

"There's only you then?"

Warmth flushed her cheeks. Was he asking what she thought he was asking? She nodded.

Lothar quieted, looked at her for a while then returned his gaze to his plate.

Erica spent an enjoyable meal with Lothar and too soon had to face the fact that she couldn't stall any longer. She'd have to go to Sam's and buy the parts she needed. That meant she'd repair her plane and fly back down to Whitehorse the next day.

Why does that make me want to chew down some antacids?

Lothar let her pay without the testosterone-induced fuss guys were known for. They were walking out when Steven caught up to them.

"Hey, Erica," he said, beaming and totally ignoring Lothar by her side.

Now was that rude or was that rude!

"Hey, Steven, how are you, bud? This is my friend Lothar. Lothar, Steven. We went to school together." Implicitly, she let each man know where the other stood. One *used to be* an acquaintance in her past life while the second was a friend *now,* in her present life.

Clearly annoyed, Lothar nodded while Steven stared. "Don't see you here often, Lautawr."

Had he butchered the name on purpose? Erica felt like pointing out Lothar pronounced his name Low-Taarr.

A standoffish shrug from Lothar was all Steven got.

She had the distinct impression each man knew the other, although it didn't seem to be a friendly connection.

Why had Steven decided today was the day he'd stop ignoring her? Through her uneasiness, Erica smiled extra wide and shoved her hands in her pockets. "So, how's Jennifer?"

"She's doing fine," replied his wife as she stepped out of the restaurant.

Erica could actually *feel* the ice forming on her wings. She had to jettison Steven and fast. Looking pissed off and edgy, Lothar was already going for the truck.

"Well," she said as she began to turn around. "It was nice running into you guys. See you some other time, right."

Then two things happened. Well, three but it was hard to count that fast.

First, Steven put his hand on her elbow to keep her from turning away while Erica instinctively tried to snatch it back.

Second, his wife stared a gun at him before cringing when he raised his fist as though to hit her. He didn't. But with a split second retrospect, Erica realized that from the angle Lothar must have thought Steven was raising his hand against her. Not his wife. But her. Erica.

And that was when the third thing happened.

With his face set in stone, Lothar charged back, grabbed Steven by the front of his sports jacket, ripping the felt sleeves instantly, and violently body-checked him into the brick wall of the restaurant. While he fisted the front of Steven's shirt, Lothar managed to haul the man high enough that his feet no longer connected to the sidewalk. An awful sound like crunching lettuce accompanied his fist when it rammed into Steven's face. Lothar had struck three more times when Erica got to him and hung on his fleece-clad piston of an arm to stop him.

Everyone started yelling at once.

Jennifer was screaming hysterically as blood started pouring—*pouring*—from Steven's mouth and nose. Erica was dividing her yelling between the wife to tell her to quiet down and Lothar to demand what the *hell* had gotten into him.

Patrons from the restaurant rushed out to latch onto Lothar's shoulders and arms and pull him back. Someone had their cell phone out and frantically punched numbers.

Then as suddenly as the whole mess had begun, Lothar stopped trying to bash Steven's head against the wall and pulled back, haughtily jerking his jacket back over his shoulders and throwing dark looks all around.

"Lothar…" Erica began, clamped her mouth shut and shook her head in dismay. Talk about a *temper*. Jeez.

She stared at him but he looked away and angrily adjusted his sleeves — making the closest people flinch nervously.

By the time the police Bronco showed up, Lothar was leaning on the bumper of his truck with three or four guys standing in an unresolved-looking barrier between him and Steven. Her ex-crush had slumped to the ground and was holding his nose by the bridge. There was *a lot* of blood. He kept pushing aside Jennifer's hands.

Trying to explain to the officer that Lothar had busted Steven's chops for…well, not a very good reason but plenty of good intentions took all her energy and left Erica drained and shaky. With typical small-town lack of sensationalism, the polite but resolute constable looked at Lothar and hooked his thumb over his shoulder. As if it were a regular event. *Okay, Angry Drunk of the Week, get in the truck.*

With a dark glare, Lothar sat in the back of the Bronco and buckled his seat belt.

Erica approached the front window. He leaned down between the two front seats and looked at her but didn't speak. His eyes looked much darker than usual.

"Are you all right?"

He nodded.

"Did you get hurt?"

A shake of his head. For the first time since she'd met him, Erica felt a very real tingling of fear tighten the back of her neck. Lothar honestly had some issues to deal with.

She cleared her throat and stuck her hand in the cabin. "Can I take your truck? I'll get my stuff from Sam and come pick you up at the station, okay?"

The keys felt heavy and cold when he dropped them in her hand. She noticed his shook.

"We'll straighten this out at the station, ma'am," said the constable before he climbed in. "It'll take a few hours though, swing by later in the afternoon."

With that, he took Lothar away.

Erica turned to face the small crowd and felt her cheeks flush. With anger or embarrassment or both she wasn't too sure. The day had started out so well.

Chapter Six

❧

"You're such a charming person, Sam," Erica sneered as she flicked the clipboard around, signed for the needed parts while he clipped her credit card in his old-fashioned slide machine with the carbon paper. She shook her head.

"I heard what happened at Jo's," Sam remarked waspishly. "I always said that foreigner was a cracked pot."

"He's been in the Yukon for almost ten years, he's hardly a foreigner."

Sam only shook his graying head. Smells of cigarette made her want to take a step back from the counter. "Cracked pot just the same."

Anger flushed Erica's face. She gritted her teeth against the remarks piling on her tongue. "You don't even know him."

"Steve's going to press charges I heard. Can't blame him."

Erica balled a fist around the pen. "Yeah, I bet he doesn't like it when other people do the punching."

A narrowing of the eyes told her she'd pissed him off. Good. Lothar may have overacted a tiny bit…yeah, well, okay, a *big* bit, but at least his intentions had been good. The look on Jennifer's face when Steven raised his fist told Erica all she needed to know. Unfortunately, the police might not see it that way. Whatever plans Lothar had for Monday, he would apparently need to reschedule.

Sam disappeared in the shop adjacent to the radio room and came back soon after with a plastic bag in his nicotine-stained hand. He tossed it on the counter and turned his back to her when the radio beeped on.

"Your clients from Blackstone called last night," he threw over his shoulder. "On the phone. Wanted to know if you were all right and where you'd be for the next few days."

"Not Blackstone, they're in Miner's Point…" But Sam had picked up his mike and was pointedly ignoring her. After flipping him the bird—something she'd never done since high school—she grabbed the bag and headed back to the truck. With the size of radial mudders Lothar had, she needed to hang on to the "holy shit" handle just to get behind the wheel.

After she did a quick stop at one of the general stores to replenish the supplies she'd used at Lothar's place, she pulled into the Royal Canadian Mounted Police station parking lot—deserted except for the constable's Bronco. Erica couldn't help feeling responsible for Lothar's predicament. He was in this mess because of her. If she hadn't proposed to eat at The Greasy Spoon, they wouldn't have met Steven. If she hadn't dropped down on Lothar, literally, he wouldn't have come to Dawson in the first place. Of course, one didn't choose where one made an emergency landing.

The heavy aluminum and glass door made a *whoosh* when she pulled it out and stepped up to the reception. White melamine and government-issued office equipment—beige or gray or a combination of both colors—were set pell-mell around the place with stacks of folders piled dangerously high on every flat surface available.

"Are you here to get him?" the constable asked when he emerged from an adjacent office. The neon lights shone against his skull through his thinning hair.

Erica nodded with a grin. "How much trouble is he in?"

"Steven won't press charges, so Mr. Kessler can leave right now."

Mental note—give that lying jerk Sam a piece of my mind.

While she filled out a long, double-sided form, she heard them come back and lifted her head just in time to catch

Lothar's reaction when he saw her. Relief. Embarrassment. Anger. Much anger.

When he signed his name—a large, looping signature fit for a king—inside one of the many spaces, she noticed his hand shook badly. His nails looked darker too, like he'd been pinching the tips to stop the circulation.

Outside, Erica meant to give him his keys but he shook his head. He looked preoccupied, kept checking his fingernails. "I'm not fit to drive."

"And I'm not fit to be driven around by you."

Her attempt at humor didn't catch. In silence they sat in the truck, buckled up and headed out of town with the sun already starting to dip toward the MacKenzie Mountains. Ominous clouds gathered like a flock of gray sheep. She rolled her shoulders when an image of their enthusiastic lovemaking flashed in her mind and created a nice little heat down there. She felt Lothar's gaze on her.

"I thought he was going to hit you."

"I know."

Several more traffic signs announcing towns hundreds of miles away flashed by in green rectangles by the time Lothar spoke again.

"Did you get what you needed for your plane?"

"Yeah, Sam had it right in the shop so it was easy. Funny though, he said my party called to ask if I was all right. I hope they don't need anything up there because I'm not due to pick them up until Sunday. They're quite the bunch, those guys. Had me going to the wrong place, can you believe it?"

"What do you mean?"

"Told me halfway up that they'd made a mistake in destination, so I had to fly up to Miner's Point Lake instead of Blackstone, which isn't anywhere close."

"They had you change destinations at the last minute and called to know if you were all right?"

Something in Lothar's tone made her turn toward him for a quick glance. "What?"

"How did they know you were in trouble? Didn't it happen after you left?"

She shrugged. "Everyone knows everything up here."

Still, the thought bothered her and it obviously troubled Lothar as well for he crossed his arms and scowled. "I don't think you should go pick them up. Let them sit there."

"Good grief, Lothar, you can't do that to clients, let them sit in the boonies. They won't have food or anything. It's part of the contract. Jeez!"

He shook his head. "When you repair that plane, you should go back to Whitehorse and charter someone else for them. I don't like it."

Erica couldn't help the twinge of anger. She wasn't prone to it. She'd had to learn patience with two big brothers! Yet, that Lothar looked so eager to get rid of her needled her pride and budding sense of affection.

"I'll start on the repairs as soon as we get back. Shouldn't take me too long before I get out of your space."

By the corner of her eye, she saw Lothar turn toward her and run a hand in his hair. It was loose. Saliva seeped under her tongue. She wanted to bury her face in that silky mane like nobody's business.

"I'm not in a hurry to see you leave. There's just something I need to deal with for a day or two. Then…"

"Then…?"

"Then I could go down to Whitehorse. Maybe see you?"

Her heart fluttered. That'd be nice. *Very* nice. "Do you hike?"

"Yes. Why?"

"Not next week but the one after, I'm off, going hiking with some friends. Have you ever been to Prince George? It's gorgeous."

He didn't reply. Was he miffed that she'd be surrounded by friends and he'd only be one of them? Or was he interested in hiking but with her alone? Maybe he just didn't care either way.

"I'd like that," he replied at length.

A smile crept back to her face. She must have spent most of the day scowling, surely a first for her. She nudged him on the shoulder. "My friend Tina is going to *love* you."

"Oh?"

"She has a thing for men with long hair."

After a quick smile, Lothar was back to his preoccupied self.

With much less speed but much more grace, she veered off onto the dirt road leading to the station, noticing only then a small sign indicated the way. The big truck leaned and rattled and groaned over rocks and roots and into puddles of mud, but at least it didn't feel like it'd tip over every ten feet. Leaning forward in the seat, she narrowed her eyes as she navigated the unstable road. Rain had reduced the narrow strip to one long mud pit with the occasional hole or bump to add spice to their life. Erica smiled with relief when she steered the truck past the last bend and spotted the station between the trees.

"There, sir," she quipped in her bad British accent imitation.

Strips of brown and purple slashed the sky, evening loomed closer as they emptied the truck of the stuff she'd bought and the couple of things for her plane. The back of her hand itched. As she rubbed it against her thigh, Lothar came over and wrapped his much large one over.

"You're going to get it infected," he said, his voice low, his eyes ardent.

Something was different about him. Erica couldn't place it. He looked fidgety, tense, as though he was waiting for something unpleasant, yet at the same time, his expression was no longer one of repressed anger but of cautiousness...someone testing the water.

Not kissing him was hard. But she had to use the little bit of sunlight she had left to start the repairs.

"Yes, Doctor Lothar."

He hurriedly released her hand and looked away.

Issues. Plenty of them. Um.

Plastic bag in hand, Erica went to check on her plane. Poor thing looked so sad tied to the pier. It still smelled of fire retardant and burned plastic. Crouching behind the front seat, she stretched out on her side so she could get at the circuit-breaker panel and replaced the faulty piece. With only a few wires to reconnect, she straightened so she could drag the toolbox to her and spotted Lothar standing on the pier with his hands in his pockets. The generous crotch of his cargo pants was filled with his fists and member. Erica couldn't repress the frisson of arousal. Was he gorgeous or was he gorgeous! The plane could wait. She wasn't in a hurry to leave anyway.

"I need to send the balloon. Do you want to come with me?"

Erica laughed. "No one has ever offered me that before. Sure I'll go watch you 'send the balloon'."

She followed him up the narrow trail to the highest part of the station where they were afforded a nice view of the rest of the buildings and the pier. Her white and red plane gleamed in the last rays of the sun.

After he unlocked the door to a small, corrugated metal building, Lothar went inside and came out holding a package of red fabric or plastic, a white box with a funny-looking tube sticking out the top and a tank.

Erica watched him get his things ready, fill the red helium balloon from the tank and hold it still while he untangled the lines dangling below it.

"Can you clip it to the probe?" He pointed to the white box.

With not a clue about what she was doing, she held the box steady while he clipped it to the lines, bunched his fist around them and raised it above his head. A bit of wind caught his loose hair and stirred it in his face. Erica resisted the urge to tuck it back for him. She wanted to touch him so much her hands itched.

"Keep the box away from me while I launch it, okay? So it won't catch in my clothes," he said between his upraised arms. A sliver of skin showed under his jacket and turtleneck.

A pang of desire made her press her lips together.

She did as he directed and both watched the balloon as it gently rose into the air then caught a gust and climbed high and away.

While he stood with his face upturned to follow the probe's flight, Erica drew near him and rested a hand over his chest, running it in a slow and gentle circle. He gazed down at her.

The sudden, feral light in his eyes stopped her breath for a good three seconds. A gasp left her when he grabbed her wrist and pulled it to his mouth, where he proceeded to rake his teeth along the tender inside. Nearly hanging by the arm, Erica pressed herself against Lothar, snaked her other hand underneath his gray turtleneck and traced an upward path over his front in a straight line, soaking the heat of his skin through the bandages, feeling the hard thud of his heart. She stayed well away from his scarred flanks.

The color of his eyes reminded Erica of her birthstone, peridot, only with a gray tint to them. His gaze never left hers. With his mouth, he tugged apart the Velcro cuff of her sleeve, bit the flap of nylon and pulled it up her arm to denude it. Fine hairs rose in waves as he lipped the tender skin. A vein pulsed rhythmically, which he felt with a featherlike touch of his upper lip. Because of the minute separation between his mouth and her arm, each faint pulse raised her skin to his in a touch so subtle, so faint, Erica had to bite her lip to keep from pressing her wrist harder against his mouth. A slight breeze sent a strand of his hair into his face but he didn't blink, didn't sever the connection.

Erica's heart beat hammer-hard as she felt his other hand rise behind her, cup the back of her head then close a loose fist in her hair. The slight pressure was the most erotic, intoxicating sensation. Subtly, she felt the balance of power shift in his direction as he held her vulnerable wrist against his mouth, bared his perfect teeth and raked them against her skin. She thought for a second he would bite her. But he didn't.

Lothar closed his eyes. "If we don't stop right now, I might not be able to later on."

Under his turtleneck, Erica pressed her hand over his left pectoral and felt his heart beat harder and faster than any she'd felt before. Almost as fast as a dog's.

"Please don't stop."

Fire accompanied the series of quick little nips he took on the inside of her forearm. His fist tightened over her hair. When he ran out of naked arm to kiss, he skipped right to her mouth and crushed it under his, biting and sucking her lips, his tongue agile at tormenting and taunting hers. The heat of his breath was like a wave as it came and went with hers. She hadn't thought it possible but the ground really did sway beneath her feet.

He pulled away to look at her while his other hand joined his first in fisting her hair. Trapped in his burning hands, spellbound by his even more scorching gaze, Erica did the same to him, snaked her good hand full of his thick golden-brown hair and raised herself to him. In a mimic of what he'd done to her wrist, she raked her lips over his eyebrows, his refined nose, his succulent mouth, down his unmarked cheek then under his chin. As Erica's progress took her under his jaw and up the other side of his face, his scarred side—Lothar tried to pull away. She held on, closed her fist fully into his hair and pressed him down harder.

He stopped trying to push her away.

Leisurely, with light kisses all along the silvery line of scar tissue, she lipped then murmured against his face…first a kiss then his name, another kiss, his name again. A pearl necklace of tender attentions. Upward over the smooth jaw, the prominent cheekbone, she followed the scar near the eyelid — he'd come so close to losing an eye, she thought with a shudder — then over the eyebrow the color of a lion's mane. Her lips became lost within the lustrous hair hanging partly over his face. It felt cool, intimate, a shield.

"I want you, Lothar," she whispered in his ear. "I want all of you."

He froze.

"But you have to want it too."

"I've never wanted anything more…but I can't. Not with you."

"Because you're afraid to hurt me?"

"You don't know what I'm capable of, what I did."

Erica rolled the notion around in her head as she kissed his hair and ear. Obviously, whatever he referred to involved violence. She'd already seen his temper get the better of him once. Did that make him a bad person? Erica didn't know. Because she never could believe that people were born mean, she had to assume someone had hurt or betrayed — or both — Lothar deeply enough for him to lash out at others.

"People aren't doomed to repeat their mistakes all their lives. Not if you know it was wrong."

Lothar inhaled deeply. "I want you so much, so *hard*, it scares me."

He drowned her reply with a long and powerful kiss. She'd been about to say "me too".

Erica didn't know how she made it down to the station, only that when Lothar shouldered the door, it clattered and hit them back as they stumbled inside, clothes in disarray, hair in their faces, their hands and mouths assailing every part they could reach.

The dying sun's rays barely poked over the mountains and cast a coppery shadow inside the living room. Dust particles flew in roiling patterns. Lothar struggled against her. Twin thuds announced he'd kicked his boots off. Her shoes followed. The nylon creaked in protest when Lothar yanked her jacket wide and tugged it down. Momentarily trapped with her arms twisted behind her in the sleeves, Erica could only moan with her face toward the ceiling while his hands and mouth pulled and tugged at her T-shirt and pants. A small ripping sound announced at least part of a seam had given. *Oh.*

She exhaled loudly when he pushed her back against the wall and pinned her there with his hips crushed against hers. His thigh wedged between her legs, he rolled his pelvis, pressed his massive erection into her while he watched her reaction. She wished she had her hands to cup all of that magnificent cock! Struggling against the crumpled jacket trapping her arms back, she twisted and arched. Lothar's eyes flared.

"Erica..."

The warning in his voice did something quite remarkable to her. Instead of slowing down, she raised her chin defiantly and kept twisting and rolling her shoulders to disentangle them. Or for the sheer pleasure of rubbing herself against him.

His hand closed over the waistband of her chinos and roughly pulled her up and even closer to him while his other skimmed a thumb over her lips, pressed against the seal of her mouth and entered her. Lothar brushed the pad of his thumb against her bottom teeth while he held her by the pants in an implacable hold. While she continued her twisting and struggling, he looked down as she sucked and mock bit his thumb. Finally, she managed to slip her arms out of the sleeves and put her hands against his chest. Pushing against him felt like pushing against a tree.

Lothar's expression softened. "Do you want to stop?"

"I couldn't even if I wanted to. Just step back a little, I need some room."

He did, relinquishing her mouth and pants.

While his hands hung on either side of him, Erica snaked hers under his fleece and slid it over and down his muscled shoulders. She grabbed the bottom of the turtleneck and pulled up but Lothar didn't move to help.

"Trust me."

They stood for a long while, facing each other, she holding his top partly up over his belly while he stood immobile. His gaze darkened, his nostrils flared. For a few seconds, she thought he'd go chop wood again. But the wave subsided. She could see it as clearly as if it were lapping against the beach. Slowly, cautiously, he raised his arms and let her take his turtleneck off.

She hadn't been able—or allowed—to see that set of scars clearly since she'd caught him fresh out of the shower. And even then, he'd practically run by before she could take a better look. So she did now. His belly contracted with his shallow and quick breathing. A grimace twisted his mouth. He looked clearly embarrassed by them. Silly man.

"You shouldn't...it's not—"

First with a single finger, she traced the one closest to his navel, then the one next to it. A sharp intake of air slowed her movement. She wanted him to trust her, wanted him to know that his scars didn't count for her, that she loved him just the same.

Liked him just the same.

Or loved?

I don't know him well enough for that.

Did she need to though?

Erica knew she'd been toying with the idea at the back of her mind. It wasn't such a big shock that she'd at last admitted it to herself. Not that she'd share the revelation with him.

Something told her that'd drive him away. So like someone who'd found a gold nugget and didn't want to alert anyone about it, she folded and pocketed the confession and tucked it away for later.

After blowing on the abused skin, Erica applied her hand and as lightly as she could, followed each silvery line, every jagged edge of scar tissue, until his breathing slowed, his fists unclenched. Approaching, she leaned over and breathed him in, his male scent, the subtle hint of soap. The first kiss she applied to his scars made him twitch.

"*Trust* me."

Erica couldn't understand how he'd survived such a vicious attack. He looked as if a rope of blades had been wrapped around his waist then yanked out. With her hands constant companions, she kissed and licked every abused part of his flanks and chest. Muscles rippled and contracted with his breath.

Her need becoming more pressing by the second, she trailed kisses up to his hard pectorals and circled his nipple with her tongue. Then up to his throat and shoulder she went. His skin was so soft, the muscles underneath so hard. She dug her nails in.

The movement must have triggered something in Lothar for he dove for her neck while her T-shirt came up at the back of her. Her bra fell loosely between her chest and his.

She wanted him. His ardor, his near brutality. Her pussy clenched while he practically ripped her shirt off. Gasping at his skill and speed, Erica stepped out of her pants and underwear after Lothar had both bunched around her ankles. Without warning, he pushed a finger into her.

The sudden invasion felt rough for a second but when he angled his hand so that his palm rubbed her clit, Erica decided to wait and see what he did next. She wasn't disappointed.

Perhaps the mix of soft and hard prompted a faster reaction. Whatever it was, she felt a veritable gush of honey seep into his hand.

"Hold the back of your neck," he told her. His voice was harder, deeper.

After a quick look down at his hand, Erica crossed her hands behind her neck as she would to do a sit-up. With a curl to his lips, Lothar placed a hot, flat hand on the small of her back and gently pressed so she'd curve into him. She wouldn't have been able to keep that pose if he hadn't been supporting her. He was dipping her like a dancer would, his finger in her becoming two, yet managed to stroke her clit at every upward push.

Heat and pressure forced her eyes closed. She waited while Lothar continued his rhythmic push in, out, in, out.

Okay, I can see the potential with this...

Not even three seconds later, Erica felt the first ripple. She came fast. The heat of his hand behind her back accentuated the pleasure. *Whew. Where did he learn that?*

Her sigh made him smile knowingly. "Exactly where I knew it would be."

She had no idea what he was talking about and frankly didn't give a damn. Spasms tightened her channel around his fingers as she rode the last of the wave.

"Spread your feet a little."

Erica did. He put one foot in between so he could keep both their balance. Then literally supporting half her weight with his hand, his muscles contracted and taut, he pushed in harder, deeper into her wet sheath, his quick and precise thrusts forcing a moan out of her. Already?

She dug her nails in her own hands as a searing jab of release shot up her womb. With a ferocity that stunned her, she cried out her pleasure at Lothar. It was so good, so good! Erica didn't care if she woke the dead. His name filled the room. But as soon as she came, he pulled out and wrapped her in his arms. Honey dribbled down her thighs. She'd never been so wet.

Erica fought against him. She wanted more. Her need was knifing at her, burning her. She could've humped her own hand.

"More," she murmured against his chest.

"You have to wait—"

"I don't want to wait, dammit, I want you to take me now!"

She must have surprised him as much as she did herself for he stood rigidly before back-walking her with a palm against her sternum, back toward the kitchen until she collided against the table. He kicked the chair aside. It clattered against the woodstove and toppled on its side. His eyes were so dark, almost chocolate brown.

Erica couldn't ponder the strange phenomenon any longer as Lothar's mouth landed on hers in a brutal kiss that left her lips throbbing. With a gasp of excitement and apprehension, she let him spin her around before he clamped a viselike hand over her nape. Relentlessly, he pushed against her. On pure animal instincts, she struggled for a second before following his lead.

Lothar bent her completely over the table, pressed down until her breasts were crushed, her belly flattened. He jammed his thighs behind hers. Then he took her.

Chapter Seven

** හ**

Lothar thought he would explode into her, that his cock would burst and split in half to release all of his seed, all of *him* in one single, blinding flash of triumph and ecstasy.

That she would use his name such, for release, for satisfaction…for *pleasure* gratified his male ego but also his blossoming affection for her. There were no words to describe it except one.

"Erica."

When he'd felt her resistance, barely a second but still, doubts had come crashing back onto him. Perhaps he was going too fast, was asking too much. But Erica had stopped struggling right away and relinquished power to him. That she'd trust him so completely made him want to howl in exultation.

Her quick panting drove him wild.

"Hold on to my wrist," he said through clenched teeth as he pulled out to his glans and waited.

Erica wrapped her arms over her head and clutched his wrist with both hands. Applying just enough pressure to anchor her but not enough to hurt her neck, he waited until she'd begun to breathe normally.

Muscles accentuated the lovely shadows pooling along her spine. That fine butt was so rounded in this position, so tempting. It reminded him of the days when women wore corsets. Even though he knew for a fact they were much more comfortable without them, Lothar still missed corsets. There was nothing quite as stimulating, quite as whetting, as slowly, deliberately unlacing one of the complicated affairs to expose the tender skin underneath. That gradual release of constricted flesh, the bone marks filling up, the fine hairs straightening. Even if there were modern versions of corsets — leather, lace or even latex — sadly, none of the thrill had survived progress.

Lothar imagined Erica's waist cinched in one…with her trim and fit figure, she would've looked particularly enticing. He rubbed his hand on her cheek in slow circles.

The clack of skin against skin reverberated in the room. Lothar froze, waiting…hopeful.

Her yelp of surprise turned into a low and throaty moan. Bolstered, he slapped her cheek again. But a more pressing urge stabbed at his hips and cramped his thighs. After he held on to the crook of her hip, Lothar thrust in deep. She was so very wet, he wasn't worried about hurting her and lavished all of his pent-up energy into her welcoming pussy. The back of her, so vulnerable and beautiful, her flesh so hot and conforming to his own pushed him closer to the edge.

Their moans grew proportionally to his piston-like momentum. Erica's honey was so plentiful he felt it dribbling along his balls, which bounced happily as they hadn't done in a while. Biting his lip hard, growling, Lothar pushed, pushed, pounded into Erica until he felt her pussy start to clinch at him again. Then he started hammering. Sweat made his grip on her hip hard to keep. He clutched his fingers tighter.

Erica cried out as she dug her nails into his wrist. Her sheath tightened around his cock like a strap of hot, wet leather. The milking movement finished him off. With a liberating roar, Lothar Kessler reached the highest, purest climax of his life and collapsed on top of the woman he loved.

* * * * *

Lothar woke to the sound of the front door closing. He snapped up in bed and listened intently. It took him a while to remember what had happened. Then he did. A grin tugged at his lips.

Erica.

How his fortune had turned for him to be gifted with such a gem!

Then a sharp twinge of pain in his knuckles reminded him of how little time there was left.

Monday.

The full moon would come tonight. His elation burst like a fragile bubble of soap. Erica *had* to leave. He'd push the damn plane down the road if he had to, but she *had to leave.* She couldn't be a witness to his transformation. He'd lose her. And the thought made him want to crawl into a hole and wait for death.

With renewed determination, Lothar grabbed some breakfast and downed the carton of milk left on the counter — she'd even set things up for him to have a cup of tea — such a sweet woman — and headed for the shower.

While he rubbed all the pleasantly tingling spots, Lothar nodded to himself at his new strategy. They could have a long-distance relationship. More and more couples lived this way nowadays. It'd afford him the privacy of changing into a horrible monster every full moon. Ha. A sardonic smile spread on his face.

He actually looked forward to hiking with Erica and her friends. Although he would've enjoyed an entire week with her all to himself so he could make love to her over and over again, in every known position in the book...a book he'd once owned and studied meticulously.

But that was a long time ago. Another time, another Lothar Kessler. He was different now. Just as Sister Jane had done, Erica was showing him how to be a human being again, had found a way into his shell, through the many — many, many — barriers he'd placed around himself.

Feeling rejuvenated, Lothar finished his shower. After wiping some of the steam off the mirror, he took the time to study himself. The man looking back at him felt unfamiliar. Had his eyes always been so bright? And that grin, it looked so silly and, well, *foreign* on him, but he couldn't wipe it off. Instead of tying his hair in a ponytail, he left it loose on his shoulders, suspecting she liked it better that way anyway since she kept trying to snake her hands in it.

"Don't mess it up," he told his suddenly stern reflection.

Erica was precious, special. There wouldn't be another like her in his lifetime, as long as it ended up being.

He was brushing his teeth with even more energy than usual when he heard an engine. Was her plane already repaired? Strange. It didn't sound like a floatplane. Too high-pitched. Were there two of them?

Lothar jogged back to his room and hurriedly pulled clothes and his fleece jacket on. It was getting colder every day. He hated changing during the winter. Waking the next morning naked on the forest floor wasn't terribly pleasant.

His heart was swelled with all this new life brimming over his horizon. He couldn't wait to drink it all in. There wouldn't be a woman on earth with a more attentive and affectionate lover. He made the vow to lavish on her a lifetime of affection and consideration. That newfound thirst for life would all be about Erica. He'd make love to her slowly, tenderly, then would take her hard against the wall, as he knew she enjoyed. With her by his side, his light, he would brave his worst fear…he'd tackle life with renewed energy. Perhaps he could even learn to trust again?

Slow down, man.

The sound had stopped when he stepped out, locked his door out of habit and bounded down the steps. Erica's floatplane didn't look as though it'd gone anywhere. Lothar felt his face tighten when he spotted two rigid-hull inflatable boats, one of them empty while two men sat in the other. A third, thickly set and gray-haired, stood near Erica.

Were those the hunting party she'd dropped off three days before? She'd mentioned how one could reach their lodge by heading north on the Yukon River.

His first indication of trouble came in the form of Erica's halberd-straight back and the way she kept shaking her head emphatically. Anger spiked in him. Lothar slowed and surveyed the peculiar scene through narrowed eyes. No one seemed to have noticed him so far. The pair in the RIB seemed to be deep in conversation as they sat facing toward the embankment.

He quickly dismissed jealousy as the source of his anger. Something bothered him about the way Erica didn't seem her comfortable, easy-going self with the gray-haired man. As Lothar drew near, one of the two in the RIB must have spotted him for he pointed up at the path and stood. Erica and the man with whom she was talking immediately spun toward the bank.

To his shock, Erica shoved the man back from her and started screaming.

"RUN! GET OUT!"

After the split-second animal response had fired in his muscles and been denied by his brain, Lothar charged down the path fast enough to kick himself in the ass.

"NO!" Erica screamed, waving frantically for him to get away. "RUN!"

The man she'd pushed whirled on her with a backhand that sent her colliding against the floatplane behind her. She floundered back and leaned against the wing for support.

White-hot rage flared. Air whistled out of his clenched teeth. How...*dare* he lay a hand on her!

Had the need to ascertain her wellbeing not overridden everything else, Lothar would've changed immediately and massacred them all.

As he barreled down the bank toward the pier, the one who'd spotted him first raised a rifle and fired once a short distance in front of Lothar. He didn't slow down.

They wanted him alive then. That was their second lethal mistake. The first had been to touch her.

With a leap, he reached the pier and landed in a shuddering thud that rocked the floating structure. His charge barely diminished, he was reaching the halfway point when another shot clacked in the air and bits of wood exploded right where he'd been about to put his foot. That man was a good shot.

Too bad Lothar didn't care.

Slowed but still running, he got to within ten paces when he skidded to a dead halt, his mountaineering boots digging in the planks and stopping him cold. He windmilled once to regain his equilibrium then let his arms fall placidly on either side of him. The rage was gone. Fear had replaced it. Abject, gut-wrenching fear. The kind he'd never experienced but had often caused. Now he knew how it felt to fear for a loved one. It was horrible.

The man by Erica's side had just yanked her back to him and put a gun against her head.

"That's some big boyfriend you have, Miss Bain," he exclaimed with a booming voice that grated on Lothar's nerves.

When she said nothing, he laughed. A jovial uncle at a family reunion. "I thought you said he was gone to town and left you here to watch the place." His smile showed too-perfect teeth within a too-tanned face. "It's not nice to lie."

She'd tried to protect *him*. No one had ever cared enough to sacrifice themselves for him before. The thought she would confront three armed men alone, lie about his whereabouts so he'd remain safe boggled the mind.

Lothar didn't think he could talk yet so he just stared at Erica for any other sign of violence on her. She had her shoulders tightly drawn in as if she expected a slap upside the head. Her pale eyes were wide and—curse them—filled with horror and fear when there'd been nothing but good humor and serenity. How he hated them for putting that filth into her soul.

"Will you be all right?" he asked of her, keeping his tone carefully modulated, reaching out to her with at least his voice since he couldn't approach.

She nodded twice quickly.

Ignoring the men and knowing it would infuriate and unsettle them, Lothar stared hard at her and only at her. "When I start killing them, I want you to run away and not look back. No matter what you hear. Okay?"

One of the men in the RIB laughed weakly. No one else did.

"Promise me."

Another quick nod satisfied him.

The one holding a gun to Erica's head narrowed his eyes and looked at Lothar for a long while. "Usually, I don't like unforeseen twists but I have to say that you've just made my day, Mr. Meteorologist. Things will be much livelier with you in the game."

"What the hell is this?" Lothar demanded.

To his infinite horror and rage, he saw a red mark darken Erica's cheek where the man had hit her. Lothar's jaw started to ache with the first twinges of the change. He fought it down. As a beast, he wouldn't be able to tell who was friend or foe and just may attack them all indiscriminately. Erica included.

"We'll tell you all about our little event once we get to the lodge," the man replied, his smile widening. Turning to his men in the RIBs, he added, "Al, get Marty to help you tie him down then put him in your boat. I'll keep Miss Bain with me in the other RIB in case he doesn't cooperate."

Lothar felt his lip twitch upward as the man pocketed his gun, took Erica's arm and guided her toward the empty RIB. Holding her hand like a perfect gentleman, he let her sit then joined her.

The two in the boat, "Al" a large bullish sort of character with black and gray camouflage clothes and the other a sinewy man with yellow-tinted glasses who Lothar assumed was

Marty, climbed out of the RIB and came for him. Al held a length of nylon rope in his hands while Marty trained his rifle on him.

"Lie down," Al said.

His gaze on Erica, Lothar slowly knelt then lowered himself onto the pier with his arms bent push-up-like. Under the cover of his colleague, Al circled Lothar and leaned over. A grunt left Lothar when the other jammed his knee right between his shoulder blades to make sure he was staying in the prone position.

Erica meant to get up on her feet. "Hey!"

"There's no need for this, Al, just tie his hands and feet then let's go back." The group's mouthpiece checked his watch. "I want to start when there's still sunlight."

Bound hand and foot, Al rolled Lothar until he lay right by the edge of the pier then waited while Marty pushed the RIB underneath before giving a final push with the ball of his foot. Lothar landed on his side against the RIB's inflatable ring and slumped at the bottom where he sat with his back against the seat so he could look at what was happening to Erica.

The mouthpiece was tying her hands behind her but didn't bother with her feet. He looked over at Lothar. The smile was gone. "If you don't play nice with Al and Marty, Mr. Meteorologist, I'm going to send charming Miss Bain over the side and watch while she struggles to swim ashore in that glacial water and all those heavy clothes with her hands tied behind her back. How long do you think she'd last? Five minutes? Ten? You wouldn't want her drowning on your conscience, would you? I hope we understand one another."

In another life, Lothar wouldn't have cared much what happened to one person. He cared now. "We do."

"Good. That goes for you too, Miss Bain. You'll need your boyfriend later on today when we start."

The sound of both RIB motors going at once scared several birds out of their nests and they flew away over the water as both boats slowly backed up along the pier, angled north and took them farther along the river.

Wind whipped at his hair when Marty gunned the engine. The river was calm at the moment but Lothar knew it wouldn't last. He could already spot a rainstorm in the making over the Mackenzie Mountains. Dark clouds masked the highest peaks.

With an occasional glance at the other RIB to make himself feel better, Lothar stared straight ahead as the boats made their way upstream until, about two or so hours later, he spotted a pier jutting far out into the river. When they'd neared it and slowed alongside, he spotted a huge lodge nestled in the hilly embankment. A narrow gravel path snaked up into the woods.

As Marty cut the motor, Al dug a hunting knife out of a sheath along his chest and cut the cord around Lothar's ankles before hoisting him up by the collar of his fleece jacket. Power was being wrestled out of his hands again, just as it had so long ago when he was being "trained" to be the perfect little apprentice to the revolting physician. Rage bubbled from the depths of his soul and pushed against a trapdoor he thought closed forever, pushed to come out and make him a monster once again, through and through. He forced his breath to slow but feared it wouldn't be enough. His jaw ached constantly now, as did his hands. His only salvation was Erica. He wouldn't change in front of her.

A quick peek revealed her worried gaze on him as her captor helped her climb out of the RIB. Lothar nearly slumped back against the seat with admiration. As soon as he saw her looking at him, he felt the beast recede. This simple act, her gaze alone, succeeded where six hundred years of merciless self-discipline had failed.

How he loved her.

Somehow, despite her own fear, Erica found the courage, the kindness to look out for him and wonder about his safety. *She* was the lone female amidst a group of men who wanted to… Lothar couldn't bring himself to follow this chain of thought. Pain waited there, pain and madness and carnage.

She was surrounded by guns and violence with her hands tied behind her back. Yet she found the inner strength to think of someone else. Her fortitude made him want to be a better man.

And her death would send him over the edge.

If they killed Erica… The images scared even him.

Should they extinguish such a light as hers, they would plunge him into such an abyss that he'd never break the surface again, would sink back to his former vicious self—and beyond—where violence reigned and even the devil didn't dare come. There would be no deed too dark, no act too vile for him. He'd tear them all apart, rend their limbs off, gut them and watch the light die out of their eyes while he waited close, close enough to hear their last ragged breath gurgle out of their ruined throats.

There wouldn't be redemption for him without her.

Erica swallowed hard as she watched Lothar stomp by, flanked on one side by Al while Marty followed a pace behind with his rifle pointed at the back of her man's head.

Her man.

The way he'd charged down the pier with his face twisted in fury, Erica's entire being had hummed with fear and love and pride. To watch Lothar run toward her, despite bullets landing feet from him, to not fear for his own life because he was coming to her rescue, did something to Erica. It made her feel special. When bullets hadn't stopped him, the mere act of putting a gun to her had frozen the charging bull in his tracks. She'd been so scared they were going to shoot him. And still was.

What could these men want with Lothar and her?

They were led to the large room with the animal heads mounted on the walls. The smell of pipe smoke tickled her nostrils. The rest of the party was already sitting there and waiting. The one who'd been sick after his flight up looked even paler. He kept rubbing his thigh and looking fearfully at the blond-bearded giant, a Viking really, standing with a plastic case in his hand. One of the British hunters, the one she'd pinned as the pipe smoker, was doing just that as he leaned against the wall.

"There," Thomson said, indicating she should sit in one of the large leather loveseats on either side of that horrid table with the hoofed legs. "Take a seat, Miss Bain."

How could the man be such a gentleman when he'd backhanded her hard enough to make her see stars? Her cheek throbbed. Crazy bastard.

"Are the chips in?"

"They are," the Viking replied.

"Good," Thomson said with a wide grin. He winked at her and sat in the opposite loveseat. "How about coffee? Would you like a cup? And you, Mr. Meteorologist?"

She shook her head and watched Lothar give one hell of a dark look at Al as the big man pushed him down into a straight-backed chair along the wall. Marty still had his rifle trained on Lothar.

"Fine, but you'll need to eat later on, to keep your energy up. I've waited four years for this and I won't have it ruined because you're too weak to run."

Primal fear clutched at her throat and squeezed. Run? Toward what? *From* what?

"Are you going to tell us what the hell is going on?" Lothar snarled.

"Where are you from, Mr. Meteorologist? I hear an accent, I think. Europe somewhere, Germany, yes?"

Lothar didn't reply and just stared nuclear bombs at Thomson. Erica was sure glad she wasn't on the receiving end of that glare.

Thomson shrugged with a genial smile. "It's simple. Every four years, my associates and I arrange a very prized, very lucrative event. Each man you see here has paid an exorbitant fee for the chance to try something they've always dreamed of, to hunt the best game of all."

Erica thought she would pass out from the sudden drop in blood pressure. She felt her entire body go numb with the realization.

"Ah, I see you're a quick one," Thomson replied, nodding.

"What?" Erica meant to stand, but her legs gave without help from any of Thomson's thugs. *Dear Lord...they're all crazy.*

Spitting something in German—she guessed—Lothar stood abruptly. "This is a manhunt?"

"Sit down!" Thomson's tone had gone from gracious host to crazy old man with a gun in the blink of an eye.

The one beside her, Baldy, made a sort of squeaky coughing sound as he rubbed his thigh with renewed vigor.

"Until you showed up, Miss Bain, Tom here was to be one of our special guests with Luke." He pointed to the other British hunter, the one sitting on a couch. He too didn't look too happy to be there. His thick russet mustache quivered as he looked down at his feet.

"They knew about the nature of the hunt, of course, only not that they'd be the ones running in front." Thomson laughed. "The look on Tom's face."

She shook her head and closed her eyes briefly. Everything began to spin. She opened her mouth to speak but nothing came out. Forcing her mind to clear, she leaned forward in the sofa. "You intend to hunt us? People? *Why?*"

"Ahh, because there's nothing like the sensation of knowing your prey is as intelligent and cunning as you are, Miss Bain, knowing that if the tables were turned, you'd be the hunted. It all comes down to our species' primal craving for dominance. To test ourselves. To win."

306

"You crazy old bastard," she breathed, unable to stop herself.

He just grinned. "Well sent, Miss Bain, well sent. It wasn't supposed to be like this, mind you. We've never had a lady join us before. You were supposed to go down with your plane three days ago, not end up here with them." He hooked his thumb at Tom and Luke, who both flinched as though he'd struck them.

The man's words sank in her heart like stones. "It was *you*. You sabotaged my plane so I'd go down right after I left."

A simple nod confirmed it. Behind him, Lothar flushed to a violent shade of red.

"We were monitoring Dawson's airwaves to learn of your demise, which never came. After a while, we contacted them. The gentleman there was very helpful that way and told us where you were staying. Marty was amazed to hear that you'd managed to land despite what he'd done to your plane. All we had to do was wait for more clement weather before we attempted to take the RIBs out.

"But I'm a man of my times," he went on. "I won't treat you any differently than I will the three men who'll join you as our special guests. Equal opportunity."

Al laughed. The rest only sniggered like the demented bastards there were.

"You can't do this," Erica said, surprised at how her voice kept rising. Not in fear but in anger. "People will look for us. They'll find us and trace it all back to you. What the hell is wrong with you people?"

They were going to gun them down one by one like rabbits. They meant to put a bullet in Lothar.

"No, they won't. No one knows we're in Canada except you and your boyfriend. Each of us has taken great care to hide our prints, so to speak. False names, ironclad alibis, conferences, meetings, everyone thinks we're somewhere else. As far as everyone is concerned, we're in Blackstone, not

Miner's Point, even Dawson's dispatcher thought so. He doesn't know where we are…nor where *you* are because we used the satellite phone. Dawson doesn't have the ability to trace them, I checked. Tomorrow, your plane will conveniently disappear at the bottom of the Yukon River while animals will take care of the rest here on land. Everyone will think we all went down with the plane, Mr. Meteorologist included since you landed at the station. They'll think you came back up for us after you spoke with the dispatcher, perhaps bringing your friend with you, then all of us disappeared. This is the High North, wilderness, the animal kingdom at its most untamed."

Understanding dawned on her. "You changed destinations midway so no one would know, so people look in the wrong place." And she'd been nice enough—dumb enough—to fly them there!

"Don't be too hard on yourself, Miss Bain. I always get what I want."

Erica couldn't help looking over at Lothar. She knew he couldn't do anything to change the situation but just looking at him made everything feel less hopeless. The sheer madness of…*everything* made her head hurt.

A manhunt? In Canada? In this day and age?

"You'll need someone else to take you back down to Whitehorse," she said through her teeth.

Thomson shook his head. "That's why we have the RIBs—oh, Marty, don't forget to fuel them, wouldn't want to be caught unawares. After we've taken care of everything, we'll get down to Keno where no one is looking for a missing plane and discreetly drive from there in a van my colleague—" he pointed to the Viking "—already drove there earlier this week. It's taken months to preposition everything, piece by piece. This isn't our first hunt, Miss Bain. I've planned this sort of event for years. Tunisia, the Russian Steppe, England."

Erica wanted to kick him. Hard. "They're going to find the plane eventually. They'll see it was empty."

He shook his head. "I've already scoured your country's board of transportation archives. Most flight safety reports of accidents that happened in remote places show that very little in terms of human remains were left in or near the different wreckages. Since the Yukon is especially...*wild*, it's no stretch of the imagination to think that our carcasses floated away and were disposed of by nature."

Out of arguments, Erica bit down and looked away. *They've thought of everything.*

She chanced a quick peek at Lothar to find him looking at her intently. Wasn't life cruel sometimes? Just as she'd found someone special... Resentment tightened her teeth. For the first time in her life, Erica would've hurt someone for the sheer pleasure of it. They were going to steal him away from her, gun them down like animals.

"I'm not some deer caught in the headlights," Erica snarled. "I'm not going to run around and make it fun for you. Just shoot me now, you ridiculous old—"

"Erica."

Lothar's warning tone stopped her mid sentence. She clamped her mouth shut and sank farther into the cushion.

Thomson's eyes narrowed, his mouth thinned with an ugly smile. "I think your boyfriend here understands much more of the nature of this hunt than any of you." He twisted around to look at Lothar and nodded. "I knew right away when I saw you that you'd be perfect. You're a hunter yourself, I can tell. You have it in you.

"Now," Thomson went on, rising. "How about we implant the chips and get something to eat? I'm starving."

Erica yelped when the Viking came over and grabbed her shoulder hard. Before she could stop him, he yanked the sleeve of her jacket down over her arm, pulled the T-shirt sleeve out of the way and stabbed her shoulder with one huge syringe.

"Argh!"

But he'd already released her.

By the corner of her eye, she saw Al punch Lothar in the belly to force him back into his chair. Marty's rifle pressing hard against his forehead was the only thing that made him sit back. The look in his eyes spelled murder. Erica shivered as she tried not to fall into a heap of sobs.

"What the hell did you do to me?"

"This is just a canine locator microchip, absolutely safe," the Viking replied as he tore the cap off a plastic cartridge and retrieved another syringe.

"You injected a *dog*'s chip into me?! That's your idea of a hunt? Isn't this whole craziness supposed to be about 'hunting the best game of all'?" She sneered the last few words, even throwing an accent in it. "Talk about being a lying, cheating sack of—" She went to stand but Thomson pressed hard on her shoulder and circled the loveseat so he could stand closer to Lothar.

"Now, we're going to inject you too, and I don't want any foolishness."

The Viking came over, cautiously denuded Lothar's shoulder and injected him with the clear liquid containing the chip. It must have been small for Erica couldn't see anything floating in the liquid.

Lothar's face registered no pain as he stared guns at Thomson. Clearly, they'd developed a special kind of hatred for each other. Erica remembered that it'd been Thomson who'd hit her and sent Lothar down the pier like a vengeful storm. Steven's bleeding face came back to her. For his sake, she hoped Thomson didn't turn his back on Lothar. For her sake, she hoped he would.

Chapter Eight

&

After orange juice and sandwiches—which tasted like ashes to Erica—Thomson had his four "special guests" line up outside the lodge while he and his four cronies checked and rechecked their gear. Her watch indicated sixteen forty-six. Barely fifteen minutes to go. Everything felt surreal.

I'm going to wake up any second.

Erica felt part of some madman's idea of a shoot 'em up arcade game gone wrong. She'd never seen half of the stuff arranged in neat piles on the ground. She could recognize some of it, like a portable satellite receiver unit and five handheld GPS like those used by fishermen and hikers. They even had night vision goggles!

She stood by Lothar's side. Their ropes had been taken off, as had anything in their pockets. Just so she could feel a bit better, she inched closer until their elbows touched. He looked down at her, his expression softening right away.

"We'll be fine."

She felt like reminding him they had demented hunters with G.I. Joe gear about to let them loose in the forest an hour before they started tracking them so they could shoot them down, one by one. So no, they wouldn't be fine, dammit! But just hearing him say it made her feel better.

Nothing like a good dose of denial.

To her left was Tom, the balding guy. He looked around him, panting hard. "Thomson...look...I can't do this. This isn't how it was supposed to be. Everything was arranged for..." He stopped, threw a quick, panicky glance at the mustachioed Luke then looked at his feet.

Thomson only smiled benignly. "No, Tom, it's not, is it? You weren't supposed to join Luke. But over the years, I found that having a surprise guest livens things up considerably. And now that we have four…well, I'd say this hunt will be the most exciting so far!"

"And I wager Luke hadn't realized either he'd be joining Tom, for that matter," added Marty with an elbow at the other Brit, who nodded his agreement as he sucked on his pipe.

They all acted so casually. What sort of men did this, this sordid double- and triple-crossing?

A wave of nausea made her bend over and take a few hard breaths. Lothar's hand on her back felt so hot, so much like a shield that she felt better after a while.

"Maybe ladies can't play with us after all," Al said. He patted his rifle. "I'll put her out of her misery, poor thing."

He went to point his rifle at her but was simultaneously stopped by Thomson and Lothar who both took a step forward.

"That's exactly what I thought," said the older man with a knowing grin. "The only thing that's keeping this one docile is her. When she goes, *that's* when the fun will start. I think this time our special guests will give us a run for our money."

He sounded excited by the notion.

Clearly irked, Al returned to checking his gear.

Erica noticed that Lothar's fist shook so violently his arm trembled. Seeking to calm him as much as herself, she slid her hand around his wrist and while the five men continued going through their equipment, she felt Lothar's fist unclench then his fingers entwined with hers. Had the situation not been so dire, Erica would've felt as though nothing could touch her. Heat transferred from him to her.

Good grief, I need a hug right now.

"Let's review the rules," Thomson said. "At precisely five p.m., our four special guests will depart, as a group or individually, that's up to them. Then sixty minutes later, my friends and I will follow, each with one of these," he held up the small GPS receiver before putting it in the breast pocket of his fishing vest. "In case one of you shows back up at the lodge with the idea to take a boat ride, Marty over there has the keys."

Marty patted his chest confidently.

"Then it's just a matter of who's more cunning than the other. Territory doesn't matter. There's nothing closer than our good friend the meteorologist's station, some fifty miles south of here. I don't think anyone can run that far!"

The first raindrop fell with a click on her shoulder. She looked up to see storm clouds massed overhead in angry gray fists. This one would be bad. By her side, Lothar also looked up. Veins showed at his temples, his lips looked tight.

"Okay, there's just one last thing we need to do," Thomson announced in his news anchor voice. "Motivate the crowd."

He pointed his rifle toward Luke, the Brit on "her" side, and fired.

Only partly drowned by the gunshot, Erica's scream reverberated while the man slumped soundlessly, the back of his skull a mangled trapdoor oozing blood and tissue. With a lurch, she fell on all fours and emptied her stomach.

"So make that five of us and *three* special guests," she heard Thomson remark lightly.

Through the haze of tears and the mad beating of her heart in her ears, she heard Thomson start a countdown from twenty seconds. A strong hand grabbed the back of her jacket and hoisted her up.

"We need to run, Erica. I'm sorry," Lothar murmured in her ear.

They ran.

With her jacket twisted up for the implacable grip Lothar had on it, they ran. Through copses of evergreens, thick and clingy undergrowth, across thin brooks that gurgled toward the mighty Yukon River, they ran. They didn't stop when Erica's foot slipped against a slimy tree trunk, neither did they slow down when Tom tripped and fell hard on his stomach.

Over fallen trees strewn about the forest floor and around boulders the size of sheds, they ran. Her lungs burned. But for a while, fear made her feel like she had wings. She silently followed Lothar as he charged through the woods.

Even when Erica began to feel increasingly heavy and uncoordinated, Lothar pulled her mercilessly, his face onward, never once looking back or down or up. Rain managed to reach them between trees and made their progress treacherous and difficult. Dirt became looser quickly for the recent rainstorm. It soon became darker for the thick cover of clouds accumulated over their heads. It felt to Erica as though they touched the treetops. Then rain turned to drizzle.

Still they ran.

Her chest burned, she gagged at every breath. From exhaustion, fear, horror at the grisly scene replaying in her head over and over, the back of the man's skull bursting open with a dark red squirt that lifted some of his hair.. His soundless slump toward the ground. Bile rose in her throat.

"Lothar...*please*," she urged, grabbing a tree to break her momentum but only tearing the skin of her hand when that didn't stop his relentless charge.

Finally, after they'd jumped over a downed tree and skidded down the muddy bank of a brook, Lothar slowed then stopped completely. His fist was still gripped around her jacket. She gave a feeble tug on it as she tried to lean against a tree. Her heart beat fast in one uninterrupted flutter against her ribs. She ached everywhere. Her face and hands burned, her bandage was torn and dirty.

Lothar seemed to snap out of his trance and looked down at her. He released her but immediately closed his fist on her jacket again when she began to sink to the ground.

"We can't rest now, Erica," he whispered, looking around. His gaze never stayed on the same spot more than a second. "Later."

"If...I...don't rest..."she panted, gagged then planted her palms on her shaking knees. "You'll have...to carry me. Too slow."

After a second, he agreed with a nod. "Two minutes."

He put one knee on the ground and took several deep breaths.

Far behind them, they could hear Tom crashing through the tangled branches.

Lothar snarled something in German.

She didn't know what he said but could understand what he meant. Tom's noisy progress would get them killed.

"Come," Lothar whispered, getting to his feet and reaching for her hand.

"Two minutes," she panted as blood continued to rush to her head. She straightened and looked behind but couldn't see the third "special guest". Not that she had an ounce of sympathy for the man. He'd come there to hunt people too.

"We'll let him go one way while we go another. He's noisy, so they'll go after him first."

Erica nodded. She couldn't believe she'd just agreed to use another human being as bait. Another wave of nausea tightened her throat. She closed her eyes and hissed.

"You're doing fine, Erica," Lothar murmured with a quick squeeze of her hand. "We need to move. Now."

So they did.

With her hand trapped in his like in a bear trap of flesh, Erica ran until her legs were so heavy, her feet so numb she was stumbling with every other step. It was getting darker too. It forced them to slow down, which was a boon in one way for she didn't think she could last much longer. Her watch confirmed it was nearly six thirty. Night would fall soon.

Another hour, hour and a half tops. Then it'd be pitch black because they couldn't even see the moon. Erica had counted on the full moon's light to help them along but with the storm, she couldn't even tell where the trees ended and where the sky began. Damn.

Drizzle hardened into hail but they didn't stop or take refuge, only plowed on through. Then hail melted again into freezing rain that seeped through their clothes, into their eyes, plastered their hair to their heads and made their shoes heavy and cold. Her teeth clattered so hard she swore Lothar could hear the sound.

The first gunshot took her by surprise.

It reverberated only once because of the rain. She was so stunned she didn't even yelp or show any outward sign she'd heard it other than a cringe. Lothar froze and crouched. She did the same. Trying to breathe through her nose so she could listen for any suspect sound, she waited as the rain pounded on her head.

A man cried out. Then another shot.

The sound of something crashing through the woods grew. Lothar pressed on her shoulder and forced her down into a prone position while he crab-walked to a nearby tree and hid behind it. His muscled legs were bent like a predator preparing to pounce.

She couldn't help the notion that he looked familiar with all this, that being chased through the woods was something he'd done before. Maybe he was just an outdoorsy type of guy. He had to be since he worked in a remote weather station.

Wheezing preceded the crashing sound with a rhythmic thud of running feet. A sob confirmed Tom was getting closer. Erica was about to crawl back to her knees when she caught Lothar's frenetic hand signals that she stay down and not move.

With her face an inch above the wet and cold ground, she tried to breathe normally before they started running again.

Dead leaves and twigs stuck to her palms, her chin. Wet smells made her cringe. Erica kept her hands pressed on either side of her shoulders in case she needed to get back up in a rush and waited.

The sound of crashing grew louder. Through the rain, she spotted movement a few feet in front of her. Branches snapped up and down as someone used them for anchors.

Her heart beat a mad cadence. He was getting closer. She knew it was only Tom, just by the sound, but she feared he'd be trailing someone behind him.

With a gasp, Tom staggered by only ten or so feet to her left. He stumbled and fell in a panting heap.

Lothar didn't say a word or show himself. Neither did she. Guilt and shame made her want to crawl toward Tom and try to calm him down so he wouldn't make such damn targets of them all. She was terrified too but could at least control herself. Just as she was wrestling with her conscience, another gunshot cleaved the air.

That one was so near she had to put her hand to her mouth to stifle the groan of despair. It resonated somewhere behind them.

With a pitiful cry, Tom floundered to his feet and scuttled in an erratic pattern, bouncing off trees, getting tangled in branches before falling again. He moaned until the sound of someone approaching silenced even him.

Despite the deepening darkness, she could tell it was Marty since he was the smallest of the lot. He appeared alone. The rifle pointed at the ground as he carefully approached, his clothes glistening with rain. Thick undergrowth hid his legs.

Lothar didn't move a muscle when Marty padded right past him on his way to her right. Her hand clamped over her own mouth, Erica followed Marty's progress with rising panic. She could tell he knew someone was around for he kept looking back and forth, his rifle sweeping the ground at the ready. Something dangled around his neck, the NVG no doubt. It wasn't dark enough yet. She wished she had a pair.

She cringed when Tom let a strangled moan escape. *Goddamn, man, shut up!*

Marty straightened from his slightly bent position and angled his rifle at where she'd seen Tom fall. Thick ferns blocked the muzzle of the rifle but she could tell he had a good shot just by the way his body seemed to relax and straighten.

Poor Tom.

"Marty, man, it's me, it's Tom. Please—"

Then something happened that made her gasp in fright and shock.

Quicker than she thought anyone capable of, Lothar left his spot behind his tree and rushed at Marty.

She felt like screaming "no" but gritted her teeth, watching the muscled man move with the speed and stealth of a great cat. Marty didn't seem to hear anything either as he cocked his rifle.

Without a sound, Lothar tackled him. The pair disappeared through the ferns with only a faint rustling of leaves to indicate two men had just gone through.

With her heart in her throat and fearing any second for the telltale gunshot, Erica pushed off the ground and darted toward the spot where they'd disappeared.

She burst out from a thick bramble just as a man "humphed". *Please let it be Marty and not Lothar.* Scanning the area, she spotted Marty's rifle lying on the ground about twenty feet away. She ran for it.

To her right, she passed the pair of men still rolling on the ground exchanging silent blows. Fear for Lothar gave her legs that extra boost she needed.

Only a few feet away now. Hurry!

Before she could bend and pick the rifle up, a weight threw her to the ground. She rolled away and kicked out instinctively.

"Stay away from me," Tom snarled as he climbed to his feet and pointed the rifle at her. At *her*!

But he didn't for long as he turned tail and took off with his prize.

"Come back," she hissed in a hoarse whisper. "Tom, fuck, come back with that!"

She spun back toward the struggling pair with the firm intention of trying to land a good kick into that slimy little shit Marty just as Lothar was getting to his knees, his fist bunched over the man's vest while he pummeled him relentlessly. Every time his fist connected, the man's head snapped back and lolled. Standing, Lothar fished around the unconscious man's vest pockets.

The keys to the boats!

Erica rushed over and watched Lothar pocket both sets of keys.

"Got them," he whispered, looking around. "Where's his gun?"

"Tom took off with it. Damn fool wanted to shoot me."

"*Verdammt!* I should've finished him too."

Finished him?

Erica gasped loudly when Lothar wrapped his arms around Marty's head and gave a quick twist sideways and down. She didn't hear anything, neither did she see any difference in the man's body. But she knew Lothar had just killed him.

His eyes were hard and narrowed against the rain when he faced her. He let the man's lifeless body fall to the ground without a look. "We have to make it back to the lodge and get a boat. It's the only way we can get out of here alive."

She couldn't do anything else but look at Lothar, unable to say a word, to form a thought. Silence settled around them, save for the intermittent ticks of raindrops on their jackets.

He drew near and Erica had to fight hard not to draw back. Not in disgust but in shock. And fear as well.

Lothar reached to her but let his hand fall by his side. "Please don't look at me that way," he said. If his eyes were hard, his tone, on the contrary, was pleading. "They're hunting us like animals."

She nodded, unable to talk. He'd just killed a man.

While Erica crossed her arms and bounced on the balls of her feet to keep warm, Lothar gave her a set of keys. "If we become separated."

She took the key and shivered when he closed his large, hot hand over hers. His large, hot hand that had just snapped a man's neck.

"Let's go, we'll follow the brook we passed down to the river and make our way back up the bank. I doubt they're expecting us to come from that way."

She agreed with a nod. He really *was* good at this. And it scared her.

Silently, she followed Lothar's wide back as he cleaved his way among glistening trees. He kept looking up at the sky whenever they'd reach a clearing or a break in the canopy of branches and dying leaves. She looked up too but couldn't find anything of interest. The rain had stopped a while back. She checked her watch. The Indiglo backlight glowed green when she pressed the button. Seven thirty-three.

They finally reached the river. For the first time since they'd begun their crazy dash through the woods, Erica felt hope. If they could get one of the boats—and keep the keys to the other so Thomson and company wouldn't get them—they could get back to the station. From there, she'd fly them both to Dawson. They'd be safe. They *had* to get that boat.

Lothar checked back to make sure she followed as often as he did the sky, and although his expression was unreadable in the darkness, she could well imagine what must have gone on in his head.

She'd looked at him like he was a monster. Poor guy had just killed a man to save both their lives and she'd acted like a prima donna.

He was the one who'd had to snap a man's neck to save their lives. She'd only watched it, but it was *his* hands that had done the deed. *Lothar* would have to live with that sort of thing on his conscience, not she. What had she done to help their escape? Nothing. A wave of shame burned her cheeks. She'd acted like a shocked virgin when she should've thanked him on her knees. Shit, she hadn't even thanked him at all!

She jogged a bit faster and slid her hand in his. He slowed down so he could look at her.

"I'm sorry I looked at you the way I did. I didn't mean to blame you or anything. I was just scared." A mirthless laugh escaped her. She sounded close to hysteria. "And I still am."

The warmth of his hands as he wrapped them both around hers was soothing. "I had no choice but I'm sorry you had to see it. I was trying to finish it before you got there."

"I'm glad you're here. I wouldn't have lasted a minute without you. So thank you, okay, you saved my life."

"And you saved my soul," he replied softly as he bent to kiss both her palms. "We're even. Now, shh."

She wasn't too sure what he meant by her saving his soul but nodded. When he turned, Lothar seemed to stumble before bracing himself with a hand against a nearby birch. After a second or so, he kept walking. Something in his gait caught her attention. He was stooped a little bit, like his belly hurt.

She hadn't even asked if he was all right! What if Marty had hurt him?

"Oh no, you're not hurt are you?" Fear for his safety made the dread of discovery pale in comparison.

"I'm fine," he replied without turning around.

"No, you're not. I can tell."

They'd reached a clear patch by the river. Pulling him back by the elbow, she circled him and stood right in front so he couldn't avoid her. It wasn't as dark as in the woods there and she could see his face a bit better. What she saw stopped her heart for a good three seconds.

"Lothar...you're *bleeding.*"

"It's okay, he must have gotten a lucky punch. I'm fine." He patted his chin, where a dark trail glistened like ink. She couldn't tell if he was bleeding from the nose or from the mouth. Or both.

She was about to ask when he pointed at something up ahead. She craned her neck and caught the distinct silhouette of something jutting out over the water. The pier. With the two RIBs moored to it.

Erica wanted to jig!

"Are you sure you're all right?" she whispered close to his face.

She saw him nod. His movements didn't seem as fluid as they'd been but awkward and jerky. Like someone in pain.

The thought of Lothar hurting stabbed her heart acutely. She loved him. She really did.

I've never had good timing with those things.

She scowled when he turned around and crept closer to the pier. The lodge was still hidden from view by the woods but even if they were close enough, she doubted they'd see anything with the cover of clouds. Speaking of which, she thought she saw a thin crack of blue-gray light right over the trees across the river.

Lothar seemed to have spotted it too for he cursed and started jogging until he was silently running along the pebbled riverbed, the only sound an occasional splash of water or sucking of the mud. Erica thought he was extremely stealthy for a man his size. She wondered what he'd done aside from working as a meteorologist and medical aide. He obviously had some sort of affinity for all this. Police maybe? Soldier?

She'd ask him a thousand questions when they hightailed out of there. She made herself that promise.

The pier was barely twenty feet away when Lothar stopped under the cover of the last few trees and scanned the area several times. Slowly, he stepped out into the open, Erica on his heels, and padded to the pier. She'd had her set of keys in hand for the past several minutes as she mentally replayed the image of Thomson starting the motor. She hoped Lothar knew exactly what he was doing. She could start a plane with her eyes closed—and fly a good bit without seeing a thing too—but had never used an outboard motor before.

Lothar froze and checked over his right shoulder, toward the woods and the lodge beyond, which they still couldn't see. Erica did too and stifled a yelp of shock when gunshot erupted, several at once, then nothing. Men's voice rose in alarm.

They must have found Tom.

Because Tom had Marty's rifle, they would know their man was dead. They'd probably figure out Lothar and she had the keys when they wouldn't find anything on the bald man.

"We have to go for it," Lothar snarled.

They both started running for the boats. Arrhythmic thuds rattled the wooden planks when they both hit the pier running. Lothar jumped in the first boat and leaped over the seat so he could jam his key in the ignition. It seemed to fit for he left it there and leaped back over the seat to give her his hand.

"You'll have to wait until you drift farther downriver before you start the motor, okay, or they'll hear it and come shooting."

You? "What do you mean, *I'll* have—"

"Remember the promise you made. Don't turn back, no matter what you hear."

"What?"

At that moment, a sharp gust of wind raised his hair and sent it in his face. Erica looked up above the trees across the river as the moon emerged from among the thick shredded clouds.

"We'll have light now," she whispered as she clasped his hand and jumped in.

But it felt wrong. Sharper, longer. *Bonier.*

She gasped when Lothar grunted and bent in half against the inflatable side. Another long groan of pain escaped him.

"What's wrong?" Erica asked, pulling on his sleeve so he'd turn around. But he wouldn't and instead yanked it out of her hand.

"Too...late."

With much more force than necessary, he shoved her away from him and toward the motor then climbed back out to the pier with obvious difficulty. His legs looked as though they wouldn't function properly. When he'd showed such strength and stamina, he now looked as if he really was at the end of his rope. Groaning in obvious pain, he clawed up to the pier, rolled onto his side with his back to her and slowly with jerky movements he stood.

She landed on her ass, pell-mell amid life vests, fuel jerry cans and nylon ropes.

With erratic movements, he yanked his clothes off, practically tore the T-shirt off his back, boots and all, and threw them in the boat with her.

"I'm...sorry — *argh.* Erica...I'll always love you."

"Lothar," she hissed in a hoarse whisper. She struggled back to her feet and hastened to the fore of the boat. "What are you *doing*?!"

"Go," he snarled, his hands shook violently as he untied the mooring. He was pushing her away from the pier! He wasn't in the boat!

"Lothar!"

He raised his head. Their gazes met. With the moon's light, Erica saw with her eyes exactly what her brain refused to believe. Lothar's face was changing, elongating, his lips curled in an awful grimace of agony.

"Go…Erica, p-please."

He seemed to have difficulty with his mouth, as though it couldn't quite form the words. Horrified, she watched helplessly as he used his foot to push the RIB too far for her to reach the pier.

"No, wait!"

On her belly, with her upper body almost over the edge, she desperately reeled the rope back to keep from getting farther away but it was no longer tied to the iron mooring on the pier and just floated uselessly in the water. When she tugged the last few feet to her and grabbed the end, a whimper of pain made her look at Lothar.

No, please.

"Lothar! You don't have to do this. We can both make it!" Desperation made her forget to keep her voice down. "*Please!*"

She saw him collapse on his knees, his back bent impossibly tight, his shoulders shaking, his hands splayed on the wooden planks. The sound of ripping and other muffled cracks she prayed weren't what she thought they were reached her. She'd broken her wrist once not so long ago and could remember the sound as clearly as if she'd broken it today. A muffled, wet "*cluk*".

The sounds coming from Lothar sounded alike, only louder and in a sickening series that seemed as though it'd never stop. He growled before collapsing onto his side. Over his wide back, what appeared to be tears burst from shoulders to waist. As if someone were pulling zippers down his back to release the too-tight skin.

Horrified and desperate, Erica tried to paddle with her hands but only ended up making an impotent rotation.

No. No. No.

Erica's heart was in her throat. Tears clouded her vision. She knuckled them away as Lothar jerked like someone having a seizure, the sound of his feet slapping against the planks something she swore she'd never be able to forget. As the moonlight shone brighter and brighter, his transformation — for indeed she could see it was one — seemed to slow down. His silhouette was wrong somehow, larger, stockier. He shifted then rose to all fours.

She gasped when instead of legs she saw…paws. Huge, muscular *paws*. A thick chest, much too large for the rest of the body, with a powerful neck and a head definitely lupine in shape. The word flashed across her mind's eye as Lothar stood on four legs and angled his long *muzzle* back toward the river, back toward her.

Like the deadly predator he appeared to have become, he padded loosely to the end of the pier. She could hear it — *him*, Lothar, her lover — sniffing, his head tilted up slightly. Then he looked directly at her. Twin embers like the eyes of animals in the darkness bore right into her soul.

Erica sank back against the seat.

Werewolf.

The word didn't just flash across her mind, this time it stayed and branded an impression of itself behind her eyelids. It left an ashy taste in her mouth, a dull buzz in her head and a hole in her heart. The man she loved was a werewolf.

He had the thickness and muscle of a lion, with the hair around his face and neck slightly longer than the rest, but while his body had the might and grace of a great feline, his neck, head and *expression* were definitely wolfish. Pointy ears stood straight up, a long and sharp muzzle graced his massive head, which he kept low over his front paws — his hands, they were his *hands*!

How could such a large being reside in another, much smaller one? The pain Lothar must have endured while his poor body ripped in shreds to let this…this *thing* out. He was still Lothar, wasn't he?

How could someone suffer so much and survive? Despite the horror and the fear, compassion for Lothar surfaced. Were all those scars his own doing? Had he clawed at himself without realizing? So much pain.

He made a soft sound as he seemed to be considering how best to leap out into the river. Erica backed deeper into the boat, her eyes never leaving his. One paw, *hand*, at a time, he took quick swipes at the water, retracted, tried again.

A sharp crack from the darkened woods made him whirl back and start growling. Another snapping sound. Then voices were heard.

Thomson and his men were coming!

While Lothar was looking back, she blindly palmed at the ignition behind her, found the key and clasped it tight.

She couldn't leave him there with those men. They had guns. He had nothing.

"Lothar," she whispered hoarsely. "Get away. Run."

As the voices grew louder, Lothar suddenly bounded back up along the pier.

"No," she called, standing in the boat. "Run *away*!"

He didn't seem to hear her or to care about what she said. His powerful legs gouged the planks and she heard them splinting from where she was. With incredible speed, he dove into the woods without a backward glance.

Silence settled, the occasional lap of water against the rigid hull the only sound.

Not ten seconds later, gunshot erupted. A lot of it. Then screams. A lot of those too. Horrible, bloodcurdling screams. The sound of carnage. Then a long howl.

With a sob, Erica twisted so she faced the motor and fiddled around the damn thing until she'd figured out she needed to lower the blades into the water first. Tears blinded her as she grabbed the throttle, twisted the key and moaned in relief as the motor rumbled to life on the first try.

Thank you, thank you, thank you!

She couldn't leave him. But he had looked so adamant that she leave and quickly. What an impossible decision to make!

He'd made his own choice, had made sure she was safe before he changed. The least she could do was get help. If anyone could help him now. She pushed the horrible images of his body pierced by bullets out of her mind so she could focus.

After some dizzying spins, she regained control of the craft and roared down the Yukon River toward the weather station and possibly help and safety, her mind set on Lothar's radio.

Behind her, the sounds of gunshot lessened. But the rest went on. The sound of men screaming…dying.

Erica left them all behind, the gunshots, the screams, that anguished howl she knew was Lothar's. She also knew she was leaving behind a large part of herself.

Chapter Nine

❧

He could smell them.

The stench of fear floated on currents of air and tickled his nostrils. He knew there were four of them, all terrified, all trying to get away.

But they wouldn't. Not from him.

They ran upright with thunder in their hands. He found the first one easily for it smelled like smoke. Its soft flesh was no match for his fangs as he tore out its throat, ending the pitiful cries in a bubbling froth. It fell to the ground but he was already on the prowl for its companion, a larger one with much pale fur on its face.

That one was a bit more difficult to see as it blended with the forest because of its mottled coat. After a quick growl, he tore forward by a few quick strides, felt the air caress his belly when he leaped high. Because of the size, he tackled it first so he could assess the threat. The being made a sound when it landed on the ground. The thunder in its hands rolled again, creating a sharp burning sensation in his shoulder. No matter. The pain was slight. He dove for this larger prey and wrestled with it, rolled on the ground. When he had successfully pinned it beneath him, he gutted it with his claws. A pitiful cry flattened his ears against the back of his head. Too high-pitched. When it tried to crawl away, a tress of its innards trailing in the mud behind it, he closed his jaws on the thing's neck and snapped it easily.

The third didn't smell as much of fear but of confusion. That one too made the thunder roll, but no burn touched him this time. Circling it, he lunged and snapped the thunder stick in half. He was about to circle it once more to get a better angle when another smell wafted to him. He recognized it.

White-hot fury sharpened his vision, flared his nostrils until he could smell nothing but this new prey.

He took a quick swipe at the present thing's throat and a gush of hot blood rewarded him. No time to revel in the kill though, for there was that last one to catch.

More cunning but older and slower, he'd wanted to keep it for last. For this one was special...it'd done something wrong, hurt something precious, beloved by him. He wouldn't kill it right away.

He stopped, raised his head to the great white light so he could voice his triumph, his primal cry of victory and bloodlust. He knew the prey heard him and he rejoiced in this. He *meant* it to hear him coming, to smell his inexorable approach and see its death in his eyes.

With a great leap, he cleared the short distance between the prey and him. Mud clung to the thing's hind legs. Thunder rolled in its hands but didn't touch him. Circling it as fast as he could, he lunged at the thing's back and tore a great chunk out of it. The thunder stick fell to the ground. When he rolled it around so it could see him clearly, he noticed how its teeth looked bright and smooth. A great anger descended over him as he listened to the peculiar sounds coming from that throat. No matter. It would suffer greatly for what it'd done. When it pushed against him and climbed back on its hind legs, he let it get a few steps ahead before tackling it down again. He toyed with it for a while, letting it get back up before leaping and tackling it down again. The stench of fear was overpowering.

Growing tired of this game, he let it get up one last time before sending it sprawling to the side with a powerful blow. This time, he pinned it by a leg. Slowly so as not to kill it, he raked a claw across its soft belly. Layers of something thin and devoid of fur gave way to denude the thing's true skin. It cried out when he curled his lips to show the thing his teeth and leaned down closer to its peculiar flat face. Baring his fangs, he breathed in the prey's smell, its gasps and stifled cries of fright. He could end it all right then, could rip the thing's face off and savage its flailing limbs. Nothing would be simpler than sinking his fangs into the supple hide, feel the beat of its heart fluttering against his tongue as he slowly, relentlessly squeezed harder until the light would leave its eyes. Or he could even end it much quicker than that and simply tear the thing's throat open and letting it bleed to death.

But he didn't. He yearned to kill it and knew he would eventually. But not now.

He wanted to make this one last.

* * * * *

Tears rolled down her eyes the entire time she rushed back to the weather station. How long did she spend with her hand cramped over the throttle twisted full blast? She couldn't tell. Spray froze her to the bones, wind stung her eyes. Yet she didn't reduce speed once, not even when she almost didn't make a bend in the river, of which there were many. Relying on her inherent sense of navigation and piloting skills, Erica bent forward in the RIB, hoping for even more speed.

Were they hurting him? Had they shot him and was he now bleeding to death, alone, facedown in the dirt? The image made her gag in fear and desperation. She wouldn't let them. If they hurt him, she'd kill them all!

The depth of her rage surprised her. But as soon as she'd vented it, fear surfaced again and choked what little flame of hope she clung to. They had guns, damn them.

Her desperation to reach the station quickly spurred her to take chances with her own life. When she would've spent a short while studying a leg of the journey, as she usually did, she just plowed through without a thought or care. Speed was of the essence. She had to get to the station and get there fast.

A quick glance skyward revealed the full moon's white face framed by shredded clouds. She still couldn't believe…

Lothar is a werewolf.

There are werewolves among us.

Her tears dried out. Because she had nothing left to cry or from a profound sense of desolation, she couldn't be sure, only that as she made the last twist in the river and spotted the white sphere behind the treetops, she leaned forward in the RIB until she was no longer seated but crouched over the throttle like a frenetic jockey on his horse.

Faster. Faster!

He depended on her to get help. He'd sacrificed himself so she could reach the station and radio Dawson. She wouldn't waste his precious gift.

Too soon, she had to fuel that damn thing, which wasted precious minutes as she lugged around the heavy jerry cans, tinkered with the motor and finally managed to pour the fuel down the plastic funnel. That she was fueling a burning-hot motor with precious little light to help didn't escape her. But damn it, she had to hurry. Lothar could be dying at that very second.

Finally, the station came into view, from a distance the cluster of white and light gray buildings huddled against the embankment resembling a pack of scared sheep. Her plane gleamed when she banked and aimed for the water's edge. No time to slow down along the pier. She was just going to beach the whole damn thing!

Spreading her feet, Erica pointed the prow of the boat right in the middle of the gravelly and rocky edge, didn't let the throttle go until she was about ten feet away then hunkered down among the inflatable seats and ropes.

With a thunderous crash, the RIB rocked sideways, clawed for the first few feet before vaulting some good three or four in the air. For a split second, Erica left the bottom of the boat and floated a few inches. She grunted when the RIB landed hard, skid at an oblique angle and finally settled with a grumble against the rocks.

Her throat raw, her eyes burning, she crawled on top of the seats, out over the edge and fell in a heap on sharp boulders and wet sand. One of her wrists began to burn. No time to investigate. They could be killing him right now!

Unfortunately, her plane wasn't entirely fixed. Some of the electrical components still needed to be reattached. She couldn't spare even a second on it. Lothar's radio was the only one serviceable right now.

After a deep breath, she sprinted up the path, slipping and falling too many times to count, twisted her ankles but the price to pay was slight compared to what she'd seen Lothar endure. The pain must have been horrible.

There was no light anywhere around the station. None inside either.

When she approached and realized the door was closed, she knew it was probably locked. Feet heavy with exhaustion and waterlogged shoes, she dragged herself onto the porch and confirmed her fear. Lothar had locked his house.

Lothar.

The name alone brought dry tears to her eyes. She'd left him behind. Left him with a gang of gun-toting maniacs chasing after him. Yet what could she have done? He'd told her to leave, probably knowing he wouldn't be *himself*. She didn't know a thing about werewolves, not even the legends or myths.

Werewolf!

What she knew, she'd gleaned from movies, which didn't mean shit. Would he recognize her? She doubted it. Lothar had been more than resolute that she leave. She gave the handle a rough, desperate shake. Snarling, she tried to put her shoulder to it, her hip. Nothing. She *had* to get inside but would need something to force the door.

The door didn't have a window, unfortunately. And the actual building's windows were too high to crawl into. So she'd have to basically demolish the door to get in, which she was more than ready to do if that was what it took! Circling the main building, she went on a frantic search of something she could use.

With the moon's light, she spotted the pile of mangled firewood. It gave her some hope. She felt so numb. If she found a nice long piece, she could bash her way in.

Tripping over everything, her feet, pieces of log, other things she couldn't identify, Erica wandered around the site, increasingly closer to the woods. She must have bled from her hands because everything felt slick and sticky.

"Christ," Erica snarled as she picked up a log, found it too light and tossed it back.

She was close to giving up hope when her foot slid along something much too smooth to be a fallen branch. After she palmed the area with her hand, Erica closed her eyes. The axe.

Panting hard enough to cause a stitch in her side, Erica hurried back to the porch. That door was coming down, dammit!

Axe in hand, she used the head of it instead of the edge and slammed it against the panel like a battering ram. Her wrists burned, her hands were so weak and slick they kept slipping along the handle. She noticed only then the bandages were gone. So many aches and pains plagued her poor body, she hadn't even noticed.

Think of him. *How many aches and pains does* he *have right now?*

She rammed the axe several times, each thud made a deeper indentation in the hollow metal panel. Too slow. Much too slow.

Erica cursed and gave that one shot her all. The narrow head of the axe crashed against the doorjamb and splintered it. Her shoulder finished the job. With a half sigh half moan, she stumbled into the house, headed for the radio room and noticed how Lothar's power bar under the computer desk wasn't on. No lights anywhere either…

The rainstorm.

There wasn't any power in the place. None. The storm had knocked it off again. She didn't know where the generator was or how to get it going again. What if it was locked in one of the annexes? No time to go hunting around.

Erica didn't even bother bringing the axe back outside and just let it thud on the floor. The moon had dipped slightly lower toward the tree line. Her watch indicated one in the morning. She was so tired, she could sleep right then and there, curl up on the ground and close her eyes.

But Lothar needed help.

Jerked alert, she jogged clumsily back down the path toward her plane. If she had to fix that radio by moonlight, she'd do it.

Her plane looked so sad sitting there tied like a forgotten beast. She patted the underside of the wing as she pulled her dead weight inside the cabin. Her toolbox was still there, the lid off, just as she'd left it that afternoon before...

Thomson. That...that *monster*.

Anger made her grab the flashlight and poke at the circuit breakers she'd bought.

On her elbows and knees, she squeezed behind the front seat and fingered the back of the circuit-breaker panel. So many wires hanging loose. Shit. Down on her side, she let her head rest against the floor and tried to finger her way over the back of the panel. She was so tired.

Erica woke with a start. Oh no! She'd fallen asleep. How could she have been so damn selfish!

"*Nooo*."

She gasped when her watch announced two fifty-seven. She may as well have killed him herself. The guilt crushed her. Despair choked the air out of her lungs.

Rolling onto her back, she tried to claw her way out of the tight spot and ended up giving a kick to the toolbox that sent it spilling over the side and onto the pier. She cursed when she realized her flashlight had been left on and was now dead.

Tears threatened to make her a complete wreck, so she forced them back and scooted out from behind the seat, sat against the edge and, after missing a couple of times, finally found the rung and stepped out of the plane. She was so tired, she could hardly manage her own body. Every limb felt alien, like they weren't hers to control.

There wasn't a single cloud left and the moon shone brightly. For some reason, Erica cursed at it, at the damn thing for hurting Lothar so much.

With a long sigh, she collapsed on her knees and started sifting through the tools. She was bending over the upturned toolbox when she spotted something by the corner of her eye. A dark shape, unmoving, with eyes like glowing embers.

He was there. Right on the pier, barely thirty feet from her. Alive!

Lothar.

He'd run all the way from Thomson's lodge to the station, a good fifty-some miles away. Torn between fear and vast—universe-encompassing vast—relief, she pulled one knee off the pier and tried not to stare while at the same time studying his behavior. Would she know if he decided to pounce? Would he kill her if he did?

"It's me, Lothar," she said gently, using her most soothing voice. "It's Erica."

He didn't move a muscle, only stood there, his chest swelling rhythmically with each cavernous breath, his disturbing gaze set on her. She tried not to show her fear but knew she was failing miserably.

Without looking down, she palmed the spilled content of her toolbox.

A deep growl rumbled in Lothar's chest. He took a step forward.

Even from the distance and the relatively poor light, she spotted the hackles on the back of him raised in spikes. Another growl rumbled deep in his chest. She could swear she felt the vibration along the planks.

Erica nearly fainted at the sound. So primal, so much like a predator. This wasn't Lothar, not right at the present. He was too far gone to recognize her. She'd survived up to then only to be gored by the man she loved.

Desperate, Erica ignored the continued and rising growl and kept patting her tools for anything she thought she could use. Lothar didn't seem to like that at all and padded a couple of feet toward her. He emitted a sort of bark-yelp, a strange combination of man-beast and even though she couldn't really understand what he'd said—if he'd said anything—she realized he was getting agitated.

She needed something to distract him. Erica couldn't bring herself to hurt him, even if that meant letting him maul her to death. She preferred dying this way than living with the knowledge she'd hurt him.

A quick peek down at the tools proved her undoing. With his vicious fangs completely uncovered, he rushed at her. Erica cringed as she closed her hand over a smooth and metallic object. The flare gun!

With much more speed than she thought herself capable of, she slammed the metal cylinder down with her palm while pointing at Lothar. Just as he was lengthening his stride, she aimed. She knew he was going to leap. Any second now…

She fired.

His sharp yelp tore at her heart. Lothar tried to avoid the blinding projectile as it shot out and hit the pier between his feet. He lunged sideways but too far and tumbled into the water with a strangled bark.

Erica didn't wait to see if he could swim. She had no doubt he could.

While he splashed around and growled furiously, like a madwoman she rushed along the pier, dashed up the path with energy born of wretched fear and leaped up the four steps without touching a single one. The door wasn't in too bad a shape so she closed it, looked around the Spartan room for anything she could drag against it and resolved to use the sofa a few feet into the living room.

Groaning, she pushed against it, tugged and finally decided to upturn it against the entrance instead. She was finishing when sounds from outside paralyzed her.

Small clicks like someone drumming their fingers against a hard surface only bigger…much bigger.

Erica backpedaled from the overturned sofa and back into the living room. Trying to keep her breathing under control so she could hear where he was moving to, she turned her head slightly, followed the clicking sound. Her heart was squeezing painfully with each beat, more like a fluttering. Her mouth was suddenly dry. She licked her lips.

Outside, the sound stopped. Another replaced it. A brisk sniffing, followed by a low growl. Erica squeezed her eyes shut when tears blinded her.

Lothar was *sniffing* at the door.

She thought she'd go mad at the terror clawing at her. With her arms outstretched in case she hit something, she backed farther into the living room. Her left hand encountered something. A chair.

Silence settled around the house. Then she heard him go down the metal steps, followed by the muffled sound of his paws in the dirt.

He was leaving?

The sudden and unmistakable sound of something heavy running forced a squeak of panic out of her. A split second later, the entrance literally exploded inward. The sofa went crashing far into the corridor with a thunderous racket. The walls shook under the impact.

Broken remains of the jamb and bent metal panels creaked and rattled when a soaking wet Lothar stepped over the debris and stopped, silhouetted in the gaping entrance. For a few seconds he stood immobile, his gaze searching the interior before settling on her.

Erica backed frantically. She couldn't speak, could only stare in mute horror as he slowly, carefully, stepped off the broken door and other bits and stalked into the living room.

His eyes never left hers. Out of desperation, Erica put the chair in front of her in an inborn urge to put a barrier between two hundred plus pounds of fang-bearing half wolf and her. For a split second, she looked like a lion tamer. The ludicrous image triggered a panicky giggle out of her.

I'm going to die.

A lightning-quick swipe of his powerful hand sent the chair smashing against the wall where it broke into several pieces. The force sent Erica back. Her hip caught against something. The table. With a partly stifled grunt, she tumbled heavily against the lone remaining chair, nearly toppled over but steadied herself with one foot. It clattered back on all four legs. Something tugged at her shoulder and she fiddled with it without looking. The blanket she'd left there to dry.

Well, that won't help.

Step by cautious step, Lothar drew near, barely a few feet away, trailing water into his immaculate home, his paws the size of squash racquets. She could smell his cologne and the thought made her want to cling to the slowly sinking hope that he was still in there, somewhere, still inside the beast. It was Lothar still—wasn't he—*her* Lothar.

He sniffed deeply once then in a series of quick little pants, as if he tasted the air. Or tasted her scent. She wondered for a split second what a person tasted like. The thought horrified her.

I'm already losing my mind.

Only five feet away now.

Lothar's head was low over his arms and tilted to one side, his vicious-looking claws clicking against the floor, his powerful shoulders rolling with each slow step. He was so big. She guessed his shoulders would reach her waist. That is, if she had the energy to stand. He was still dripping wet but Erica noticed it wasn't just water landing in clicks on the floor…

Was he hurt? Was that his blood?

The thought of what he'd done, those horrible cries as she floated downriver threatened to sink her hopes for good. *Push it away.* Erica blinked then focused on his face. Fangs like her baby fingers protruded from his lips. At least his hackles were down.

Maybe it's just the water flattening it.

With moonlight stabbing inside the room at a sharp angle, Erica saw his face clearly then. A rosy scar cut the regularity of his golden-brown coat. It ran from his temple down along his muzzle and curved under his jaw. Just as she was used to seeing on his human face. His eyes too were the same gray green, held the same intensity. It *was* Lothar in there. She could still see a sliver of the man beneath the beastly façade. Erica clung to it, to the belief that somewhere deep inside him remained the heart of a man with whom she'd fallen in love.

He extended his powerful neck and took a quick, tentative sniff with his mouth parted. Erica heard the chair creak when she leaned as far as she could, literally molding her back to the backrest. But he kept going, didn't stop at her chest and reached with his quivering nose over her shoulder to smell at something behind her. Barely daring to turn her head, she peeked down and noticed the blanket draped over the backrest. The same one she'd used to protect him from the rain when he'd rushed outside naked. He must have smelled them both together on it.

"Lothar," she murmured close to his powerful neck. The smell of him felt so incongruous to the image of his hairy— *furry*—body. "It's me, Erica."

A muscle twitched on his shoulder amidst the mass of them. His ears quivered when he drew back. Erica swore she could see his eyebrows wrinkling, his eyes narrowing, his expression turning utterly, unmistakably *sad*. Her heart went out to him.

Lothar whimpered deep in his chest. The sound conveyed so much grief, so much despair that she had to fight the urge to wrap her arms around him and hold him tight.

With a long sigh that swelled his massive chest, Lothar sat very much like a dog, with his legs tucked under him and slowly, his gaze on her face still, laid his great head on her lap.

"You're in there, aren't you? You're still my Lothar."

Burning tears rolled down her cheeks. She licked the salty taste off her lips as she placed a light, *very* light, hand on the back of his neck, where she proceeded to caress him in calm and deliberate strokes. Water from his drenched coat seeped into her pants. His breathing deepened, that cavernous sound like an engine, then slowed. His eyes closed.

"You'll be okay now, Lothar. I'm here and I'm not leaving. You can trust me."

Her murmured promises and encouragements seemed to appease him for soon the depth of his breath told her he was sleeping. Lothar had actually fallen asleep on her lap! His trust touched her for she suspected how difficult it was for him to trust anyone, even himself. She had no idea what could have happened to make him the way he was—werewolf and everything else—but whatever it'd been, it must have been cruel and profound. A betrayal of the worst kind. She could feel it. But not tonight. Even in his "altered" state, he'd trusted her, laid his life down between her hands, confident she wouldn't hurt him.

While her voice and her hands soothed Lothar with words and caresses, Erica watched the moon dip below the trees across the river. She witnessed the sky turning brown and purple with the occasional strip of burgundy. Her hands never stopped caressing Lothar's neck as the hours passed. She never stopped loving him.

Chapter Ten

∞

Pain lanced his face and body and limbs. Something was trying to claw out of him! He heard himself howling without cease. Fire entered his mouth and nose, flooded his guts, ripped its way out of every pore as everything began to dull and fade. Through it all, a being—female by the smell of it—kept making soothing sounds. He knew she was doing it for him and he was thankful for it. Then merciful darkness enveloped him.

* * * * *

Lothar felt himself again. His body throbbed, his teeth felt loose and ached. Swallowing proved hard. But the pain didn't compare to the agony of his very first awakening. He'd had no idea von Innsbruck had infected him and didn't know what was happening to him, only that his entire body felt on fire. Thankfully, he'd changed into a beast rather quickly since his body was already so weak from loss of blood. But the change back into a man...now *that* had been hellish. The shock, the humiliation of waking naked, bleeding and on the verge of total breakdown had all but driven him mad. And if he took it better after six hundred years of practice, it still left his body racked with grief.

It was time to drag his body back home.

He opened his eyes and realized he was sitting on the floor of his living room, facing the window and front door.

Verdammt, the door!

The extent of the damage stunned him for a second then the sinking feeling he'd done something horrible closed in on him.

What have I done?

Wood slats dangled from the destroyed entrance where smears of caked mud and blood in prints he knew too well revealed he'd been the one to force his way in. He'd never done that before, try to break his own door down. What could've compelled him to? What could've been inside that he'd want so much?

Then he remembered. Everything. The demented hunt, the frantic dash through the darkened woods, his desperate hope to save her before he changed and Erica's horrified face as he pushed the boat away. She must have succeeded and come back to the station.

And he'd followed her there.

The mud and blood didn't lie. Revulsion forced his eyes closed.

When he thought he couldn't possibly loathe himself more, that the things he'd done so long ago would drag him to hell despite his pitiful "comeback", he'd committed an even worse crime. The one fear that had forced him to cooperate with those lunatics, the one thing for which he would've done anything, anything at all, even lay down his own life. His light. It was gone. He'd killed it himself.

Erica had died with that last image of him, a creature of rage and violence. She hadn't even had time to learn who he was. He had so wanted to tell her everything but had been too much of a coward. He'd delayed the inevitable until it was too late. He'd learned to live with guilt, the devil knew he had, but this time, he wasn't sure he would. The irony stung him deeply—he'd been given a second chance in life and he'd wasted it. Again.

First with Sister Jane, his one-time mentor and friend. Probably his only true friend. A woman who'd given him a place to call home, for a time anyway, had found him work in New York when he'd just immigrated there with a wave of others like him, looking to make a new life for themselves. She hadn't judged him, not once, even though his temper would have warranted many times. With his skills as physician, he'd worked at her charitable organization and been able to repay her kindness that way.

Then his other second chance had come with Erica. Another who'd shown him patience and kindness. And so much more. She'd shared her body with him, had let him touch her, love her. To repay that sort of trust, Lothar had forced his way into her shelter and murdered her.

It was all too much.

When a muscle twitched at his jaw, Lothar felt something soft and warm underneath his face. He realized then the peculiar position in which he sat, only partly upright while his legs were folded underneath him. A small weight pressed on the back of his head. When he looked up, he spotted the cuff of a red nylon jacket he recognized.

Please, please.

He repeated the desperate plea in his head as he slowly followed with his gaze the cuff, higher along the sleeve, a shoulder, the torn collar, dreading the mangled mess he'd find in the end. Erica's beautiful face was covered in superficial scratches and dirt. Her eyes were closed.

Despair engulfed him whole and he wished he could die that very second.

But her chest rose slightly. She lived!

Lothar was ready to melt with relief when the next thought stopped him. He'd been in contact with her as the beast yet she lived. Impossible. Unless…

No.

He'd infected her! He'd made her like him.

Lothar reached up with a numb hand and gently traced the curve of her jaw. None of the injuries he could see looked deep enough to allow for the blood to flow and mix with his own. With a start that cramped her entire body, her eyes flared wide.

The horror still filled them. He thought his heart would stop. Then she looked down, her pupils contracted and recognition settled in the pales orbs. He felt her relax immediately. A flicker of smile curved her lips.

Had Lothar believed in a god, he would've thanked him on his knees. But he'd lost the ability to believe in the divine. The notion of something pure and good had long ago been corrupted out of him. Still, to see Erica safe and sound had brought him as close as he'd ever been to enlightenment.

Without waiting to hear from her that he'd dared touch her body with his monstrous hands, Lothar floundered to his knees and frantically patted her shoulders and arms, her neck, her face, which he twisted left and right to look for his handiwork. Finding none, he sat on his heels and framed her head with both hands.

"Please forgive me," he murmured. His throat was raw and tight. He wanted to say more, so much more, but for now could only fill his eyes and heart and soul with her. Time for words would come soon enough.

"You haven't hurt me, Lothar, it's okay." She cringed and shifted in the chair.

He rose, tried to find the other but noticed the broken pieces strewn along the wall. He shook his head. Everywhere around him were reminders of his nature. How he hated himself right then. It wasn't enough that he'd been an odious man in his life but he had to be an outright monster as well. Inside and out.

"Erica, I don't know how I could have been here with you and not…you must know. Everything."

She gave a sad little nod as she stood on uncertain legs. "I know. But first, we have to call the police." Her hand came to rest over his on the table.

He nodded and slid his hand away.

There was still no power to the station, so Lothar fired up the generator and radioed Dawson. He couldn't believe how calmly he announced that there'd been some trouble at a lodge upriver from him. For once, Sam only listened and told them both to sit tight, that the police would be there soon.

When he faced her, Lothar noticed the dark circles under her eyes. "They won't be here for at least an hour, even if they come by floatplane."

She nodded, her chin trembling even as she put on a brave face. He loved her more for this than anything else. She was just unflappable. His rock. His light.

"I'll get your clothes from the boat," she said, turning around and stepping over the demolished entrance.

Picking his way carefully, Lothar followed her down the path. A cold mist hung to the ground and drifted in tendrils over the quiet river. Cold seeped into his bones. By the time he reached the pier, Erica was coming back with a bundle of clothes under an arm and his boots in the other.

"You might want to rinse some of the blood off."

He looked down at himself and cringed. Shivering with cold and humiliation, Lothar knelt by the riverbank and scrubbed his arms and legs clean. Dried blood rubbed off in flakes. His right shoulder stung where a bullet had grazed him. He'd seen enough wounds in his life to categorize them and knew what this one was even if he couldn't remember being shot at.

When he was done splashing his body, he cupped his hands, filled them and rubbed his feverish face. He could still taste the metallic tang of blood in his mouth when he rinsed it. The blood of his victims.

She gave him his clothes piece by piece, caring enough to give them to him in the proper order, from underthings to jacket and boots.

Dressed, he surveyed the pier and the toolbox with its content strewn around in a wide circle. Even there, signs of his passage were clearly visible with bloody prints on the pier itself. A long, black scuff caught his attention.

Erica must have seen him looking at it for she followed his gaze. "Oh that's the flare."

"You fired a flare up here? There's nothing around for at least a hundred miles."

"Not to draw attention to myself but to keep it away from me. I didn't have a choice." She smiled tentatively. "Sorry."

Sorry?

He was the one who should grovel at her feet begging for forgiveness. She shouldn't have to feel sorry for defending her life against him.

Erica suddenly appeared miserable and shaky. She looked up to him with tears in her eyes. "Can I have a hug?"

Lothar almost cried himself when he wrapped his arms around her and held her tight. Leaning his chin over her head, he breathed in the smell of her, forced every nerve ending to remember the feel of her body pressed against him, the warmth, the pure joy. He willed himself to live this moment to its fullest, because he knew it'd be the last time he touched her.

"You deserve to know who I am," he said slowly, each word a dagger in his heart.

"Not now."

"Yes, now. Or I'll never have the courage again."

He told her everything then. All he was, all he'd been and done. His true age—almost six hundred and seventy-one years—and where he was from. Lothar left nothing out as he mercilessly plowed through his former life, how he'd been subjected to the worst form of abuse and how in turn he'd done the same to others. The years of shame and powerlessness to stop his "tutor" and his friends from using his body as they pleased then the years afterward when he'd unleashed his rage on others, seducing them, using his pleasing appearance so he could exploit them as he'd been exploited. He shared with Erica how he thought that wrestling power away from others would keep them from trying to control him, how he'd vowed to never again trust another human being and would consume what he needed and discard the rest.

Lothar disclosed the episode of Katrina and her abhorrent scheme to get her hands on a relative's fortune and how he'd willingly helped her. Lothar left nothing out when he shared his abusive treatment of von Innsbruck, his twisted obsession with Scarlet and how much he'd hurt that woman in his hunger to possess her. He revealed how he'd fought and lost against von Innsbruck in 1373, a year he'd come to view as cursed, and been left for dead with his face in the dirt, how that fitting end had never come and he'd woken with the disease that made him a beast every full moon. He'd lost everything, his practice, his assets, his future. From physician and sought-after bachelor, he'd become a wild man living off the forest, isolated and distrustful, a hermit, before slowly coming back to civilization a couple centuries later. He'd then been a courier during the Napoleonic Wars and used his great knowledge of his country's forests and mountains to help the war effort. He told her of his subsequent immigration to the New World in 1872, of Sister Jane and her obstinate hope in his redemption, her death in 1899, when nothing had kept him in New York and the siren's song of the Gold Rush had lured him to Alaska, where he'd lived for almost a hundred years, moving from place to place. Lothar told her about his recent life, acquiring dual citizenship during the last decade through forged papers and his subsequent profession as meteorologist and assignment to Dawson in 1997. He remembered every date, every name, every place he'd called home before being forced to uproot himself and start all over again. How he wished he could've forgotten at least half of them!

He talked.

Lothar talked long after he knew he'd lost her, each additional word driving her away. But he told her everything. Erica deserved to know the truth even if it meant losing her.

* * * * *

Erica pulled away when he began his tale about a woman he'd loved long ago—or thought he loved. What he'd done to her and her man shocked Erica. And it hurt her.

She hugged herself as she took a step back and watched Lothar spill his heart at her feet. She had no way of verifying his claims but she knew he was telling the truth. No man would share such intimate, damning details if they weren't true. He had no reason other than his wish to inform her about the kind of man he was or had been at one point. Erica wished he'd stop. She didn't need to know...nor did she *want* to. It occurred to her she didn't want to know Lothar's past because she'd suspected all along the violence in it, even if she couldn't have guessed any of the details. She was also afraid of knowing his past because it'd force her to either love him in spite of it or take her love away and leave him behind. Neither choice felt right.

I'm such a coward.

Lothar easily could've told her some story about becoming recently infected and his changing into a werewolf. There was no need to add anything else. She couldn't have known it wasn't true. But Lothar would know. And for this, he was baring his soul, showed her every little dark corner. The least she could do was listen. And she did. Listened to every word, every confession, every fault he put on himself. The entire time, Erica wanted to reach out and comfort him but couldn't bring herself to.

He spoke quickly, as if he were afraid to run out of time, that he'd be struck dead in the next minute and wanted to get all of it off his chest first. Erica tried not to feel burdened by all these admissions but soon found herself staring at the ground under the weight of them. And he'd lived with this all his life!

When the sound of a plane drifted closer, Lothar was still talking, although by then his voice was hoarse and shaking. But he finished his tale. Erica nodded when silence settled after his last word. She trudged up the path and went to sit on the porch, her knees drawn up under her chin, her arms wrapped around her shins.

Lothar plodded in the opposite direction, down along the pier, waiting to help moor the floatplane after it'd made its approach.

She didn't even look up when constables spilled out of it and began talking with Lothar or when much later, several SUVs roared out from between the main building and the annex and stopped beside Lothar's truck. While nameless, faceless police officers came and went and asked questions and communicated with the other team farther north at the lodge, Erica tuned them out.

She remained sitting on the steps, stupefied, numb. Lost. A blanket had long been wrapped over her shoulders, a juice box placed in her hands. Constables had come and gone, sometimes in pairs, sometimes in small groups, asking questions. Always the same.

Had she seen what kind of animal it was? No.

Could it have been a bear or a group of wolves? She didn't know. She couldn't remember much.

Had the hunters been alive when Lothar and she had escaped by boat? Yes, she could hear gunshots.

Did she know any of them, who they were and how they'd organized the manhunt? She only knew what information Thomson had given her for the flight. He'd paid cash. Five thousand. No, she'd no idea they would start shooting at each other.

Had she seen the weapons they'd put in her plane? Not really, everything was packed or in bags. But she could tell it was large game hunting gear.

Did they know how lucky they were to be alive, Lothar and she, with the beast trying to get inside the station? Yes.

Would she mind if they checked her plane? No. They could also see the damage the fire had caused when one of the hunters had sabotaged her circuit-breaker panel on Friday.

Could they keep the floatplane temporarily as evidence? Yes.

Would she be up there or in Whitehorse if they wanted to reach her?

"Whitehorse," Lothar replied for her.

She looked up to find him standing a few paces behind, likewise with a juice box in hand. He hadn't opened it. "Erica lives in Whitehorse and that's where she'll be."

When the constables were gathered around their trucks and their own floatplane, Lothar approached and sat beside her. Heat from his elbow reached her knee. The urge to touch him tingled her palms. But she didn't know how safe it'd be to touch him. Not because she feared he would hurt her. She wasn't sure touching Lothar was a good idea since he looked bent on seeing her off back to her own life. If she clung to the barrier he'd just put between them, that past life filled with so much pain and violence, she could at least pretend she no longer loved him, she could believe her life would get back to normal when she returned to Whitehorse. The truth was, she cared about what he said because of the reason he said it, not necessarily the details of it. Sure, that he'd been such a brute once mattered to her in the sense that it helped to understand him, but when she looked at it directly, Erica realized she didn't really give a damn. Maybe she was worse than he'd been. *Maybe that's why they call it denial.*

After spending several seconds looking at her while she obstinately stared at the tip of her shoes poking out from underneath the blanket, Lothar sighed. The sound felt like a razor across her heart.

"They're going to take you home now."

"Why did you tell me all this?" Erica asked suddenly, snapping her gaze to his face. She caught it then, the pain, the loneliness and misery. The regret.

He immediately put the mask back on. It didn't fool her. "You have a right to know. I wish I would've told you before."

"But now that I *do* know, what am I supposed to do with it?"

"Do with it as you wish, Erica," he replied softly. His waved at someone down the pier then turned to her. "They're waiting for you."

"I don't care," she snapped back. "I'm asking *you*, what did *you* want me to do with your story? Judge you? Punish you? What?"

He raked a hand in his hair, opened his mouth to speak but nothing came out.

"That's what I thought. Well, I'm not going to judge or punish you, Lothar, and I'm not going to run away screaming. I'm staying right here."

Hope, shock then horror flared his eyes. "You're leaving if I have to carry you to that plane. It's much too dangerous for you here. You've seen what I can do!" He rose and stepped past her on his way inside the house. "Leave."

Erica stood as well, whirled back toward the door with her hands on her hips and a good bit of arguing at the ready but lost her chain of thoughts when she spotted Lothar walking away. The way he held his head and back, one would've believed he was carrying a house on his shoulders. Or the weight of a thousand regrets.

Someone whistled. With a curse, Erica marched down the gravel path and joined the pair of constables waiting for her at the floatplane. A team was already on its way up to the station to repair hers and fly it back down to Whitehorse so the RCMP could do its investigation. Erica gave a tender pat to her aircraft as she plodded by. Expecting every other second to see Lothar run out of his demolished doorway and wave frantically for them to wait, Erica kept her face pressed against the window while they prepared for takeoff. When it became clear he wasn't going to make one last attempt at keeping her with him, she leaned back and laid her head against the backrest.

Erica didn't sleep on her way back home though she wanted to. Each hour asleep would be one less to endure knowing she'd lost him. It'd be sweet oblivion. So why couldn't she sleep?

By the time they reached Whitehorse, Erica was expecting journalists to flock the small airport and camp outside like on the news. One of the constables explained that one of the hunters was a prominent American businessman and a publication ban had already been levied on the whole thing. Erica was glad. She didn't want to tell anyone anything. She wanted to crawl back home and lie in bed for six months. She knew she wouldn't, only wished she could wallow in self-serving misery for a while.

Instead of the peace and quiet she so longed for, what waited for her at home were two suddenly affectionate brothers and a pair of clingy parents.

When everyone had been properly made to feel better and hugged and told everything would be fine, Erica closed the door on the last back and locked it.

Dirty and numb and ringing with emptiness vast enough to make her fear about her sanity, she collapsed facedown on her bed and didn't even bother to stifle her sobs in her pillow. She cried. She cried for her loss. She cried for Lothar, who'd obviously suffered enough for ten people.

How could she have gone from bliss to despair in the span of a weekend? Erica had no explanation for it. For the first time in her life, Erica Bain had no logical explanation, no joke to take the hurt away and no hope that she'd ever be able to laugh again.

For the first time in her thirty-two years, she allowed herself the luxury of falling apart.

Chapter Eleven

ಐ

It took Lothar a week just to put the station back in order. During that time, he tried not to think about her, not to think at all. Everywhere he looked, there was always *something* to remind him of her. A faint tone lingered in the air, like the last second of a tuning fork's reverberation, which served to emphasize to him how empty the place was without her laugh. He would turn around and expect to see her standing there with her arms crossed and that freckled nose crinkling with laughter. But it was better this way. For her anyway.

Driving down to Dawson City for supplies proved even more difficult. Facing the awkward congratulations or questions from people left him tight and cross and he'd had to get back in his truck and forget groceries. For the worst part was that they kept asking how Erica was doing. And he had no answer for them.

After a couple of weeks, they stopped asking. Shockingly, the unpleasant affair blew itself out without the added fire of an extensive media coverage. One wouldn't have known there'd recently been seven murders, that some rich, bored businessmen had started hunting one another before a rabid pack of wolves — the investigation's conclusion — had massacred them all. An abattoir, some of the constables had called the scene. Lothar was glad to put all the pain and the guilt behind him. Again.

* * * * *

Erica sat at her rented office by the wharfs and surveyed the empty room and the carton of files and other documents. Where were her maps?

355

"Oh there," she murmured when she spotted the extra-thick briefcase by the window. *Last batch.*

She checked and rechecked that she hadn't forgotten anything in the drawers or under the desk before giving one last look at her office—her first real office all to herself—and switched off the neon light. The last carton under an arm, she pulled the magnetic placard reading *"Get There Now"* and put it between her teeth as she locked her door. When she passed the receptionist, she relinquished the keys with a little twitch of melancholy. But it was for the best. She couldn't stay in Whitehorse. She'd tried. It hadn't worked.

Outside, October wet snow plastered her hair to her forehead. She tried to keep the hood of her parka over her head but it kept flying back over her shoulders. Down the slowly swaying pier, her plane bobbed in the water, its red and white body gleaming like a jewel. Lengthening her strides, Erica carried the carton up to her plane, pulled the cargo doors wide and sighed when she realized she'd have to repack everything because she had too much *stuff.* Everything she owned basically fit in her plane. Well, mostly. Muttering, she wasted half an hour pulling bags out, putting cartons in at the bottom then the luggage on top. She changed her mind then redid it all. A quick glance at her watch made her grit her teeth. Mid afternoon already. Not much daylight left. Plus there was some serious snow in the forecast. She better hurry.

One last look behind, she climbed in the cockpit and flicked on her instrument panel. If she wanted out of Whitehorse, she had a tiny window of opportunity before the snowstorm. She wanted to be far from there when it hit. She wanted to be far, *period.* The dull ache in her heart intensified every time she thought about him.

With a quick shake of her head, Erica pushed him out of her mind and focused on flying. Always on flying.

Pre-checks done, engine rumbling as she held back the throttle, she radioed the tower.

"Edmonton Center, this is Floater zero one taking off Lake Laberge."

"Floater zero one, Edmonton Center, do you have the latest special weather report for Dawson City?" crackled the male voice in the radio.

"Negative, go ahead with Dawson's SPECI for Floater zero one."

"Dawson special weather report valid for the next twenty-four hours. Winds zero six zero degree, fifteen gusting twenty-five, visibility two miles with snow showers, ceiling is broken at one thousand feet."

"Floater zero one, copy all, thanks."

She was pushing the weather but nothing, *nothing*, would keep her grounded that day. She *had* to leave. Her sanity depended on it. After waiting in vain for Lothar to contact her, she'd lost all hopes he ever would. No use for her to stay in Whitehorse when her heart was no longer there.

By her side on the forward seat rested her magnetic placard. She looked down at it, gave it a quick pat before returning her hand to the yoke. Erica angled her plane away from the pier toward the middle of the wide Lake Laberge, pushed the controls to the maximum, the plane shaking as it cleaved through ripples then she took off toward her new life.

* * * * *

Lothar was glad for the thin layer of snow covering the land. It made everything seem clean and new. After he shook it from his hair and kicked his boots off, he brought the armful of firewood into the living room and set it down to dry by the woodstove, blazing hot and filled to capacity. After he fixed himself a nice strong tea, he went to his office and sat at the computer for the hours of work he'd managed to generate for himself by offering to go back through the archives. Of course, his supervisors had been more than happy to grant him access to the long-neglected files so he could input them into the computerized records. One of the many projects he'd taken on so he wouldn't have too much time to think.

Outside, the wind intensified. Snow stuck to the windowpanes. He gazed out over the river, gray and forlorn, at the way trees swayed under the gusty wind. Power should cut anytime soon. With a snort, he leaned his temple on his fist and pulled the first file to him.

A tiny sound caught his keen ears. He looked out the window but saw nothing. Going back to his work, he sipped at his tea and was turning a page when he heard it clearly. An engine?

Who would be crazy enough to drive up there in this weather? Didn't everybody know they—hell, *he*—called for below-freezing temperatures to hit sometime that night? He'd given his report to Sam early that morning. No one could claim not to know by now.

But the unmistakable sound of an engine forced him to grab his fur-trimmed parka and mitts. Cursing the fool's recklessness, he stomped outside, circled the building and waited to see who'd managed that bit of driving. No headlights disturbed the darkened woods beyond his home. Yet he could still hear the engine and it was definitely coming closer. Craning his neck, he tried to see around the bend in the dirt road. Nothing there. He should see them by now. Then it hit him. The river.

"*Verdammt.*"

He jogged back around the main building, muttering and cursing that he'd be stuck with visitors again—undoubtedly much less charming than his last—when the power would go. Nice and cozy. Great.

Through the thickening snow, he spotted a tiny light in the late afternoon sky right above the tree line. The police? He couldn't tell yet. Lothar waited as the plane executed an impressive drop that took it barely ten feet above the water. He'd seen that bit of wild piloting before. Without knowing what else to do, Lothar waited with his heart beating madly and his fists clenched to his sides.

He refused to hope, just *refused* to.

By the time the floatplane turned to aim at the pier, he could see the color and markings, recognizing Erica's aircraft. Despite his best intentions, hope flared in his chest. Why had she come? He'd told her to leave, to stay away from him. He was dangerous.

As much as it shamed him to admit it, Lothar was secretly happy to see the red and white plane. Engine roaring, Erica pulled up along the pier where Lothar was already waiting and cut down the throttle. What he thought at first were passengers turned out to be cargo. It filled her plane almost right up to the windows. He made quick work of the rope and tethered her float securely to the mooring loop. With the winds announced for that night, he didn't want the thing to float away. She'd need it to go back home.

Because she *was* going back. She couldn't stay, even if he wanted it more than drawing his next breath. It wasn't safe.

He straightened just as the door opened. Without a word, Erica reached to her right, pulled something from the next seat and jumped out of the cockpit.

"Hi. Did you get a new door?"

He nodded, unable to talk just then. She wore an olive green parka, cream-colored turtleneck and still had cowlicks from wearing the headset for three hours. A hint of lip-gloss shone on her lips. She was mesmerizing.

"Is it metal like the last one?"

"Yes."

Lothar drank her in, her freckled face, her pale eyes, the way she looked up at him before...*walking right past?*

Stupefied, he followed her up the path. Her boots left large prints in the thin layer of snow. Once she reached the porch, she climbed, spun around so she could look at him while she slapped something on his front door. It landed a bit crooked but he could read the placard nonetheless.

"Get There Now," he said, reading the tilted sign. "That's your company."

Erica nodded. "Yep. Things are going to change around here, I'm afraid."

Like someone had punched him in the gut, he could only watch in silent awe as she climbed back down, slowly reached behind his head and pulled the elastic from his hair before pocketing it.

"I like it better that way," she murmured in his ear as she stepped back and smiled.

She was in his arms before a single thought had formed. Lothar squeezed her hard, reminding himself not to squeeze *too* hard, but it was so difficult when he wanted to mesh them both into one person. The mix of cold parka, wet snow and warm skin against his cheek proved the ultimate cocktail that sent his senses into a spin. Knowing he was grinning like a damn fool, Lothar pushed her at arm's length. But as soon as elation swelled to unprecedented proportions, it burst. He felt his cheeks, his whole face, sag.

"You shouldn't have come back—"

"Look," she replied, cutting him right off. "I've seen you at your worst, with a mouthful of nasty pointed teeth and your hair sticking up like this." She splayed her hands out on either side of her head. She looked like she had antlers.

Torn between joy and misery, he shook his head. He couldn't accept her gift. She was too precious. "It's dangerous up here for you. I told—"

She put her gloved hand over his mouth and nodded. "I know, I know, you get cranky at full moon. I get cranky too sometimes, PMS and all. But I have just the plan. Get this…every full moon, I fly you out farther north, let's say the day of, then I come pick you up at some spot we'll have staked out beforehand. If it's too cold to fly up there, then I'll take the truck and spend the night in Dawson, not too often to make people wonder, but once in a while, you know. Makes perfect sense."

He wanted to argue. He really did. But as much as he tried to find a fault with her plan, he couldn't...which made him happier than he'd ever been. Yet there still remained some uneasiness at having her around. It wasn't just the full moon that could make him change. What if he did it out of anger?

"It's still not going to work, Erica," he began.

She never let him finish as she grabbed him by the fur-trimmed hood and pulled him down to her.

When her lips pressed against his, all thought other than their naked bodies together in his bed left his head. His hands found her zipper and pulled it down so he could touch her.

Pulling back, she stared at him in a way he'd never seen from her before. She wasn't joking. "I want you to make love to me, Lothar Kessler, and I don't want any of that craziness about holding back. I want you and I want *all* of it."

His first instinct was to object then it occurred to him Erica could handle much more than he'd so far given her credit for. After everything she'd lived through during her passage—including armed men chasing her through the woods! He hadn't wanted to let his darker side take over while they made love in case he scared her away or worse, hurt her. But he knew now that she could take him. And the thought stiffened his cock with amazing fierceness and rapidity. He hadn't been this turned on in his long, long life.

"Let's get your stuff inside before the storm hits," he urged, practically running down the path to retrieve it.

They must have made ten trips. Who knew a single-engine Otter would contain so much stuff! When he was doing what he guessed would be his last trip, Erica came up behind him, pocketing her keys. With a barely suppressed groan of impatience, he slid the carton inside the house with the ball of his foot and meant to ask if that was all.

Lothar rocked back against the front door, which clattered against the wall when Erica jumped and wrapped her legs around his waist. Her slim figure strapped to him provoked all kinds of responses in his already fired senses. She planted a passionate kiss on him, even bit his lip. Had it not been October in the Yukon, with a snowstorm looming, he would've taken her right outside on the porch.

"Inside." The sound of her voice came muffled against his neck as she play bit and kissed with loud wet sounds. "Hurry…shower. Bed. Sex."

"I think not," he snarled as he swung around and slammed the door with his foot before holding her against it with his hips. Working a hand under her, he unzipped his pants and freed his aching cock from the boxer briefs. "Sex now *then* shower, bed, sex."

He let her slide to the floor so he could yank the chinos open. The Velcro closure's ripping sound made him gnash his teeth with anticipation. With Erica helping, Lothar pulled her pants and underwear down around her ankles—so thankful they were wide enough for her to kick out of, boots and all—and stepped between her feet.

A finger confirmed she'd have pleasure as well for the moisture already slicking her folds. After he gathered her thighs in his grip, he stood with a simultaneous tilt forward of his hips. She knocked her head back and closed her eyes when he pushed inside. So wet, so tight. Encouraged by her pelvic roll, he thrust up to his full height, took her hard and fast while she bit her bottom lip and hung on to his neck and waist. The knocks of their disorderly and frenzied coupling reverberated along the wall as the door rattled rhythmically in its frame, ever faster sound soon accompanied by their joined groans of excitement. Pleasure flared to his every pore. He came with a deep upward push that made her pant his name.

Satiated, they slowed, panting against each other's necks, hair in disarray, clothes twisted.

"Whew," she wheezed, a big grin on her face. "Damn, that was good."

Lothar shook his head as he let her slide off him. "Modern women."

"Shower," she announced, marching for her destination as she shed the rest of her clothes.

Lothar realized they'd made love with their parkas still on. That had to be a record somewhere. He couldn't resist giving her butt a sound smack. She whirled around, looking outraged, aroused, flushed with impatience. Exactly how he felt himself.

"The *things* I want to do to you, Erica," he murmured low in his throat.

With a lascivious grin so unlike what he'd come to expect from her, she stepped inside the bathroom and activated the shower. He would've loved to come with her but barely fit in the narrow stall by himself as it were. So he stripped, waited and feasted his eyes while water and soap lather made her body a form of psychological torture. He had no idea where the strength to stay put and only watch came from. They switched with a quick kiss then he was the one under close scrutiny. For her viewing pleasure, he rubbed the soap around his body, knowing it was pleasing to the eye and feeling proud of it too. He was rinsing himself when the lights blinked out. The water would turn icy cold in a few seconds.

"Perfect timing," she remarked. He couldn't see her clearly but knew she was grinning.

She pressed a towel against him when he came out of the stall, which rattled when he stepped off. It was a bit colder in the bathroom and he longed to return to the living room where he'd stuffed the woodstove right to its glass window. An image of the fire's amber glow and how it'd reflect deliciously on Erica's body flashed in his mind. Oh it'd be perfect.

As they made their way there, he picked up the bits of clothing lying about and dumped it all on the sofa. The blanket he'd lent her was there, folded neatly. Lothar unfolded and laid it out on the floor in front of the woodstove.

"Now," he said, standing in the middle and beckoning to her, "we can play all night."

With a grin, she joined him.

Lothar circled her and placed his hand over her shoulder when she looked about to turn around. "Stay put."

By the fire's glow, her skin came alive with amber tones and furtive shadows, goose bumps and forgotten water beads along her spine, that special place he loved so much at the small of her back. Back in his halcyon days as favorite to many in Vienna's court, he'd embraced many a small back but never one quite like Erica's. Hers was both well-defined because of her trim figure and invited his gentle caress, but at the same time a delectable network of muscles played under her skin and this incited in him more than a light touch. But what he enjoyed most—and hers would bring unparalleled exhilaration—was to watch the small of a woman's back bending, bowing with her behind raised in surrender to him. The sweetest gift.

While Erica stood in the fire's golden glow, Lothar circled her many times, slowly, drinking his fill with the sight of her. Once in a while, he'd unexpectedly stroke a thigh or blow on a shoulder. Her body would then answer his touch with a tightening or a frisson. He loved it.

"Do you get pleasure from this?" he murmured in her ear when he stood behind her.

A simple nod answered him. "Are you absolutely sure you wish to continue? If this is too much, say it now, because…"

She planted her pale gaze on him. "All of it, Lothar. I trust you."

Closing his eyes against the swell of emotions assailing him, he gathered her hair in a hand and raised it on the back of her head so he could trail gentle kisses along her nape.

"Look down at your feet."

She did. The vertebrae pushed up against the skin and created a perfectly formed little mound that he kissed and licked while a violent shiver shook her. Using the pad of his forefinger like a pen, he wrote her name on her back then his. He explored every recess, curve and prominence. His practiced eye let him know this body was strong and fit, which pleased him for he wanted to do things a frail woman wouldn't bear well. He wanted to love Erica without holding back. Something he'd never done since Katrina, so long ago in her native Germany.

His lips against her spine made her hiss a long sigh. Lothar kissed her between the shoulder blades, watched them swell when she shivered. Then lower over her waist, keeping the small of her back for last, denying himself temporarily so the pleasure would be even more acute when he did press his lips against that special place. He kissed the dawn of her tailbone and finally closed his eyes so he could enjoy the experience to its fullest before touching her spine where the curve was at its sharpest. Erica started.

"Most men don't know about that place," Lothar whispered as he blew air then kissed her again. "Most women don't know about it either."

"Where did you…*ohh.*"

His tongue silenced her right away. Lothar licked her from tailbone to waist, in a straight line then in a series of dashes, as if his mouth were sending Morse code. Her bottom squeezed. A smile denuded his teeth, which he raked up right to her nape. She was so responsive to his touch. Now for the front.

Circling her again, letting the suspense linger a while, Lothar stopped in front of her, let her feel the might of his arousal against her hip before pinching her chin and turning her face away from his. With a snarl, he mock bit her neck. Her response nearly made him lose his focus. She gasped and grabbed his wrist at the same time. The combination of voiced tension and physical restraint served to pour oil over an already raging inferno. It'd been so long since he'd allowed himself that sort of luxury.

He pretended to bite her neck again just to enjoy her reaction one more time. Since she hadn't relinquished her hold on his wrist, she accentuated the pressure. After one last feint, he bit her for real. Erica let out a sharp little yelp that he readily drowned with his mouth. Forcing hers wide, he thrust his tongue in deep, twirled it and retreated with a quick nibble on her bottom lip.

Her eyes were large as she watched what he did to her. He fisted the back of her hair and took a deep whiff of it, filled his head with her intoxicating scent until he thought he would no longer be able to smell anything else but her. Staring at her, Lothar thumbed her jaw then her lips.

"Take it in."

She reached up to hold his hand steady but Lothar pushed it back down and shook his head.

"Just your mouth."

Her lips glistened when they parted and allowed his thumb in. He ran it along her bottom lip then over her teeth before sinking in to the first knuckle. With just the right amount of pressure, he pulled his thumb out and down so her bottom lip would follow. Saliva made the tender flesh look like a ripe fruit. And he was a starving man.

Lothar dove for her mouth and captured it with his. His tongue and teeth proved merciless allies as he attacked from every angle. His fist still in her hair, he forced her head back so he could better devour her. When he left her mouth, Erica was panting. Her lips were swollen and red. So tempting. Sexual hunger pulsated in his balls but he denied himself. He'd come earlier for that exact reason—devote all his time to her pleasure. Watching her come and lose control would be the ultimate release for him.

Leaving her face, he kissed her neck, the delicate collarbones, the dip above her sternum. Her breasts rose with each pant. But he didn't kiss them yet though he knew she was desperate for it. She'd have to wait a while longer.

After he released her hair, Lothar traced a path with an index finger, down her shoulder to her breast, circled the areola a few times to see it tighten then followed the curve underneath so he could reach the other breast without breaking contact. That was of the utmost importance when pleasuring a woman. Break contact as little as possible. Serpentine shapes along her chest forced a series of spasms to tighten her belly. Lothar could see the muscles clenching along her abdomen and flanks. He couldn't wait to feel them from the inside as she wrapped him with her pussy and squeezed.

"Do you want me to kiss your breasts?"

She nodded. Her eyes narrowed when Lothar grinned and shook his head. "Later perhaps."

He returned to tracing swirling shapes over her skin. After dipping his finger into her mouth, he circled a nipple, ever closer. He knew the anticipation was burning her. He could tell by her rapid breathing and dilated pupils. Just so he could enjoy watching her pleasure, Lothar added another finger, his middle, and slid her pebble in the V of his two extended fingers. When it came to rest between his knuckles, Lothar slowly, inexorably brought his fingers closer together, squeezed her roseate point until it darkened and he felt the faint pulse in it. Erica stopped breathing for a few seconds. He waited for the perfect moment when he knew pain would replace pleasure then released her. Color spread to the entire breast. Erica's eyes squeezed shut. The faint odor of female musk reached his keen nostrils. So responsive.

With a grin he knew by experience looked half wicked half seductive, he leaned over, his mouth parted so she would guess his intentions, came very close to actually taking her nipple into his mouth before he retreated and waited for her reaction.

"Lothar," she growled.

She breathed heavily, which caused a spine-tingling wave of violent arousal in him. He loved the sight and sound of a woman's panting. Lothar repeated the process with her other nipple, trapped it between his two fingers while his palm raised her breast higher. Grinning wider now, Lothar bent over her chest while he still trapped one breast in his hand and let his mouth hover close for a full ten seconds. When he knew Erica was ready to either push his head down or smack it, he parted his lips, let his breath caress the imprisoned nipple before wrapping his mouth over it and sucking. Hard.

"Ahh."

Her sharp intake of air rewarded his male pride as nothing else. He knew how to pleasure women, had been "trained" at a young age. But what he wanted most was to please this woman, *his*, please her as no other man had before him. If that required all his skill and all night, he wouldn't complain. He was patient and he was *determined*.

While he seized her other nipple, Lothar curled his spine so he could face her breasts and lavished all his love on them. He sucked and licked, kissed and bit, he blew air and drew them between his teeth then pressed them together so he could ravish both at once. Then he did it all over again.

Erica was making little whimpering sounds in her throat. She wrapped her hands over his head and dug her nails in. His scalp burned but he didn't care.

"Harder?"

A moan and a nod swelled his chest. He dove back in. Lothar made love to her breasts in ways he hadn't before, harder than even he'd ever done it. And the devil knew he'd bruised a few in his passion. Erica's tolerance to his stimulation frothed his desire to drive himself in her right that instant. But he waited. He knew it was worth the wait. *She* was worth the wait.

When he could tell by the grimace on her face the pleasure-pain was slowly sliding toward the latter, he abandoned her breasts so he could tease her belly instead. Her navel provided the perfect sheath for the tip of his tongue. Then kneeling before her, Lothar licked long and slow lines from her pubis up to her waist, each one taking him closer to her sex. He hadn't touched it at all, had denied himself that bliss so he could keep it for later. It was time.

"Spread your feet," he commanded as he planted each about the width of his shoulders.

Because she was fairly tall — women were getting so much taller with every generation — she didn't look too spread out and uncomfortable. In the fire's trembling glow, her narrow ebony patch glistened invitingly. Saliva pooled under his tongue at the thought of eating her.

With precise and deliberate fingers, he parted her so he could see her dark, rosy flesh, so ready for him, so willing. Her juices had seeped out like melted butter and coated her entire cleft. Lothar looked up into her face and caught her staring down at him. Oh she wanted it desperately. Therefore she would have to wait.

He blew on her engorged lips, drew near enough to touch her nether mouth with his but left her on the brink of contact. Muscles contracted on her thighs. He couldn't wait to feel those around his waist as he plowed into her wonderful pussy. This time, Lothar knew he wouldn't hold back. He was long past the ability to hold back.

"Do you want my mouth on you, inside you?"

She didn't even nod or say a word and only stared guns down at him. He grinned widely. After a languorous pass over his upper lip, he flicked his tongue and barely touched her flesh. Erica shivered violently. Lothar indulged the woman so she wouldn't attack him, just to keep her on the edge but not enough to give her actual pleasure. That would come later.

His knees were tight between her ankles and hurt his throbbing cock. A small price to pay for a woman's unrestrained pleasure. While he kept his gaze on her face, he curled his tongue and did a sort of come-hither movement that stroked her bud with a touch he knew was much too light. So he did it again. And again.

Erica's belly constricted, her thighs trembled. Still Lothar used his tongue like a finger and beckoned her into his mouth. Honey now dripped onto his tongue in salty-sweet rivulets. An overwhelming urge to possess her made him growl as he pushed his mouth against hers hard, selfishly. He gorged on her until the first sign of climax tightened her pussy. Then he stopped.

"No, don't stop," she urged by pressing his head to her pelvis. "Come on."

Much stronger than she was, Lothar planted his palm on her mons and kept her away. "Not yet."

She tried to tilt her pelvis so his palm would rub her aching sex. "I'm going to lose it."

While she gyrated in mounting frustration, Lothar forced her still with his hand against her mound and his other around her waist. She quieted with a muttered curse. She'd lost it. Lothar grinned.

She'd find it again. Soon.

Chapter Twelve

ॐ

Erica could've cried with frustration. He'd brought her so close...she could already feel the first tingles as her orgasm swelled. But then he'd abandoned her right there on the brink. She looked down while he knelt in front of her and caught the look of satisfaction etched on his handsome face. A dark light shone in his eyes.

Oh and he knew what he was doing too.

He stood, his muscled body flexing and bulging as he rolled those impressive shoulders. With a hard look, he indicated the floor at his feet. "Now it's your turn to kneel."

With no inhibition or sense of modesty, Erica sank to her knees and looked up into his face. His great cock bobbed inches from her mouth. With his gaze alone, he let her know what he expected from her.

Hands shaking, she gathered his heavy balls in one hand while she fisted his cock. He watched her with the intensity of a predator as she licked his glans, around and under before sinking midway down the long length of him. He must have been ten inches long and her fingers didn't touch around his girth. It was a wonder he could fit at all. In her mouth or in her pussy.

Hard and hot and smooth, his shaft glided in effortlessly over Erica's tongue and throat. The salty taste made her salivate and pump her fist.

"No," he snapped with a sharp slap on her wrist.

Dammit, she wanted to fist him as if there were no tomorrow! Instead, she forced her hands to work slower as her mouth sank deeper around him. She yelped in shock and thrill when he bucked and penetrated her deeper. He pulled away before a gag reflex even registered in her. Erica looked up at him in wonder. Now, that was a man who *knew* how things worked.

When he wrapped a hand over the back her head, thrill and alarm fought inside Erica. He was so large, he wouldn't fit all the way in. With every stroke, Erica was expecting Lothar to force her head against him. Yet he didn't, only fisted her hair and let her do her own thing. Muscles bunched and twitched along his thick thighs. Good grief he was gorgeous.

The very last row of abdominals strained for the weight of his meaty cock and rippled when Erica fisted him, drawing him in hard. His belly contracted. The awful scars around his waist glistened like rained-on earthworms.

Then he did it. He clamped his hand around the back of her skull and plowed in. Erica growled with sheer primal hunger. She fisted whatever part of him she happened to hold and knocked her forehead against his hard lower belly. When a sharp gag reflex tightened her throat, Lothar must have felt it for he released her and pulled all the way out.

"Wait here," he said as he strode over to the sofa.

She watched him rummage through their clothes and pull something out of the pile. When he turned, Erica swallowed hard.

He held his belt folded in half with a fist over each end. A sharp tug made the belt clack loudly. No practice shots either.

Lothar's smile was both menacing and sexy as he drew near and indicated she should turn around. He did this with his index finger pointing down and moving around like a spoon in a mug.

But Erica couldn't take her gaze off the belt in his block-like fists. She wasn't too sure about it anymore. Um.

He knelt by her side and kissed her forehead. "What do you think this is for?"

"I don't know but I'm not sure I want to play anymore."

"Do you trust me?"

Erica looked into his eyes then at the belt taut between his fists then back up into his face. "Yes."

"Then turn around."

She scooted around still kneeling until she faced the woodstove. Lothar remained behind. She couldn't see what he was doing.

As much as it alarmed her, the thought of whatever he was going to do titillated her senses as they'd never been before. She'd never, *ever*, had sex like this. It was so damn good so far. Why not give him the benefit of the doubt? She'd know soon enough if she didn't like it. And she trusted him implicitly to stop if she asked him to.

"Back away from the stove."

She did, moved back a couple of feet. Heat still reached her but comfortably so. The sun had long ago disappeared below the treetops and evening had settled in. The only sound in the house—the entire universe to her agitated senses—was the logs' merry crackling.

She felt him drawing near, felt his hot breath against her shoulder. He wrapped the belt around her waist, keeping the buckle behind her. "Put your hands behind your back," he murmured in her hair.

Slowly Erica did as he instructed. He slipped her wrists beneath the belt and tightened it. She now knelt with her hands strapped behind her back and a very large, very aroused man kneeling behind her. A nervous giggle tugged at her throat. She pushed it down.

"I made you lose it earlier, didn't I?"

She nodded, remembering the almost painful twang of orgasm that had never come. She'd felt so, *so* frustrated.

"I won't this time."

Heat like a fever rushed to her cheeks and forehead.

"Bend over until your chest rests on the floor."

"I can't, I'm going to tip over."

"Here," Lothar replied, putting his hand under her chest and lowering her gently so her shoulders would rest on the floor while her bottom stuck way up in the air. The vulnerable position wasn't lost on her. Nor the thrill it triggered. She remembered vividly his capacity for violence, could still see Steven's bleeding face as if he stood before her, neither would she ever forget the sight of Lothar's poor body twisting and ripping apart as he changed into a werewolf. Lothar knew all about pain.

Yet she'd seen the gentler side of him. It was *there*. The sliver of his personality that perhaps would've been the true Lothar had life not been so difficult in his early years. She wondered what would've become of the young Lothar had the physician not taken him back to the city. He wouldn't have met that woman Katrina and never would've been infected with the werewolf…whatever it was, virus, curse. A shameful, selfish part of her was glad he'd lived the life he had, if only for the purely self-centered reason of her meeting him.

While he knelt behind her, she heard him rubbing his hands briskly then clap them together a few times. Oh. She barely had time to grit her teeth.

The slap he gave to her backside stung and tingled, skirted the edge of hurt. Another clack resounded in the room. But instead of continuing, Lothar stopped, blew on her stinging cheek and kissed it tenderly.

Oh. My.

She was bracing for another one when instead a soft, hot and wet *something* touched her pussy. She twisted to see his head hovering near her ass. *Ahh.* This would be good.

And it was.

First, he made it extremely light. Like a silk ribbon brushing against her. In slow, measured strokes, he licked her from throbbing bud to coccyx. Then he made it wide, gave her cleft thick, broad licks that pulled at her lips and rolled her clit. She felt herself melt between the legs. After this, he dove in and furiously ate her out with his entire mouth and lips and tongue. Erica could feel how wet she was just by the smoothness covering her fissure and by the way his tongue glided effortlessly in and out. With a rumble deep in his chest, he stabbed his tongue in. A sharp little yelp of pleasure left her. She hadn't come but, boy, was she close.

Just as the wave intensified, a resounding *CLACK* cleaved the air. Erica cried out. This time her butt burned like fire.

"Did you think it'd be that easy?" Lothar demanded as he leaned over her back and cupped a breast in his hand. "Were you close?"

"Oh yes," she replied breathlessly.

"Good."

He gave a ruthless squeeze to her breast before bouncing it in his large palm as one would a baseball. Erica bit her lip when he pinched her nipple and rolled it.

"You wanted it all, didn't you?"

With her cheek resting on the floor, she gave a vigorous nod.

"Still do?"

Another nod.

She didn't feel his hand move until his fingers were in her. Lothar was watching her reaction closely as she bit her lip and tried to push back against his hand. But he pulled back as soon as she moved and denied her climax again.

He left her side so he could kneel behind her and finger her pussy to his—and *her*—heart's content. No words were necessary as he took her close to the edge, only to deny her yet again. Unspent release tightened her whole body, cramped her back and legs. She wanted to *come*.

Lothar pulled his fingers out so he could make room for his mouth. A sharp precursor of climax tightened her pussy but Erica tried to suppress any outward sign that she was close to it. She bit down and forced her legs still, her butt cheeks relaxed but inside, in her chest and in her throat, Erica was beginning to ride a wave.

Don't let him see it, she kept chanting in her head.

Somehow, even despite her self-control, Lothar must have felt the difference and pulled away so he could slap her ass again. When she felt another one coming, she angled her cleft to receive the stinging palm and yelped when it did. The throb at the sudden contact of his hot hand against her vulva almost made her come. Almost, dammit.

She heard him chuckling. Bastard.

"If you want to ride something," Lothar said as he spread her thighs with his knee, "ride this."

He slipped his muscled thigh in between hers and rubbed it in a seductive fashion along her drenched cleft. Shamelessly, Erica twisted for all she was worth as she drove down hard, back up then down again over his thigh. Desperate for release, she whimpered when Lothar reached under and captured a breast while she humped his leg.

"Argh, Lothar, come on, don't make me beg," she snarled with a roll of her pelvis that only frustrated her by its failure to relieve the pressure building inside her like a raging volcano.

He slipped a hand over his leg, palm up, and rubbed at her aching clit. "There's nothing wrong with begging as long as both lovers want it."

He would make her beg. A man would make a woman beg to be screwed. *That's a first.*

Yet as much as the thought shocked and irritated her at first, she was past caring about restraint and politeness. If he wanted to hear her beg, then she'd beg, dammit. And he better deliver!

"You don't agree?" he asked as he slipped a finger in her and followed a slow, torturous cadence.

"Please, Lothar," Erica murmured with her eyes closed.

She felt him stiffen behind her.

"*Please* take me."

The belt tightened even more. Her hands tingled behind her back. What was he doing? She twisted and saw him close a fist around the belt. That was what had tightened it.

He raised himself up on his knees and caused the belt to tighten a bit more. Erica knew what was coming and spread her knees wider to accommodate him. With the belt as an anchor, Lothar parted her lips with his glans and waited there, forcing a whimper of anticipation from her, making her close her eyes and grit her teeth and ball her fists.

Instead of a forceful penetration, she hissed when he sank in slowly, all the way in and stayed there. His massive cock filled her so tightly it burned at first. Then her channel molded to his thick girth. But no blinding stab of pleasure rewarded her. Erica breathed through her nose with the rising tension. She wasn't going to come that way. At first frustrated, Erica sought to release the pressure herself and bucked back against him. But he placed his other hand, palm against her cheek, and kept her from moving back. Or forward.

Then it began.

A tingle developed at the base of her neck, spread down her back, tightened her anus and cheeks, burned her spread-out thighs and converged into a localized, sharp twinge right at the entrance to her pussy. When spasms began to clinch her channel around Lothar's cock, he stabbed deep into her before pulling back to the glans and waiting.

Erica panted hard. Ohh. *Ohh.* "Again, *please.*" She stretched the last word without meaning to. She really was begging. Not just saying the words.

He thrust in and retreated again.

Fire licked at her cleft. Her toes curled in. "Please."

Another shove, that one so deep she felt him push against the end of her channel. "Ohh, Lothar, take me, please, take me."

While she whimpered her need for release, he slammed into her, his balls connecting with her flesh. She couldn't feel the buckle and suspected he had his fist over it to protect her skin. The belt dug into her hipbones but she wouldn't change a thing in the world as he held on to it with both hands and delivered the most brutal, precise and passionate hammering she'd ever taken from a lover. In her favorite position too.

When pleasure finally hit, Erica let out such a high-pitch keen she thought she'd break the windows. It escalated into a staccato before crashing to moans that would've shamed her any other time.

While she came like a vengeful storm, Lothar pounded away.

Sweat connected them and soon her juices as well. Fiery rings tightened the base of his cock. He'd never had to fight so long and hard to keep his pleasure at bay. Never in his entire life had Lothar been forced to bite his lip to keep from spilling his seed prematurely. When he prided himself on being in complete control of his sexual appetite and responses, Erica, with her pure and unadulterated delight, had nearly undone him. That he could pleasure her this way made him proud and content.

He exploded in her tight, clenching pussy in violent bursts that made him see stars. Biting his lip hard, he gave one last push and was rewarded by her gushing climax. His name came out of her so often and in so many different ways, Lothar wasn't sure where the first instance ended and the next followed, and when her voice broke under the intensity of her climax, the sheer wall of primal release, he felt a languor deaden her body.

Lothar slowed then released the belt, which he untied and pulled away. He tenderly smoothened her hair back from her face and guided her behind down so she could rest on her side.

Bain's Wolf

Panting hard, he lay down behind her and draped his arm along her side and hip. His head in a palm while he propped himself up on an elbow, he kissed her neck. "Thank you."

"For what? You did all the work." Erica yawned and snuggled closer into him.

"Thank you for trusting me. Thank you for seeing something in me that I couldn't see myself."

"It was there all along, you just weren't letting it out very often, that's all."

Lothar closed his eyes at the words. She had no idea what they meant to him.

His palm burned from the metal belt buckle digging in it but rubbing her hip soon alleviated the small discomfort.

"Erica," he began, stopped to admire her back when she rolled onto her stomach and propped her chin in her palms. A pool of shadows filled the small of her back. He placed his hand over it and splayed it so his thumb and baby finger would reach on either side of her. Heat transferred up to him then back down to her.

Her pale gaze bore into his as she angled her chin to better look at him. She must have liked what she saw for she sighed and grinned. "What were you going to say?"

"Your trust means everything to me. I'll cherish and protect and nurture it as long as…"

He couldn't finish. His condition came back to him in all its jagged greatness. He was well over six hundred years old. Erica wasn't even forty.

"As long as I'm alive, you mean?" she asked astutely.

To his shock, she shrugged and never lost that grin he'd come to love so much, to depend on so much. "I still can't wrap my brain around that one. You're six *hundred* years old…you fought against *Napoleon*." A flicker of a grin played at the corner of her mouth.

Lothar could tell she had something to say about it. How she could find his age amusing baffled him. Everyone had his or her own solace. Hers was humor…and his was Erica Bain.

"I age very slowly and unless there's an accident, I'll outlive everyone you know." And everyone he knew or had ever known. "And that forces me to move often so people don't start wondering how come I'm still around looking the same when everyone else has grown older and gray."

She raised her hand like a student in a classroom. "Have plane, will travel."

Lothar found the strength to smile. Unflappable. "There's also the slight chance that our blood would come in contact. As I told you, that's how one becomes a werewolf in the first place. Diseases of the blood used to be called curses before the word virus was adopted. Although not many believe in mine."

"Are there many people with the werewolf virus?"

"Except for the one who infected me, none other that I know, although I'm sure there are more like me. Especially considering all that is required for infection is contact with blood."

She seemed to toss that around for a while. "No bite or anything, right, just blood going from one person to the other…it's so anticlimactic."

This time, Lothar laughed outright. "It is very 'climactic' when you're the one bleeding everywhere, believe me." He quieted down to better gauge her reaction.

Her gaze hadn't left his nor had the grin diminished as he'd been afraid it would.

"Are you looking at me because you want me to become like you or because you're afraid I'm going to ask?"

"Both," he murmured.

The thought of Erica dying in his arms scared him to his core. Not only for the eternal solitude that would be his lot upon her passing but in case she died in pain, tired and worn because of his nature or if some heart-wrenching illness would come to steal her away from him prematurely.

Yet to know that as a werewolf she'd have to go through the agonizing transformation and become a mindless beast didn't make him feel any better. But it was her choice. He'd respect whatever she chose to do.

"I'll be like you, Lothar, believe me. I'm not going to just sit around and wait for rheumatism and liver spots. But I don't think it'd be a good idea just now. I think one of us has to stay 'grounded' for a while. What do you think?"

She'd be like him. Not then but some day, she'd be like him. He wouldn't go on and on alone as he'd always been. He looked at her, her tousled hair, the freckled nose crinkled with a grin. How he loved her!

Unflappable *and* sensible. Lothar feared that if his heart swelled any more it'd explode in his chest. "The choice is yours to make, my love. I'll do whatever you ask."

"So you're letting me control that bit, eh?"

How shrewd she was. He nodded.

"I trust you completely, Erica Bain."

For the first time in his life, he gladly relinquished power to someone else. Because he knew in his heart and soul she wouldn't turn it around on him, wouldn't use it against him. Lothar trusted her implicitly and wholeheartedly. His rock, his light.

* * * * *

Lothar's presence by her side filled the cockpit. He was looking down through the window and couldn't see her eyes filling with happy tears. She wiped them away with the back of her gloved hand and patted his thigh then pointed down at the tranquil lake glimmering in the distance. She showed him a "thumbs-up" so he'd have time to brace for landing. People usually ended up bracing for her landings anyway, might as well forewarn him.

Cutting down the engine, she angled her floatplane toward the lake they'd chosen for his monthly transformation. His "time of the month" she'd called it teasingly. Lothar had been horrified at the comparison at first, but seeing that Erica wouldn't relent, he'd come to accept it. It was his third "time of the month" since she'd come to live with him.

Lothar had argued long and hard that she should drive to Dawson and wait out the full moon there instead, but Erica had finally convinced him that her idea was best. First, people in Dawson might get gossipy if she spent a couple days there every month—they were so nosy—on top of booking a room at the lone hotel, and second, it took longer to drive down then fly up. It made logistical sense to keep to themselves until they found another way. Lothar had proposed to barricade himself in one of the annexes but Erica wasn't too sure the structure would hold and the idea of him being caged like a beast didn't please her. She preferred to drop him off and pretend he was camping for a night instead. The lesser of two evils, right. Because it was nestled in a protected area, no one ever came up to Blackstone Lake. He could have all the privacy he needed yet keep her a mere radio call away. She could be there within an hour to pick him up. Eventually though, she realized they'd have to find another, more convenient way for him to change. Maybe the padded cell idea wasn't so bad after all…especially when she'd begin to change as well. She doubted she'd be fit to fly so soon before or after. The prospect of her new "life" left her tense but determined. No way she was getting old and dying in his arms!

Lothar leaned back in his seat as she dropped from the sky like a dive-bombing sparrow and leveled off at the last possible minute. After a particularly pronounced flare, she let one float touch the surface then the other. She saw Lothar let out a long sigh when the plane finally started to rock and shake as it touched down and roared toward the opposite bank. The sun was high in the crisp, beautiful January sky. Snow twinkled like a blanket of stars on the ground. Erica caught herself smiling broadly. Life was good.

A hundred feet or so from the bank, she cut the throttle down and let the momentum carry them to the edge. Lothar already sat sideways ready to jump out.

That butt.

While she still had a bit of steering left, she tilted the yoke and brought her plane perpendicular to the embankment so Lothar wouldn't land in water. He readily tied it to the same tree they'd used every time.

After she flicked everything off, Erica slung her headset around the steering column and squeezed out of her seat so she could push out the cargo doors and pass the supplies to him.

Brisk winter air filled the plane as she tossed Lothar the different bags he needed, ending with his pair of cross-country skis in case something happened and she couldn't come back. He'd have something like a hundred miles to do, which would be a drag in the best of times but it was better than living in the woods for weeks while he hiked back home.

"You know," Erica said, kneeling in the cargo area and rubbing her chin. "We might have to do it your way, with the annex I mean. I won't be able to fly both of us when I get my 'time of the month'."

Lothar grimaced. "I told you my idea was better."

"Okay, okay, don't rub it in. It was my whole angle for coming back up to Dawson in the first place."

He stopped lugging bags around to look at her. "And I'm eternally glad you came."

"Eternally? A *pun*, my, my!"

"Quite unintentional," he muttered.

When the plane was empty, she jumped on the embankment and windmilled once before Lothar caught her wrist and reeled her in.

After planting a passionate kiss that left her breathless and hungry for more, he went back to his task of pulling the one-man tent from its bag. With a brisk shake, he set the pop-up tent down in front of him and pulled the straps and lines tighter. The oval-shaped, bright orange and purple nylon contrasted sharply against the white and dark green surrounding. But that was the point. She wanted to see him right away when she'd come back. Lothar had said that if he were alone as a werewolf, with nothing distracting or threatening, he didn't tend to wander.

"Tea?" he offered as he held the thermos in his hand. The blue nylon mitt basically covered the entire length of the thermos. The guy had big hands. Her butt tingled at the memory of that large hand landing on her.

Erica shook her head then winked. "No, it's for you. Keep it for later when I'm gone and there's nothing left that's hot around here."

He shook his head. Erica had noticed he did that a lot. Must have been her charming personality.

"Everything in order?" she asked, going through the stuff herself in her best mom imitation. She pulled the flap aside and peeked inside the tent. "Lamp? Check. Radio? Check. Extra batteries? Check."

"There's extra *everything*, Erica. Stop fussing."

"Look, I'm leaving my favorite person alone in the woods with all kinds of hungry animals running wild, just let me fuss a bit before I go. Okay?"

"Come fuss with this then," he said as he closed a bear paw in a mitt over the front of her parka and pulled her to him.

They were in each other's clothes within minutes. Sunlight reached them tinted through the orange and purple nylon while they lay squeezed inside the narrow tent. His feet pushed against the zipper. She'd have to find a bigger one for him. This was supposed to be a "one-man" tent but there always ended up being two inside.

Lothar kissed her deeply, his lips like silk against her mouth and chin and cheeks. The man knew how to kiss. And after spending three months with him, she'd learned that he didn't only know how to kiss. His skills were incredible as was his *experience*.

A giggle escaped her.

"What?" he asked, nibbling at her earlobe the way she liked best.

"Your belt...would you have it with you by any chance?"

He arched an eyebrow. "Yes... Why?"

"You *know* why."

The look on him!

"If it weren't so damn cold, I'd ask you to tie me to a tree or something. Wild monkey sex!"

"That can still be arranged," Lothar replied as he came up on an elbow. Muscles rippled over his pectorals.

"Nah, I'm too much of a wuss. It's cold out there, sir."

She only had time for a gasp before Lothar grabbed her by the wrist and rolled her on her back. While gathering both her wrists in a hand, he fished behind him for a while, yanked the belt from his pants and skillfully looped it around her hands, which he pulled high over her head. The end of the belt he wrapped over his fist.

"You're not taking me outside, are you?" Erica asked, unsure about the suddenly dark look in Lothar's eyes. "It *is* cold."

"Not outside," he snarled, his upper lip curling up over his teeth. "But taking you I *am*."

An adrenaline high tightened her nipples and pussy as Lothar forcibly kept her hands above her head while he rolled on top of her and spread her knees with his.

"Spread your legs."

The abrupt tone sparked a sequence of frissons all over her skin, creating a mesh of sensations that crisscrossed and rolled along her limbs and back and even inside her where her channel clutched as it awaited the pounding coming its way.

"What do you want me to do, Erica?" Lothar murmured against her mouth, his gaze never leaving hers. "How hard do you want me to take you?"

She replied with her hips, which she tilted against him despite the great weight crushing her against the hard frozen ground underneath the air mattress and tent floor. His rock-hard cock compressed her belly, painfully so, but she didn't care. Another roll of her pelvis made him growl—literally *growl*.

When he blinked several times and audibly ground his teeth, Erica knew he was fighting the transformation. It shocked her how close he could come, how much near the surface the "beast"—how she hated that word he kept using, she'd have to find another—managed to rise yet never completely overwhelm him. He'd told her that he never used to be able to skirt the line so tightly, until he'd met her. The implicit trust on his part warmed her heart. She closed her eyes.

"Look at me."

Her eyes flared when Lothar retreated so he could snake a hand down between her thighs. "Spread them wider. Flat on the ground."

Erica did, spread her feet until each touched a side of the narrow tent. When his fingers invaded her, she gasped. His experienced hand raided her sex, tormented, bruised and branded her clit, drew her juices and spread them around so he could enter her more deeply, more forcefully until spasms pulled at her quads and calves. God!

"Clutch at my fingers," he urged, now pumping rhythmically. "Tighter."

Muscles burning, she milked his fingers with everything she had. A moan rose up her throat, forced her to let it out through her nose for her jaws were locked so tight she could barely swallow.

"Tighter," he growled before bending over and giving her a sharp little nip on the shoulder. "I want you to be tight for me when I fuck you."

Erica squeezed her eyes shut when climax tingled along her spine, spread to her butt cheeks before rolling upward and firing a series of contractions that made her pussy fist Lothar's fingers as if she meant to break them. His fist around the belt tightened, cut circulation to her hands. Like she cared! Her arms stretched up high, she arched her back when she came.

Without a word, he pulled his fingers out, climbed back on top of her and let his weight bear down. Fire heralded his thick cock when he thrust in. His muscled thighs barely fit between hers since he wanted her flat on the ground, but the pressure added to the excitement of Lothar's brutal lovemaking and his ferocity. Ramming, hammering, pounding. He fucked her exactly how he said he would. Hard.

Her cries filled the tiny tent. Without warning, he pulled out, yanked her hands down by the belt so he could put the end of it between his teeth. Snarling something in what she guessed was German, he hooked her knees up over his shoulders, keeping her hands in between with the belt tight around her wrists. Hazel eyes fixedly on her, he loomed like a snarling, bronze-haired archangel before stabbing in.

Air left her in a great humph. The shock—and the apprehension—dispersed in a thousand quivers that rocked her entire body. Her long scream surprised even her.

With his hands merciless around her knees, Lothar took her, raided her, demanding yet loving in his passion. The belt dug in her wrists and at the corners of his mouth but he didn't seem to notice nor to care. Neither did she.

Erica came for him. And he came for her. Sweat united their skin, ecstasy their bodies and love their hearts.

When he released the belt, Erica didn't have the strength to keep her arms upright and they limply fell above her head as blood slowly returned to her deadened hands. She spread her knees wide so Lothar could lie in between and rest his head against her belly. He panted hard.

"It's good that I didn't know about this until I met you. I would've gone mad without it."

Erica brushed his hair away from his face. That gorgeous hair! "Didn't know about what?"

"This," he replied after blowing a strand of hair out of his mouth. "You. Us. I didn't know what I was missing, that I could feel this way."

"Yeah, I know what you mean." She curled her toes upward. "Man, my butt hurts."

She saw him rolling his eyes.

"Something I said?"

"You have to be the only woman who can't 'share her feelings' without turning it into a joke."

"That's all part of my charm, right? *Right*?"

Chuckling, Lothar squeezed beside her and lay on his back. He checked his fingernails and cringed. "It's getting close."

"I know." Erica raised herself on an elbow and spotted the mess of semen on the sleeping bag. She couldn't help the smirk. "Something tells me you'll be back here tonight, sniffing around."

"Arghhhh, Erica!"

She laughed while he shook his head and retrieved his underwear so he could wipe the mess away.

"Not that I want you to go but you still have a bit of daylight left. I'd feel better knowing you're safely home."

Home. That sounded so delicious in his decadent mouth.

She nodded as she clawed back into her clothes and out of the tent. Lothar followed her outside, dressed haphazardly and gazed out over the lake where the edges had frozen. A big intake of air swelled his chest.

There was always a sense of desperation and hurry in their lovemaking, knowing she'd have to leave him behind. A part of her stayed each time. She crossed her arms and rocked on her feet.

"I was thinking the other day—I try not to do that too often but you know me—and, well, maybe it'd be fun to visit Europe. I've never been there."

Lothar was shaking his head emphatically before she'd even finished her sentence.

"Okay then, Las Vegas?"

After a quick smile, he shrugged. "If you want to go to Europe, we'll go. But there's nothing there to see but decaying buildings and crowded streets."

"I take it you don't like your homeland much anymore."

"North America is my home now. It's whole and big and clean. Nothing here reminds me of the past and I like it that way."

Desperate to lighten the mood, she grinned and tapped her shoulder. "Wherever we go, since we've already been tagged, we should get a GPS receiver. That way we could know where each of us is."

Her grin wavered then she let it fall completely. Why the serious face, she wondered.

Lothar didn't smile. Not even a little. "You won't need to look for me. I'll be right beside you. Always."

"I know."

After one last kiss, she gave him a bone-crushing hug, which he returned just as fiercely, even rumbling deep in his chest, then she climbed back into her plane and waited until Lothar had untied it and moved away several paces.

Electrical switches on, she started her plane and angled it away toward the opposite bank. Before she'd gained enough speed, she pushed against the door and let her upper body hang out the opening so she could blow him a kiss. The broad grin on his face made tears of joy spring to her eyes. *Jeez, woman, get a grip.*

With a last wave, she sat back in, gunned the engine and took off.

Why an electronic book?

We live in the Information Age—an exciting time in the history of human civilization, in which technology rules supreme and continues to progress in leaps and bounds every minute of every day. For a multitude of reasons, more and more avid literary fans are opting to purchase e-books instead of paper books. The question from those not yet initiated into the world of electronic reading is simply: *Why?*

1. *Price.* An electronic title at Ellora's Cave Publishing and Cerridwen Press runs anywhere from 40% to 75% less than the cover price of the exact same title in paperback format. Why? Basic mathematics and cost. It is less expensive to publish an e-book (no paper and printing, no warehousing and shipping) than it is to publish a paperback, so the savings are passed along to the consumer.

2. *Space.* Running out of room in your house for your books? That is one worry you will never have with electronic books. For a low one-time cost, you can purchase a handheld device specifically designed for e-reading. Many e-readers have large, convenient screens for viewing. Better yet, hundreds of titles can be stored within your new library—on a single microchip. There are a variety of e-readers from different manufacturers. You can also read e-books on your PC or laptop computer. (Please note that Ellora's Cave does not endorse any specific brands.

You can check our websites at www.ellorascave.com or www.cerridwenpress.com for information we make available to new consumers.)

3. *Mobility.* Because your new e-library consists of only a microchip within a small, easily transportable e-reader, your entire cache of books can be taken with you wherever you go.

4. *Personal Viewing Preferences.* Are the words you are currently reading too small? Too large? Too... ANNOYING? Paperback books cannot be modified according to personal preferences, but e-books can.

5. *Instant Gratification.* Is it the middle of the night and all the bookstores near you are closed? Are you tired of waiting days, sometimes weeks, for bookstores to ship the novels you bought? Ellora's Cave Publishing sells instantaneous downloads twenty-four hours a day, seven days a week, every day of the year. Our webstore is never closed. Our e-book delivery system is 100% automated, meaning your order is filled as soon as you pay for it.

Those are a few of the top reasons why electronic books are replacing paperbacks for many avid readers.

As always, Ellora's Cave and Cerridwen Press welcome your questions and comments. We invite you to email us at Comments@ellorascave.com or write to us directly at Ellora's Cave Publishing Inc., 1056 Home Avenue, Akron, OH 44310-3502.

erridwen, the Celtic Goddess of wisdom, was the muse who brought inspiration to story-tellers and those in the creative arts. Cerridwen Press encompasses the best and most innovative stories in all genres of today's fiction. Visit our site and discover the newest titles by talented authors who still get inspired - much like the ancient storytellers did, once upon a time.

CERRIDWEN PRESS

www.cerridwenpress.com